The Gods of Newport

Also by John Jakes

*Savannah (or) A Gift for Mr. Lincoln**
*Charleston**
*On Secret Service**
California Gold
The Bold Frontier

The Crown Family Saga
*American Dreams**
Homeland

The North and South Trilogy
North and South
Love and War
Heaven and Hell

The Kent Family Chronicles
The Bastard
The Rebels
The Seekers
The Furies
The Titans
The Warriors
The Lawless
The Americans

*Published by Dutton

THE GODS OF NEWPORT

A NOVEL

John Jakes

DUTTON

DUTTON
Published by Penguin Group (USA) Inc.
375 Hudson Street, New York, New York 10014, U.S.A.
Penguin Group (Canada), 90 Eglinton Avenue East, Suite 700, Toronto, Ontario M4P 2Y3, Canada (a division of Pearson Penguin Canada Inc.); Penguin Books Ltd, 80 Strand, London WC2R 0RL, England; Penguin Ireland, 25 St Stephen's Green, Dublin 2, Ireland (a division of Penguin Books Ltd); Penguin Group (Australia), 250 Camberwell Road, Camberwell, Victoria 3124, Australia (a division of Pearson Australia Group Pty Ltd); Penguin Books India Pvt Ltd, 11 Community Centre, Panchsheel Park New Delhi - 110 017, India; Penguin Group (NZ), cnr Airborne and Rosedale Roads, Albany, Auckland 1310, New Zealand (a division of Pearson New Zealand Ltd); Penguin Books (South Africa) (Pty) Ltd, 24 Sturdee Avenue, Rosebank, Johannesburg 2196, South Africa

Penguin Books Ltd, Registered Offices: 80 Strand, London WC2R 0RL, England

Published by Dutton, a member of Penguin Group (USA) Inc.

First printing, November 2006
1 3 5 7 9 10 8 6 4 2

LIBRARY OF CONGRESS CATALOGING-IN-PUBLICATION DATA HAS BEEN APPLIED FOR.

ISBN 0-525-94976-3

Printed in the United States of America
Set in Janson Text
Designed by Spring Hoteling

PUBLISHER'S NOTE
This book is a work of fiction. Names, characters, places, and incidents either are the product of the author's imagination or are used fictitiously, and any resemblance to actual persons, living or dead, business establishments, events, or locales is entirely coincidental.

For Rachel, first and always

CONTENTS

I
1893 and Before

II
1894

III
1895–1896

IV
1897

The Gods of Newport

The upheaval caused by the war, the quick boom in railroads and industry at its end, and the vast opportunities for wealth offered by an expanding people, made the nation suddenly outgrow rules that formerly had sufficed to keep illegality somewhere within bounds. Self-sacrificial patriotism was out of style. The profit motive went on a glorious spree.

—W. A. Swanberg

They danced and they drove and they rode, they dined and wined and dressed and flirted and yachted and polo'd and Casino'd, responding to the subtlest inventions of their age; on the old lawns and verandahs I saw them gather, on the old shining sands I saw them gallop, past the low headlands I saw their white sails verily flash, and through the dusky old shrubberies came the light and sound of their feasts.

—Henry James

A fortune of a million dollars is only respectable poverty.

—Ward McAllister

What do I care about the law? H'aint I got the power?

—attributed to Commodore Vanderbilt

In the years between the Civil War and the twentieth century, America experienced astonishing change and growth. Railroads and the telegraph joined the oceans; the Atlantic cable joined the continents. Giant steam engines, printing presses, looms and Bessemer converters shifted the base of the nation's economy from farms to factories. History calls some of the legendary capitalists who made it happen "the robber barons," because the progress they created along with great personal fortunes carried a high price: laws ignored or broken; judges and legislators bribed; big-city political clubs organized into engines of corruption.

Searching for a summer retreat in these turbulent years, New York society turned to Newport, a quiet Rhode Island village at the southern tip of Aquidneck Island, in Narragansett Bay. Earlier, Newport had been a smuggler's haven, a garrison for redcoats during the Revolution, a home port for shipowners whose vessels brought human cargo from Africa, a favorite escape from hot weather for Carolina planters. A summer colony of intellectuals flourished. It included Henry Wadsworth Longfellow, Oliver Wendell Holmes and Julia Ward Howe.

Lured by the reputations of these relatively poor but famous Americans, wealthy newcomers created a short season of eight to ten weeks, July into September. Some of the so-called robber barons managed to launder their fortunes and pedigrees and join the migration. The old-money elite and the newly rich turned Newport into "the Queen of Resorts," known around the world and unmatched for reckless extravagance and ruthless social climbing.

Some who sought acceptance in the summer colony succeeded; others failed, ending their struggle tragically. Beneath the glittering veneer of glamour and celebrity lay hidden strata of frustration, depression and even insanity.

Thus Newport's golden summers at the end of the nineteenth century were, by turns, melodramatic, comic and sad but always uniquely American.

I
1893 and Before

1
Fisk's Blood

Jay Gould thrust a sealed envelope at him.

"Give Jim this warning. Ned Stokes is looking for him."

"What for?"

"What for? Did someone turn you into an idiot? To murder him. Don't let Stokes get the best of you. Don't let any of them get the best of you."

Gould used the familiar formless threat on employees to instill a sense of falling short; predictably, this produced redoubled effort, all conscience abandoned. Sometimes Sam hated Gould, small, bearded and sly. Sometimes Gould treated him as if he weren't an Erie insider—vice president, special operations, responsible for knocking heads when heads had to be knocked.

He shoved the envelope into his pocket. "Where is Jim?"

Gould regarded him with murky brown eyes. "Grand Central Hotel. Do you know where that is?"

Absurd question. "Of course I know."

"Then get going."

Sam rushed down the great staircase of the Opera House and through the lobby doors to 23rd Street. It was a strangely lurid afternoon, with swift clouds racing over the noisy street. Between the clouds, bands of orange and green streaked the sky.

He hailed a hansom, jumped in and shouted his destination. The cab's dusty interior smelled of cigars and some tart's perfume. He examined the mysterious envelope. He slid his index finger under the end of the seal but no matter how he pushed or tore, the envelope wouldn't open.

Outside the cab, the clouds alternately closed above the buildings, dropping the street into darkness, or flew away swiftly and brought flooding, blinding light. A sense of dread overcame Sam as the cab swung into Broadway and fought its way south through the noisome tangle of fine carriages, clanging trolleys, horses dropping dung, hogs wandering, pedestrians cursing the congestion.

An overturned omnibus blocked half of Broadway and backed up traffic. The delay seemed interminable. Finally the ride to the hotel at 3rd and Broadway ended with the hansom at the curb next to the Grand Central's entrance for ladies. Jim used that entrance when he didn't want to be seen by reporters. Sam left the cab without paying and ran inside.

"Colonel Fisk?" he shouted to a young porter polishing gas fixtures. From atop his ladder the porter pointed to the grand staircase. A strange multicolored light dappled the steps—light of the kind that fell through stained glass. Halfway up the stair, Jim Fisk, round as a fairgrounds balloon, froze under the gaze of a handsome black-haired young man half visible in a clot of shadow on the second-floor landing.

Big Jim's tawny red-gold hair and waxed mustaches gleamed. On his starched shirt bosom shone his ever-present diamond, big as a baby's fist, bright as a locomotive headlight. He raised one hand, as if pleading. Petrified, Sam watched the handsome young man point a revolver and fire. The bullet drove Fisk backward; he sat down on the stair, against the wall.

The shooter, Ned Stokes, was a playboy, Jim's sometime partner and a rival for the favors of Jim's mistress, the actress Josie Mansfield. Recently the two men had confronted one another in court.

Stokes fired again. Fisk cried out, jerking against the wall, clutching the bosom of his dark blue admiral's coat heavily ornamented with gold frogs and epaulettes. A bloodstain bloomed on his corpulent belly. His eyes, usually so full of mirth and bonhomie, bulged. Sam held out the sealed envelope, trying to convey its urgency. Nothing came from his mouth but a frustrating croak.

Hotel staff from the second floor swarmed around Ned Stokes, disarmed him and wrestled him to the carpet. Fisk sat against the wall, breathing noisily, bleeding all over his fine uniform. . . .

Things blurred briefly. Sam found himself in room 213 where Fisk lay on a divan, his coat off, his right sleeve and shirtfront two bloody messes. A doctor bent over him. "The bullet is more than four inches deep, Colonel. In your bowels. I can't find it."

Someone said, "Telegraph his wife."

"Where?"

"Lucy's in Boston, as always."

Someone else said, "Better notify the papers. He's a celebrity."

A police captain shoved disheveled Ned Stokes to the fore. "Is this the man who shot you?"

Fisk peered, whispered, "Yes, that's Ned Stokes." *Never let them get the best of you.* . . . Sam lunged for the shooter's throat. A police nightstick jabbed him and stopped his charge. The captain dragged Stokes out of the room, roughing him up in the process.

Sam knelt beside the divan, showed the envelope. "I'm sorry I was late. Mr. Gould sent this urgent message."

Fisk's big round eyes, usually so jolly, were full of mist and pain. "Nothing's urgent anymore. I go where the woodbine twineth." It was one of Fisk's favorite expressions, brought along from his youth as a peddler on the back roads of Vermont. Jim Fisk was a young man, not even forty. The newspapers might laugh at his excesses of drink and dress and convivial good humor, but they always wrote about him. Sam raised his hands in front of his face. The fingers and palms were coated with Fisk's blood. But he was sure he hadn't touched . . .

Somewhere glass broke.

The scene—Fisk half on, half off the divan, gasping like a beached whale; Sam kneeling; dark observers round about like mourners at a bier—rapidly shrank, boxed by darkness until it was no more than a small diorama-like rectangle in the distance. Sam began to toss and thrash. Sweating and gasping for air, he came out of the nightmare.

He sat up in the dark, still gripped by the spell of the dream. The windows of his bedroom were open on the sultry air of early June. Far away over the Atlantic, heat lightning flashed.

He cudgeled his memory until things began to right themselves: This wasn't 1872, when Fisk died at the Grand Central, this was 1893. He was in his sixteen-room summer house by the shore at Long Branch, New Jersey. He heard the sea curling and murmuring below the open windows. He smelled the salt air, and his own night sweat.

Gould had sent him to the Grand Central with a message for Fisk that afternoon, but it wasn't in a sealed envelope, it was a verbal summons for Fisk to return to Erie headquarters on an upper floor of the Opera House for a consultation pertaining to a stockholder's threatened lawsuit. Because of traffic Sam didn't even reach the hotel until after the shooting. He joined the others in the deathwatch in room 213 where Fisk lay breathing his last. But in the dream, which had recurred many times, Fisk's blood always stained his hands. Somehow they got the best of him, whoever "they" were. . . .

Sam heard a second crash of glass, someone moving on the ground floor, someone else on the staircase. Was his wife out of her bedroom? Or his daughter? Who was the intruder? A common thief, or someone else? Sam had legions of enemies but he never imagined any would follow him all this way to a summer resort. The coachman asleep in the coach house was the only help close by. . . .

Samuel Stephen Driver, the millionaire railroad baron, swung his bare feet off the bed, picked up the hem of his red-and-white-striped cotton flannel nightshirt. He left his red leather mules under the bed and stole barefoot past a wardrobe crammed with nightclothes, bought by his wife, that he refused to wear: a padded banyan, a pair of new-style pajamas decorated with Chinese characters. At the door to the hallway, he heard pegged flooring creak, then his daughter's voice.

"Who is there? Who is it?"

Sam slipped toward the stairs. His heart pumped with fear, but the invasion of his home generated resolve more than wrath. He wouldn't let himself or his loved ones be threatened this way. He was a survivor; the others—Vanderbilt, Drew, Boss Tweed, poor lusty Jim whom everyone liked for his generosity and youthful exuberance—they were all gone. Gould too, last year, dead of tuberculosis at fifty-six. Sam was still standing. On the wall of his New York office hung a plaque illuminated like a medieval manuscript.

NEVER LET THEM GET THE BEST OF YOU.

He'd lost count of all the things he'd done to live up to that motto.

To the left on the ground floor, a gaslight sputtered and brightened in the front parlor. Sam's hair hung over his brow. His sweaty hand slid on the balustrade as he crept down toward the light a step at a time.

2
Intruder

Offshore, flashes of white lit the greasy swells. French doors opening to the broad porch had been forced, two small panes broken, scattering the Persian carpet with shards that reflected a dim gaslight he assumed his daughter had turned on.

Jenny's strained oval face was turned toward him, her wide blue eyes startled and uncertain. Jenny was eighteen, with her mother's slender but ample figure and auburn hair, plaited in a single long braid. Her night robe, persimmon silk, showed costly touches of russet piping on the lapels.

"Papa, I heard the glass break, so I ran down—"

"Stand aside, Jenny."

He advanced another step into the suitably cluttered Victorian parlor. The intruder skulked near the broken doors. Sam was hanged if he could dredge up a memory of who the man might be. He was small, middle-aged, handsome in his youth perhaps, but now with sagging dewlaps and pouches under his eyes. A sweat-grimed collar showed beneath his seersucker coat.

Sam was inclined to throw the man out by force but that would deprive him of the pleasure of turning him over to the Long Branch constabulary. "What the devil are you doing in my house, sir? Tell me your name."

Defiant, the intruder pulled a pasteboard square from his side pocket. Upstairs, Sam heard his wife call his name.

"Stay there, Grace. Don't come down."

Sam's voice was strong, deep, belying the emotion he felt. He believed in hiding fear from enemies. It was one of the principles that had raised him to his current eminence. At fifty-two he was one of the richest men in America. Shorter than Jenny by two inches, he was stocky, with large freckled hands and curly brown hair graying and receding from his widow's peak. He resembled a butcher or a cabman more than what he was, although his eyes, dark and darting, suggested a man of formidable intelligence and cunning.

Sam read the soiled card. "T. Adolph Riley. General contracting. Swarthmore, Pennsylvania." He tossed the card on the floor. "I don't know you."

"Oh, you do, Driver. By God you know me. I lost the bid to build your hospital."

Someone creaked a stair step.

"Grace, do not come in here. I'm handling this."

The stair creaked again.

Sam began to sweat. He said, "I've built nine hospitals and I'll build more." Before old Dan Drew died at eighty-two, he'd inspired Sam. Or, perhaps better, jabbed his conscience. *Samuel,* Drew had said, *philanthropy is a rag for wiping dirt off your hands. Every rich man I know owns one.* Uncle Daniel—the Deacon, some called him—read the Bible for recreation. He knew scores of passages of Scripture by heart and prayed in church every Sunday.

He endowed seminaries with one hand while he destroyed stock market rivals with the other. Sometimes widows and orphans were victims of his maneuvers. The Deacon shrugged it off.

"Nine," Sam repeated. "I have no idea which of them you refer to."

"Chester, Pennsylvania. Saint Michael the Archangel."

"They're all named Saint Michael the Archangel."

"So you're a Papist as well as a crook."

"Michael is the patron saint of soldiers. I was in the war. I was born a Lutheran, if that's any of your damn business. Now what the devil are you doing here?"

"I'm bankrupt. I've lost my home, my wife's in an institution for dipsomaniacs."

"You sound like you'll soon follow her."

The wrong thing to say; Riley shouted at him. "Goddamn you, I submitted the low bid for the Chester hospital. Thousands below the others." Riley's reddening cheeks told Sam this was passing beyond the boundary of argument into hopeless, unreasonable confrontation. Sam moderated his tone.

"Oh, yes. I remember. Why don't you have a seat? We'll discuss it."

"Discuss? Why?" Riley clawed at an inner pocket of his wrinkled coat. "You won't beggar anyone else, I came here to make sure."

And there it was, an old but dependable .31-caliber Colt pocket pistol, the barrel but two and a half inches long. Sam recognized the weapon because he'd carried the same kind more than once. It was unfailingly accurate at close range and powerful enough to knock down a stevedore.

A shadow fell across the carpet at Sam's right. Jenny said, "Mama, go back." Sam didn't dare turn but his stomach roiled; she'd defied him.

"Riley, listen to me. I regret your personal situation but I couldn't allow you to build the Chester hospital. We looked into your record. One of your buildings collapsed. Two more were denied permits for occupancy. I couldn't endanger the lives of patients by letting a contract to a man who skimps and cheats."

"You're so very righteous. You're a cheat too. God knows how many men you've driven to the wall with your tactics." Riley's eyes shifted to Sam's wife standing behind him. "Woman, step out here where I can see you."

"Grace, don't," Sam said as the shadow at his feet changed position. He pivoted, swept one arm behind him, grasped Grace's waist and shoved her so that his shoulders and torso shielded her.

Jenny again: "Papa, be careful, he—"

Grace, simultaneously, pulling against Sam's restraining arm: "There's no need to berate the poor—"

Riley, fairly screaming over both:

"I didn't come here to argue with stockjobbing scum." He cocked the single-action pistol, then clapped his left hand over his gun wrist to steady it. Sam grappled Grace around the waist to fling her aside. Riley fired.

The bullet shattered an oval mirror beside the archway to the hall. Sam slipped, fell to one knee. Grace stood just beyond him, an upright target. He reached for her in one awful, attenuated moment that seemed to last and last, until Riley shot a second time.

With a gasp of surprise, Grace stared down at the bosom of her nightdress. She fell sideways, smoothly, as if some memory in her lithe body still remembered her days as a dancer at Fisk's Opera House. Sam gained his feet, snatched up the nearest chair. Riley back-stepped to the broken doors. Sam smashed the chair on Riley's head.

Riley fell on his spine, his neck gashed by a triangle of glass left in one of the window frames. Sam leaped on top of him, insensible with rage. He was cursing and snorting and pounding Riley's head with reddening fists when someone heavy-footed came into the parlor.

Jenny: "For pity's sake, Viktor, pull him off. Mama's badly hurt."

The bald coachman, an émigré from Riga, wore only his trousers with galluses over bare shoulders. He tugged and pried and by sheer strength separated Sam from the half-conscious intruder. Riley's nose leaked blood and mucus. His neck poured blood onto his jacket collar. Gradually the light of sanity replaced Sam's glazed look.

Jenny groped behind her for a chair, as though her legs wouldn't support her. Sam stared at Grace lying at his feet, shot through the breast and barely breathing. "Oh my God, no."

He crashed to his knees beside her. He'd been unfaithful to her more times than once but he'd never loved anyone else. Hesitantly, he inserted his right hand under her neck in an effort to elevate her head. She had the same auburn hair as her daughter, though gray-streaked now. Her skin gave off the familiar lilac smell he loved.

Her right hand closed around his left. Her eyes filled with luminous joy. "Sam dearest. The overture's begun. I must take my place. I'll see you after the performance."

Tears ran down his cheeks. She was already leaving him, smiling as she exchanged the present for the past, the wrecked parlor for the shadows backstage where young ladies of the dancing chorus lined up for their entrance and Jim Fisk stood by, squeezing Sam's shoulder and congratulating him on his eye for beauty in the person of Grace Penny. . . .

"Grace, Grace." He chafed her hand. It was cold. Jenny knelt to ease his fingers away, cradle his head against her shoulder.

"It's too late, Papa. She's gone. Viktor, please get dressed and fetch the police."

3
Sam's Epiphany

An Erie Railroad locomotive drew the funeral train through a downpour. In the fading daylight, whitecaps showed on the Hudson, streaming away behind the private coach carrying Sam and Jenny northward on Grace Driver's last journey.

Between the coach and the engine, an otherwise empty freight car bore Grace's remains in a plain coffin of pewter finish, with silver handles and a silver plate engraved with name and date. Sam had telegraphed the mortician in Rochester to be ready to prepare Grace's body in the traditional white robe and cap, with a large bouquet of red roses, which she loved, to be clasped between her hands.

Rain beat at the window beside Sam's swivel chair. The cigar in his teeth etched a spot of fire on the streaked glass. The car was one of three Sam owned, finely appointed with rosewood paneling, upper windows of etched glass, two sleeping compartments and a small galley. On the rain-splashed lacquer of the car's exterior, rococo lettering spelled PRIDE OF OHIO.

A week had passed since the fatal shooting. Riley, a weeping, babbling wreck, had been driven off to the lockup that same night. A cash payment of $5,000, slipped to a circuit judge by Sam's longtime assistant, Mozart Gribble, guaranteed that Riley would never again walk free, no matter how skilled his defense lawyer.

The weather was cold for early summer. The rain had fallen without letup since they left the city's Grand Central Station. They were traveling on Vanderbilt's New York Central tracks, "at water level," because the Erie's main line ran too far south, across New York's Southern Tier. Once, the Central, like the foul-mouthed old Commodore himself, was to be avoided, but the railroad wars of the late 1860s and '70s were largely over, though enmities lingered; men who lost huge sums to other men didn't forgive.

Old-fashioned lanterns glowing with John D. Rockefeller's "Standard" brand kerosene swayed on the ceiling, alternately revealing and hiding Jenny seated some way up the aisle. She was reading a tabloid paper, the notorious *Town Topics*, a New York weekly published to chronicle the doings, respectable and otherwise, of members of "the 400." Where that name came from, no one was certain. Some said Ward McAllister guessed at the number of people who could fit in Mrs. Astor's ballroom. Sam and Grace had never been invited to one of Mrs. Astor's famous winter balls.

Even deep in grief and depression, Sam struggled to look ahead. With a small gold-cased pencil he wrote in a memo book on his knee. *Aft. 1 yr. mourning, Gribble to send cards inviting calls by friends.*

The locomotive whistle wailed. The train was running through a patch of river fog. He tossed his half-smoked cigar into a spittoon and walked down the aisle to an empty swivel chair next to Jenny's.

"Anything of interest in that rag?"

"In the Saunterings column, Mrs. Astor announces an Arabian Nights fete."

"In Newport?"

"Yes. Late July."

In 1885, when Jenny was ten, Grace had wanted to build a summer home in Newport, as other wealthy families were doing. She complained that Long Branch and similar resorts on the Jersey shore were already "a trifle tawdry." Long Branch itself had suffered a decline of status after the late President Grant and his wife ceased their summer visits. Sam's assistant, Mozart, had contacted Aquidneck Island real estate agents. He'd come back with a disheartening caveat:

"They won't let you in."

"What the hell do you mean? My money's as good as anyone's."

"Oh, there's no problem about buying a lot, or hiring contractors. It's social acceptance. Mrs. Astor and her adviser, McAllister—"

"Her court jester. A prancing little fop. I could put him down with one punch."

"Absolutely. But he's influential. He has the ear of the grande dame. He heard of your interest, and I'm afraid he categorizes you as a swell." Mozart Gribble, a bachelor of forty, had a long jaw, spaniel eyes and a melancholy air. Since he worked in a dim study in Sam's Fifth Avenue mansion, he could dress any way he pleased, including his old black velvet smoking cap with no brim and a shoulder-length tassel. He wore it indoors or out. He had been with Sam over twenty years.

"And what, may I ask, is McAllister's definition of a swell?"

"A man of new money. McAllister favors those with older

wealth. Three generations is preferable. Nobs, he calls them. Also, your past business associations are a detriment."

"Fisk, Gould, those fellows?"

"Yes." Mozart hesitated. "Shall I continue?"

"On what subject?"

"Mrs. Driver."

Sam stiffened. "Be careful."

"Yes, sir, but it's well known that she was an actress."

"A dancer. A damn fine one."

"Whom you met at the old Fisk Opera House. Actresses are unwelcome in Mrs. Astor's circle."

"The doors in Newport are barred even before we knock, is that it?"

"Not barred literally. You may build and move wherever you wish. I'm only relating what has been conveyed to me, namely that Newport would likely be an unhappy experience for Mrs. Driver and your daughter."

"Arrogant sons of bitches."

"No denying that. Still, they rule the gilded roost. More accurately, their wives do."

So the lot wasn't bought, the preliminary architectural sketches were rolled up and stored. For once others got the best of him.

The following year, a sprawling house on the beach at Long Branch replaced the Drivers' modest cottage two rows removed from the ocean. Sam would never go back to the beach house. The day after Grace's death, Mozart was ordered to sell it.

The railway car lurched; the wheel trucks clacked. The whistle sounded again but the river fog was dispersing. Sam asked, "Would you like to be invited to that Arabian Nights affair?"

She thought a moment. "I suppose I might, though I'm not

sure striving to be approved by Mrs. Astor is a worthy ambition. She treated Mother badly without knowing her."

"They met once, at the Metropolitan Opera. Your mother was cordial. Mrs. Astor cut her dead."

"That's what I mean. Newport's still a fortress."

"No fortress is unconquerable."

Jenny shrugged and turned away. Passing lights from a trackside inn threw patterns of descending raindrops on her cheeks. Sam decided this was neither the time nor place to continue the discussion.

In Rochester, distant cousins from the Penny family of the Finger Lakes district gathered under a green canopy at Mount Hope Cemetery. Rain fell without letup; elaborate floral tributes from Sam's business and club associates were beaten into dripping drabness. Mozart stood a respectful distance behind father and daughter, who had been given chairs.

The minister was bareheaded and uncomfortable even under the canopy. He read familiar passages from Scripture. *In my Father's house are many mansions. I go to prepare a place . . .*

Which she couldn't find here on earth, poor dear woman, Sam thought with bitterness. At that moment, for whatever reason, a vision came.

He saw a round, misty atrium or entrance hall, architecturally vague but aesthetically magnificent. A full-length oil portrait of Grace dominated the space. Half again life-size, the painting showed her as a young woman, gowned, a splash of red roses in a tall vase behind her. As you entered the great hall you couldn't avoid Grace's lovely, thoughtful eyes following you. The vision was so intense, Sam felt almost drunk.

Force them to look. Force them to admit she was a great lady. They denied her once and I let them, for her sake. They won't do it again.

Were there images from which a portrait painter could work? Yes, two ambrotypes that captured her beauty, and a small oil hastily rendered by a Manhattan street artist and bought as a lark on an afternoon stroll.

And the Newport door was open again, however slightly . . .

Without admitting it to Jenny, Mozart or anyone, Sam kept an eye on society's doings. It was unavoidable, really; all the New York papers, including the most popular and innovative, Gordon Bennett's *Herald*, printed endless columns of society news. The upper classes were celebrities. Readers lusted to vicariously experience the lives of their fancied betters.

Mrs. Astor still dominated the social scene, but with advancing age she'd relaxed her control on the summer colony, yielding to a triumvirate consisting of Mrs. Stuyvesant Fish, Mrs. Herman Oelrichs and Mrs. William K. Vanderbilt, wife of the Commodore's inadequate son. Sam had met Mamie Fish, Tessie Oelrichs, Alva Vanderbilt and their husbands casually, at charity affairs. The Fishes belonged to McAllister's original 400; the Oelrichses and Vanderbilts did not.

The old bandits with whom Sam had schemed and fought were gone. Other capitalists of dubious reputation remained, certainly: Carnegie the steel magnate in Pittsburgh; Rockefeller the Cleveland oil king. But they were pious do-gooders compared to roistering buccaneers like Jim Fisk. Rockefeller, a hymn-singing Baptist, made no secret of his dislike of Newport's ostentation.

The drenched cemetery workers lowered Grace's coffin. Sam put a hand over his eyes. Jenny laid a black kid glove on his black wool sleeve. Her face was uncovered, as fashion prescribed; her black tulle veil fell behind her ears, to her shoulders.

"What are you thinking, Papa?"

"I'm thinking how much I loved your mother. And I'm thinking we should go back to Newport."

"Certainly, if the idea suits you."

"I didn't like running away the first time. I did it to spare your mother's feelings. She was better than the lot of them. You might find Newport a good place. Full of eligible young men."

Jenny avoided a direct response. "Doesn't Brady spend his summers there?"

"I believe so."

"Do you want to face him? Deal with him?"

Sam fell back on a familiar thought:

"No fortress is unconquerable. If there's any such place as heaven, I'd like to have your mother looking down and approving of what we do. How we succeed. Because we will."

"Well, the choice is yours."

And already made. Brady or no Brady.

4
Some Citizens of Newport

On a glorious June morning two weeks after Grace Driver's interment, three Rhodys—Rhode Islanders, born and raised in Newport—went down to Long Wharf to watch the arrival of the Fall River steamer *Puritan*. The overnight boats from New York usually docked at 4 a.m., then carried most of their slumbering passengers over to Fall River itself, for a more leisurely return. A severe storm had delayed *Puritan* in Long Island Sound, much to the pleasure of locals who otherwise wouldn't have gotten up for the arrival.

The 400-foot steamer with FALL RIVER LINE blazoned on the bow was a multistoried beauty. White as a wedding cake, she carried upwards of 950 passengers, a good many of these already crowding the rail to disembark. At one time Jim Fisk and Jay Gould had controlled the Old Colony Steamboat Company, forerunner of the Fall River Line, Fisk adding the title admiral to his other military honorific, colonel.

The clear sky promised a beautiful day. The harbor sparkled, already busy with traffic: a ferry bound for Jamestown; a three-masted naval training vessel weighing anchor under the Danish flag; fishing skiffs; even a few rowboats on the water for pleasure. Sweet scents of honeysuckle and hawthorn masked less attractive odors from local cesspools. For all their cynicism, the three residents were, with some exceptions, proud of their old wooden town whose off-season population was about twenty thousand. Here the Rhode Island general assembly met from time to time, coming down from Providence. To say you lived in the only state with two capitals was worth boasting about.

Eldest of the three watching the arrival was Titus Timmerman, who reminded many people of a turtle. Titus had appropriated the only available seat, a rotting keg at the head of the pier where drays lined up to receive luggage for hotels and guesthouses. Titus owned a Thames Street grogshop named Ye Snug Harbour, an orthographic conceit he long ago decided would attract tourists in search of New England quaintness.

Titus lived most of the year on the profits of July, August and September. He welcomed vacationers to his tavern in obsequious fashion but secretly loathed them; he seldom made any money from the howling swells who had begun putting up their huge "cottages" out along Bellevue Avenue.

Hands on the tarnished knob of his cane, sharp chin resting on his hands, eyes bright as a raccoon's, he watched the docking vessel.

"Season's started, boys," he said, stating the obvious.

To Titus's right, dressed in a loose white cotton shirt only half buttoned over his chest, stood Titus's handsome nephew, Prince Molloy, his sister Maureen's only child. Poor downtrodden Maureen had justified the unusual name by saying, "I called him Prince because that's what he'll be someday."

In the V of Prince's open shirt hung a cheap tin-plate medal, another legacy of his mother's. The medal was a stylized head of an owl. Prince didn't know what it signified and he didn't much care. He liked the trinket and its sentimental association.

Prince's father had been a mechanic from Cork, Ireland. He was employed as a coach finisher in Newport's best carriage shop on West Broadway. There he'd worked alongside Negroes and Bohemians without a second thought. His wife was a local girl, fair-skinned, deeply religious. While Regis Molloy was alive, his young son never realized the family lived in poverty, or close to.

Prince loved growing up in Newport. The green hills and open farmlands, the play of light on the ocean, the bracing air when the wind changed, made daily life a delight. He rolled a hoop, dove into the breakers at the public beach, watched sailboats tacking in the bay and wondered whether he'd ever be able to afford even a small skiff.

Prince had a cheerful disposition back then, bordering on the cheeky. His good humor didn't endear him to autocrats, of which there was at least one at St. Mary's school. This particular nun had not yet had him in class but had observed him, and thus managed to take an immediate dislike to the Irish boy.

Because of its close connection with the sea, Newport's population was an eclectic mixture of nationalities and backgrounds. As a boy, Prince formed a friendship with a baker named Marcel Youmansky, who owned a shop two blocks from the groggery belonging to his uncle.

The bakeshop was small, narrow and dark. The front window had an equally modest aspect, saying no more than FRENCH BAKERY in six-inch letters. But when the front door stood open in the spring or fall, appetizing odors of cinnamon and almond, butter and yeast and warm bread were sufficient to dizzy those passing by.

Marcel was a Jew. He worshipped at the Touro Street synagogue. He closed his shop before sundown Friday evening and reopened at nine Sunday morning, which the goyim regarded as a blessing for their Sunday dinner tables. Marcel was a small-boned, slightly built man in contrast to his wife, Berthe, who towered over him. Prince loved to listen to them shout at one another in French.

"You like to hear the language, eh?" Marcel asked once.

"Yes, but it's like monkeys chattering," Prince said. "I couldn't learn it."

"Why not?"

"For one thing, some of the nuns think I'm stupid."

"Their mistake. You could learn French if Berthe and I spoke more slowly."

"Why don't you?"

Marcel scratched his ear. "I think because we're French."

Prince stopped at the French Bakery often. His favorites were the short toasted bread sticks flavored with tomato and basil, two for a penny. Marcel gave Prince three for a penny.

"But I thought tomatoes were poison," Prince said the first time he bit into one of the delicious sticks.

"Nonsense. The tomato traveled from South America to Europe. Only the nobility could afford to eat the red fruit—yes, yes, I know, tomatoes are classed as vegetables but they are not; they have seeds. The poor could not afford tomatoes. The nobility ate them from pewter plates. Acid from the fruit absorbed lead from the plates. That's how tomatoes became poisonous. You see how ignorant people are?"

"I wish you taught at my school," Prince said, being in fourth grade then.

"*Merci*, but I have all I can do seeing that my dear wife heats the oven correctly."

One Sunday when Prince was eleven, Mr. and Mrs. Molloy took a rare holiday, leaving the boy with Maureen's unmarried brother, the stubbornly atheistic Titus. The Molloys rode the ferry across Narragansett Bay, intending to enjoy a carnival set up in Jamestown. A boiler exploded and those who couldn't swim to shore drowned. Regis Molloy drowned.

Maureen Molloy and her son moved to smaller quarters. The quality and quantity of food on the table declined noticeably. Prince sought what jobs a boy could find after school. He began to understand the meaning, the feel, of poverty. Prince's mother took one of the few jobs open to a woman of her limited skills and education. She became a maid at the Ocean House Hotel, up the hill from the harbor.

Prince's separation from the process of education, perhaps inevitable from the start, happened a year after Regis Molloy's death.

St. Mary's, at the rear of the church of the same name at Levin and Spring, was Newport's largest parochial school. Here, Prince and regimentation were never on the best of terms. He laughed too freely, too often. His developing good looks, together with the lack of a father, tended to stigmatize him as the possessor of a limited intelligence and a bent for trouble. He was always assigned a desk at the back of the room. There he slouched, letting his eyes rove everywhere but the lesson board. The nuns, generally patient and kindly, couldn't help but notice Prince's demeanor. Being strict disciplinarians, they occasionally rapped his knuckles.

After his father's death, Prince became more sullen, often responding with a saucy mouth when one of the nuns criticized him. The worst in this regard was Frances Mary, a portly sister near retirement but still swift and adept with the hickory switch. She brought a fresh one to the seventh-grade classroom every Monday.

When he couldn't answer a question, said he'd forgotten his times tables or certain answers in the catechism, she ordered him to hold out his hands, then whipped them.

"Master Molloy, with that attitude you'll never get on in this world. You may grow up to chase balls at the Casino but I can't imagine you achieving anything better."

Prince slid down on his spine again and squinted at the grimy windows. What she said about him was not new; no one except his mother thought much of his chances.

His career at St. Mary's ended abruptly one May morning when Sister Frances Mary seemed in an especially foul mood. She whipped Prince's hands twice. The second time, his lower lip jutted.

"Sister, may I ask you a question?"

"What is it? Quickly, please."

"Aren't you supposed to be the bride of our Lord Jesus?"

"That is very close to blasphemy, young man. But the answer is yes."

She held out her right hand to display a plain gold ring.

"I'm surprised He even looked twice at you."

"What are you saying, you vicious boy?"

"Why would He? You never shave your mustache."

When he walked home shortly afterward, never to return, his buttocks were striped red under his trousers. His opinion of himself was, and would remain, low, no matter what his mother said.

Perhaps to make up for Prince's punishment, and his insistence on leaving school to find work that would help support them, Maureen told her son that he would have a grand future. She added that he shouldn't continue to grieve too much for Regis Molloy because Regis wasn't the boy's father, only a surrogate for a rich rake she refused to name "until the time's right."

The time was never right. Maureen Molloy passed away

when Prince was almost fifteen. Her secret, if any, died with her. Prince wasn't sure he believed it anyway.

Maturing, growing handsomer, Prince showed his Irish heritage more strongly: curly black hair, vivid dark eyes, a smile that could shine like the sun, all charm, no guile, whenever he chose. Few guessed that Maureen's death had twisted and soured something inside him. He harbored a hatred of an entire class—the nameless, faceless people who'd kept Maureen Molloy bent over soiled beds at the hotel until she died of penury and despair.

Outwardly good-looking and carefree, inwardly Prince seethed with resentment, and a desire to repay some of those who had wronged his sainted mother.

The third onlooker, younger than Prince by six months, was his friend Jimmy Fetch. Jimmy was likewise an orphan. He and Prince had been tennis ball shackers at Gordon Bennett's Casino on Bellevue Avenue for several years, their nominal Catholic faith qualifying them for the jobs. In the winter they worked on an ice-cutting crew that sawed blocks from frozen ponds so a goodly supply of ice could be brought from storage to cool the drinks and bedrooms of the summer visitors.

Jimmy was a small, round-faced lad, heavily freckled, and perpetually squinting under the brim of a grimy plaid cap. Prince never altogether trusted Jimmy. Their friendship, as far as Prince saw it, sprang more from loneliness than liking. Jimmy followed his better-looking friend like a willing dog.

"Hope it's a richer summer than last," Titus grumbled. Prince laughed.

"You're only happy when the tally goes up, Uncle. Same as last year won't do in a Newport business."

"Not in mine it don't," Titus said, whacking the ferrule of his cane on the earth between his shoes.

Jimmy peeled off his cap and mopped his perspiring

forehead. "Lots of swells on the steamer. She must of been sold out."

As *Puritan* warped in, deckhands threw heavy mooring lines to the pier. Officious pursers stood guard while gangways were let down and secured. The steamer's passengers were a varied lot, ranging from the affluent with many trunks and portmanteaus to poorer families escaping New York heat for a refreshing night cruise. Passengers could book a luxurious suite or a low-priced berth in what amounted to belowdecks dormitories. The cheapest fares allowed sleeping on deck in sling chairs. Prince had been aboard a Fall River boat once, making a delivery for Titus. He remembered a splendid interior of gold leaf and polished wood where a string orchestra serenaded the guests.

The gangway ropes fell; the arrivals began streaming off. Jimmy nudged Prince. "Pipe the third bunch coming down midships. Handsome little tart, huh?"

Prince followed Jimmy's pointing hand. The man leading the way, probably a father, looked coarse and rather ordinary despite his striped blazer, white trousers, white gloves and straw boater with a wide band patterned like a peacock's tail. A flunky in an old black smoking cap snapped his fingers at luggage porters. The object of Jimmy's approval was the third of their party, a young woman under a pale emerald parasol. Her auburn hair, more red than brown in the morning light, shimmered with highlights.

"Pretty," Prince agreed. "Never seen her before. You, Uncle?"

Titus jutted his head forward like a curious turtle. "Nope. Man's got a familiar phiz. Picture in a paper maybe?"

Jimmy scratched his privates with no concern for people close by. "I'd like to get acquainted with 'er."

"So would I," Prince agreed, smiling in an oddly cold way.

He might well like to know her, but not for reasons Jimmy, or the girl herself, could guess.

To the clamor of arriving passengers, the maneuvering of the hotel wagons and drays, there was suddenly added a commotion from the direction of Washington Square. People scattered as a brass horn tooted, clearing the way for a magnificent four-in-hand coach wheeling up to the wharf in billowing dust.

Titus made a sour face. Another of the howling swells of summertime was out for a dash through town. A trim and mustached gentleman rode beside him and two grooms hung on behind. The driver's waving whip and florid face showed his displeasure over so many commoners, and common vehicles, jamming the pier head.

Prince recognized the coach, though not its owner. It was a road coach, offspring of English stages of past days. The side panels were bright yellow, waxed and buffed. Indigo lettering, small and artfully done on the quarter panels, identified the coach as ROCKET. Bouquets of artificial flowers decorated the throat latches of the four matched grays.

The driver wore white shirt and trousers set off by a high silk hat, yellow waistcoat, gleaming boots. For more formal drives and races he would have sported a white cravat and green cutaway.

While "Rocket" was temporarily halted by the roadway congestion, a mulatto urchin broke away from his mother and did a jig in front of the lead horses. This infuriated the driver:

"Get out of my way, you guttersnipe."

Someone shouted, "Don't be so cheap, Brady. Toss 'im half a dollar, he'll move."

"I don't reward show-offs."

The child's mother snatched his suspenders and dragged him away from the horses; the pause in their progress allowed the animals to relieve themselves hugely and noisily in the street.

"Brady," Titus Timmerman said from the side of his mouth. "William King Brady the Third. Wall Street. Old money. Cottage out Bellevue some ways."

"Who's the gent with him?" Jimmy asked.

"O. H. P. Belmont." O.H.P. as in Oliver Hazard Perry, one of the famous Perry sea dogs from Newport.

"The lot of you, stand away or I'll run you over," Brady shouted. Then something midway along the pier caught his attention. Prince craned around. Brady was staring at the rough-looking passenger, his attractive daughter, and the flunky in the smoking cap.

"I'll be damned," Brady exclaimed. "He has the nerve to set foot here? We'll see."

W. K. Brady III popped his whip over his matched grays, O. H. P. Belmont held on to his hat and the four-in-hand lurched through a break in the traffic, no doubt bound for a breakneck run on one of Newport's dangerously narrow country roads. One famous whip, Gordon Bennett, who built the Casino in retaliation for a fancied social slight, had been notorious for racing his coach on moonlight nights along back roads, howling drunk and stark naked.

Prince fixed his eye on the young woman. "Sort of feel sorry for that family."

"Ah, why?" Jimmy scoffed.

Titus explained, as if to a witless child. "Because, boy, if Brady don't want people here, he can make life hell for 'em. I wouldn't give you tuppence for their chances of lasting the season. 'Less of course they're complete fools, which the rich sometimes are. I'm going back to the groggery. The season's begun, alright."

5
Sam's Rise: The Civil War

Sam Driver's long march to acceptance by the Newport elite began years before he heard of the place. He and his older brother, Sebastian Drubermann, were born in southern Ohio. Their father, an 1837 immigrant from Swabia, drove switch engines in the Dayton yards of the Chicago, Hamilton & Dayton Railroad Company. The pay was low but Sepp Drubermann loved the modernity, the size, the violent power of the "steam horses" pulling his adopted country into the industrial age.

Sepp's boys fell in love with the chuffing, sparking monsters just as their father had. Sam was partial to 4-4-0 locomotives produced by the Rogers Works of New Jersey. Even in foul weather he'd tag after Sepp and stand in awe of the huge wheels driven by pistons, the gleaming steam domes over the great boiler, the unforgettable shape of the balloon stack, the great oil headlight that could illuminate a rainy evening as though day had dawned. The sight of a CH&D 4-4-0 rolling out of the yards convinced Sam that he was living in a marvelous new age. Any man who wanted to embrace the future should follow the trains, wherever they led.

As a student Sam was mediocre. English poesy and Latin verbs might as well have been written in Arabic for all the interest he had. He responded to numbers, sums, multiplication tables, division problems. But even these weren't attractive enough to keep him trudging a mile each way to the rural schoolhouse after seventh grade.

Sepp's wife, Hildegard, died of consumption in the spring of 1858, three years before the explosion at Fort Sumter. Abolitionist fever infected the boys. Sebastian enlisted in a Cincinnati infantry regiment. Sam, already at work as an apprentice fireman on the CH&D, persuaded his reluctant father to intercede with Congressman Clement Vallandingham, a Democrat even more antagonistic to Lincoln than Sepp. "Valiant Val," as his constituents called him, recommended Sam for service under Gen. Herman Haupt in the newly formed U.S. Military Railroad corps.

Sam was posted to Grafton, the staging area for McClellan's campaign to drive the rebs from western Virginia. He soon saw his idealistic vision of the war destroyed by reality. In trackside field hospitals no better than mortuary waiting rooms, young men lay in their own filth and died of dysentery brought on by spoiled food sold to the army by unknown contractors. In a heavy snow, a pair of new government-issue shoes dissolved on Sam's feet. He picked apart the remains and found mostly cotton wadding and lacquered paperboard.

Sam was promoted to corporal and shipped to the Alexandria terminus of the Orange & Alexandria line, a strategic sixty-three miles of roadbed running down to Lynchburg. After Shiloh, Sam received a letter from his ailing father. Sebastian had died in the second day of fighting at Shiloh, not from an enemy's ball, but from metal scraps that tore his face apart when his defective carbine exploded as he fired.

Sam went home to visit Sepp. He arrived two days after Sepp succumbed to pneumonia and despondency. So much death brought about a sea change in Sam. Henceforward, he carried out his duties with an underlying sense of the fraud and deceit that allowed a few phantom profiteers to enrich themselves behind the lines while whole regiments perished.

One February night in 1863, Sam was riding shotgun on a supply train heading south to Lynchburg. Three miles from the O&A roundhouse the train ran through deep woods. A sniper picked Sam off, blew him off the train and hurled him into a ditch, where he lay unconscious while the train chugged on.

He woke in pain and confusion, seeing the round face, straggling gray hair, nondescript clothes of a benefactor who examined him by lantern light. On the road beside the ditch stood a mule-drawn farm wagon, a tarp hiding its bulging load.

"Howdy, son. Guess I chanced along just in time. Seen you fall. Shooter got away, I reckon." The old man had a curious and unfamiliar nasal accent. "I'm bound for Washington city but I'll find you a field hospital."

Sam started up. "Oh my God, no, they'll saw off my leg."

"Reckon they will, but what's the choice?"

"I'll take my chances in Washington."

"You telling me you want to desert?"

"This isn't the war I bargained for—cheats and crooks getting rich while our boys die. Leave me in an alley somewhere."

The old man scratched his gray-speckled chin. "No, sir. In Vermont we don't dump wounded on a trash heap. Something's got to be done with you. I'll figure it out."

He extended a large, callused hand into the spill of kerosene light. "Fisk's my name. James Fisk, Senior."

Old man Fisk helped him hobble to the wagon, boosted him

up the wheel spokes to a precarious seat next to the driver's. Sam's left trouser was a sticky wash of blood. The pain was excruciating but he made no sound.

He lifted a corner of the tarp. When he turned back, he stared into Fisk's furious eyes, and the round muzzle of an army Colt.

"You're right, son. Bales of cotton. My boy, Jim Junior, deals in it. I'm going through the lines with a forged pass. You yell or fart or do anything to attract notice, you won't live to regret it. Won't live at all, if you take my meaning."

Sam nodded and held fast to the seat as the mules lurched the wagon forward.

So it was that Sam awoke in the suite of Jim Fisk, Junior, at Willard's Hotel on Pennsylvania Avenue.

Sam was clean, bathed, his left leg dressed and splinted. He lay under a starched sheet while a balloon-shaped young man with rosy cheeks, popping blue eyes and a drooping red mustache surveyed him through a wave of cigar smoke. Fisk the younger was sartorially elegant compared to his father. Embroidered flowers decorated his satin waistcoat; fawn breeches fit snugly on his fat legs.

"I hear you wanted Pa to leave you to rot in some alley where the woodbine twineth. Pa's a sentimental old rip. He brought you here. I paid for the doc. Jim Fisk's the name."

Sam shook a handful of fingers that resembled white sausages.

"You're cotton smugglers."

"Why, that's a mighty self-righteous tone, Mr.—"

"Drubermann."

"It's Confederate cotton. I have agents from here to Tennessee rounding it up. I ship it to the mills of my partners at the Jordan, Marsh company in Boston. They turn it into shirts and blankets for our boys. One hundred percent quality goods, no shoddy. So before you climb on your high horse, let me explain something. Jeff Davis and his vermin don't get any benefit or profit from stolen cotton and that helps defeat the damn rebs. Second of all, the cotton's milled into the goods I mentioned, and that helps defeat the damn rebs too. I'm as patriotic as yourself, maybe more so."

A coarsely pretty young woman in a purple hoop skirt glided into the room in a cloud of scent. Her scooped bodice barely contained her huge overhanging bosom.

"How's he doing, Jimmy?"

"Coming along just fine. Mr. Drubermann, this here's Lottie Hough. She's chums with lots of the officers at the War Department. They generously arrange our passes through the lines. Lottie's very persuasive, aren't you, dear?"

"So long as you keep me in clothes and champagne, Jimmy. I'm going shopping."

"Don't spend too much." As the door shut, Fisk sighed and rolled his big blue eyes. "As if I could do anything about it."

He hitched closer to the bed, his bulk making his chair sway and creak. "You want a job? I can always use another top-notch driver. Now and again, I regret to say, one or another of mine gets picked off or slammed into the stockade by the bluecoats. I make the pay worth the risk."

"Well, I'm not going back to the service. Why not?"

"I'd recommend a change of monikers. Provost marshal's men may be on the search for Mr. Drubermann."

Sam thought of the powerful Rogers locomotives. "Driver. Sam Driver'll do."

"Jolly good." Fisk clapped Sam's splinted leg without thinking. "You seem like a bright fellow—sharper than most who work for me. The war won't last forever, and I mean to move on. I'll take loyal soldiers with me."

"Where?"

"New York. I've always wanted to beat the tar out of that Wall Street crowd. Show 'em that a Vermont country boy can play their game and win handsome." He gave Sam a smile so broad and winning, Sam laughed despite the pain in his leg.

"You think you have a chance going against those sharks, Mr. Fisk?"

"If Jim Fisk don't, nobody does."

Years later, Sam often recalled that conversation. Fisk had supreme confidence, never mind that his ill-informed competitors on Wall Street called him a sappy rustic, and the newspapers treated him as a clown. Old Cornelius Vanderbilt thought so highly of Jim's business acumen that after the shooting in 1872, he spoke of hiring a medium to contact Fisk in the spirit world, to secure stock tips.

That night at the Willard, Sam rolled over and slipped into a contented drowse, imagining lurid financial victories built on Jim Fisk's declarations, but none of the struggles and dangers he'd find when he followed Fisk to New York.

6
Sam's Rise: On Wall Street

In 1652, the citizens of Nieuw Amsterdam built a defense wall at the south end of their island settlement, to protect against fancied threats from the New England colonies. Twelve years later the British overran the Dutch enclave in a bloodless attack. The crumbling wall lasted until it was razed in 1698 but the name of the street remained. The first commodities traded on Wall Street near the East River were African slaves.

Sam reached tumultuous, trash-strewn New York soon after Appomattox. Many newcomers were overwhelmed and defeated by the hectic pace and cutthroat activity of the city but not Sam. He felt he'd found his metier, especially in the financial district. Because of his facility with numbers he slipped easily into a clerk's post at Fisk's new brokerage at 38 Broad.

In those days government bonds and corporate shares were traded at several locations. The original mart, on Broad Street below Wall, and since 1863 called the New York Stock Exchange, held two sessions daily, at 10.30 a.m. and 1.00 p.m.

Although raucous songs were sung, and peashooter wads fired back and forth for the amusement of those assembled, the presiding officer's gavel kept a minimum of order as he called out the various issues for consideration: federal bonds, New York bonds, railroad shares such as the Pennsylvania and New York Central.

Other deals were made, prices quoted, shares traded at the so-called Open Board that met from 8:30 to 5:00, and also at Gallagher's Evening Exchange that ran twenty-four hours a day in a posh hotel on Madison Square. If those marts were too slow or formal, there was always a handy piece of curbstone where shares could change hands under lamplight, or as the sun rose—in fact anytime.

Fisk's firm was famous for the fat man's hospitality: champagne and raw oysters, roasted pigeon and foie gras, Cuban cigars and other deluxe offerings available gratis to all who dropped in. Genial Jim presided, uncorking the bottles and proudly showing off a tinted daguerreotype of his wife, Lucy, a permanent resident in Boston. "By godfrey, the finest, most dependable wife a man could have. She never, ever pays me a surprise visit."

Sam didn't as yet understand the intricacies of deals consummated with handshakes and whispers, but he soon understood that the naive Fisk, an inexperienced lamb, was being devoured by the wolves he welcomed to his fold. Within months the brokerage closed. On a nasty November afternoon, Jim Fisk shook his employee's hand on Broad Street.

"Don't leave town, Sam. I'm off to Boston to prospect for more capital, and if I ain't back in a month, operating full bore, I'll eat nothing but stone soup till judgment day. Wall Street ruined me, and by God, Wall Street will pay."

"You gave it a fine go, Jim."

"No, sir. I let their smiles and flattery gull me into making a whole lot of bad investments. I didn't understand the number one rule in this business, namely, there are no rules."

And off he went into blowing mist, leaving Sam to survive as best he could.

Sam moved from his residential hotel to a miserable waterfront doss-house and sank to the bottom of the labor pool. He worked for a private trash hauler, dragging odious bags of waste out of alleys. After a fistfight with his crew boss, he hired on at a brewery. Like similar establishments, the brewery kept a dozen cows, fed them with fermented mash and sold what the city referred to as swill milk, impure but cheap. Cholera and tuberculosis were blamed on swill milk. The brewers and distillers looked the other way.

Frequently Sam ate but one skimpy meal a day, bought at one of the new "lunch counters" opened to serve the always-hurrying members of the financial fraternity. Sam used his extra pennies to buy newspapers that informed him of the ways of the street for which he'd formed an attachment. Moralizing editorialists didn't think much of Wall Street, calling it "a cockpit of besotted habitual gamblers," and "a modern Colosseum where bulls, bears, and other ravening beasts gore and tear one another for profit." Sam was not put off.

Swill milk encountered competition from fresh milk arriving in Jersey City along with strawberries and butter on the cars of the Erie Railroad, an expanding short line. The Erie's board included both Commodore Vanderbilt and Daniel Drew, by reason of substantial loans each had made to the railroad.

The Erie was disreputable. "The graveyard of investors" and "a darling of speculators" were two of the kinder terms used to describe it. Dan Drew, who kept all his accounts in his head, boasted of jiggering Erie stock up or down according to his needs and whims. The primary rule of trade being an absence of rules, he dumped or withdrew shares to influence their price. "Daniel says up, Erie goes up. Daniel says down, Erie goes down." The widely quoted witticism was truthful.

Good as his word, Jim Fisk returned and opened a new brokerage, Fisk & Belden. He found Sam in the doss-house and rehired him. "Special clerk's your title but part of the job's bodyguard. I don't trust some of these stockjobbers, 'specially if they get hurt in the pocketbook. Buy a pistol. Buy two. I'll advance the money."

So Sam came into possession of a pair of .31-caliber Colts he carried under his frock coat, in an elaborate shoulder harness.

Fisk acquired an unlikely associate, a small, dark-bearded leather merchant named Gould. He might have once been Jason but he answered to Jay. He might have been Jewish but professed to be an Episcopalian. He had a family, and was as scrupulous about morality as Jim was dismissive. Fisk was outgoing, boisterous, forever the generous, optimistic front man. Gould sat hunched in his office totting up figures and scribbling computations. It was hard to say which of the two was smarter.

Both men were elected to the Erie board in October 1866, part of a deal that involved a group of Boston speculators. Sam transferred to a desk at the Erie's Manhattan headquarters, at the foot of Duane Street by the Hudson. Here, one day, a spike-haired man with a knife invaded the waiting room, ranting about losses on Erie stock that had recently tumbled. Gould was passing through to Fisk's office. The investor charged Gould with the knife raised. Sam leaped over his desk, yanked his pistol from its shoulder harness, and put two bullets in the wild man's leg.

After a patrolman carried the man off, pocketing a generous tip from Fisk, Gould invited Sam to dine with him that evening at Delmonico's. Over lobster thermidor and a white Volany, a wine Sam had never tasted or even heard of, Gould chatted on a number of topics, one of which played directly to Sam's interest in railroads:

"Short lines, especially failing ones, they're the thing. Buy them cheap. Squeeze them for all you can. Print bonds convertible to stock. Keep the shares, or distribute them to friends you trust. Make some cosmetic improvements if you must. Then, when omens are favorable, sell high, to one of the big trunk lines such as our dear friend Vanderbilt's New York Central. Alternatively, sell short and draw in some fellow you despise, so he takes a drubbing. Short line railroads. That's the ticket, Sam."

Upon that bit of conversation Sam Driver founded his fortune.

Slowly, he learned how to play Wall Street's peculiar game without rules. He met Vanderbilt several times, and while he didn't care for the Commodore's constant profanity, he never forgot Vanderbilt's boast: "What do I give a goddamn for the law? Ain't I got the power?"

He learned that having the services of compliant but greedy attorneys was crucial to success. "No problem there," Fisk assured him. "Throw a penny with your eyes shut in any part of town, chances are you'll hit a lawyer like that, maybe a dozen."

Gould often took the night steamer up to Albany carrying two satchels and returning with one. "We like to be sure we'll be looked on favorably by judges and members of the legislature," he advised Sam.

"So the Erie's bribing them?"

Gould's little shoe-button eyes remained unfathomable. "Nothing so undignified. The term is retaining. We want to be sure they never get the best of us."

"They?"

Gould's wave encompassed the world. "Our enemies. The ones we know, and the ones we don't."

Fisk presented Sam with 500 shares of Erie stock, currently selling at 66 and a fraction. Hesitant, Sam asked how much he owed for them.

"Oh, well, I could charge you for the paper, and the ink, and the pressman's time, but we can absorb that. Consider it a reward for good service. You don't have to keep 'em, you know."

Sam didn't; he pledged them at 40 on a short sale to a cooperative curbstone broker who sold them when they went to 75. The buyer was the widow of an Italian barber whom Sam fortunately never had to meet. When he covered the shares at the due date, he realized $33.60 per share.

In March of 1868, Commodore Vanderbilt called on his corps of captive lawyers and judges to oust Uncle Daniel from the Erie board on grounds of malfeasance. Injunctions and counterinjunctions flew from courtroom to courtroom while Vanderbilt pursued a corner on Erie shares. The more he bought, however, the less control he seemed to exert.

Sam guarded Jim's person, and the portmanteau he carried to the William Heath brokerage on Broad Street. He understood Uncle Daniel had paid similar visits to the firm before. Jim's round pink face glowed with satisfaction as he unlatched the portmanteau and flung sheaf after sheaf of Erie convertible bonds on the table.

"There they are, boys. Good for fifty thousand shares. If our good old printing press don't break down, we'll give the old hog enough Erie to choke on."

At that inopportune moment, a door opened from the office of one of the senior partners. Sam was rudely pushed aside by a stout, strong-looking young man with broad shoulders and imposing Burnside whiskers. He was grandly outfitted against bad weather in a long overcoat of green wool tweed and a high-domed hat of brown felt. Sam immediately assumed him to be a crony of the Commodore's because Fisk snarled at the senior partner. "Doing business on both sides of the table, Norval?"

"Mr. Fisk, we were merely conferring about—"

"Hold your clapper, Norval," the stranger said. "As for you, Fisk, never mind what we're conferring about. I see how you're playing the game."

"To win, sir. To protect our legitimate interests and those of our stockholders."

"Bullshit. Your stockholders are about as far from your concern as Sitka, Alaska. You're watering the stock." The phrase had come into use after Uncle Daniel's days as a cattle drover; he'd kept his herds thirsty, then let them lap up water just hours before they were weighed for sale.

The stranger laid a walking stick on the banded bonds. "I'll bet the ink on these certificates isn't even dry."

Fisk flicked a look at Sam, who fanned back his lapels, letting the stranger see the forward-facing butts of his holstered pistols. The stranger's eyes, a chilly gray, focused on Sam's face. He lifted his walking stick off the bonds.

"We'll talk later, Norval."

The young man strode out. In profile his well-shaped face suffered. His nose became a beak; his chin receded weakly from his plump lower lip. Sam learned he'd just met the blue-blooded Wall Street speculator W. K. Brady III.

On the morning of March 11, 1868, the mood at the Erie's Duane Street headquarters was triumphant. The Commodore had bought and bought, until Messrs. Fisk, Gould and Drew had bitten into his fortune for some $7,000,000, cash. Jim Fisk poured champagne, although it was still an hour short of noon. Uncle Daniel hunched in his chair and intermittently chuckled with what Sam thought was insane glee. Little Jay Gould stroked his beard, smiled and even told a joke. A runner from their captive law firm interrupted the celebration:

"Court order's being issued over in Brooklyn, citing contempt."

Fisk's eyes bugged. "What the devil for?"

"Refusal to obey the injunction against issuing more bonds. You'll be served before the day's over. The sheriff will want to lock you up in a cell at Ludlow Street."

Uncle Daniel leaped from his chair like a man a third his age. "Not me, I'm too old."

Fisk began pounding on closed doors. "Everyone out. Clear the safe—greenbacks, ledgers, correspondence files. Everybody carries part of the load. Don't leave so much as an ounce of spit. Catch the ferry to Jersey City and we'll take over Taylor's Hotel, near the Erie depot. Vanderbilt can't touch us in another state."

At half past twelve Sam dashed from headquarters with two valises. By day's end most of the Erie staff had escaped to what the press christened Fort Taylor. That night, Fisk and Gould remained behind to dine at Delmonico's in a show of bravado. Warned of deputies on the way to seize them, they fled to the river, hired a rowboat and crossed to Jersey City in a dangerously thick fog.

Taylor's Hotel was soon guarded by three twelve-pound cannon, by units hired from the Jersey City police and the Hudson County artillery, and by a company of wharf rats Sam recruited and commanded. Sam was fully occupied with securing Fort Taylor. He forgot William King Brady III—dismissed him as one more effete Wall Street dabbler puffed up with self-importance. No threat.

Or so he thought at the time.

7

SAM'S RISE: THE DANCER AT FORT TAYLOR

Sam sat on a bollard, smoking a cigar and watching gulls, trawlers and a great Cunarder outbound for Liverpool. Twilight was settling. An onshore wind brought the scent of the salt ocean to cleanse the stench of the river. Twenty yards offshore, in a semicircle of four rowboats, Erie men armed with old muskets kept watch.

Five days had passed since the occupation of Fort Taylor. Several times, roughnecks almost certainly hired by Vanderbilt had drifted up to the front of the hotel. They were quickly sent off by the hired police. Gould had taken the train to Albany, there to attempt to persuade state legislators to pass a bill removing legal barriers to stock watering and banning New York Central directors from holding seats on the Erie board. His persuasion consisted of a trunk full of packets of thousand-dollar bills.

Bored, Sam began reading a used book bought from a push-cart. *A Pocket Guide to Gentlemanly Conduct.* He used a stubby pencil to underline key passages he wanted to remember.

Do not dress like a "dude" or "swell." Do not wear anything that will make you conspicuous or offensive to others. He lifted his pencil, amused. Fisk, with his scarlet frock coats and diamond-patterned vests, didn't believe such advice.

A shadow fell over the paving stones; Dan Drew, leaning on his walking stick. The old pirate's wrinkled face looked more sad than predatory. Sam hitched over to make room on the bollard. Uncle Daniel's eyes misted as he stared at the lights of Manhattan.

"I hate this. I miss my house in Union Square. I want to go home."

"Don't we all," Sam agreed. More footfalls then; a second arrival, Fisk. Uncle Daniel stood, his face briefly showing dislike of his partner. Hostility was brewing between the two, fueled by Drew's ceaseless complaints of homesickness.

"Out for the air, Uncle Daniel?"

"Better than staying in that stuffy, smelly hotel."

"Sorry you feel so." Drew started away. Fisk looked nonplussed. "Good evening, then." Drew walked on, unresponsive.

After a moment Fisk squeezed Sam's shoulder. "How's your old tin oven, my boy?"

"Holding up, sir."

"Mind checking out a pair of fair doves in the dining room? They have the look of performers."

"Does Miss Mansfield know them perchance?" Josie Mansfield, barely into her twenties, voluptuous and black-haired and, in Sam's opinion, icily ambitious, had recently joined Fisk at the hotel. She was said to be his kept woman, though not his only one.

"She don't. You might inquire of their names, so we could be properly introduced."

"I will."

Sam responded without enthusiasm. He didn't mind roughing up men but he disliked pimping. Fisk never concealed his fondness for pursuing women. *I am married to the dearest girl in creation*, he liked to say, *and she will remain that so long as she remains comfortably in Boston. As for myself, I am a bad man—born bad, and if God almighty is going to damn me because I love women, let Him go ahead and do it, but right now I'm having a good time.*

Sam asked, "Any report from Albany?"

"Gould's opened the liquor bar in his parlor at the Delevan House. Unfortunately some poltroons who may be working for Vanderbilt have a suite upstairs, where equal amounts of ambrosia are flowing. Votes are for sale in both the House and Senate, so it's a bare-knuckle bang-up to see who wins. The House already voted no on our Erie bill but Jay says that ain't the end of it. The pivot is the Boss"—William Marcy Tweed, leader of the city's notorious Tammany ring—"begging your pardon, Senator Tweed."

A sickle moon hung above them now. Fisk eyed it. "Time for the dining room, wouldn't you say? Before those charmers finish supper."

Sam found the two young women dining on low-priced entrees of whitefish and boiled potatoes. The homelier of the two wore the brighter dress, plum-colored, with a matching jacket tightly buttoned. Her companion's dress was some gray material, with blue buttons down the front. The young ladies looked stylish but not extravagant; he supposed actresses knew how to dress without buying French imports.

He bowed to them. "Excuse me, ladies. Mr. James Fisk has taken over a good part of the hotel on behalf of the Erie Railroad. He hopes you haven't been inconvenienced."

"Not so far. We aren't rooming here," said the homelier one. Neither could be much older than Josie Mansfield. From the maturity of twenty-eight, Sam had a confidence and swagger which didn't seem appreciated by the prettier of the pair.

"My name's Samuel Driver. I work for the Erie. And you ladies are—?"

"Dorcas Flugel," said the homelier one. Her mouth overflowed with large upper teeth, but her sultry eyes and warm manner overcame that. Like her companion, she was slender from the bust downward. "This is Miss Grace Penny. We're dancers with Madame de Rosa's ballet, part of the Broadhurst company opening at the Jersey next week."

"Offenbach's *Orpheus in the Underworld*," said the other, with what Sam perceived as reluctant politeness.

"That a fact. You ladies are theatricals." Sam had heard about the notorious cancan dance in the French operetta.

Miss Flugel seemed eager for male attention, and eager to induce it with effusive speech. "The show is definitely risqué. It played Broadway seven years ago, but everyone in that company spoke and sang German. We were too young to be permitted to see it, Grace and I. Even if we had been, girls from Rochester couldn't have afforded train fare."

"Not on a parson's salary," said the other. "Both of our fathers are ministers."

Dorcas Flugel giggled. "And neither one knows what kind of job we have in New York. They think we're shopgirls. It's a terrible fib but there's no other way we could audition and be hired as dancers."

The conversation sagged into silence. Sam blurted, "Offenblick, you say?"

"Bach. Offenbach," said Miss Penny. She was kind enough not to roll her eyes. Sam's neck turned red.

"Our version's English, less suggestive," Miss Flugel said. "The cancan's the same, though. People sometimes walk out."

"Your name is Grace?" Sam said to the other.

"Grace Penny, that's correct. Is there anything else we may do for you, Mr.—?"

"Driver." He was annoyed yet piqued by the girl's fresh, assertive style. She tilted her head slightly, her blue eyes large, unblinking. An invitation for him to leave? He wouldn't be so easily put off.

She saw the Colt pistols hanging inside his open coat. He tugged his lapels together. "I'm sure Mr. Fisk would be delighted to offer you a sherry or cordial when you finish your supper. His parlor on the second floor is quite elegant."

Grace Penny sat back in her chair, allowing Sam full appreciation of her shapely bosom. The gaslights shone in her auburn hair but there was no warmth in her response. "I'm sorry, sir. The reputation of Mr. Fisk has preceded him in many a newspaper."

"You mustn't believe all you read."

"Better a reporter's account than the word of an employee. However pleasant." The last was an afterthought, as if to make hasty amends for a needless rudeness. She reached to a vacant chair for her flat straw hat with a blue velvet band. "Please excuse us. We have an early rehearsal."

Dorcas Flugel collected herself and headed out of the dining room, her lower lip jutting to show her annoyance. "You pay, Grace, we'll settle later."

She vanished in the lobby. Grace Penny had to stop at the headwaiter's podium for settlement of their bill, which allowed Sam to hover.

"Miss Penny, we've gotten off to a poor start."

"Haven't we," she agreed with a cool smile.

"My fault entirely. Mr. Fisk meant no harm with his invitation." Which was of course a damned lie. "Might I see you again?"

Grace Penny contemplated his face, his wrinkled frock coat

and trousers. “Of course you may if you buy a seat at the Jersey any night during the engagement. Otherwise, I think not. Good evening, Mr. Driver.”

He watched her glide after her friend, attracting the stares of several of Fisk’s hired ruffians lounging in lobby chairs. Sam scowled at them.

In the gentleman’s bar, he planted his elbows and ordered a double rye whiskey. He’d tell Fisk that one of the ladies swallowed a fish bone and rushed out, violently ill. As for the pretty one, Grace with the biting tongue, her tartness challenged him. Her unpretentious charm appealed to him. He’d see her again, damned if he wouldn’t.

8
Sam's Rise: Confronting Brady

Ferries and chartered launches carried swells from Manhattan across the water to the Jersey Theater, there to enjoy the high kicks and red underwear of Offenbach's cancan dancers. Sam bought a seat in the smoking loge at the rear of the auditorium. He got a jolt when the spill from the proscenium lights revealed W. K. Brady with several friends in one of the boxes. When the dancers were onstage, Grace and Miss Flugel among them, Brady peered through opera glasses like a man about to devour a succulent steak.

The keeper of the stage door shoved Sam away when he tried to enter after the performance. Several top-hatted gentlemen, better dressed, passed bills to the doorman and slipped inside. Sam had nothing more than a half dollar. He slunk away through a lineup of hired carriages waiting to take the swells and their companions to supper, and God knew what else. Of Brady he saw no sign.

In Newark, Sam surveyed the rusting rails and sun-blistered rolling stock of a foundering short line, the Trenton & Teaneck Rail Road. He remembered Jay Gould's advice about milking, then unloading short line railroad stock. He marked down the T&T as a likely target.

The siege of Fort Taylor limped to an end in April. First, Dan Drew sneaked off to Manhattan, where one of Sam's men tracked him to Vanderbilt's town house on Madison Square. Presumably a deal was made there; the Commodore abruptly stopped putting money in the pockets of Tweed and his fellow legislators and the Boss about-faced to align his group with the Erie.

The two houses in Albany passed the Erie bill, lifting the ban on excess Erie stock. A complicated settlement netted Vanderbilt nearly $5,000,000 and led to his intercession with a captive judge who voided Manhattan arrest warrants for the Erie directors. The defenders of Fort Taylor recrossed the Hudson having won a victory that left them poorer.

Fisk shrugged off the loss. "We'll make it back. I'd rather have a Fisk palace here than a stone palace at Sing Sing." For meritorious service, Sam was promoted to vice president.

The line, meantime, was dealing with a tragedy brought on by Uncle Daniel's greedy refusal to replace rusted rails when he was Erie treasurer. A nine-car Erie express heading for the city took a curve at a reckless thirty miles an hour. The last four cars broke loose and plunged into a ravine. A coal stove in a sleeping car caught fire. The conflagration spread. Forty died in the accident, and a storm of editorial scorn descended on the Erie. *Many are the roles assumed by the tricksters in charge of this endless swindle*, said one paper. *To this we now add the role of public executioner.*

"Time to lie low, boys," Fisk advised. Gould concurred, and they did.

A man presented himself at Erie headquarters, seeking a job. He impressed Sam as more alert and intelligent than the usual gutter rats who lurched to his desk. Mozart Gribble was a long-faced, melancholy chap who reminded Sam of the Sephardic Jews seen about the city. He insisted he was a Boston Unitarian who had slipped over to New Hampshire in the late unpleasantness, there to enroll in Company E of Berdan's U.S. Sharpshooter regiment.

"Then I assume you shoot well?" Sam said.

"I can put a hole in the capital B of the Holy Bible's cover at fifty yards, without fail."

"Have you ever killed?"

"Gettysburg, Chancellorsville—quite a few. I never stopped to ask their names."

"If I hire you, Gribble, you can't wear that peculiar Turkish hat around these premises. Not indoors."

"Then, sir"—gravely, Gribble stood and brushed specks of a breakfast roll off the front of his old army greatcoat—"I must thank you and take my leave. Where I go, my smoking cap goes. It belonged to Grandfather Gribble and I refuse to part with it for a minute."

Sam sighed. "Sit down, sit down. Maybe in this case I can make an exception."

At Fisk's urging, the Erie bought Pike's Opera House at 23rd Street and Eighth Avenue, with elaborate plans to refurbish the marble building and convert the upper floors to the railroad's headquarters. Hardly had this program gotten under way than Fisk began dickering on a lease for Brougham's Theater on West 24th near Fifth, then a second lease on the Academy of Music on 14th. He boasted that he planned to be the town's foremost theatrical impresario, with a mission of bringing "culture and education" to his stages. It was remarkable hubris for a man who'd had even less schooling than Sam.

Fisk's penchant for continually expanding his horizons astonished his associates. Early in 1869 he bought a steamship company consisting of two vessels plying between New York and Fall River. Lavishly redecorated and rechristened the *James Fisk Jr.* and the *Jay Gould*, the steamers featured full-length portraits of both gentlemen in each vessel's grand salon. A caged canary added charm to every stateroom; Fisk loved canaries. The most important part of his new role seemed to be the admiral's uniforms run up for him by a tailor. Dark blue and heavy with braid loops and sleeve stripes, they were identical to U.S. Navy uniforms except for the line's emblem generously displayed.

Fisk had his nose in all sorts of deals and, to Sam, some of them smelled bad. He didn't like the smarmy good looks of the playboy Edward "Ned" Stokes with whom Jim went into business as partners in a Brooklyn oil refinery. Stokes seemed as interested in Josie Mansfield as he was in manufacturing kerosene and lubricants.

Gould tolerated his partner's excesses and kept busy with his own pursuits. His eye fell on another short line, the Albany & Susquehanna, built by a Scotsman named Ramsey. The A&S was a 142-mile right-of-way linking Binghamton with Albany. The Erie had a major junction at Binghamton, and from Albany, all the markets of New England would be open to expanded Erie service. Further, the A&S used the same six-foot rail gauge as the Erie, making transfer of rolling stock easy.

"We want it," little Jay declared. "We'll do whatever it takes to get it."

What it took was the usual small-town coercions, injunctions and cash bribes. Unlike the Fort Taylor affair, the A&S raid didn't end peacefully. In August, Sam rode the line hiring a small army of thugs, wine bibbers and other denizens of local vice dens. On the night of August 10, two hundred of these were aboard flatcars on an Erie train chugging through the 2,200-foot Long Tunnel east of Binghamton. Sam and Mozart Gribble, the latter with a Sharps rifle, rode the foremost flatcar.

Sam viewed his improvised army with considerable reservation: “Half of them are ready to fall off drunk.”

“Pick of the litter,” Mozart said with a shrug. “Can’t expect to do better when the litter’s poor.”

The engineer blasted his whistle. Men shouted, exclaimed and suddenly turned white in the glare of the great headlight of a second train climbing the same grade the Erie train was descending. “There it is,” Sam exclaimed. All day, telegraph wires had carried warnings of an A&S train of armed men steaming to confront them. “By God I think he means to crash into us.”

Seconds later, the terrified Erie engineer braked and jumped out of his cab.

The two trains collided with jaw-rattling force. Sam was thrown off, and many of his besotted soldiers with him. The headlight of the A&S locomotive tilted crazily in the dusk as the front wheels ran off the track. A whistle jammed open, shrieking without letup.

In the twilight of a summer evening the rival armies fell on each other with shovels, wrenches, clubs, pieces of lumber. The A&S men, more disciplined and sober, also had more firearms.

A bullet tore Sam’s .31-caliber Colt out of his right hand, destroying the gun. All around him, men swung weapons and cursed with an appalling variety of blue language while the jammed whistle screamed.

Sam tripped an A&S head-knocker, seized the man’s two-by-four as another assailant scrabbled up the shale slope with a pitchfork aimed for Sam’s belly. Sam swung the lumber two-handed, and too hard. The left side of his assailant’s head exploded. Blood splattered Sam's face. The man fell, dead before he landed on his chest. Only by force of will did Sam keep from throwing up.

"Jesus Christ, Mozart, I killed him."

"So he wouldn't kill you. War's war."

The Battle of the Tunnel ended with both sides withdrawing into starry darkness, leaving wounded to be dragged away later. Steam hissed from the stalled locomotives; mercifully, someone's rifle had silenced the whistle. There were few fatalities, but the one for which Sam was responsible never left his conscience.

Managing the battlefield from Albany, Fisk arranged the arrest of three principals of the A&S line. A judge retained by Ramsey issued a writ of habeas corpus and an order for Fisk's arrest. Fisk fled down the Hudson in a chartered steamer. After additional injunctions, lawsuits and countersuits, the Erie takeover of the short line was thwarted.

Gould was petulant about it, Fisk nonchalant. "Nothing was lost save temporary honor," Fisk said. Sam remembered his own blood-slicked face and reflected that he'd lost a good deal more than that.

Newspapers laughed at Jim's latest folly, the Erie headquarters redecorated and renamed the Grand Opera House. The railroad took the top three floors, leaving the entrance hall to impress patrons with its enormous staircase, its marble paving, its magisterial bronze bust of William Shakespeare.

The second floor was a marvel of extravagance: metal gates for the anteroom, the inner office of the vice president and managing director featuring a desk on a dais and a throne chair studded with gold nails. Telegraph wires at Fisk's elbow connected him with offices in the building, as well as with Jersey

City and other important stations along the line. In the ceiling, painted ovals edged with gold repeated the Erie name.

Gold-flecked carpet sank beneath a visitor's boots. Even Fisk's washstand received a decorator's attention; painted nymphs sported in the marble bowl, their naked breasts gleaming. An inevitable canary twittered in a gilded cage.

Sam recruited a half dozen doorkeepers and armed each one, to guard against the intrusion of process servers and detectives hired by enemies.

For the opening attraction of the auditorium, Fisk continued the run of *La Périchole*, another opéra bouffe composed by Monsieur Offenbach. Once again, Madame de Rosa's ballet girls formed part of the company. Caterers delivered champagne and pickled oysters to the stage door on a nightly schedule. A riot of carnality pervaded the marble building after hours. Sam learned to knock before entering even the most public room. Once, sent by Gould to retrieve some papers from the managing director's office at half past midnight, he barged in too hastily and saw Fisk's immense half-moon buttocks bouncing up and down on the spread legs of a danseuse gasping and groaning on a divan.

"Come back later," Fisk panted without looking around. He continued bouncing while his caged canary sang. Sam backed into the anteroom, hot and embarrassed. He knew Miss Penny was in the de Rosa company and prayed to heaven that hers wasn't the face hidden by Fisk's bulk.

Fearing that he might learn something he didn't want to know, he avoided the dressing rooms of the ballet girls. Most nights he perched on a stool beside the keeper of the stage door, monitoring the pomaded dandies who presented themselves for admission with appropriate bribes for the old man on duty.

W. K. Brady appeared, bouquet of yellow roses in hand. Sam stepped up to bar his way.

"Looking for someone?"

"Miss Penny of the dancing chorus." The beaky man stood half a head taller than Sam, and let him know it by peering down.

"She expecting you?"

"She will be as soon as I speak with her."

"I'm afraid she has a prior engagement."

"With whom?"

"With me."

The lie put Brady on the defensive, but only for a moment. He reached for Sam's lapel to drag him aside. "I'll speak to someone in authority, if you don't mind."

Sam knocked his hand down. The doorkeeper stared; a number of other swells crowded in to watch what might become lively fisticuffs.

"Is vice president of the Erie enough authority for you? Get out or I'll call the guards."

Brady leaned in, blowing stale breath in Sam's face. "You're a damn nobody."

"Not in this building. Leave."

Brady withered him with a look, then battered his way through the gaping spectators.

Sam waited in the hall leading to the dressing rooms until Grace Penny appeared, dressed for the street. They'd seen each other on previous evenings—a nod from her, a smile from him—but always hastily, in passing. Tonight he blocked the hall.

"Miss Penny."

"Mr. Driver. You're an important man around here, I understand."

"Important enough to save you from the attentions of a nasty gentleman from Wall Street who, I suppose, intended to buy you supper at Delmonico's."

"Truly? You turned him away? What if I'd wanted supper at Delmonico's?"

"Then I'll be happy to provide it. Unless of course you have a prior obligation to someone? Mr. Fisk, perhaps?"

"He's asked me to supper twice. Both times I declined. A parson's daughter has no business visiting privately with a man of Mr. Fisk's—ah—colorful reputation. He has a wife in Boston, a sweetheart living half a block away and, from what I hear, concubines throughout this building."

Hurrah! She wasn't the girl in the upstairs office.

A smile spread across his rough face. He saw no need to tell her that he'd already bribed a headwaiter at Delmonico's with several free Erie passes, which Jim Fisk distributed generously to employees and friends.

Sam offered his arm. "Shall we, then?"

Her blue eyes changed from cool speculation to warm amusement. "I don't see how I can refuse such a gallant offer."

"I knew we'd be friends."

"You knew better than I." She took his arm and let him guide her into the night.

"But perhaps you were right," she said. "My father is seventy-nine, retired from his pulpit. I could introduce you without the slightest hesitation. One day perhaps I will."

Two nights later, when Grace was indisposed, Sam was one of the last to leave the Opera House. At the corner of Eighth, a pair of men came from the shadows of the wall. One stepped in front of him with a cigarette.

"Spare a light?"

Suspicious, Sam nevertheless pulled out his matchbox. As he struck the light he sensed rather than heard motion behind him. The second man slammed a lead pipe into the backs of his legs.

The first man batted the match and box from his hands and kicked his groin. Sam went down, retching and scrabbling on the pavement. The first man had a hickory billy. Together, the assailants landed a half dozen blows. One broke open Sam's forehead, which leaked blood.

"Brady sends regards," whispered the first man. The two dashed into Eighth Avenue, nearly run down by an omnibus before they vanished.

Sam lay in his own blood, gasping and nauseous. A patrolman poked him with his boot and rolled him over.

"Public drunkenness is a crime, lad."

Sam was too dizzy and weak to argue.

So much for interfering with Mr. W. K. Brady III.

9

. . . And Getting the Best of Him

Sam pocketed $42,000 in the run-up to what was called Black Friday, September 24, 1869. Jay Gould's scheme to corner the U.S. gold supply was predicated on anticipated collusion in the Grant White House. It never materialized, and the attempted corner, while enriching a few, ruined hundreds. Sam banked his money and waited for an opportunity to deal with Brady.

It came a year later, when a consortium of investors bought up outstanding shares of the foundering Trenton & Teaneck Rail Road. Sam read in Gordon Bennett's *Herald* that a newcomer had joined the board of the short line and had been named interim president. Sam took his case to his employers.

"I'd say you're due a pound of flesh," Fisk agreed. He was just returning to the good graces of the financial community. The "honest crook" or "the crook-in-chief," depending on which paper you read, had been tarred with the scandal of the attempted gold corner.

Gould fingered his black beard. "Vanderbilt should covet the T&T if it's cheap enough. What's the quote today?"

"Forty," Sam said.

"Let's see if we can get hold of it. Drive up the price, then pounce. I've never liked Brady. Old money, but he swanks it as though he earned every penny. He didn't; it all started with his grandpa's concert saloon on the Bowery. The old man kept soiled doves for rent on the second floor. Brady the First rolled his money into a fleet of garbage scows that founded the fortune."

Fisk suggested that they employ Uncle Daniel's well-remembered handkerchief trick. Gould looked dubious. "That's a pretty hoary stunt."

"Sure, but it ain't been used in a while. Don't forget, Brady's a snob. Fancies he's a whole lot smarter than us rural fellows. His biggest enemy's his swelled-up opinion of himself."

Gould's little button eyes flashed with what might have been amusement. "You sometimes amaze me with your labyrinthine logic. How would you propose to proceed?"

"Tell your spies to keep track of a Brady luncheon reservation at your club. Then invite me for the same day."

In a week, the stars were in proper alignment; Fisk joined Gould at the prestigious Union Club, 21st and Fifth. Every influential businessman and stockjobber in the city belonged. Brady was dining alone at a window table. Fisk and Gould sat within nodding distance but paid no more notice than minimum politeness required.

Fisk seemed to have a case of catarrh. He reached into his pocket frequently for a linen kerchief. The fourth time, the kerchief dragged out a scrap of paper. On the paper was a scrawled memorandum. *C.V. wants T&T for NY Cent. Buy!!*

The scrap fluttered to the carpet near Jim's beautifully

polished half boots. He appeared not to notice. He and Gould left soon after.

Next day T&T shares closed at 55½.

"Brady's buying all he can, I have it on good authority," Fisk said to Sam. "The Erie picked up a few T&T convertible bonds. Let's take them to the cellar."

In cobwebbed gloom that smelled of ink and paper, Fisk turned the bonds over to a round-shouldered engraver. "We want to be able to print these here. As many as we need. Can you make the plates?"

"More'n likely. Just give me a few days."

T&T bonds convertible to common stock were soon spewing from the Erie's underground steam press.

Brady or his representatives continued to buy shares aggressively. When the price reached 98, Gould called Sam to his office.

"I'm releasing and converting our bonds tomorrow afternoon—that is, three dummy companies upstate will do that without revealing our involvement. Jim, are you comfortable with calling on the Commodore?"

Fisk chuckled, his various chins jiggling. "So long as I don't have to turn my back on him."

Gould was too busy for amusement. "We must be on solid ground with the old man regarding his intentions. As soon as we are, twenty thousand of sixty thousand new shares will be dumped on the market by our friends upstate. After a suitable wait for the trap to spring, I will issue orders to sell short."

The trap closed smartly: Brady personally took all 20,000 shares then selling at 97⅛. His contract called for delivery of the [illegible] twenty days, at an agreed upon $96 a share. The Erie surrogates promptly began selling at 40. Desperate to recover cash, Brady sold heavily. When the stock dropped to 22, the Erie in the persons of Messrs. Gould, Fisk and Driver snatched up everything in the market, until Gould told them they had all they needed.

Sam took the train down to Trenton with a heavy valise. Uninvited and unannounced, he barged into the seedy second-floor boardroom of the Trenton and Teaneck. A half dozen directors, all but one a septuagenarian, sat at the table with Brady, in shirtsleeves, at the head. Sam set the valise on the table.

"Gentlemen, the Erie owns fifty-one percent of the outstanding stock of this line."

One of the elderly directors sniggered. "How much did you print yourself?"

Sam ignored him. "The Commodore does want the T&T for the Central system. In due course we'll sell it to him. As for you, Mr. Brady, we require that you vacate the presidency."

"You arrogant little bastard. You dare address me in that tone?"

"I do. Get out of your chair. Collect your things. Now. You other gentlemen may stay until we elect a board of our own choosing. I'll tell you one more thing, Brady."

Sam leaned across the table. "If you send plug-uglies after me once more, I won't bother to chase them, I'll come after you."

"I—I—I refuse to countenance—" Brady's voice trailed off. "Gentlemen, excuse me. We'll soon have an injunction to stop this act of piracy."

But the Erie had alerted its retained lawyers and judges, and the Brady injunction was voided. That day in Trenton marked the last time Sam was in the presence of W. K. Brady III until the summer morning in 1893 when Brady spied him on the pier at Newport.

Fisk cheerfully loaned one of his six fine carriages to Sam, so that he could drive Grace up the Bloomingdale Road and tell her of his success. It was a soft moonlit night. Fragrant apple orchards sweetened the air. Only an occasional rider or coach passed them bound for New York.

"Do you remember William Brady, from Wall Street?"

"Oh, yes. Dreadful man."

"I threw him out of the Trenton and Teaneck president's chair day before yesterday. I replaced him with a gentleman who's sitting close to you this moment. Jim's been generous. If this deal goes as I hope, I might make close to a million dollars. So I have something to ask you. If I make that much, will you marry me?"

Shadows of moonlit clouds flew across Grace's face. The surprise was quickly replaced by a gentle joy. She laid her gloved hand on Sam's.

"Long ago, Sam, I changed my mind about you. I'll marry you even if you never make a million dollars."

"Let's keep it the other way. A greater incentive, don't you see?"

Grace laughed and fell into his arms while the team grazed at the roadside. A night omnibus from Westchester rattled by; with their arms around one another, the lovers paid no attention. Someone in the omnibus yoo-hooed and whistled, then the omnibus passed over a hill.

"Grace, I want you to know"—he kissed the soft breath on her lips—"Jim Fisk is my friend. I work for him. But I'm not the kind of man he is. One woman, the right woman, is all I want from life."

"And children?"

"A dozen. We'll watch our grandchildren when we're ninety."

Not quite the way it turned out: She could bear only one child before the doctors forbade more. But it seemed the sweetest of dreams, that night on the Bloomingdale Road.

10
Mr. Make-A-Lister

Sam Driver knew that he hadn't lived a spotless, irreproachable life, but thus far he'd lived more successfully than not, rising out of the smoke and noise of Dayton's CH&D yards to a position of wealth and eminence in his industry.

Not to complete success, of course—not success in what America termed "society." But that would come; he would outlive his past, or at least render it meaningless. He would create a place for himself and Jenny in Newport—a fitting memorial to his beloved wife.

Thus he faced the sparkling June morning in 1893 with confidence, even joy. Never mind that Brady summered on Aquidneck Island; he'd defeated Brady before and would gladly do battle again.

A porter delivered nine pieces of luggage to the Ocean House on Bellevue Avenue immediately south of the casino. The hotel had a faintly rundown air: patches of peeling paint visible outside, faded carpets and ferns in red stone tubs looking starved and dusty inside. A garrulous passenger on the steamer had informed Sam that the Ocean House was over sixty years old, no longer fashionable as in years gone by. But it remained the only hotel in Newport worthy of the name.

In their suite, Sam stretched his legs in a chair and said, "Tomorrow I plan to call on McAllister. The desk told me he's in residence."

Jenny unpinned her hat, twirled in front of a gilded mirror. "If you still want that, Papa."

"I think it would be advantageous for you to join the summer crowd."

"So you can play matchmaker?"

"Well, someone must. Perhaps we can enlist one of the grande dames to take you up, as the saying goes."

"With Brady looking on?"

"Who gives a damn about that? I just want to be positive that you'd like to crash these golden gates."

She hardly hesitated. "The prospect seems very attractive."

"Then leave the rest to me."

Handsomely turned out in a pale gray seersucker suit and straw boater, Sam left the Ocean House early the next afternoon and turned left on Bellevue Avenue. He'd sent Mozart to the Lyman Cottage on Leroy Avenue requesting an appointment with Samuel Ward McAllister, Esq. The appointment was a necessity, he'd been told.

Mozart returned to say Sam would be received at one.

The shingled cottage sat on a small lot on a shady street leading to the ocean. Sam rapped the silver head of his cane on the darkly stained door. A dour butler answered. Sam identified himself.

"Mr. McAllister is expecting you in the sun parlor."

The uncrowned, possibly deposed king of society rose from

a wicker chair. Sam had heard him referred to as "a discharged servant." If so, he seemed unaware of it.

"Mr. Driver. Forgive me if we don't shake hands. It's an unsanitary habit. I believe we've met before?"

"At the Union Club." Sam had seen him there, but never spoken to the man the papers had christened Mr. Make-A-Lister. The roster of "the 400," McAllister's creation, finally had been revealed the previous year, with only 319 names on the rolls.

"Please, be seated. Sarah will be here shortly with tea and scones." McAllister's speech seemed an odd, forced mixture of British upper class and the soft syllables of his native Savannah. He had family connections in Newport's intellectual colony: His mother was an aunt of the famous Julia Ward Howe.

The little lawyer struck Sam as quite ordinary. Portly, with a receding hairline, he sported a fashionable Vandyke and mustaches much like Jim Fisk's, only gray. Sam guessed him to be about sixty-five. What wealth he possessed had been built from handling gold rush claims in San Francisco. He brushed an invisible crumb from the cuff of his fine linen smoking jacket.

"Your principal business is railroads, as I recall."

"Yes, although I have only one board position now, treasurer of the San Antonio and Sonora. Quite a profitable little line. We haul ore from Mexican mines and carry fripperies back across the Rio Grande for the ladies. I've disposed of substantial holdings in Union Pacific and Western Union, both run by my friend the late Jay Gould."

"The little Jew."

"No, he wasn't. But he liked to have people think so. He felt it enhanced his reputation for clever dealing. I found it a peculiar attitude, frankly."

"I'll wager he was really Jewish."

Sam kept silent. This arrogant little toad, together with Mrs.

Astor, had kept the doors closed to Grace while she lived. The Drivers had never been invited to subscription balls presented by the New York Patriarchs, the clique of select gentlemen McAllister had organized twenty years ago.

Sarah McAllister arrived with the dour butler, who rolled a tea cart. Sarah was said to be a Georgia heiress. She was a pale, shy-seeming woman of almost excessive politeness. She expressed sympathy over Grace's death, which she'd read about. Then, with a swish of skirts and a trace of fragrant powder lingering behind, she vanished for the rest of Sam's visit.

"That will be all, Johnson. I'll pour the tea," McAllister said. The butler left. McAllister noticed Sam glancing at a dozen books stacked on a table in dappled sunshine.

"Ah, my modest memoir. Allow me to present you with a copy, already inscribed."

He pressed the gold-stamped volume into Sam's hands. *Society As I Found It* had been published the preceding year. Sam had read almost 290 turgid pages before giving up. McAllister congratulated himself endlessly; parties in his "circle" (notably those arranged by himself) were "the stepping-stones to our best New York society." He dwelled on his expert knowledge of food and wine, larding his text with annoying French phrases he didn't translate. He described the proper way to *frappé* champagne: in a pail of alternate layers of ice chips and rock salt, so that the champagne reached "perfection" in precisely twenty-five minutes, with "little flakes of ice" among the bubbles. He seemed to consider this one of his life's highest accomplishments.

Although McAllister's self-glorification made clear that he mingled with the best people, and they with him, he didn't name names or trade in gossip. Even so, this hadn't prevented his decline in status; the book was simply too pretentious to be taken seriously. Who wanted to be associated, however dimly, with such a pompous fool? New Yorkers snickered and turned away; papers west of the Hudson jeered at the literary pretensions of "the head butler" and "the mayor of Cadsville."

"You are a recent widower, Mr. Driver. I add my condolences to Sarah's. How may I be of service?"

Sam set his cup aside. "I'm in Newport for two reasons. I intend to build a summer residence—"

"Oh, many of the best people are doing that, yes. Might I ask where your cottage will be located?"

"Nothing's been decided. I presume some locations are better than others."

"By all means. Anything between Bellevue Avenue and the ocean is acceptable. The west side of the avenue, while marginal, is also acceptable. West of that, no. But renting for a year or two frequently is preferable to a headlong rush to build."

There followed a somewhat didactic discourse on a local gentleman named Alfred Smith, whom Sam had not heard of before. Smith recognized the real estate opportunity Newport afforded and, before his death in 1886, had amassed millions by laying out and selling lots on Bellevue Avenue, Ocean Drive, Indian Avenue and other desirable venues.

"He also ran an excellent rental agency for many years. Quite frankly, Newport's summer trade could not have survived and thrived without it, because many come here only to leave after one or two seasons, while others find themselves perfectly at home, accepted, and therefore they put down roots. A fine example is one of our leading grande dames, Mamie Fish—Mrs. Stuyvesant Fish of New York. She has always been quite comfortable with seasonal rentals."

"I'm afraid I am not. I'm no longer a young man, and I consider myself competent to deal with architects and contractors. That may not be the case in the Fish household. I believe Mr.

Fish occupies his time running the Illinois Central. But a house is secondary to my other purpose. I want to introduce my daughter, Jenny, to Newport in the proper way. In that area I'm woefully ignorant. I decided to call on the man who knows all about such things. I've heard stories about your vast knowledge of European society. Your ingenuity in designing entertainments—"

"Spectacular ones, if I may say. I think the most elegant was my Star Quadrille, all the ladies gowned in flattering colors of my selection, and one of Mr. Edison's electric lights softly glowing on every tiara." McAllister pulled out a pocket kerchief and dabbed his brow. "May I be perfectly frank about the workings of Newport, Mr. Driver?"

"That's the only way, sir."

"Acceptance in the best circles does not come easily. It takes three or four years for anyone, even those eminently qualified, to establish themselves. Those years must be spent on what I call the stool of probation."

Sam clenched his jaw and murmured sympathetically. Full of himself, McAllister failed to notice the crimson in Sam's throat.

"The cost is escalating rapidly. A young lady entering the social whirl must have an extensive wardrobe. A new gown for every occasion. Small dinner parties for important guests are passé. Large fetes are favored—a theme, an orchestra, a multitude of servants. Before beginning all that, I advise young ladies to enjoy a summer at Bar Harbor, learning to flirt, to mingle with young gentlemen of the better class."

Sam shook his head. "No time, sir, as I indicated before. Can you estimate how much a three- or four-year probation, as you call it, might cost?"

"No, sir, I can't. But you surely know the old saying. One million is only respectable poverty."

"Money's no problem."

"Good, that's an auspicious start." He bit off a small piece of blueberry scone, chewed it and dabbed his lips with his serviette. "We might begin to lay out a program, then."

"Which, of course, I'm prepared to compensate you for organizing."

"Kind of you, sir. Very kind." As if it could have happened any other way. Sam had asked many questions of his informants. If they didn't know Mr. Make-A-Lister personally, they knew his style of operation.

More animated now that he knew Sam was willing to pay, McAllister said, "Perhaps we might consider one of my fêtes champêtres—my famous little plein air picnics that I hold at Bayview Farm farther up the island. Guests typically arrive in gaily decorated wagons. The atmosphere is heightened by sheep grazing, and a few head of cattle. I rent the animals for the occasion. Some additional locals might be hired and dressed in rural costume to enhance the atmosphere if you wish."

"Interesting. Please go on."

"Guests hobnob and sip champagne under a canvas pavilion, then sit down to one of my Saratoga-style banquets—Spanish mackerel, soft-shell crabs, woodcock, partridge and many other delicacies. I select the wines personally. Afterward, there's dancing on the lawn."

Sam had trouble stifling disbelief bordering on disgust. This is how the elites spent their time and money? Had Grace truly known what it was that she wanted? He was a simpler man. He would swallow the ostentation, and the accompanying bills, for Jenny's sake.

"It sounds perfect." He hoped the words carried conviction.

"Jolly good. Might I be so bold as to ask whether your daughter is attractive?"

"I consider Jenny a beautiful girl. Of course I'm her father. Judge for yourself." From his waistcoat Sam drew a gold locket that had belonged to Grace. He snapped it open, handed it to his host.

McAllister inspected the miniature oil portrait framed in the locket. "Oh, right you are, sir. Right you are. This tells me your daughter has already met the first of my requirements for Newport. It's beauty before brains, and brains before money."

He returned the locket and they began a discussion of details. Leaving the house, Sam asked whether McAllister wanted a cash payment on the spot.

"No, no, my banker will be in touch about such matters," said the mayor of Cadsville, throwing up his hands in mock horror.

Sam's pocket watch showed a few minutes past two. He'd promised to meet Jenny but the interview with McAllister had left him uneasy, and tired. At the Ocean House he flung off his boater and sprawled on a couch for a short nap. He presumed Mozart had retired to his own room.

Churning up from darkness, fighting for air, Sam saw his assistant's face looming.

"What is it, sir? What's wrong? I heard you calling out."

Sam raised his hands before his face. His fingers and palms were dry.

"I'm fine. Bad dream, that's all. I'm sorry I disturbed you. I'm late for meeting Jenny."

Sam busied at the mirror, straightening his cravat, combing his hair. Was he guilty of doing the wrong thing for his daughter? Was that the meaning of Fisk's blood spilled again in his dream?

No, he wouldn't believe that. They'd never get the best of him, these shallow, self-important lords and ladies of this little town.

Mozart hovered in silence until Sam bid him a terse good afternoon and left the suite.

11
At the Casino

While Sam sat down to negotiate with McAllister, Jenny walked from the Ocean House to the Romanesque arch leading from Bellevue Avenue into the Casino. It was an eclectic building, ivy-covered, shingled and gabled, with retail shops on the street side. The soft thump of a tennis ball soundly struck was punctuated by occasional applause from the sunlit courtyard.

Jenny paused in the warm gloom of the passage, pondering the significance of the moment. The Casino, built by James Gordon Bennett, Jr., the raffish journalist and millionaire whose Italianate mansion, Stone Villa, rose up directly across the street, was a centerpiece of Newport life. This was so even though the publisher was something of a local pariah. By passing through the tunnel to brilliant green lawns overlooked by a horseshoe piazza, Jenny knew she would be taking a first step toward committing herself to Newport's ways.

She wasn't fearful so much as skeptical of the wisdom of the venture Sam had launched with her consent. Clearly her father wanted recognition, acceptance for the two of them. Was he trying to ameliorate guilt because he'd been unable to provide recognition and acceptance for his wife a decade ago, when Mrs. Astor and her peers scorned men of new wealth?

Jenny's mother, God rest her, had always wanted to be part of society, even in her girlhood at a Rochester parsonage, where she'd secretly read about the travels and romances of "the 400" in old copies of New York papers, especially Gordon Bennett's *Herald*, which Jenny's grandfather wouldn't allow into the parsonage, deeming it coarse, if not salacious. Jenny remembered Grace describing how the Reverend Penny had pounded the supper table and railed against the "godless doings" of the New York and Newport elites:

"Go out to the entrance to the chancel. Read the plaque I put up when I was called to this pulpit. The law Moses brought down from the mount. 'Thou shalt have no other gods before me.' Have those depraved children of Mammon ever practiced the First Commandment? Are they even aware of it? I think not."

Despite Grace Penny's upbringing, she craved admittance to the world of the privileged who lived on Fifth Avenue's "Vanderbilt mile," some ten blocks north of the Drivers' relatively modest fifteen-room house. Once when Jenny was small, she spied on her mother, who was standing by a window overlooking the avenue.

A strange, almost grieving expression strained her mother's face. Jenny sensed the moment too deep and intimate for interruption. She stole away and slipped down marble stairs in time to glimpse a great four-horse carriage rolling south. Instead of a coachman, two smartly dressed postilions bestrode the near horses. Everyone knew the Parisian *demi-daumont* owned by the short, homely wife of Commodore Vanderbilt's grandson.

The rhythmic beats of a tennis volley brought her back to

the dim tunnel. Was she doing the right thing? She'd never know until years had passed and she could look backward.

Then what was the sense of hesitating? She stepped out briskly, toward the rectangle of sunlight ahead.

The Casino offered two venues for tennis, a large green building at the rear of the property where court tennis was played indoors on a wood floor, and three outdoor courts, for lawn tennis. Court tennis, a favorite in Britain, had not caught on in America, whose sturdy citizens seemed to prefer matches in bright sunshine.

On the Bellevue Avenue side of the property, a Tiffany clock tower rang the half hour. Prince knelt at the end of an outdoor net, shacking balls for Dickie Glossop, the bachelor architect who'd learned his trade in Richard Morris Hunt's studio. Prince knew Glossop and didn't care for his elegant manners and overtly disdainful air. Glossop had chosen Jimmy Fetch to volley with him.

Glossop wore smart white flannels, marred only by a grass stain on the left knee. Jimmy was his untidy self, wearing knickerbockers more gray than white, a sleeveless sweater with holes, his shabby cap. Glossop was of moderate height, lithe and limber; Jimmy, stouter, moved more slowly.

Glossop delivered an overhand serve that brought ladies to their feet under the piazza umbrellas. Jimmy returned it lamely, into the net. A few spectators scattered around the Casino bleachers applauded; guests and employees called the bleachers "the typewriter," because the round metal seats resembled the keyboard of one of those new writing machines.

A bleacher spectator whose clapping was less than strident was a muscular young man in his early thirties, with mustaches large and graceful as gull's wings. When the Casino opened, a committee of members had seen fit to hire Thomas Pettit away from the Court Tennis Club of Boston. The young Englishman was a strong player, and had won matches from Richard Sears of Harvard, the first Lawn Tennis Association champion, as well as from the reigning champion, Henry Slocum. In Newport, Tom Pettit found his services more in demand as a mentor for lawn tennis than for the unpopular indoor game for which he'd been hired. Tom liked Prince and from time to time coached him in the fundamentals of the lawn game.

Prince's attention had wandered from the volleying to the new arrival. She made a fetching picture in pale yellow lawn, with matching gloves and veil securing her wide hat under her chin. Dickie Glossop screwed up his sunburned face and shouted. "Hey, Paddy, wake up. Gawk on your own time."

Prince's jaw reddened. He scrambled after the ball. Glossop trotted back to the service line with a new ball of white wool. All the shackers at the Casino were Catholic, recommended by a parish priest. "Paddy" was no insult, or so Prince tried to tell himself.

Two serves that blazed past Jimmy finished the game. Glossop left the court without tipping Jimmy or even thanking him. Parties of ladies were chatting and gathering their effects to move into the shade for refreshments. The young beauty in yellow still stood by herself, smiling and composed but clearly unacknowledged; ostracism of newcomers was not uncommon at the Casino.

At courtside, Prince handed Jimmy a scrap of towel. "Sloppy play, Jim."

"Sure, why not? He knew he could beat me. He's too smart to go against you."

"Happen to notice that new lovely? It's the girl from the pier. Hold on, wait till she looks the other way—"

Jimmy's half-uttered question coincided with the young lady turning to survey the piazza. Prince snatched Jimmy's ball and racket from the ground. A quick lob sent the ball sailing to within a foot of Jenny's skirt. She turned in time to see Prince dash up to her and scoop the ball into his hand.

"My apologies, ma'am. My friend's a tad careless with his aim."

Her blue eyes appraised him, not in an unfriendly way. "No harm done. That was very quick of you."

Grinning, Prince pocketed the ball. Out by the net, Jimmy tumbled to the deception and walked away shaking his head. Prince swept off his cap. "Would you care to sit down? I'd be glad to bring you a refreshment."

"My, my. Do you wait on trade as well as chase balls?"

"When the trade's as pretty as you." The sally didn't seem to offend her. "Prince Molloy, at your service."

"That's a strange first name."

"A little notion of my mother's. She thought I'd live up to the title one day. So far I haven't," he added with a disarming smile. He liked these pretty belles of summer. The prettier they were, the more they fulfilled his purpose.

"Are you what they call a Rhody, Mr. Molloy?"

"Yes, ma'am, born and bred here. The old Fifth Ward. Might I know your name?"

"Jennifer Driver."

"New to the town?"

"Relatively." She snapped her parasol open, the sun through the ribbed silk patterning her face. "Shall we continue this conversation where it's cooler?"

"My apologies. Why don't you take that table and I'll bring you a cold drink."

"Lemonade, please. And one for yourself."

"No, ma'am. Casino employees aren't allowed to sit with visitors."

He brought the tinkling glass to her table on the horseshoe. When he bent to put the glass and serviette in front of her, she noticed the tin-plate owl at the throat of his open shirt.

"Is that a religious medal?"

"Not in the way you mean. I'm Roman Catholic, least I am when the priests corner me. This was a present from my mother."

"Does she live in Newport?"

"She's dead."

"Oh, I'm sorry, forgive me."

"Nothing to forgive. Happened some time ago."

"Does the owl have special significance?"

"If it does, I don't know about it. Just a souvenir she liked, I guess." He decided he'd better press his advantage while he could. "Miss Driver, would you take an evening stroll with me along the Cliff Walk?"

"What is that?"

"A public path that runs the length of Bellevue Avenue, all the way to Bailey's Beach. You can see the grand cottages on one hand and the Atlantic on the other. The people who own the cottages tried to keep townies off the walk but they lost in court, because an old law says Newport fishermen have access to the sea forever. Cliff Walk at sunset's very beautiful."

Jenny didn't reply immediately; he had a feeling he'd persuaded her. She was a pretty package, alright. He admired the round curves of her bodice, ample but not overstuffed like those of so many of the young ladies he considered bedding.

"I'm sure I'd enjoy that, Mr. Molloy. On the other hand, while I don't know a great deal about Newport as yet, I do know that young ladies must walk during the day, not the evening. Even then, to avoid scandal, they must be accompanied by their father. My own father's assistant, Mr. Gribble, told me so."

While he reconsidered his strategy, a rough voice intruded.

"If you're through bothering my daughter, I'd appreciate it if you'd move along."

Prince spun around, confronting an older man standing there in seersucker finery. Jenny said, "This is my father."

"How do you do, sir? No offense intended. Good evening."

He walked past Sam, separated, for the moment, from the young woman he'd chosen as likely quarry.

12
Warfare Begins

Sam peered into the shadows under the balcony at the rear of the property, where the boy had disappeared. "That young lout had no business annoying you."

"I discouraged him, Papa. Actually, I thought he was rather good-looking."

"I'll speak to the managers about him."

Her hand on his sleeve drew him back. "Please don't make an issue of it. You have to admire his cheek."

"In seeking an obviously attractive and no doubt rich young lady to chat up? I do not have to admire that for one minute."

Noting Jenny's frown, he left it there. He supposed the young man's good looks accounted for her leniency, but he still thought the upstart deserved a thrashing.

"It isn't my intent to regulate your life, Jenny. But this afternoon I made excellent progress with McAllister. I don't want your reputation sullied before it's established."

"There's no need to worry, I won't see the boy again."

"Happy to hear it."

He offered his arm, which she took. Secretly, she hoped to see Prince Molloy again, and very soon.

Outside, a line of expensive carriages proceeded along Bellevue Avenue at a leisurely pace. Many were open to the warm weather. Sam tipped his boater to a woman likewise watching.

"Beg pardon, ma'am, is this some sort of parade?"

"No, sir, just the usual afternoon ritual of distributing visiting cards. Every day at three, unless the gentlemen are showing off their coaches."

He thanked her and she moved off with a condescending nod. Jenny's hand tightened on his sleeve. A half-top phaeton drew abreast of them, side panels a rich shimmering indigo with a thin yellow stripe running horizontally. Two ladies sat behind the liveried coachman, intently staring at the Drivers.

The younger woman, raven-haired, oval-faced, with a light olive tone to her skin, could have been a beauty save for a small, thin mouth. The corners turned down naturally in a kind of perpetual pout.

The older woman looked like her daughter, but her face was rounder, with an unfortunate resemblance to a pug dog's. Someone had trimmed her garishly tinted russet hair so that it hung halfway over her forehead. Her eyes had a grimy, sunken appearance not helped by a heavy application of some sort of violet eyelid paste. Sam was no expert on unhappy women, but in this case he could make a reasonable guess. The phaeton passed on to the south, the half-top hiding the occupants.

"Who are those people?" Jenny said. "Do you know them?"

Sam said, "No, I don't believe so," although he'd seen the older woman in New York, from a distance, more than once.

Mrs. Emmeline Stackhouse Brady.

Next day, Saturday, William Brady began his campaign.

Inquiries had confirmed that Driver and his daughter were not merely weekend visitors, but had plans for a summer residency. Brady launched his attack at the old Newport Reading Room.

The gentleman's club presented a modest appearance on Bellevue Avenue, north of the Casino. Its building lot was small, its frame construction relieved only by a cupola and a broad piazza for members to take their ease in warm weather. Yellow-painted siding was beginning to fade and peel. Over the past decade membership standards had been lowered; Brady now had to share the club's amenities with coal pit operators from Indiana, gas fixture tycoons from Ohio and the like.

For lunch Brady ate a bowl of canned clam chowder and soda crackers; the club served nothing else. He preferred soup and crackers to sitting down with the Tigress, as his wife was called behind her back, and his daughter, Honoria. The worst part of Brady's life was the weekend, when propriety required that he board his yacht *Ozymandias* and sail up to Newport. He'd have preferred the company of his current mistress, a soubrette from a comic opera company who had a mediocre singing voice but remarkable talents in bed.

After lunch he retired to the main reading room. One member slept with head thrown back, mouth open, bandaged foot resting on a gout stool. Passing across the room to join a couple of acquaintances still showing signs of consciousness, Brady noted a discarded copy of Colonel Mann's detested but avidly read *Town Topics*, the New York paper more famous for omitting scandal, if the subject paid enough, than for printing duller items of social news.

"Do either of you know Samuel Driver?" Brady asked as he sat down with Catullus Howell, the elevator millionaire from

Chicago, and Arleigh Mould, the hotel man from Cincinnati. Howell picked his teeth with a fingernail.

"Driver the railroad man?"

"Yes. He arrived on a Fall River boat day before yesterday."

Mould belched without apology. "Don't believe I've had the pleasure."

"Don't count it a pleasure." Brady smoothed his thinning brown hair, its artful streaking of lighter strands the product of a chemist's bottle. "He has a lot of dirt on his hands. For a while he partnered with Fisk, and that crook Gould."

"I don't think so badly of Gould," Howell said. "I won contracts for my first two installations with a Jay Gould loan."

Brady clipped the end of a green Havana. "Past history. I'm told that Driver wants to join the summer community. We don't want or need his kind. If you encounter him, I suggest you do all you can to make him unwelcome."

They were well positioned to do it. Howell belonged to the exclusive Clambake Club, and Mould had just moved from one of the second-row cabanas at Bailey's Beach to a much more prestigious waterside cabana, a social advancement that typically required a wait of several years.

Mould leaned forward like a prosecutor. "This a personal matter for you, Bill?"

"Not personal at all. I have the well-being of Newport in mind. This is a special place. We don't want men like Driver setting themselves up among us."

Howell frowned. "That bad, is he?"

"Unprincipled. Slit your throat for a nickel."

"We'll keep it in mind," Mould said as he hoisted himself from his deep chair. "Where's the steward? I'd like a whiskey and a nap on the porch before I go home."

"I'll join you if I may," Brady said. Almost anything was preferable to returning to his cottage and spending time with his wife. Em had brought seven million to their marriage, from the Stackhouse meatpacking empire centered in Poweshiek County, Iowa. She had also brought a noxious prudishness about marital relations, but this Brady didn't discover until their wedding night. As a consequence Em gave him but one child.

The sun was setting toward Narragansett Bay when Brady left the porch and reluctantly began his bracing hike southward along Bellevue Avenue to Sunrise, his forty-room residence on the water between Mrs. Astor's Beechwood and Alva Vanderbilt's new Marble House. He'd enjoy a peaceful evening in his study, provided Em wasn't in one of her states, as he called them.

Alas, when he entered the vast sitting room, she rushed him like a predatory animal:

"Do you know who I saw outside the Casino this afternoon? Can you imagine?"

Brady slowly stripped off his gloves in an effort to remain calm. "Grover Cleveland campaigning for president?"

"Don't make snide jokes, Bill." Em stalked across the immense Persian carpet, kicked the train of her skirt, reversed her course and stalked back. Brady longed for the soft arms and inane cooing of his mistress.

"Where's Honoria?"

"Lying down. She identified that rotten man who forced you out of the T and T presidency."

Brady walked to the tall window overlooking the broad lawn and the Atlantic off Sheep Point Cove. "Sam Driver. I know he's here. Looking to become a permanent member of the summer colony, I'm informed."

Em Brady beat her ring-bedecked hands on her hips. "I won't have such trashy people moving into our circle."

He couldn't resist a sarcastic, "It does clutter up the social ladder, doesn't it?"

She slapped him with all the strength of her thin arm. He seized her wrist, bending her so she sagged toward the floor. "Woman, I told you never to raise your hand to me."

She began a singsong litany. "Oh, Bill, Bill." He shouted to be heard:

"Do you think I want Driver here? Do you think I'll sit by and do nothing?"

"Bill, Bill, Bill—"

"Go to bed, collect yourself, and when you come down in the morning, try to behave like a sane woman."

He left her and stormed into his sanctum, the glass-walled study; by his order, she was allowed in it only to care for the potted plants.

Her sobs faded, together with her erratic steps on the great front stair. There were enormous pressures on someone who couldn't quite gain the status, the entree, that Em craved. She wanted to be Mrs. Astor's lapdog. She wanted to be included whenever Tess Oelrichs or Alva Vanderbilt organized a committee. The trouble was, the Tigress—a mocking allusion to her striving—although rich, was too emotional, thus widely disliked for her erratic, often abrasive behavior. After years of marriage, Brady had no illusions.

At the whiskey sideboard he reached for the decanter of good Kentucky but withdrew his hand and studied the sherry bottle. Only a third remained. He never drank the stuff.

Thieving servants?

No. He had another suspect in mind.

13
Dickie Decides

Richard Rutledge Glossop, "of the South Carolina Glossops," kept his main office near Union Square in New York. In Newport he maintained smaller rented rooms on Touro Street. Cottage commissions were becoming more numerous and profitable as the craze to build and live in the summer colony accelerated.

A week after Sam's arrival, Dickie sat at his drawing board, pondering an unsatisfactory sketch of a three-story entrance hall for a new residence for Howell, the elevator millionaire. Following the advice of the famous architect with whom he'd apprenticed, Dickie had already decided on a heavy use of gold leaf and pink and green marble. All he needed now was a suitable design to incorporate those expensive materials, and more.

Dickie's family, South Carolina landed gentry since the early 1700s, owned a 400-acre rice plantation on the Edisto River below Charleston. For many years Dickie's forebears had fled the Low Country's pestilential heat to summer in Newport. The threat of civil war ended the vacations in 1855, a year before Dickie was born.

As a young man he spent one season in Newport, in a temporary project office of his mentor, Richard Morris Hunt. The master had taught him not only architecture but significant life lessons:

"Never forget, Dickie, as a class the rich are insecure. Anxious about the permanence of their wealth, doubtful of their entitlement to it. Reassure them of their worth and security by spending their money lavishly, as though funds were inexhaustible, and tomorrow didn't exist. In the end they'll thank you, and bring other clients to your door."

Four years ago, with Hunt's approval, he'd launched his own firm and done well. He was facile at adapting architectural fashions to the American market, and his gracious Southern manners and gift for flattery pleased clients.

He was relieved of further agonizing over the Howell job by the jingle of the bell above the street door, and the breathless entrance of Honoria Brady.

"Darling, wonderful news. Alva Vanderbilt's invitation arrived this morning."

"Her extravaganza to show off Marble House?"

"So exciting—the largest and most expensive summer home in America. We'll go together."

Dickie buttoned his waistcoat. "Certainly, if I receive an invitation."

Honoria tossed her glossy dark hair. "Well, sir, you had better, or I'll find another escort."

"Oh, we wouldn't want that to happen," he said with a faintly sour smile. The pertness, not to say rudeness, of rich society girls was a cross that gentlemen quickly learned to bear without protest.

He lifted his coat from the antler of a mounted stag's head.

"You really must excuse me, Honoria, I have a ten thirty appointment."

"You'd abandon me for some grubby old client?"

"Would-be client. The railroad man, Driver. I'm not sure I want to work for him."

Honoria's downturned mouth set the tone for her reply. "Don't even consider it. My father detests Samuel Driver."

He tugged on one gray glove, then another. "Trouble in the past?"

"The details don't interest me. I only know Papa doesn't want Mr. Driver in Newport. Or his daughter for that matter."

"Daughter," Dickie murmured, tilting his hat at a jaunty angle. "I wasn't aware he had one."

"I'm sure you won't be meeting with Driver long enough to make her acquaintance." Honoria said it sweetly, but there was no disguising the warning. She presented her cheek for a perfunctory kiss. Dickie obliged, then strolled out to issue instructions to his draftsman in the outer office. He and Honoria said good-bye in the shade of Touro Street. He set out for the livery where he kept a smart spring wagon with oversize rear wheels, two luxurious black leather seats and optional poles for a single horse.

Dickie was a young man who recognized and pursued the main chance. Bill Brady was wealthy, and that was Honoria's trump card; she believed Dickie wouldn't damage his opportunity to marry the Brady heiress. He'd groped Honoria a few times but never gone beyond that. He found her inexperienced and expected her to be the same way after marriage, lacking the passion of the girls he'd met during his year of study at the École des Beaux-Arts in Paris.

The clatter and bustle of the town improved his spirits, but driving past the Casino reminded him of Jimmy Fetch's friend,

Molloy. The shacker was an insufferable threat to someone of Dickie's position because, good though Dickie was at lawn tennis, Molloy was better. Dickie's deepest, darkest wish was not only to defeat Molloy on the Casino court, but to humiliate him.

Sam Driver and his assistant, a taciturn but somehow intimidating person named Gribble, were waiting on the Ocean House piazza. Dickie jumped from the front seat to greet them and shake hands. Sam Driver said, "I've found a property that's ideal for Red Rose."

"What, you've already named your cottage?"

"I intend it to be somewhat larger than a cottage, Mr. Glossop."

"In Newport, sir, the word *cottage* is used in the European sense, to denote a residence occupied only part of the year."

"That so?" Sam sounded annoyed. "Well, cottage or house, red roses are important. My wife loved them. Space for a large garden is critical."

"I'm eager to see what you've discovered," Dickie replied, though he wasn't. Dear Honoria had spelled out the rules. Driver was not to become a client. "Please, sit up front with me, Mr. Driver."

Sam took the suggestion. The odd chap in the smoking cap lounged in the second seat. Dickie shook the reins over the back of his dapple gray and off they went along Bellevue. It was a splendid morning; showers during the night had left the leaves of old oaks and elms glistening like displays of jewels.

On Sam's instruction, they drove out Narragansett to Ochre Point Avenue, where Ogden Goelet's magnificent Ochre Court rose in marble splendor. Dickie identified the style as Francois I, pointed out the slate roofing, the multitude of gables and mullioned windows. "Gargoyles on the water side," he added as they drove on.

Going south for two blocks brought them to the oceanfront on Leroy Avenue. Leroy ended at the Cliff Walk that ran from the Forty Steps to the foot of Bellevue farther on. Gribble opened the rusting gates of a weedy lot, three and a half acres, and so heavily treed as to be enfolded in darkness despite the sunshine. A grape arbor virtually hidden by dead vines bordered more than half of the south side.

Amid the trees stood a dilapidated Stick Style house with much of its half-timbering rotted away. "Fellow who owned this had traction franchises in St. Louis," Sam said. "Things went bad and he turned his pistol on himself. The attorneys for the estate reduced the price."

"It's dreadfully run down," Dickie said. "What would you hope to make of it?"

"Nothing. I'd raze it. I want a new house on this lot."

The Atlantic shimmered in the brilliant sunlight; unseen waves broke on rocks below their vantage point. Dickie didn't want to sound too negative so he said, "An excellent view. Certainly makes the property worthy of consideration."

"Consideration was yesterday. I've bought it. You can make your own inspection of the interior if you wish. We need to settle details of your employment."

"I'm the only architect you've consulted?"

"Frankly, no. First I went to the man in greatest demand, your teacher. Mr. Hunt can accept no more commissions at the moment."

"I appreciate your candor," Dickie said, determined to have nothing to do with Samuel Driver.

"Shall we walk the lot?" Sam said, already moving into the weedy fringe of the property.

After their inspection Sam suggested a drive past the brightest stars in the constellation of newer cottages: farther along Ochre

Point Road, The Breakers, which Hunt had agreed to remodel for Alice Vanderbilt, Alva's sister-in-law and bitter social rival. Then over to Bellevue, and Rosecliff, the cottage of Mr. and Mrs. Herman Oelrichs; south to Beechwood, the relatively modest property enhanced by the occupancy of Mrs. Astor, and the ballroom she'd added; William Brady's Sunrise, an ersatz Tuscan villa; finally, the newest sensation, Marble House, a Greek temple filtered through the sensibilities of a French architect under orders to create an American version of the Petit Trianon at Versailles. At each cottage they saw squads of gardeners, and a profusion of flower beds, massive banks of blue hydrangeas predominating. "Newport's favorite," Dickie told his guests.

He drove back to town along Coggeshall Avenue. By the time they reached the Ocean House, he'd silently rehearsed his little speech declining the commission. In Driver's suite they settled in the sitting room. Dickie consulted his pocket watch. Going on toward noon—not too early for a bracer, which he needed. Driver was a forceful man.

Seating himself, Sam said, "Let's discuss your terms, Mr. Glossop. And a completion date."

Dickie tugged his tight collar. "Your project presents an interesting challenge, but I'm afraid I must tell you—"

The suite doors opened. A stunning young woman entered, bringing with her the fresh scent of outdoors, and three hat boxes.

The men jumped to their feet, Dickie so hastily that some of his whiskey slopped on the knee of his trousers. Sam said, "My dear, let me present our architect, Mr. Richard Glossop. My daughter, Jennifer."

"Honored," Dickie said, bowing.

"Mr. Glossop was taught in the studio of Richard Hunt."

Jenny put her boxes down and took Dickie's hand without shyness or ostentation. "I'm pleased to meet you." Her smile was sweetly genuine, her blue eyes fine and deep. The effect she had on Dickie was immediate and overwhelming. She was a flash of sunshine, not bitter darkness like Honoria. She could be worth the risk.

"I trust you'll enjoy building Red Rose for us," Jenny concluded.

"I know I shall." Dickie bowed again. "The pleasure's all mine, Miss Driver."

Driver's man Gribble followed him down to the lobby, a brown paper cigarette smoldering on his lower lip. "May I ask a question? I hope you won't consider it impertinent, but I'm curious. Why do people spend so much money to build those monstrosities we saw?"

Dickie bristled. "You disapprove of our cottages?"

"Personally? Yes. The houses are pretentious. Visible insults to the poor. Why do people build them?"

"Because they can. The rich have always built monuments to themselves. Mr. Driver's no different."

"I would hope he'll be more restrained."

"I too have an impertinent question, sir. Are you an anarchist?"

Gribble blew smoke from his nostrils, reminding Dickie of engravings of dragons in children's books. "No, sir, but Newport's excesses might drive someone that way."

"I wouldn't tell your employer."

"Our employer, Mr. Glossop. Good day."

14
At Bayview Farm

Sheep bleated. Cowbells clanked. Champagne corks popped. A string quartet scratched out "After the Ball" beneath one of several open-sided tents. McAllister ran from point to point to make everything perfect. So far he'd succeeded. Sam felt the bucolic outing was a huge success.

Yesterday he hadn't been so certain. Black skies threatened rain. He'd contacted McAllister, asking about an alternate date.

"Oh, never, never, never," Mr. Make-A-Lister exclaimed. "As I advise the Mystic Rose"—Mrs. Astor—"and the other leading hostesses, it is axiomatic that one never cancels a dinner party, for any reason."

That seemed to banish the possibility of inclement weather. The skies cleared, bringing a glorious September afternoon. The lawns of Bayview Farm shone a vivid green. McAllister's property was located on Brown's Lane, three miles or more above the village of Middletown. It had a splendid view of Narragansett Bay. Silver highlights danced on the water. The slant of the sun lent a charming melancholy, reminding guests that the season of 1893 would soon be over, servants packing up, yachts and private rail cars carrying the cottagers back to New York for the winter.

Sam stood in the shade of the house, enjoying his cigar and a glass of claret. Ever the proud father, he watched Jenny circulating and flirting judiciously, greeting strangers and making friends. She was closely followed by young Glossop, who seemed to have attached himself to her now that he'd accepted the Red Rose commission.

For their first formal discussion of that subject, Sam had strolled to Touro Street. Dickie had an elaborate silver coffee service waiting for him, foolscap pages with an expensive tooled leather cover open, and questions.

"We've already spoken of the need for ample garden space, Mr. Driver. For the cottage itself, what architectural style or period do you have in mind?"

"That's your decision. I'm not educated about such things."

"But what impression do you want the cottage to convey?"

"Money. Lavishly applied."

Sam's unexpected candor stunned Dickie; clients didn't behave this way. They descended on him with thick dusty books of engravings of classical buildings, old Parisian newspapers, Italian postcards, pieces of molding, boards daubed with paint samples, fabric swatches, catalogs from European antique houses, even a few wet-plate photo prints of the Duomo, the Alhambra, the Parthenon. A client's portfolio of suggestions always shrieked "money" without uttering the word.

The meeting quickly abandoned aesthetics in favor of practicalities. Sam forced the young architect to promise conceptual plans and elevations by November 1, and a contract with a builder by New Year's. He wanted to host a party at the new house by next September. The cottage needn't be completely finished, but it had to be enclosed.

Dickie had resisted. "Opulent houses usually require two years, minimum."

"You'll receive a fifty-thousand-dollar bonus if you meet the deadline. Does that change the picture?"

"Somewhat. But I'm not the contractor."

"You'll supervise the contractor, won't you? You and Mr. Gribble. Every week the project's delayed after September First entails a penalty of five thousand dollars. The contractor agrees to the same bonus and penalties or he doesn't get the job."

"Your terms are hard, Mr. Driver, but the incentives compensate."

Sam smiled. "I knew you'd see it my way."

Among the fifty or so picnic guests at Bayview Farm, the host had snared a goodly number of Newport's elite. Sam had met several Livingstons, a Lorillard cousin, two maiden aunts of the Rhinelander family and a stone-deaf Schermerhorn matron. Mrs. Astor and the Vanderbilts had eluded McAllister's net, but Sam still considered it a worthy aggregation, with two real catches. The first was Mrs. Stuyvesant Fish, squat and homely as a bulldog but with keen black eyes and a likable openness of manner. Her summer gown of pearl gray cloth surely came from London or Paris, surely cost a thousand or more, and sagged and bunched on her stout body like a potato sack. She showed not the slightest concern.

The other catch was McAllister's acknowledged successor, the blond, pink-faced Harry Lehr. Sam had overheard maids at the hotel giggling as they competed with imitations of Harry Lehr's famous high-pitched laugh. Sam heard the real thing somewhere in the crowd.

Since it was a weekday, more women than men were present. Males were represented by some older eccentrics such as Casper Criswell, a millionaire who hung fourteen-karat apples on trees in his yard, and Girard St. Ong, an unread poet who strutted in a tailcoat with a red sash and gaudy decorations. St. Ong's memory had abdicated in favor of a delusion that he was either Prince Albert or Otto von Bismarck, depending on when you asked.

Mamie Fish worked through the crowd with the speed and drive of a steam train. Before long it was Sam's turn to be accosted.

"Howdy-do, howdy-do. Mamie Fish, pleased to know you."

"Likewise, Mrs. Fish. Samuel Driver."

"Oh, my sweet lamb, I am so poor at remembering names. Lovely picnic. One of Wardie's best. My husband will be sorry he missed it. He's in Chicago on railroad business. You're the papa of that little girl we all came to meet?"

"Yes, and proud to be."

"She's a beauty. Not uppity like some. I can't stand uppity. You and that lovely child must have dinner with us on Gramercy Park this winter, no excuses. By the by, I like the smell of your cigar. I'd ask for one but my reputation can't stand any more damage this week." She brayed her amusement at her own remark. As she waddled away, Girard St. Ong caught her and fluffed his chin whiskers with the back of his nails.

"Madame Fish? H.R.H. Prince Albert, in case you've forgotten."

"My sweet lamb, I wish I had. Give my regards to Queenie when next you see her. Ta-ta." She curled her fingers in farewell. H.R.H. harrumphed and fluffed his chin whiskers.

McAllister flitted among the guests, clapping and exclaiming, "Supper in ten minutes, ladies and gentlemen. Please proceed inside. We'll have a dance floor laid down when the meal is over. If we're generous with our encouragement, perhaps Harry will play for us."

Sam saw Jenny link her arm with Glossop's and follow the crowd, both of them chatting and laughing as though they'd known each other since childhood. He thought it would be entertaining to snag Mrs. Fish for a partner but Harry Lehr glided up to him before he could act. Lehr was a pudgy, vaguely androgynous young man, early twenties, splendidly turned out in a white blazer striped with pink, white trousers and two-tone shoes of white canvas and black leather. Sam understood that Lehr seldom spent a cent of his own for anything. Fine restaurants such as Sherry's and Delmonico's fed him on the cuff, and the best haberdashers were happy to dress him so long as he circulated their names among his acquaintances.

Lehr draped a white hand across Sam's wrist. "Lovely daughter you have, Mr. Driver. Sure to be a leading belle of the town."

"Thank you."

"I notice that Dickie Glossop is quite taken with her. Everyone assumed he intended to marry Honoria Brady."

"Things perceived as done have ways of coming undone, Mr. Lehr."

Lehr leaned closer, his long-lashed blue eyes darting around as though he were about to impart state secrets. "You do know that Bill Brady is busy blackening your name."

"I wasn't aware but I'm not surprised."

"That doesn't affect your decision to build here? Or to return next summer?"

"If anything, Mr. Lehr, it encourages me."

"Please, it's Harry. We must become better acquainted." Another caress of Sam's sleeve; he was beginning to find Lehr's attention distasteful.

"I understand you're a fabulous pianist, Harry."

"Performing for a crowd has always attracted me. I grew up in Baltimore and took part in many amateur theatricals. Usually playing feminine roles, which I adore. Shall we take supper together?"

"I'm sorry, I've promised someone else."

"Pooh, too bad. I shall be watching your daughter's progress most carefully. The old Tigress, Mrs. Brady, may not take kindly to having her poor child thrown over, but those little calamities save life from dullness. The cardinal sin for anyone or anything is dullness, don't you agree?"

He capped his remark with a giggle as high-pitched as his voice. When he'd gone, Sam searched for someone he might dragoon as his supper partner.

After supper Harry Lehr entertained the crowd with one of Mendelssohn-Bartholdy's *Songs Without Words*. Before playing he reminded his audience that the composer was Queen Victoria's favorite. Gratified sighs and applause greeted his remarks; Americans adored and aped the ways of European royalty. Only Mamie Fish looked pained by Lehr's music.

Couples went out to the lawn to waltz under Japanese lanterns on the small dance floor servants had laid down. Amply fortified with McAllister's food and drink, Sam watched the revelers from the sidelines. Jenny's hair glowed with red-gold highlights as she whirled in Glossop's arms. The architect was besotted with her and, for the time being, that was acceptable, since it should help speed construction.

Except for Lehr's gratuitous warning about Brady, Sam counted the picnic even more of a triumph than he'd imagined earlier. McAllister darted up to reinforce this by saying, "A huge success. Many, many compliments." Sam supposed a $500 tip to the host wouldn't be rejected.

Farther down the island at Sunrise Cottage, there was no gaiety or festivity. Most of the cottage was draped in a somber darkness, with here and there a lonely gas fixture flickering to light a corner or a stair. Em was furious that her husband thus far had balked at the expense of installing electric lighting.

Brady was in New York, as was his weekly custom. No doubt he was rutting with whatever little tart he was currently supporting. He didn't mind spending money on selfish things. Em had no illusions about her husband's morality, or his behavior when he was out of her sight.

The Tigress prowled through the cottage with her nerves drawn screamingly tight. Her uncombed hair straggled around the shoulders of her dressing gown, whose quilted lapels were spotted and stained by the soup she'd eaten in the kitchen. She'd ordered cook and her helpers to leave the premises so she could sulk and brood in private.

Yesterday, Alice Vanderbilt had called, her sole purpose, Em was sure, to cattily inform her that she planned to attend a garden party in Providence today, hence couldn't accept the invitation for McAllister's picnic to introduce Jenny Driver. No such invitation had come to Sunrise, though Em didn't admit it to Alice. She sneered that McAllister's picnics were gauche and she had no intention of being seen at one. The absence of an invitation hurt, of course. Em was wracked with anger, and familiar feelings of insufficiency.

September dark engulfed the house. A tall Swiss clock in the foyer rang the hour. As the chiming faded she heard another sound from far away upstairs. She stole to the foot of the main staircase to listen.

Honoria. Sobbing . . .

Had word reached her about the fickleness of that opportunist Dickie Gloop? He'd begun squiring Driver's daughter to tea; even broken into his morning routine to take her to an 11 a.m. concert by Mullali's Orchestra at the Casino. He'd excused himself from Alva Vanderbilt's evening gala at Marble House on the ground that work was pressing him. Despicable liar.

Screeching demons invaded her head. They came every time she fell into one of her states. There was only one antidote. She ran to her husband's forbidden study, knocking over an ornamental taboret in the dark. She heard wood crack; she didn't care.

Pale light from the moonlit ocean beamed into the glass-walled room. It guided Em across the cold marble floor. She unstoppered the sherry bottle and drank hungrily to silence her demons.

15
Plans of Attack

Prince nudged Jimmy with his elbow. "Take off that hat."

"Why? Your Uncle Titus give it to me."

"Not to wear indoors and make a fool of yourself." The hat, brown tweed, had a high crown and a brim turned down all around. The brim helped hide Jimmy's squint.

"Shit, what do I care about them people? To them we're just the rubber plants, good for laughing at."

Prince knew it was true but he was fixated on the auburn-haired girl waltzing with Glossop, among a swirl of other dancers below. The scene on the floor of the Casino theater was one of fine gowns, jewelry, gloved gentlemen, a small orchestra on the stage boisterously playing *Tales from the Vienna Woods*. Scents of perfume and powder rose up to the railed balcony where Prince and Jimmy and other locals sat on high stools, observing their betters. Admission to the balcony cost ten cents. Jimmy was out of sorts about paying the price at his friend's insistence; he hadn't bothered to bathe.

Prince was the better dressed of the two: dark gray trousers with a loud black check, a black silk coat of vaguely Chinese cut, a stiff white shirt, the tin owl hidden in the mat of his chest hair by an emerald green railroad bandanna. He'd doused his hair with water before he combed it; tiny drops still gleamed under the Casino lights.

Jimmy was dilatory about the hat. Prince snatched it off.

Jimmy grabbed it back.

"You're just sore because he's dancing with her."

"Let him. I can take her away from him anytime it pleases me."

"So when's it going to please you, Mr. Fifth Ward nobody?"

"Won't be long."

Prince leaned both elbows on the rail, watching as Jenny Driver hung in Glossop's arms, whirling, turning, her hair shining, her laughter showing teeth white as porcelain. Images of his late mother flickered in his thoughts: Kneeling to tuck in sheets at the Ocean House. Holding her nose to remove a slops pot. Coughing her last on a cot in the charity ward . . .

Applause from the dance floor signaled an intermission. Jimmy saw the odd look on Prince's face. "I can't figure you, Molloy. Do you fancy that girl or do you hate her?"

"People like that made my sainted mother an old woman before her time. People like that killed her."

"So you take the society girls into the moonlight an' get real friendly an' then you toss 'em over?"

"That's been the way so far."

"How many times? How many you left sitting on their asses and bawling?"

"Four."

"One got a baby in her belly, you said."

"Almost. She took care of it."

"You give her anything?"

"Sympathy."

Jimmy shook his head. "An' that one down there, she's number five?"

"She will be."

Miss Driver was peach pretty. Bright too—the best of any he'd pulled into his net. He almost regretted choosing her. But vows at his mother's grave mattered more than temptations of the flesh.

"What if she tumbles?"

"She won't, not till I want her to know she's punished. Wait, the swell's traipsing off to the punch table."

He waved. Jenny inclined her head, signaling that she'd seen him.

Jimmy said, "Sometimes I think you're a real bastard."

"The world makes it easy, pal."

Back came Glossop with punch. Jenny Driver's eyes closed briefly, the end of the silent colloquy between dance floor and balcony.

"She'll be going home to New York, won't she?"

"She'll be back next summer," Prince said with cheerful confidence.

Sam hated to be identified as a doting father, though it was exactly the role that fell on him. No one was more responsible than he was. He thought Jenny quite the loveliest young woman in the Casino theater, gowned in white satin with two dark blue ribbons trailing down her bodice to her hem and a pair of dyed blue egret feathers in her hair. He hadn't seen the bill for the imported dress but he didn't care how much it cost. Grace would have been so proud of her only child.

Old Arleigh Mould approached. Mould had watery eyes and a wife whose rheumatism kept her from the dance floor. "Well, Driver, for me it's back to the Queen City soon."

"New York in my case, Arleigh. How are you?"

"Working diligently on your behalf."

Sam raised an eyebrow.

"I've arranged for you to take over my second-row cabana at Spouting Rock." The offshore formation of boulders, where the ocean created a geyser at certain times, furnished another name for Bailey's Beach. Spouting Rock was a popular trysting place, and a tourist attraction.

"What a grand surprise. How did that happen?"

"I went around Brady, to friends on the membership committee. Brady asked us to make you persona non grata at every opportunity."

"So I've heard." Dickie Glossop, a member of the Reading Room, had reluctantly told his employer that Brady promised a black ball if Sam's name was brought up.

"Frankly, I was offended by Brady's gall. I've never liked the fellow. You may wait till your dotage to move up to a cabana by the water, but at least you're one of us."

"Can't thank you enough, Arleigh."

"If you see Mr. Brady, feel free to inform him that he was foiled."

Mould winked; they wished each other safe journeys to their respective homes and Mould hobbled off, only slightly less rheumatic than his wife, who sat fanning herself nearby.

Sam had begun a mental ledger of acceptance in Newport. Mould's news went into the plus column, along with the invitation to dine with Mr. and Mrs. Stuyvesant Fish at their New York mansion. In the negative column was lack of an invitation to Mrs. Vanderbilt's Marble House gala closing out the season next week, but then he hadn't expected one. The threatened black ball at the Reading Room was another minus. Still, Sam felt good about their first Newport season. The war had been declared. Like an old cavalry horse too long in the barn, Sam was eager to charge to the guns. Jay Gould's admonition about besting enemies known and unknown was never far from his mind.

"Carry something for you, miss?"

Startled by the voice, Jenny turned. The sun-splashed wharf was a scene of commotion, if not confusion. The Fall River boat was boarding, everyone crushing to be first. Before Jenny could answer the Irish boy, Gribble intervened:

"We have our porters. Be off."

Jenny flashed him a look, then concentrated on Prince, whom she hadn't seen since he watched her in the Casino. She enjoyed Dickie Glossop's company—he was well brought up, educated, successful—but he didn't flutter her stomach or overheat her cheeks the way the entirely unsuitable town boy did. Prince Molloy was perversely handsome, and smooth.

"Hurry, please, your father's waiting," Gribble said, moving away.

Jenny smiled at Prince. "I'm leaving for New York."

"Sure enough, else why would you be taking the boat? Sorry I can't afford a trip. I'll wait right here."

Their gazes held a long moment. "That's good. I'll be back."

She waved as she followed Gribble to the gangway.

Six months later, across the ocean, Emmeline Brady and her daughter visited a delightful new shop at No. 23, Plaza di Spagna, at the foot of Rome's Spanish Steps. Two English ladies had started Babington's Tea Rooms because of so many English and American tourists flocking to this quarter of the Eternal City. Tea served "in the traditional English way" was not available elsewhere in Rome.

Southern Italy's mild winter sunshine had restored Em's spirits and temporarily banished the demons that shrieked in her head when she was upset. She was pleased by everything except Rome's high concentration of Papists.

"It's time we had a little talk, Honoria."

"On what subject, Mother?"

"Jenny Driver. That young woman is unscrupulous. A social climber of the most brazen sort."

"I agree, Mother."

"She's robbing you of a very desirable beau, a young man with a sterling future."

"Dickie?"

Em nodded. "If you want him, and I believe you should, you must fight back. But not openly, in a manner that declares your hostility. Breach the other girl's defenses. Pretend to be her friend."

"That's quite a reversal, isn't it?"

"Yes, but I've thought about it for months and I'm convinced it's a sound strategy. Attach yourself to Jenny Driver. Dissemble. Learn all you can about her vanities, her flaws. That way, you'll be equipped to bring her down."

Em's new scheme left Honoria stunned and incapable of saying anything but, "How?"

The Tigress summoned the waiter, a greasy peasant who reeked offensively of garlic. She was ready for her nap in her suite at the Hotel Hassler, at the summit of the Steps.

"I can't say, my dear, but when the opportunity presents itself, you'll know."

Em finished her tea.

"Women always know," she said.

II
1894

16
"If Winter Comes . . ."

Through dreary days of sleet and murk, Jenny seldom left the house. Bargains offered at A. T. Stewart's and other retail emporia failed to lure her. She buried herself in books. *The Strange Case of Dr. Jekyll and Mr. Hyde. The Prisoner of Zenda.* George Du Maurier's *Trilby*, with its alluring portrayal of bohemian life in Paris.

She often turned to Shelley's "Ode to the West Wind," which perfectly expressed her longing. *O Wind, if Winter comes, can Spring be far behind?* . . .

With dirty snowdrifts piled along Fifth Avenue, she thought longingly of summer in Newport. And of the Irish boy.

Dickie met Sam's first deadline with concept sketches for a thirty-five-room cottage, 32,000 square feet, in the Beaux-Arts style taught in Hunt's atelier on Tenth Street. He peppered his presentation with the word *palatial* and made sure his unsophisticated client knew they were looking at an Americanized version of a château in the Loire valley.

Which Sam rejected:

"Too big. Too French. I want it expensive, but I want it livable."

Dickie came back with a different design, twenty rooms, 15,000 square feet.

"This is Colonial Revival style. The foremost exponent is the McKim, Mead and White studio. Of course I'm familiar with their work."

And willing and able to imitate it, Sam thought.

"I'm sure you are. Bring me new sketches by a week from today."

Sam and Mozart met a short, fat contractor named Rocco Ianelli at the Touro Dining Rooms on Washington Square (MEALS SERVED AT ALL TIMES, announced a big wooden sign outside). A Negro with grizzled hair led them to the table where Ianelli waited. The contractor informed Sam and Mozart that they'd been welcomed by one of the Allen brothers, entrepreneurs who also had the franchise to operate the congressional dining rooms down in Washington. Over a delicious luncheon of fried clams, corn bread and beer, Sam settled the arrangements quickly; Ianelli came well recommended.

"You don' mind doin' business with a dago, Mr. Driver? Some do."

"I don't mind if your work's good and finished on time. If not, I might drown you in a vat of tomato sauce."

Ianelli laughed. "Good by me. Shake on it."

Servants in the household hummed "The Sidewalks of New York." Jenny pasted together an album of souvenirs from the World's Columbian Exposition, which she and her father had visited last year before it closed. It was in Chicago that Sam had acquired his dislike of Richard Hunt's "Frenchified" Beaux-Arts style, exhibited most notably in the World's Fair administration building. He'd reacted enthusiastically to the "hootchy-kootchy" dance as presented on the Midway, and scoffed at clerics who called it a menace to morality.

In February they dined at the Fish mansion on Gramercy Park. Stuyvesant Fish, bearer of an illustrious name in the history of the city and the nation, seemed a retiring sort, almost overawed by his garrulous wife. Mamie Fish's reaction to William King Brady III was the same as Arleigh Mould's: Brady had a distinguished pedigree but an objectionable personality, a situation not helped by his tactless wife.

"In my opinion," Mamie said of the Tigress, "she has more than one cracked bell in her tower." Evidently you admired the Bradys or you did not; there was no middle ground.

Mamie liked Jenny, and promised to show her the protocols of Newport society when the season began. Jenny was elated.

The nation's economic weather was as cloudy and depressing as the winter afternoons. Financial panic was in the air. Mozart brought his employer reports of shrinking profits of Sam's investments.

Rumors reached New York about a coming strike at George Pullman's mammoth works in Chicago. An obscure Indiana man named Debs was stirring up rail workers with plans for a trade union, an idea Sam hated. He heard of a planned march on Washington by the unemployed, to "take back" the government from plutocrats.

One afternoon in early March he encountered Brady at the Union Club, where Sam had been admitted through his connection with Fisk and Gould. As he entered the busy dining room he spied Brady lunching alone at a window table. Instead of veering off to avoid contact, Sam strode ahead. Brady saw him, motioned to an empty chair.

"Hallo, Driver. Care to join me for a coffee or a pick-me-up?"

Instantly wary, Sam controlled his emotions. "Not just now." What he felt like saying was, *Not with you.*

"I don't believe I've ever expressed my condolences over the loss of your wife."

"Thank you." Sam felt his pulses speeding. What was the game?

"She was an attractive woman. Unfortunately I was never able to learn much more than that."

Raking up the Opera House incident, was he? God, how long the defeat must have festered. Sam was tempted to mention the plug-uglies Brady had sent to waylay him but this was a new era, and much as he wanted to shove the past into Brady's face, he wouldn't.

Other diners were turning to stare. Brady pushed his silver soup tureen to one side. "You've balked me in any number of ways, haven't you? You deliberately humiliated me in front of the entire board of the Trenton and Teaneck."

"Bill, that was business."

"The hell you say. That was a vendetta. I hope this summer you're not planning to inflict yourself once again on those of us who love Newport."

"Certainly I am. I love it too. We have a cabana at Bailey's Beach, haven't you heard?"

Of course he had. "Do you have any ambition to join the Reading Room?"

Sam shifted his weight, widening his stance. The dining room seemed unnaturally quiet. A waiter slipped around Sam with an apology so soft as to be inaudible.

"What if I did? It would be useless, you holding that black ball in your pocket. You'll have to play your little games elsewhere."

"Games? I have no idea what you mean by that."

"Do you mind if I respond candidly?"

"The only way between gentlemen," Brady said.

Sam leaned over the table, his smile unwavering.

"If you claim you don't know the games I refer to, you're a fucking liar."

Brady reddened. Trembling hands seized the tureen. Before Sam could dodge, Brady threw the contents in Sam's face.

In some contexts it might have been comical, Sam standing there with creamy chowder dripping from his nose and chin and staining his cravat. His good intentions blew away like thistle seed in the wind; he hauled Brady out of his chair by his lapels.

Brady batted at Sam's wrists but it was ineffectual. Sam punched Brady's jaw, knocking him sideways. The legs of Brady's table snapped under his weight, spilling him on top of jangling silver, smashed crystal and plate. The hushed room exploded into gasps and exclamations from the goggling diners.

"Bastard—you bastard—" Brady was huffing and floundering amid wreckage on the carpet. The headwaiter ran up, saved from reprimanding the brawlers by the arrival of the club steward, who seized Sam's elbow.

"Sir—Mr. Driver—I must request that you leave the dining room."

"Gladly. I've lost my appetite."

"Mr. Brady, I must ask you as well."

"Shut your damn mouth," Brady panted, crunching Wedgwood and crystal with his knees as he levitated his rear in a clumsy effort to rise. Sam's heartbeat slowed.

"So long, Bill. I'll see you in Newport, if not before. I'll send you the charges for cleaning my suit."

Brady's gray eyes glared. Sam managed to look almost nonchalant as he strolled out, still wiping chowder from his cheeks.

The following Tuesday, a messenger delivered a note from a man Sam had never met, Col. William d'Alton Mann, publisher of *Town Topics*. He invited Sam to join him at his regular luncheon table at Delmonico's, to look at a proof of an item about the brawl. He proposed to publish it in next Friday's Saunterings column, but it could be withheld, for a price to be negotiated.

Sam handed the note back to the messenger. "Tell this bogus colonel—"

"Sir, he rode with General Custer."

"I don't give a damn if he rode with the hounds of hell, I don't do business with blackmailers. Mozart, show this man out before I give him what I gave Brady."

Jenny raised the subject of the Union Club during an intermission at the Metropolitan Opera. "I certainly don't blame you for being angry, Papa, but the old days of fists and guns and ax handles are gone."

"Don't be too sure."

"But where will this Brady thing lead? When will it end?"

"When one of us falls and can't get up. It won't be me."

A bell rang to signal the next act. Sam took Jenny's elbow and steered her toward the stairs to their box, grateful to end the conversation.

Pullman workers struck. "Ought to hang them," Sam's friends said.

Coxey's army marched on Washington. "Ought to shoot them," Sam's friends declared.

Eugene V. Debs whipped up enthusiasm for a rail union. "Ought to lock him away for life," Sam's friends insisted.

Sam worried more about Red Rose, traveling every other week by overnight boat to check on Ianelli's progress. The trips were so inconvenient, and mixing with the traveling public so demeaning, he began to consider buying a yacht.

Fortuitously, he ran into Harry Lehr. Harry was having a midnight supper in the grand dining room of the Waldorf—crispy breast of duck washed down with Mumm's finest. Evidently he'd come from a fancy soiree; he wore a tailless dinner jacket, which the uneducated called a tuxedo. His companion was a peculiar flat-chested woman whose cheeks had the angular planes of a pugilist.

Sam accepted a glass of Mumm's but set it aside. After pleasantries, he said, "I'd like to discuss a fete at my new cottage late this summer."

Lehr patted his companion. "Go powder your nose, Giselle. It's shining like the evening star." When the creature left, Lehr said, "I understood Wardie handled such things for you. I can't poach on Wardie's territory. He paved the way for me in Newport."

"We both know McAllister's star is descending. You're the man Newport turns to for grand events with a theme, costumes—the whole concept. I want mine staged at Red Rose, early September."

"Will the cottage be finished?"

"It will be closed in. The architect and contractor assure me the electricity will be installed and working. Guests may have to dance on unfinished floors, but we should be safe from the weather. I'd like your recommendations."

"The kind of evening you propose is never cheap. Fifty thousand. And up."

Sam held a burning match near his cigar. "Cost doesn't matter. Only an impressive result."

Harry's delicate blond eyelashes fluttered. "My dear man. I knew from the moment we met that I liked you."

Prince passed the cold months in less comfortable circumstances. In November the Casino closed for the winter, along with the resort hotels. Prince and Jimmy took up their second occupation, harvesting pond ice. Prince's beard grew thick and black. The beard tended to hide bruises acquired when he and Jimmy fell into ferocious fistfights with men from a new artificial ice plant at Perry Mill.

Out before daylight, Prince trudged back and forth across Almy's Pond behind one of Mr. Pell's nags, dragging the plow that scored blocks of ice to a depth of eight inches. A work gang sledded the ice away to storage until summer. The worse the weather, the better the harvest, so Prince grudgingly prayed for freezing temperatures, but cursed them by the time a long day ended.

Uncle Titus's groggery stood on narrow, cluttered Thames Street between Ann and Levin, both of which ran down to the wharf side. Prince pronounced Thames to rhyme with shames, as did Titus, a lingering protest against the British. Those more willing to forgive and forget called the street by its London name, Thames rhyming with gems. Historians claimed no such logical grounds for Prince's version existed but he was loyal to his relative, and to hell with what some half-wit professor said.

Often before returning to Ye Snug Harbour he stopped at the nearby French Bakery for a baguette Marcel saved for him. By the time he reached his garret room over the barn behind the dramshop, the bread had lost its warmth. He wolfed most of it and fell asleep with his teeth chattering, unbothered by the drunken singing of his uncle's patrons. In the winter Titus kept his doors open for locals with a drinking habit and naval cadets who sneaked out after hours.

Heated dreams of Jenny Driver came to him frequently. He dreamed of her body, her mouth, her pale hands touching him. He dreamed of her with wet desire, not recrimination, something he puzzled over when he opened his eyes in the predawn darkness.

Chores for Titus canceled any rent Titus might have charged for Prince's pitiful quarters; Prince routinely saved a few coins in a tin box to entertain himself. One such night, April, but still cold and cloudless, he trudged to lower Spring Street in the Fifth Ward, to a two-story tenement where Mags Hogan kept house in stuffy upstairs rooms.

Mags was older, a full-bosomed seamstress in the employ of a local dressmaker. She supplemented her income by taking on gentlemen customers at night. She and Prince romped in lively but mechanical fashion, then fell asleep and snored. He was booted awake by a bare foot.

"You fish-eating son of a bitch. Get your skinny ass out of my bed."

"Mags, what's wrong?"

"You grabbed my tits when you were still asleep. You cooed like a dove"—she boxed his ears, making him yelp—"who's Jenny? You called me Jenny three times."

"Oh, Holy Mother—I can explain."

"No, you get out right now or I'll scream loud enough to bring the coppers, you two-bit cheater."

So Prince found himself barefoot on Spring Street. He sat on the tenement stoop, put on his shoes but didn't lace them because Mags raised a second-floor window and emptied a chamber pot. He sprang up and dodged the contents.

He fled around the corner into Extension Street where he

stepped on ice, slid and crushed something in a patch of melting snow.

In the starlight he examined a pale flower his toe plate had broken off. At the taproom, while Titus threw eggs in a skillet for their breakfast—it was Sunday, church bells ringing—he showed his uncle the crushed yellow flower. "What is it?"

"You don' know? Didn't the sisters teach you nothing while you were in school? It's a crocus. Spring's coming, and about time. We need the damn tourists."

Prince saved the crocus in the tin box where he kept extra coins, for reasons he couldn't or didn't dare explain just then.

17
REUNION

In the hard New England ground, Ianelli's crew dug a great hole with picks and hammers, chipping away stone, pounding in steel spikes to split the rock. They did it with cursing and sweating and a steam drill from Providence, the kind that famously failed to beat the legendary John Henry in a steel-driving contest in West Virginia. On the second day the steam drill broke down and mules hauled it away. Ianelli declared his distrust of the newfangled machine, which Dickie had rented.

For the cellar floor, a layer of rough concrete went down first, then brick. The rock walls of the excavation were parged, smoothed with rough masonry. Room partitions were built with more brick. Dickie insisted that the whole be painted eventually, for dryness and sanitation.

Sam liked the local men Ianelli hired. The contractor chose them for brawn and energy, not color. On a visit early in May, Sam counted three Negroes, two swarthy chaps who could have been Italian or Greek, a pale Swede, and a burly Ashkenazi

Jew from Roumania. Irish laborers made up a second, smaller crew bossed by a ruddy man named Paddy Leland. Ianelli hired Leland to lay pipe and install the centerpiece of the garden, an expensive ornamental fountain that Dickie had ordered from Italy.

The Irishmen wielding shovels were mostly older. Sam inspected them carefully, satisfying himself that he didn't have to put up with the brash young fellow who'd displayed an interest in Jenny last year.

One morning in late May, Dickie was perspiring and yelling at carpenters positioning floor joists. Work came to a halt as Dickie threw a sheaf of plans on the ground and kicked them. Workers rolled their eyes.

Standing to one side, Ianelli said to Sam, "He's young. Always trying to show who's boss. But he had good teachers, so I let it pass. I notice he's here a whole lot more when you visit."

"Probably hoping to see Jenny."

"Probably wanting to sniff your pocketbook," Ianelli said, though with such a broad wink and smile, Sam couldn't take offense.

When father and daughter returned for the season at the end of June, Harry Lehr presented his idea for a fete. Transported with enthusiasm, he fairly danced around the Ocean House parlor as he described "The Forest of Arden"—guests costumed as Shakespearean characters, "arbors twinkling with fairy lights."

Jenny liked the idea. Sam objected, without explaining that his lack of education made him a stranger to the works of Shakespeare.

Harry pouted. "Don't be a stick. This has never been done. It will appeal to the cultured element."

"It has intellectual cachet," Jenny agreed.

"You'll come as Bottom the weaver, one of the rude mechanicals, but transformed as he is in *A Midsummer Night's Dream*. I know a Providence craftsman who's an absolute master with papier-mâché. He'll make you a cunning ass's head."

Quite without wanting to, Jenny thought of Grandfather Penny's jeremiads about the First Commandment. But this was 1894, Newport, and she was part of it, willingly.

"How much?" Sam said. "Fifty thousand dollars?"

"Closer to seventy-five or eighty, I should imagine."

Jenny said, "I just had a marvelous idea. I can dress as Titania, the fairy queen."

Harry slapped her hand. "Oh, I'm so jealous."

Sleek yachts with large crews dropped anchor in Newport Harbor. Tall-masted ships of the navy's Atlantic fleet joined them. Coaches for racing or parading appeared from shuttered stables or rolled off ferries from the mainland. Party invitations arrived like flocks of migrant birds. Everyone anticipated celebration of the "Glorious Fourth," the New York Yacht Club's annual sail-in during August, the lawn tennis tournament to crown a national champion.

After a winter of despond, merchants such as Titus refreshed their optimism with beer and cleaned their premises to welcome new customers. The sun shone warmly, the nation's labor strife was far away, and Newport's summer elite reveled in the grandeur and stability of an America in which any government was ideal "so long as it's Republican."

Jenny emerged from the Ocean House one cool June morning to visit a milliner. Up from a rocker bounded a man with turned-up collar and a long-billed cap. He bumped Jenny, then apologized as he dashed into the street, quickly lost in the avenue's horse and wagon traffic.

An older guest approached. "Are you hurt?"

She assured him she wasn't.

"Do you know that young lout?" The word *young* triggered a sudden tension but Jenny said she didn't think so. The guest presented her with a folded paper.

"He dropped this."

When the Samaritan moved on, she opened the note. The pencil was blunt, the handwriting atrocious.

Eastons publik beach, befor dark, any day.

The beach for Newport's common folk lay at the east end of Bath Road. A few run-down houses and a small grocery stood on the rutted way under wind-whipped trees. Jenny hadn't found a chance to slip away from her father until two days after the note fell into her hands.

Tree limbs lashed back and forth, shedding new leaves that swirled around her. The road opened to a sandy expanse stretching down to a boiling surf. Magenta clouds darkened over the Atlantic. A trawler lumbered home through deep wave troughs. The inclement weather had cleared the beach of all but a couple of lonely strollers in the distance. Sand blew. A broken storm shutter clacked on the bath house. The wooden picnic pavilion appeared deserted. The flagstaff where a red pennant signaled MEN ONLY in the afternoon was bare.

Jenny braced against the keening wind, both hands on her hat. A spot of orange light brightened inside the pavilion, dimmed, then brightened again.

She ran down the beach to the pavilion. Prince's silhouette gradually emerged; he sat on a bench, smoking a brown cigarette.

"There you are," she cried, dashing into the shelter. He tossed his smoke away and stepped on it. When he grasped her forearms she almost fainted. Jenny was a virgin, with no experience of men except in daydreams and ladies' novels.

"I know you got the note but I wasn't sure you'd come."

"How"—she cleared her throat—"how many days did you plan to wait?"

"Every day until the season's over." He released her, indicated the bench. "Please. Be comfortable. No one can see us."

"Thank you." She seated herself on the rough planking. "That was daring of you, what you did at the hotel."

"I didn't trust anyone to deliver a message. Did I spell everything right?"

She laughed. "Not exactly. But I understood."

He perched on the other end of the bench, leaving a proper distance between them. In the northwest, over the trees, lightning flickered. Several seconds later thunder rumbled.

"It'll rain soon, so I'd better say what I came to say. I'd have written you last winter, except I didn't know where to send a letter, and I'm pretty dumb about spelling and such. As you figured out when you read the note. I want to see you this summer but I don't know how, or where. How do you feel about it?"

"Do I want to see you?" Jenny was dizzy with strange warm sensations. She was excited, afraid, mesmerized by the young man who reminded her of Svengali in Du Maurier's novel. "Yes, very much."

"I know your pa's building a cottage. Could I get hired?"

"The men putting in the fountain are Irish. The name of the boss is Paddy something."

"If it's Paddy Leland, I know him. Maybe Paddy can use an extra man."

"It would be risky. My father's often on the site. I wouldn't want him to see you."

"He remembers me from last year?"

"I'm afraid so."

"And he doesn't approve."

A wan smile. "That's like saying Niagara Falls is a freshet."

"Don't worry, Miss Driver, I—"

"Isn't it a little silly using proper names when we're planning trysts? My name is Jenny."

"Jenny it is."

He drew her to her feet, gazed at her in the sudden brilliance of another lightning flash.

"Dear Jenny."

Her notions of propriety, safety, conscience, collapsed; she flung her arms around his neck, let him feel her breasts against his coat, let him taste her kiss. His mouth was hard, masculine, strong with tobacco. She wanted to run away with him. He broke the kiss and said again, "Dear Jenny. Thank you for coming. Best you leave before it rains. One day soon, look for me at Red Rose."

"Prince, I—"

"Hush, hush"—fingers caressing her lips—"go on."

She left the pavilion and hurried to Bath Road in the first spatters of rain. Lamps had gone out in the grocery. She looked back at the deserted beach. She could see nothing in the blackness inside the pavilion. He'd disappeared like a wraith.

18
Lessons from Mamie

Mamie Fish, this year renting a cottage on Ochre Point, renewed her acquaintance with the Drivers. Mamie had three children, fed separately before she breakfasted in bed, but she adopted Jenny like a grown daughter. Mamie liked Jenny for her maturity and lack of guile.

Dickie endorsed the new relationship. "Mrs. Fish is a remarkable woman," he said to Sam during a meeting to decide on gold or silver fittings for the baths. "Her father, William Anthon, was a successful lawyer in the city. Mamie had opportunities for education that were denied to her friends Tessie Oelrichs in Nevada and Alva Vanderbilt in Alabama, but Mamie didn't take advantage. She can hardly spell. She never reads newspapers unless the item concerns one of her parties."

"How old is she?"

"That's a closely guarded secret. I would say forty."

"Even at that, her black eyes are very seductive."

"And her spine is steel. She's not one to be crossed. Be happy Jennifer's on her good side."

Mamie saw that Jenny was outfitted in a proper bathing costume: heavy shoes, cotton stockings, pantaloons under a short skirt, a jacket with a high collar and long sleeves, and a bonnet to protect her face from the sun.

"Black is the most popular color," Mamie said, "but younger persons may wear navy or dark green." Jenny chose conventional black.

"And remember, my dear, the rule is, display no flesh below the neck, except for hands. If you did, the result would be ostracism, not only at Bailey's Beach but everywhere." Mamie said it as though it were the most natural thing in the world.

At half past ten one sunny morning, they rode down to the beach in Mamie's carriage, a luxurious victoria. Jenny said, "I'm looking forward to bathing."

"The object of visiting Bailey's is not to be refreshed, but to be seen. Our cabana overlooks the water, with a lovely porch. You may sit in the shade and be noticed without risking undue exposure to the sun's rays."

Dressed so heavily she felt as though she were trekking in Africa, Jenny followed Mamie to a turnstile guarded by an old gaffer in a pretentious gold-braided coat. He greeted Mamie with obsequious deference. His smile for Jenny was less welcoming.

They spent an hour on the cabana porch, chatting and sipping iced water brought by an attendant. Then Jenny ventured down to the surf carrying her dark green parasol, which she planted in the sand before she waded. The chill water lapped over her shoes and dampened her stockings. She noticed that she was closely watched by ladies and gentlemen lounging under their parasols or in cabanas. A few frowns indicated disapproval of Jenny's behavior.

What nonsense, she thought. But if Bailey's Beach had its own peculiar rules and customs, she supposed she must abide by them to be accepted.

Mamie took her on an afternoon carriage ride to distribute visiting cards at the homes of friends.

"One never leaves the carriage," Mamie said. In a slow procession of equally expensive vehicles the victoria rolled along Bellevue Avenue, top folded down, sunlight flooding in. Both ladies protected themselves with parasols. Carriages turned off or stopped frequently to allow a footman to run to this or that cottage with a card and return with another card given him by the butler.

Mamie pointed to a carriage ahead of theirs. "That belongs to Lucille DeMint. Her husband's in lumber in Indiana. My carriage may overtake and pass hers because it's generally accepted that I am above her socially. Don't look at me that way, sweet lamb, I don't make these rules. One never, ever passes the carriage of any lady deemed to be one's superior."

"And if I did? More ostracism?"

"Oh, yes. Social suicide."

"This is a very strange place."

"It's Newport, dear."

She poked the driver on his high front seat. "Go around the DeMint rig, Ernest, it's damn hot back here."

Viktor, the family coachman from Latvia, had died the preceding summer of heat prostration; Sam had yet to find a satisfactory replacement. Thus Jenny hired a local hansom to carry her down the avenue to Beechwood one pleasant afternoon following the three o'clock coaching parade. Mamie had arranged an invitation to tea at Mrs. Astor's. Jenny had debated the wisdom of attending, fearing memories of her mother might undo her

A discussion with Sam convinced her that despite the risks, she shouldn't snub the great lady.

Beechwood was an older cottage compared to Sunrise next door and The Breakers to the south. Basically a Florentine villa, Beechwood dated to the early 1850s. William Astor had acquired it in 1880, his wife engaging Hunt to add a ballroom and refurbish the house originally designed by the architect Calvert Vaux. It was Mrs. Astor's arrival to take possession of Beechwood that gave Newport the imprimatur of social acceptance.

Jenny stepped down from the hansom under the carriage porch. She passed through the vestibule to an opulent reception hall and there immediately confronted her hostess.

The former Caroline Schermerhorn was, as gossips maintained, dumpy as a Dutch housewife. She was in her early sixties, with a wrinkled countenance no amount of powder and rouge could hide. Her gown of pale blue satin was devoid of the diamond chokers and stomachers she wore at night. Harry Lehr, it was said, had brazenly told her that her excessive display of diamonds made her look like a chandelier. Inexplicably, the Mystic Rose was amused by the remark.

Fortunately Jenny didn't have to deal with her hostess by herself; Mamie was there:

"Caroline, may I present Jennifer, the daughter of Samuel Driver?"

"Ah, Driver. I seem to recall that name from some years ago." Mrs. Astor's plucked eyebrow rose. "Driver the railroad man?"

Jenny quickly decided she didn't care for Beechwood, or its mistress; the former had a cold, museumlike air, the latter an obvious haughtiness. She called on some reservoir of acting talent and returned a sweet smile.

"Oh, long ago. He's largely retired. Tending to investments."

"I see."

"So kind of you to invite me today."

"Tea will be served shortly in the drawing room." Mrs. Astor indicated a large doorway on her left and floated away to greet new arrivals.

Mamie Fish took Jenny's arm. "Nicely done. Come along, I see Tess and Alva in there. You'll enjoy them. They aren't harpies; they only behave like it now and then."

In the drawing room some two dozen ladies, mostly older, chattered and laughed and kissed each other's cheeks. Loudly, Mamie introduced Jenny to Tess Oelrichs, a tall, pale woman with hair black as a raven's wing. Theresa Fair's father had grown rich from silver in the Comstock Lode. She'd married the American representative of the North German Lloyd shipping company. Mrs. Oelrichs was polite in a perfunctory way but after a brief conversation she left.

Mamie nudged Jenny. "Did you notice her red knuckles? Tess is insane about cleanliness, heaven knows why. Scrubs her own floors. She'll be buried with a cake of lye soap on her bosom instead of a lily."

Next Jenny met Alva Vanderbilt, a stout woman whose red hair hinted at a tempestuous nature, just as her soft accents hinted at her upbringing on a Southern plantation. There was nothing soft about the woman's delivery: She'd gathered a group and was haranguing them like a stump speaker. Her flashing eyes dared anyone to disagree with her, or that was Jenny's impression. She barely had time to acknowledge Mamie's introduction and greet Jenny before continuing her sermon on "the insufferable bondage to which American men subject their wives."

Jenny and Mamie listened awhile—the lady had very liberal ideas—then glided away. Mamie said, "All is not happy in that household. Like Caroline's husband, Vanderbilt spends more time carousing with showgirls on his yacht than he does attending to his spouse."

Three powdered footmen served tea at small tables ranged around the drawing room. Footmen charged an extra $5 for powdering their hair, Jenny was told. The footmen wore a rich blue household livery, the same color as the upholstery in Astor church pews.

"I'm afraid the old girl may be getting a bit dotty," Mamie murmured behind her teacup. "Lexie Van Hool said Caroline claims that the Diamond Horseshoe at the Metropolitan Opera was named for her gems." Jenny laughed; she was beginning to feel relaxed, even pleasant.

One of the younger guests approached. She was a radiantly pretty girl, perfectly featured except for thin lips that made a smile seem a struggle. She extended her hand.

"Hello, you must be Miss Jenny Driver."

Jenny stood. "I am. And you are—?"

"Honoria Brady. I live next door, at Sunrise." She leaned into Jenny in a confidential way. "Before you say more, I know your father and mine aren't the best of friends. But you are my age, you're from New York, and I don't believe sins of the fathers should be visited on children, or interfere with friendships. I want us to get acquainted, with or without parental approval."

Disarmed, Jenny said, "That's very kind. Won't you sit down?"

Mamie excused herself and bustled off to bray a greeting at friends: "Well, there you are, ladies—older faces, younger clothes."

"I admire your dress," Honoria said with sweet sincerity.

"I can say the same about yours."

"A little trifle from Paris." Honoria ruffled her skirt. "Are you looking forward to Tennis Week?"

"Oh, yes. Last year I only saw a bit of the doubles contest but I thought it very exciting."

"The Casino governors are seriously thinking of allowing carpetbaggers into the tournament, can you imagine?" Honoria summoned a footman for more tea for the two of them.

"What are carpetbaggers?"

"College boys, not necessarily of the proper family background. I've heard some of them drink like fish, and pool their money for a traveling masseur to knead the alcohol out of their systems." Honoria giggled. "Of course the first champion came from a fine Boston background. Dicky Sears of Harvard. Did you ever watch him play?"

"I'm afraid not."

"He won the singles championship for the last time nine years ago. Before then you couldn't stop him, though how he survived in August wearing a blazer and necktie and knickerbockers and wool socks I don't know. Dicky had this habit of playing with his tongue hanging out, like a little doggy's. So cute."

Jenny laughed and sipped her tea. She was glad to have a friend her own age, even if the friend seemed a trifle garrulous and, perhaps, vapid. Still, it was comforting to sit in a drawing room in a famous house, young ladies of idleness, and chat of inconsequential things. Did Honoria like lobster steamed in seaweed, a local favorite?

"Oh, yes, divine. I know where we can get them reasonably down on Thames Street."

"Then we must go. And one morning we could stroll along the Cliff Walk, without our fathers, if the weather's fine."

A sour look greeted that suggestion. "I hate to tell you, Jenny, I abhor sunlight. Too much color in the face and hands immediately identifies a girl as coming from the wrong social class."

"The working class."

"Commoners," Honoria agreed with a faint shiver. Jenny didn't comment. She liked nothing better than to be abroad on a bright, sunny day, but she understood the stigma. Many women feared it, and went to great lengths to avoid the sun.

They chatted a while longer, then Honoria rose. "There's an orchestra concert at the Casino tomorrow morning, would you like to attend? It's light classical, nothing heavy."

"What time?"

"Eleven."

"I'll be there at half past ten."

"Oh, capital. So glad to get to know you. We'll be friends, I'm sure of it. Till then." She waved as she left.

Soon Mamie returned. "You and Miss Brady getting on, are you?"

"Very much so."

"I wouldn't trust that one too far, my lamb."

"Why not? She seems quite friendly."

"They're a sick lot, that whole family. Tread carefully."

Jenny pressed Mamie to say more but she wouldn't.

19
Sam and the Commodore

Mrs. Ogden Goelet, mistress of Ochre Court and wife of the New York banker and real estate developer, treated two hundred people to an evening dinner party without hiring extra servants. Jenny and Sam weren't invited. Mrs. Goelet continued to maintain Caroline Astor's standards for guests: no entertainers; no Catholics; no "codfish aristocrats"—those still deemed to be "in trade." Mamie Fish shared Harry Lehr's belief that the cardinal social sin was dullness, and talked of inviting Broadway performers to her parties. Mrs. Goelet's invitation to the Fishes was, to say the least, reluctantly given.

Mary Goelet's fantasy version of Nippon featured servants in ukatas imprinted with fire-breathing dragons, and artificial ponds raised above each dining table. In the ponds, captive carp swam. A trio played samisens behind an Oriental screen throughout the seven-course, three-hour meal.

Jenny learned all this from Honoria one evening shortly

afterward, when her new friend called at the Ocean House. The two strolled arm in arm on the hotel grounds where cicadas buzzed and fireflies winked in the July dark. Jenny and Honoria were spending one or two days a week together, scurrying in and out of shops to try on dresses, lunching on oysters and champagne, listening to music or watching tennis at the Casino.

When Honoria went home in her carriage, Sam was waiting in the lamp-lit parlor. Jenny saw his thunderous visage and knew she was in trouble.

"You've a new acquaintance. She visited you here tonight."

"William Brady's daughter. Who told you?"

"Mozart. Duty compelled him. Bill Brady is a scoundrel, Jenny. He's doing whatever he can to bar us from the best houses in Newport."

"He may be your enemy but he isn't mine. Honoria's a different sort of person."

"You're foolish if you believe that. I forbid you to see more of her."

Jenny dabbed her perspiring upper lip with a square of linen. "I'm a grown woman. I'll see whomever I want to see."

"In other words you defy me on this?"

"Oh, that's so old-fashioned. It isn't a matter of my defying you, but of you letting go of the chains all men wrap around women."

"Who's filled your head with such rot?"

"Alva Vanderbilt, among others. There's a new century coming, Papa. Women won't be held down as captives any longer."

She glided toward him, intending to soothe him with a filial kiss. He stepped away.

"That's your final word?"

"On the matter of Honoria, yes."

And the Irish boy . . .

He left the parlor abruptly. The door of his bedroom

slammed. Jenny sank down on a divan with her hand over her eyes. She and her father were at odds on two fronts, her new friendship and her fascination with the Irish boy. In the privacy of her thoughts she could admit that fascination was rapidly becoming infatuation. She knew she'd ruin her relationship with Sam if he ever found out.

How far, then, was she prepared to go? In flights of fancy she went with Prince Molloy to places she'd never dreamed of going before. Would she do that in reality? Would temptation be too powerful? She feared the answer was yes, but only the immediacy of a real situation would answer the question.

Her father was cool toward her for the next few days. Jenny continued to gad about Newport with Honoria, doing her best to think of Sam's behavior as an unfortunate relic of another generation.

A 900-ton steam yacht dropped anchor in the crowded harbor. This was *Namouna*, owned by James Gordon Bennett, Jr., the publisher of the *New York Herald* and its Paris counterpart.

Gordon Bennett had inherited the New York paper from his father, an immigrant Scots printer who rose from poverty to riches. Junior grew up as a hard-drinking son of wealth and privilege, his life a delirious mix of success and scandal. When hardly old enough to shave, he was admitted to the New York Yacht Club. His keel-fitted *Henrietta* outsailed two vessels with centerboards to beat them into Cowes Road and win the first transatlantic yacht race.

Other exploits were less lustrous. On New Year's Day, 1877, Gordon Bennett, like most young dandies, roared around New York's icy streets in a sleigh, paying calls and drinking too much at every stop. At the home of his fiancée, he unbuttoned his trousers and urinated in the parlor fireplace. For this drunken escapade he was stalked by the girl's brother, who lurked outside the Union Club until the malefactor emerged, then had at him with a horsewhip.

Gordon Bennett escaped the whip and issued a challenge. The two fought the last duel on American soil at Slaughter's Gap, a venue either in Maryland or Virginia, depending on which side of the line you stood. Shots by both duelists went wild, some said intentionally.

People craved invitations to Gordon Bennett's lavish all-night parties in Newport but didn't care to be caught in the path of one of his midnight coach runs on the island's back roads. Sometimes, inebriated, Gordon Bennett hadn't bothered to wear clothes.

His equine invasion of the Reading Room was equally infamous. He'd dared a polo-playing crony, one Captain Candy, to ride his pony up on the porch and into the club rooms. This brought down the wrath of the elderly members and resulted in a reprimand. Gordon Bennett was insulted by this humorless ill-treatment and retaliated by building a town showplace, the Casino, directly across the street from his villa.

Gordon Bennett's life wasn't entirely devoted to sin and self-indulgence. He revolutionized the stodgy world of journalism by reshaping his father's paper with sports stories, lurid accounts of crimes, and spectacular stunts, as when he sent reporter Henry Stanley to Africa on a yearlong quest for the famous Scottish physician, missionary and African explorer, Dr. David Livingstone. Staffers at the *Herald* building on Broadway at Ann Street feared the proprietor's unannounced visits, because each arrival usually signaled drastic changes of personnel, policies or both.

The morning after *Namouna* anchored, Sam visited the construction site, trying as usual not to dwell on Jenny's maturity and defiance. He then proceeded in his carriage to busy Thames Street, and Merken's Barber Shop. Despite Brady's machinations,

Sam had been granted his own gilded and monogrammed shaving mug on the shelf reserved for privileged customers.

He doffed his straw hat and laid it on his copy of the *Newport Mercury*. The shop's proprietor said, "Arthur will take you, Mr. Driver. I'm just finishing the Commodore." There was but one Commodore in Newport.

All Sam could see of Merken's customer were long legs in immaculate gray trousers, and fine calfskin boots. From the waist up, including the face, the Commodore was swathed in towels. He heard the conversation with the proprietor and pulled a towel off his face.

"Hello, who's that?"

Gordon Bennett was lean and splendidly mustached, with the kind of agate eyes that inspired fear. He and Sam were roughly the same age. "Mr. Samuel Driver," the barber said obligingly. "Mr. Driver, Commodore Bennett."

Bennett sat upright. "I know your name. Ran it in the paper more than once. You hobnobbed with Fisk and those other bandits."

"At one time."

"Bill Brady's bosom chum, yes?"

"Not quite."

Gordon Bennett extended his hand. "I was joking. Your attitude puts us on the same side of the fence." They shook.

Sam and Gordon Bennett hit it off at once. Early afternoon found them climbing from a launch piloted by a crewman to the deck of *Namouna*. Sam, not unaccustomed to displays of wealth, nevertheless gaped like a schoolboy at the yacht's decor: Persian rugs, marble bidets, a music room with a pipe organ, medieval tapestries depicting knights on chargers and ladies coyly glancing from behind their veils. Throughout the vessel there was a kind of ostentation that said *If you don't like it or can't afford it yourself, go to hell.*

The Commodore invited Sam into the grand saloon to relax while a luncheon of herring salad, batter-fried clams and fresh cod fillets was prepared. A steward filled water glasses with ice from a silver bucket whose hammered lid was shaped as an owl's head.

"Ever travel to France?" Bennett asked.

"I visited once, when my wife was alive. Never got outside of Paris." He savored his host's single-malt whiskey.

"Marvelous country, France. Despite a passion for the Papacy, the people are much more open and alive than these New England puritans. The mademoiselles have warm loins and few inhibitions. One searches hard for their equivalent in New York. Sometimes I have good luck, though, especially in the theater."

"Jim Fisk felt the same way."

"I've two talented young ladies traveling with me, if you're interested."

Since Grace's death Sam had been living like an anchorite, refusing Dickie Glossop's offer of an introduction at Blanche's, the town's most refined whorehouse. ("Of course I don't indulge personally," Dickie had assured his potential father-in-law.) Gordon Bennett's invitation threw Sam into sudden confusion.

"I do have a four o'clock appointment with my architect," he began.

"Saw your new cottage when I drove around the island yesterday." Bennett broke wind without apology. "Going to be a handsome place. Let the architect wait. I can't handle both these ladies in the same afternoon."

"I suppose I could help out," Sam said, though still unsure.

"First rate. They say I'm an old rip. Happy to meet another."

Thus, on a steaming July afternoon, with the water of the anchorage lapping at the hull, Sam Driver closed a stateroom door and sat down beside the nude young woman to whom he thought he should introduce himself before he went further. He felt nervous as a schoolboy.

She had round, rosy breasts with nipples big as marbles, a smooth amber complexion, and eyes that lent her a fetching, vaguely Semitic look. She wasn't naturally beautiful so much as warm and curiously endearing; her smile and her large dark eyes combined to suggest she was at ease and totally interested in whomever she was with.

Abruptly, Sam said, "Do you mind if I smoke a cigar first?"

The fetching creature pouted. "Oh, must we get off on the wrong foot? I hate the smell."

"Then permit me to smoke outside."

"As long as you come back. I don't want to grow old waiting."

Sam fairly bolted from the stateroom and leaned on the rail. He struck four matches before a fifth lit his cigar.

Throughout his marriage he'd occasionally strayed from the path of fidelity—that was the accepted way for American husbands of a certain rank, wasn't it?—but that had in no way diminished his devotion to his wife. Grace's death rose like a bleak barrier between past and present. If he returned to the young woman in the stateroom would he be dishonoring Grace's memory—?

He yelped in alarm, having forgotten the smoldering cigar in his hand. He flung it into the harbor.

"Grace, will you think ill of me?" he said to the empty air. She of course was in no position to say yea or nay.

Sam continued thinking in a somewhat muddled way.

He experienced the stirrings of his middle-aged body.

He reckoned a widower should not have to remain unloved forever.

He decided he was a sinner and always would be.

He went back inside.

The young woman looked relieved to see him. She didn't comment on the odor of tobacco on his clothes. Sam sat down on the bed a second time, dropped a shoe.

"What's your name, my dear?"

"On the bills for Gregory's Burlesque Troupe, I'm Tessa Blue. I was Gert Blauberg when I was born in Gallipolis, Ohio. A Presbyterian deacon deflowered me when I was fourteen. I fixed him. Before I ran away to the bright lights of Cincinnati, I spread the story. He hung himself, the rotten son of a bitch. So I'm Tessa or Gert. Which do you prefer?"

Sam began to unfasten his cravat. "We'll get acquainted and find out."

"I advise you to pull the sheet up, it's chilly in here. A gentleman your age needs to look after himself. You don't want to catch *la grippe*."

It was not chilly in the stateroom; far from it. Sam looked down into those round, seemingly depthless brown eyes.

"You want to mother me, do you?"

"Not exactly what I had in mind, Samuel. May I call you Samuel? Really, though, you must cover up."

What a curious young woman. The way she spoke so protectively should have been an omen for the future but he was too busy stepping out of his pants. He wanted her. Peering with frank curiosity at his underdrawers, she could tell.

"Ooo, aren't we going to have a good time?" she said.

20
CLIFF WALK

After a day on the job Paddy Leland customarily refreshed himself at Reilley's Ale House in a poor section called New Town. Prince knew the routines of most of the working-class Irish, hence found Paddy where he expected to find him. He slid onto the bench opposite Paddy and warmed himself. Cold air from the north had dropped the temperature throughout New England; a small fire burned in the inglenook.

"Greetings, lad. Buy you a pint?"

"No, thanks, I'd rather have work."

Paddy blinked his watering eyes. "What's wrong with shacking balls at the Casino? This is high season."

"I'm tired of helping to entertain a bunch of snobs."

Paddy drank from his tankard, taking his time, reflecting. "That's it? You just got an itch to do landscape work all of a sudden?"

Prince nodded.

"Why do I not entirely believe you, lad?" The burly contractor leaned into the firelight.

"Leave me tell you why I don't. I heard old man Driver talking to Ianelli. I heard your name. Driver met you at the Casino. He don't like you. He don't want you prowling around his daughter. Glossop chimed in. He feels the same. Is that what you're after, an heiress?"

"I'm after a job. You know I'm steady and sober."

"An' you surely know my risk if I take you on. Me an' my whole crew could be replaced in a trice."

Prince waited, counting on the old bonds of Newport origins, Irish blood, to exert their influence.

Paddy Leland sighed.

"Feeney's tree men cut all the big oaks around the digs for the fountain and the garden. They pulled out the stumps an' the sun shines bright on that part of the yard. Best I could do is put you to one side, cleaning out the grape arbor and then knocking it down. It's work nobody wants. Dirt, brambles—you won't like it."

"I'll do it."

Paddy looked doleful. "Damn my soft heart. I knew your ma, Maureen. She was a peach. I'd have tried to get round her if I hadn't already had Dolly and my five brats. All right. Come to work."

He wagged the tankard under Prince's nose. "But you got to wear a hat, no matter how hot it gets. And I don't want to know a damn thing about your romantic intentions. Bring me another pint. You pay for it, considerin' my generosity. Get off your rump, lad. Time you learned to follow orders."

Paddy was right, the work was onerous. Prince left his garret before sunup and limped back after dark. Often his sleeves were in tatters, his arms bloodied from brambles. When he finished clearing a section, he chopped down the arbor itself. He worked from the house outward, toward the sea, because moving in that direction afforded the greatest solitude. He avoided contact with Glossop.

The cool weather didn't last; the temperature shot up, reaching into the low nineties by midday, unusual for a Newport summer. He pulled off his secondhand army campaign hat only when the other men were busy. He opened his lunch sack by himself, on the far side of piled-up vines he'd cut and dug out. He felt resentment from Paddy's crew, from Ianelli's as well. He didn't give a damn.

Twice in the first week a fine carriage boiled the dust in front of the rising cottage, and Sam Driver inspected the property with Ianelli and the architect. A third time, Prince saw a skirt flutter as Driver handed Jenny down from the carriage and the two disappeared in the house. He grinned and yanked at a stubborn vine, tore it out of the ground with enthusiasm.

His high spirits didn't last long, nor did the cloudless sky. Summer storm clouds sailed over. He watched the rain advancing from the ocean, a misty gray rampart. Before he knew it he was soaked. The Driver carriage rattled away, tossing up mud behind the rear wheels. He squatted in the rain, upset because he'd missed seeing Jenny's face.

She and her father came back two days later, at the noon hour. Dickie Glossop put on a straw hat to hide his peeling sunburned face and ran to her side. Driver went into the house again, stomping and shouting. Jenny took Glossop's arm. They strolled toward the Cliff Walk that ran nearly level with the property.

Jenny was on Glossop's right. While the architect picked a stone out of his shoe, Prince waved. Jenny saw him. He put a cautionary finger to his lips. Glossop straightened up and he and Jenny walked on, turning south, soon out of sight.

Prince lingered on the site until dark but he never saw Jenny again that day.

He waited two more nights, fruitlessly, hope draining away a little more each night. As dusk settled on the fourth night, he decided: This would be the last vigil. He was gloomy and frustrated and thinking perhaps he had completely imagined her interest.

A fiery red sun sank and disappeared behind the tree line. One of the last carpenters to leave was a dim-witted lout named Scoppo, who made no secret of disliking him. Prince had accidentally flung a tangle of dead vines on Scoppo's head just as Scoppo was passing behind him. An apology did no good. Tonight the surly carpenter stared at him, spat between his shoes and walked away into the dusk.

It was a balmy, starry evening. Prince had no pocket watch so he had to estimate the passage of time as he wandered down to the Cliff Walk. He sat several feet back from it, knees drawn up, melancholia consuming him. Couples strolled by, visible against the background of the opalescent sea. A yacht strung with lights steamed northward toward Boston. One of the strolling swains saw Prince and said hello. Prince waved but said nothing.

He guessed he'd waited an hour and a half. Long enough. He stood, brushed dirt off his corduroy trousers, turned around, startled. Across the lawn there came a filmy white blur. In a breathless rush, she stood face-to-face with him.

"I didn't know whether I'd find you," she said.

"I didn't know you'd come."

"I saw you the other day. Dickie didn't. How long have you worked here?"

"Almost two weeks. I quit the Casino."

"Because of me?"

"Yes."

One arm curled around his neck; her mouth came up to his with sweetness and passion. Her hair smelled of soap, her skin of a vanilla perfume. Her other hand dropped to her side, clutching his. Prince held Jenny's waist. They kissed long and deeply.

When the embrace ended he said, "Let's walk."

She took his arm; he felt the roundness of her breast touching his sleeve ever so gently.

"How did you manage to get here?"

"Papa's in New York for a few days. He said it was investment business, though I think he's involved with a woman. Every day he drives home from Merken's Barber Shop smelling like a bay rum factory. He never did that before. I just hope she isn't some cheap actress. My mother was a dancer, but absolutely respectable. Papa never could find her equal. She was gold. Since she died I suppose he settles for the dross."

"Well, love changes people in strange ways." It sounded less like an assertion than a rueful admission.

"Love, or lack of it," Jenny said.

"Were you safe walking down here?"

"Safe enough."

"You told me that a young lady out alone, after dark, wasn't respectable."

"Then I guess I'm no longer respectable. Don't tell the town."

They reached the Cliff Walk and stood there, arms around each other's waist, entranced by the murmurous tranquility of the ocean, the star-flecked surface where now and again an unseen fish jumped with a loud splash. They had little to say to each other, happy for the dark. They kissed repeatedly.

Prince wished he could hold the moment forever. He didn't know how. No thoughts of his mother entered his head. The reason he was romancing Jenny on the Cliff Walk seemed obscure and, for the moment, not relevant.

Going home at the end of the day, Scoppo had forgotten his lunch pail. Scoppo's domineering wife flew into a rage and ordered him to go back for it, they couldn't afford another. Scoppo protested that he'd have to walk nearly two miles each way. His wife elbowed him out the door and latched it.

Scoppo reached the site well after dark. He found his pail where he'd left it, behind the padlocked toolshed on the ocean side. Two people sitting on the edge of the Cliff Walk caught his attention.

He hid behind the shed. Against the faint light of the stars, he watched the man kiss the girl. He recognized Driver's daughter, and one of Paddy Leland's boys, the one Scoppo couldn't abide. Lousy mick never mixed or joked with the other fellows. He always opened his lunch sack in the arbor, by himself.

Scoppo crept away, almost forgetting his lunch pail a second time. Next morning he drew Ianelli aside and spoke to him.

Before sunset, Ianelli spoke to Dickie Glossop.

21
Dickie's Challenge

Every summer, Titus Timmerman brought in a lean, tall Negro woman, Mary, to cook. Prince took suppers at the tavern when he could, because Mary's food was delicious. The evening after meeting Jenny, he sat at a rear table hungrily spooning up peas and stew meat from Mary's cottage pie.

Noise in the taproom diminished suddenly, a reaction to the entrance of someone who didn't look like a regular or a tourist. Men's clothes of French or English cut were seen in Newport when the New York swells arrived, but you seldom saw anyone dressed that way in Ye Snug Harbour.

The pegged floor squeaked as Dickie approached Prince's table. After a sweaty day at Red Rose he'd washed up, brushed up, and donned a two-piece high-collar seaside suit, dove gray. The band on his straw boater matched.

"Hello, Glossop."

"I wish to speak with you."

"Fine, go ahead."

"May we step outside?"

"What's wrong with here? Sit down."

"No, thank you."

"Then say your piece."

Dickie turned the brim of his boater in both hands as he answered. "I didn't know you were working for Paddy Leland until Ianelli conveyed that news. As you might imagine, I have more important things to do than keep track of the local help. You hired on with Leland so you could compromise Miss Driver, didn't you?"

Prince laid his spoon next to the cottage pie bowl. "What's this about? I do my work, I get paid, that's all there is to it."

"No, that is not all. You are having secret meetings with Miss Driver. You were seen on the Cliff Walk last night."

Prince shoved the table back and stood. He grabbed the lapel of Dickie's linen coat. "You have spies on the site, do you?"

Patrons stared. At the bar, Titus leaned on his polishing rag, a worried observer.

"I suggest you speak to Jenny," Prince said. "Maybe she likes an evening with someone who isn't a stuffed shirt."

Dickie reacted with a huge backward heave that freed Prince's hand. Prince was shaking with anger but he got it under control. A glance signaled his uncle that he didn't need help.

"Get out of here, Glossop."

Instead, the architect yanked a chair from a nearby table and sat opposite Prince, fists white and pressed to the scarred wood. For the first time Prince smelled whiskey; Dickie Glossop had braced himself for their encounter.

"Not till we settle this dispute."

"How do you propose we settle it? Out behind the barn? Glad to oblige if you let me finish my supper."

"Gentlemen don't fight gutter brawls. I'll take you on another way. At the Casino court."

For a moment Prince was too surprised to believe what he'd heard. He managed wryness. "Sorry, I can't get in. I don't work there anymore and I'm not a member."

"I know the person to pay. He'll leave a back gate unlocked. Early, before the Casino opens."

"You're saying we play tennis?"

"With a prize for the winner."

"What prize?"

"Miss Driver. The loser leaves her alone, for good." Dickie threw an arm over the back of his chair, relaxing a little. "Unless you're afraid it would be no contest."

The atmosphere in Ye Snug Harbour had become palpably tense. Even though the two young men kept their voices low, the ferocity of their expressions promised a coming eruption. Tall Mary emerged from the kitchen with plates of fried oysters. She gave Prince an anxious look as she served the oysters to a customer.

"I know you're an excellent player," Prince began, wondering whether Dickie honestly believed he could win. Perhaps he did, and perhaps he could, never mind Jimmy's sycophantic flattery.

"Then what about it? The loser leaves Jenny alone."

Seconds passed.

"Alright. You're on." Prince extended his hand.

Dickie stared at the hand and thus ignored it. He pushed his chair back, tilted his boater on his head at a jaunty angle.

"We'll settle details tomorrow. I trust you to be a man of your word."

"Yes, can we say the same for you?"

Dickie called him a name, spun and walked hurriedly toward the entrance, as though caught in a sewer and anxious to escape. The door to Thames Street opened and shut. Prince asked himself if he could beat the architect. Or had he stepped into a trap precisely as Glossop intended?

22
The Tigress Slips and Falls

Animals appealed to the summer crowd. One grande dame kept a pet pig, another a pair of monkeys who perched on her shoulder during the afternoon carriage promenade. The wealthy bachelor Oliver Hazard Perry Belmont, whose father had represented Rothschild banking interests, fancied fine horses and devoted the ground floor of Belcourt mansion to a stable. But not an ordinary stable; his was designed by Richard Morris Hunt. In luxurious stalls, O.H.P.'s horses were pampered by grooms and bedded down on expensive linens monogrammed with the Belmont crest.

The passion for pets didn't exclude what the Bradys and others referred to as "the lower orders." Prince, two days away from his agreed-upon match with Glossop, found a stray mongrel behind the dramshop one evening when a light rain fell. The dog was mostly white, with a black patch on his left eye and black socks; someone had cropped his tail to a stub. Prince took some scraps from Mary's kitchen, fed them to the stray on a tin plate, and made a friend for life.

Unimaginatively, he named the dog Rex. He welcomed Rex into the loft where he slept. After an experimental prowl and considerable sniffing, Rex settled down, content to be out of the rain and adopted.

Prince slept poorly, waiting for the tennis game. During the day Glossop avoided the arbor, where Prince's cutting and chopping were bringing the job to a close. He saw Jenny once, riding in an unfamiliar brougham, showing off Red Rose to Honoria Brady and two girls Prince didn't recognize. He kept his hat brim low and his back toward the house until the brougham had gone.

Professor Potiphar Silliphant was a Boston pianist and pedagogue invited to present a recital for selected friends of Mrs. Oelrichs. A few husbands were present among the fifty guests perched on gilt chairs. Mrs. Astor attended, regal and aloof as always. Mamie Fish was absent, but everyone knew she loathed musicales; if forced to attend one, she would withdraw to another room and carry on a loud conversation with servants.

Harry Lehr fluttered his blond eyelashes and applauded prettily as the professor concluded every number.

Refreshments and a lavish buffet service followed the program. Honoria Brady busied herself with her new friends Mona Van Hool and Gwyndolyn Tankersley, the latter an overweight girl fond of hinting that she was sexually experienced but resistant to providing details.

The Drivers, father and daughter, were not present, which pleased Bill Brady. He was unhappy with his campaign to bar Sam Driver from the better houses and clubs, because it wasn't universally successful. Driver had a cabana on Bailey's Beach, and a personal shaving mug at Merken's shop. Brady had more to do.

Unfortunately his wife occupied his attention most of the evening. He was afraid Em had tippled as they dressed in separate bedrooms. At the party after the concert, she asked for a glass of wine twice as often as anyone else. It made him fume.

Then, as she blathered to a trio of ladies, she gestured too grandly, struck a lady's gloved elbow with her glass, and shrieked as the glass broke on the floor. Sherry spattered two fine dresses as well as her own.

With a rigid smile, Brady took her arm, squeezing hard and saying apologetic good nights. "Repair or replacement of those damaged gowns will of course be my responsibility, ladies." When the senior Bradys left, Honoria stayed behind with her friends.

The Tigress could barely stand. Her left knee buckled. Had Brady not been holding her arm, she would have sprawled on the marble floor, which Mrs. Oelrichs would surely attack with scrub brush and cleaning compound tomorrow morning.

On the carriage ride back to Sunrise, Em tried a feeble apology. Brady showed his back and didn't speak. Only when they were alone in the great house did the storm break.

"Goddamn it, Em"—he ripped off his cravat and flung it on the floor—"you managed to disgrace us again."

She twisted a handkerchief. Tears leaked from her puffy red eyes. "Bill, they'll forget."

"The hell. The ladies who rule this town are like elephants. And twice as ugly."

"I'll make amends, I promise."

"You'll do more than that. You'll stay dry or I'll send you back to the goddamn corn belt for the goddamn Keeley cure."

Her weeping turned into great gulping sobs. "Bill, please don't threaten me, I'll be good, I promise, only don't send me away—"

Once more he pried her hands loose.

"Go to bed and sleep it off, I'm sick of looking at you."

He banished her with a slam of the study door. In the starlit silence he raked his hair off his forehead. "What the hell am I going to do with her?" he asked the empty room.

The Tigress staggered upstairs. She hadn't told her husband about Honoria's feigned friendship with Jenny Driver, or the reason for it. That was lucky; he'd only seize on it as one more excuse to flay her. Thank God she kept a flask of fine Spanish sherry hidden in her wardrobe.

Tuesday, six days after the debacle at the Oelrichs cottage, William Brady left his Wall Street office and took a hansom to the famed Delmonico's restaurant, a temple of fine dining since the 1830s. The restaurant had recently moved north from the financial district to a new corner at Fifth Avenue and 26th Street.

Brady presented his card to the maître d'. "Colonel Mann expects me."

"At his usual table, sir. Maurice will show you."

The waiter bowed him into the presence of the sender of the written invitation. Col. William d'Alton Mann, sometime Union soldier, postwar expatriate in Dixie and rumored stalwart of the Ku Klux Klan, proclaimed himself a reformer of high society. Brady and many others translated *reformer* as "blackmailer."

Brady hadn't met Mann before. The colonel hardly fit the mental picture he'd created. Mann was a Father Christmas, a corpulent fellow with unruly white hair, thick white mustaches, sparkling blue eyes and a nose as red as a bordello lantern. His gaudy red necktie flowed over his gaudy red vest. His heavy walking stick lay across one of the empty chairs, and as he leaned forward to shake Brady's hand, his coat fell away to reveal a holstered pistol under his left arm. Those were the tools of a reformer?

"Delighted you could join me." Mann's voice bore the syrupy accents of Alabama, where he'd spent time after the Civil War. "Care for champagne? Or a cocktail?"

"Nothing, thank you."

Mann pointed to his empty flute. A waiter rushed it away. Mann handed his guest a multipaged menu thicker than most almanacs. "You have a choice of many fine dishes, but for luncheon I recommend the mutton chops and candied yams."

"Nothing," Brady repeated. "I'm experiencing some stomach problems."

Brought on by the colonel's written summons to lunch, *in your best interests*. He was sure *Town Topics* didn't entertain readers out of the goodness of its editorial heart.

"Might we get to the business at hand, Colonel?"

"Certainly. I was so terribly sorry to hear of your wife's indisposition at the Oelrichs musicale last week. Too much claret, was it?"

Brady wanted to jump across the table and strangle him. "Did you hear about it in Newport?"

"Oh, I've never set foot in Newport; I consider it a cesspool of vice and hedonism. I look upon my little paper as a force for the defeat of sin, though I prefer to spare the innocent when possible." The existence of a network of Mann informants in Newport was well known, although names of individual spies were secret.

From an inner pocket of his frock coat the colonel pulled a proof. "We plan to publish this in my Saunterings column on Friday unless there is a compelling reason why we should not."

The item was only a few lines long. A woman "often called a feline queen of the social jungle" had "embarrassed herself and fellow guests" by a "drunken display" at a "Newport soiree featuring the keyboard harmonies of a noted Boston virtuoso."

Brady's hand shook. Sweat trickled from his side-whiskers. "How much?"

A waiter arrived with two half heads of lettuce. After appropriate flourishes of oil and vinegar cruets, Mann tucked his napkin in his collar. Unperturbed by Brady's hostility, he sampled the refilled champagne, then attacked the lettuce in the European manner, fork in his left hand, knife in his right.

"How much to suppress it? How much is a good lady's reputation worth? Shall we say a modest fee of three thousand?"

Brady's jaw clenched.

"Two."

"Twenty-five hundred. We may refer to it as a loan, an advertising contract or a stock purchase. The choice is yours."

"I have no choice in this," Brady growled. "And I don't give a damn what you call it. You'll have my check tomorrow."

Having concluded his deal with the devil, Brady jammed his tall hat on his head and fled Delmonico's.

While Em's husband was in New York, the Tigress set out for the morning concert at the Casino. She took particular care with her appearance, donning a new Worth gown, a translucent white confection with an all-over pattern of blooming hydrangeas.

Departing in her carriage, she paid no attention to the young men hired to weed flower beds but spending more time leaning on their rakes and hoes and chatting. Jimmy Fetch was one of them.

Caroline Astor sat with Tessie Oelrichs on the Casino terrace while the orchestra tuned. Two chairs at the table were vacant. Em screwed up her nerve.

"Tess—Caroline—I must apologize again for the illness that caused my terrible little scene at the party. I hope you've forgiven me."

"Of course, dear," Tess Oelrichs said, staring elsewhere.

"Might I join you?"

"I'm sorry, dear, these are taken. We're expecting guests," Caroline Astor said.

Em feared she'd fall as she slunk away. She recognized ostracism because she'd given the same treatment to others. Ten minutes later she was in her carriage.

As the vehicle rattled and bumped along Bellevue Avenue, Em cried out to the driver. "Can't you go any faster for God's sake?" She needed the consolation of the sherry cabinet.

23
The Game

Although Prince no longer worked at the Casino, his friendship with the club professional drew him there. He found Tom Pettit clattering around the floor of the court tennis building on roller skates. Tom forehanded balls over the net as he skated. When he saw Prince, he braked.

"Bloody crazy way to play, eh? The members like a little novelty from their hired man. What brings you back, lad?"

"I need your advice. I'm going to play Dickie Glossop, for high stakes."

"Is it a lawn or court match?"

"Outside. The grass."

Tom pulled a towel off the net and wiped his ruddy face. "What stakes?"

"I'd rather not say."

"Then I'd rather not offer advice, much as I dislike that bloke."

Prince didn't hesitate long. "The winner has the right to court a certain young lady."

"Do I know this charmer?"

"I expect so. Sam Driver's daughter."

Tom whistled. "That's a prize more precious than money. So you want to know how to beat the uppity Mr. Glossop. Well, you already know his style. Puts finesse above strength. Lots of darting and dancing. Mebbe he thinks he's a ballerina. Play the opposite way. Hammer him. Smash it over—brute force. Do you have a backhand?"

"Not to brag about."

"Find a wall and practice."

"Tom, you know I can't afford equipment."

"I'll loan you a two-dollar Sears racket, and balls. Is this match public?"

"No. We're to play before the Casino opens."

"Anyone officiating?"

Prince shook his head.

"Then watch his feet. No leaving the ground to serve. No stepping out of bounds, even for a moment. I think the man's a bit of a trimmer." Tom unstrapped his right skate. "By heaven I wish I could watch you trounce him."

"Try to trounce him," Prince corrected.

"Ah, lad, you will, I have faith. Remember the stakes." He removed the second skate. "Let's go outdoors and practice a while. I'll whip you from here to the Isle of Wight."

Summer dawn comes early in New England. On the morning of the game, Prince watched it arrive; he was nervously awake an hour before the sky began to pale outside his grimy garret window.

He nudged Rex off the bed. At the washstand he'd saved half a glass of lager from last night. He poured the stale stuff over his curly hair and took a few licks as it dripped off his nose. He applied his comb, leaving his hair damp and beery.

While he shaved with his straight razor he let Rex out to run. His hand jittered more than he liked. He nicked his chin and stopped the blood with dabs of alum. He told himself to calm down.

He tucked the tin-plate owl into his singlet and pulled on his only good cotton shirt. He buttoned the shirt cuffs and hitched up his knickerbockers. He thought of Jenny but that only made him more nervous.

He owned no knee-length socks, so his usual gray ones had to serve. He laced up his high-top work shoes, again not proper attire but the best he had. Jimmy had given him a cap, garishly checked, with a large bill. Prince thought it looked silly but Jimmy had paid for it or stolen it, so he put it on with a rakish tilt. In the scrap of mirror he used for shaving he squinted at himself. The best he could do.

Rex trotted in the half-open door. Prince fed him two sausages from the tavern. "Wish me luck, boy." Rex went on gobbling the sausages. Prince left carrying his borrowed racket.

The morning smelled sweet and fresh, the eastern light slanting through the dewy treetops. He walked quickly up the hill into Bellevue Avenue, then turned left before he reached the Casino. In back, at one corner of the court tennis building, a black shay waited by a green slat gate. The horse was already eating from a nose bag.

Dickie appeared from the shay's dark interior. He was dressed as smartly as if he were playing a match against the reigning champion. His jacket of cream linen with broad vertical stripes of royal blue fit him perfectly. He wore a short striped tie, blue and gold, a starched high collar, and a striped cap that matched his blazer.

Dickie threw a canvas tennis bag at Prince without a by-your-leave. Prince caught the bag, heard rackets rattle. Dickie treated his opponent to a condescending smile and stepped to the gate.

"This way."

They walked along a service hall at one end of the court building. Neither spoke. On the tennis lawn the steam engine used for rolling the lawn stood idle. Grooming of the grass with the machine's front and back rollers usually took place about this hour. Had Glossop paid to forestall that too?

Prince thought he heard something; a door in the court building was slightly ajar. Dickie dismissed it: "Tramps sometimes hide after the Casino closes and sleep here. Harmless, most of them."

He advanced onto the near court, brilliantly green and smelling of damp earth. While he slipped out of his coat he said, "May we have the rackets? The wooden one's yours."

Prince unbuttoned the bag. He discovered a tilt-top racket, years old. Leather wrappings hung loose on the handle. One catgut string was broken. The other racket was a new-looking Slazenger Demon, with the familiar horned devil symbol engraved in the wood above the grip. "That one's mine," Dickie said.

"I'll play this one. I've never used a tilt-top." Which, he supposed, was Dickie's reason for bringing the antique. He handed the better racket across the net and took a couple of experimental forehand swings. Dickie piled four cloth-covered Wright & Ditson balls at one end of the net, whose tension he tested.

"You know the rules. Toss a coin for service?"

Prince agreed and called heads. The gold dollar spun into the grass.

"Sorry, tails. Choose your end of the court."

More out of irritation than practicality, Prince said he wanted to reverse their starting positions. They circled to opposite ends of the net. Dickie pocketed one ball and stepped to the right side of his baseline to serve the other.

Dickie's strong overhand serve would have been easy to return had Prince's heavy left shoe not slipped on the damp grass. Both legs flipped up and he sat down hard. Dickie's ball landed neatly within the box. Dickie laughed and danced left and right, one foot to the other, as though on marionette strings.

Prince scrambled up, red with humiliation. He promptly missed two more returns that scored points for his opponent. He bashed a third one far out of the court behind Dickie, who thereby took the game.

The sun climbed higher; the court grew brighter. Prince tugged his cap brim low to compensate. The sun's angle favored his opponent but when they reversed their court positions after three games, the sun would be Dickie's problem, then his again at the end of five.

Dickie shifted to the right side of his baseline. The second game began more favorably for Prince, but he quickly fell behind. When it was Dickie's ad, something distracted Prince, some blur of movement behind one of the grimy windows of the court building. Frantically, he reached for Dickie's return and missed it by two feet. The architect had him by two games.

After three, they changed ends of the court. Prince faltered badly, winning only one game out of the first set, which Dickie won 6–1. Prince put his hands on his knees and took several deep breaths. Time to put Tom Pettit's strategy into play . . .

Prince's first overhand smash missed Dickie's service box by a yard. So did his second, putting Dickie up love–15 with no effort. Dickie seemed to grow more energetic, fairly dancing on his shoe tips. Prince shifted to the left service position and from there rammed the ball across so hard that he heard one of his racket strings snap. 15–all

The second set seesawed between players, until Prince,

beginning to hurt in his calves and thighs, put Dickie down 6–3. The tie-breaking set began with both players dripping sweat, shirts stuck to their bodies, no noise on the court other than the *whap* of struck balls and the accompanying grunts of the players as they hit. Somehow, despite the strength of Prince's forehand and backhand returns, Dickie seemed to gain the advantage, lifting his whole body up high with each serve. Quickly, Prince lost games one and two. In the third game, diving to backhand Dickie's volley, he slipped again. He fell on his side in the fragrant grass, cursing his clumsiness. Pain lanced his right leg from his ankle to his hip.

Dickie ran to the net. "I say, are you alright? Shall we call it my match?"

"Not just yet, thanks."

Prince pushed himself up, fighting the pain of the wrenched leg. Dickie's smile spoke of the inevitability of his victory. He danced back to serve.

Prince blinked into the blinding sunshine. Dickie seemed to rise again like—what was Tom's term? A ballerina. The ball dropped between Prince's legs just inside the baseline.

"Won't be long now," Dickie called cheerily.

Prince smashed Dickie's next ball back at him. Dickie's backhand stroke missed. Prince hit the ball with every bit of strength in his aching right arm. Charging the net, dropping back, reaching high to send the ball screaming over like a round from a cannon, his furious attack wore away the architect's bravado.

Dickie's face grew oily with perspiration. Though he moved more slowly, he fought hard. His lead widened. With one devastating backhand, he took the set 6–0.

Prince's shoulders slumped. Sweat fell off his brow so steadily, he could hardly see. His leg threatened to buckle. His stomach heaved. He felt like throwing up, not only because of defeat.

He muttered congratulations. Dickie appeared not to hear, fiddling with his cravat and avoiding Prince's eye. A sudden sharp noise made both players look to the dark green court building.

Tom Pettit stepped out the door.

"What the devil are you doing here?" Dickie demanded.

Tom stroked one of his gracefully drooping mustaches. "I've been watching for some time, with great interest."

"You saw that I beat him."

"In a manner of speaking." Tom walked out to the net. "Admirably played, young Mr. Molloy. You might have had him but for Glossop's attempts to bilk you."

"Bilk? I don't like your language, Pettit."

"Be that as it may, Mr. Glossop—and believe me when I say I hate to speak critically of a club member—during your serves in the third set, your foot left the ground more than once."

Dickie reacted with rage. "Are you claiming I cheated?"

"Oh, I would never have the temerity to say that to a member in good standing. I do observe that you committed a foot fault three times. Perhaps there were others that I didn't see."

"What are you, a damned spy for this guttersnipe?"

"I am a tennis professional, sir. I play as I was taught—by the rules. If one doesn't play that way, any outcome is meaningless. Your foot left the ground not once, or twice, but three times. That much I saw, and I would swear to it if you dragged me before the United States Supreme Court. Say what you will, sir, you lost the match by disqualification, and you also lost whatever wager you two gentlemen agreed upon."

"How much did he pay you?" Dickie snarled, too exercised to notice the hint of glee in Tom's eyes.

Pettit said, "This young man? Nothing. All I want is fairness. When one player breaks the rules, the other wins, no matter what the final score."

Tom Pettit clapped Prince on the shoulder. "Enjoy the spoils, whatever they may be."

Dickie threw away his racket in a great end-over-end arc. "Damn you, Pettit, I'll have your job."

"Welcome to try, sir. Of course we shall have to discuss the match before the rules committee, in detail."

Dickie gave them hateful looks, picked up his racket and vanished down the corridor where they'd come in. Something wicked in Prince made him call out.

"Don't bother to tell Miss Driver who won. I'll take care of it."

24
Twists and Turns

Prince cleaned up, changed his shirt and reported to Red Rose by midmorning. Dickie Glossop was nowhere visible. Apart from the idle stares of a few workers, Prince's lateness went unremarked.

Two huge drays rolled onto the site at noon, the draft horses lathered and snorting. Large wooden crates in the wagons bore customs seals and showed signs of hard travel. All of their markings were in a foreign language—Italian, Prince supposed, when he saw the same legend stenciled in black on each crate. FONTANE DI FIRENZE.

The garden centerpiece had arrived.

Someone tapped Prince's shoulder. He turned to find Dickie, wearing a fresh new outfit.

"Collect your pay, Molloy. You're done here."

"When?"

"Now."

"I work for Paddy Leland."

"Paddy does what I tell him. Leave."

Prince held up a fist. "Alright, but you'd better not break your promise about the wager. Otherwise I'll break your damn face."

"You're trash. I want nothing more to do with you. If Jenny does, God help her."

He walked into the house, shouting orders.

Prince found Paddy and asked for his pay. Paddy muttered something about being sorry as he counted out the money. No one called good-bye when Prince left the site. He strode away beneath dusty trees that hadn't known rain in some time. How would he find Jenny? Tell her of the match, and the outcome? He wouldn't spare Dickie or prettify the architect's behavior, that much was a given.

Em Brady's carriage driver had quit abruptly to marry his third cousin in Bangor. It wasn't a hard decision since the Bradys made working at Sunrise unpleasant. The summer season was nearing an end; all the best servants were employed. Em had to take what she could find, a straw-haired chap named Dimmy Sneeden.

A former steward at the Naval War College, Sneeden claimed he'd been unjustly dismissed by "the stinking navy." Had Em checked his story, she would have discovered that Dimmy Sneeden was dismissed for drunkenness. Had he earned a place in Tess Oelrichs's file of servants present and past, he wouldn't have been listed with the "good," or even the "bad," but among the "rotten."

The Brady carriage joined the 3 p.m. parade on the afternoon of Prince's firing. Sneeden drove, an older footman riding beside him to deliver and collect visiting cards. Within the overheated coach, three young ladies tittered and gossiped: Honoria, Mona Van Hool, banned from any pretense of beauty by small eyes set too closely, and the libidinous Gwyndolyn Tankersley. Jenny had been invited but declined, pleading indisposition of the kind that sent her to the couch for a day or two each month.

When Dimmy Sneeden climbed up the wheel to the box, he missed a spoke and fell. Honoria leaned from the carriage to chastise him. Sneeden dusted himself off and assured her he was fine. Soon they were rolling along Bellevue Avenue in the procession of grand carriages.

Gwyndolyn fluttered a Japanese fan in front of her round rouged cheeks. "My brother Sydney sent me the most delicious novel from London."

"Another of those obscene yellow-backs?" Mona Van Hool said.

Gwyndolyn giggled. "All about a young lady named Fanny, who keeps encountering these gentlemen incredibly endowed with gargantuan *instruments* or *machines*"—Gwyndolyn rolled her eyes—"do you grasp it?"

"The meaning, not the machine," Honoria said tartly as the carriage turned a corner and stopped.

The footman ran to the mansion door. Dimmy Sneeden checked the shady street and reached under his Brady livery. The bottle flashed in sunlight as he refreshed himself generously. The young ladies in the carriage couldn't see him.

Under way again, the carriage returned to Bellevue Avenue. Sneeden swayed on his high seat. His eyelids drooped. When he dropped the reins, the footman grabbed them but yanked too violently. The team bolted and surged to the left, passing a coach whose occupant glared. Mona Van Hool fell back against the cushions.

"My God. Alva Vanderbilt."

Honoria blanched. She hammered the ceiling. "You cretin, get those horses under control."

"Trying, ma'am," came the footman's strangled voice above the clatter of wheels. A collie darted out of the path of the lurching carriage, which passed a second vehicle, the open victoria of Mamie Fish.

A block farther on, Dimmy Sneeden slowed the team. Honoria shrilly ordered him to drive with more care. When they arrived back at Sunrise after delivering the Misses Van Hool and Tankersley to their cottages, Sneeden fell off the wheel a second time. The footman, an old man long in service of the Bradys, looked on disapprovingly.

"Stand up!" Honoria screamed at Sneeden. He floundered on hands and knees in the crushed white marble of the drive. A green bottle slipped out of his coat.

The footman looked grieved. "I should have warned you, madam. I inhaled the strong odor of spirits when he took the reins."

"You're discharged," Honoria cried.

Dimmy Sneeden rolled over and vomited into a flower bed.

Honoria imagined all sorts of suitable punishments: pulling out his fingernails; scalding him with hot oil; stretching him on a medieval torture rack. She wanted to weep. None of the punishments would damage him to the extent that she'd been damaged by the gaffe on Bellevue Avenue.

Mamie Fish called at the Ocean House and related the incident. Jenny still languished on the couch in the still, stale summer air.

"Our little Board of Social Strategy convened this morning for breakfast," Mamie said. "We are dropping Honoria Brady. Alva was adamant. You know her temper."

"Really, Mamie, is overtaking two carriages such a serious offense? Mozart heard about it last night. The Bradys' coachman was in his cups."

"Makes no difference. The deed was done, and the rules are

firm." Mamie grew confidential. "I agree that we might have been more lenient, were it not for certain remarks about you made to Alva by Miss Brady."

Jenny sat up and tossed the crocheted coverlet on the floor. "What sort of remarks?"

"I won't repeat them. They were all about your character. Your lack of refinement. Oh, little Honoria passed them off as jocularity, but the intent was transparent. She meant to stab you fatally."

"I can't believe it. She's my friend."

"No, pet, she only pretends friendship. If you were wiser in the ways of this town, you would appreciate the difference. In any case, the decision about Miss Brady is final. We discussed you at length this morning and I'm happy to tell you that Tess and Alva and I agree that we must and we shall take you up. See that you receive the best invitations—meet the best people. Eligible young gentlemen, perhaps European, with titles."

Mamie's face fairly radiated joy. She patted Jenny's hand.

"Your place in society is assured."

25
The Fete

Ianelli's cousins, stonemasons from Connecticut, uncrated and assembled the fountain. In the center, a nude water nymph cradled a large bouquet in the crook of her arm. Although cut from pink marble, the flowers represented a Florentine version of red roses and artfully concealed those parts of the nymph's anatomy that might offend the prudish. Thus the sculpture, with its eerily blank eyes, conveyed youthful innocence rather than prurience. Around the fountain's rim, larger roses with inward-bending stems jetted water into the basin.

While the fountain and its piping came together, gardeners dug and spaded beds for artificial moss and ferns. Next season, real roses would take root and struggle to survive in the New England climate. Workers brought in arbors of white latticework, thick with green crepe paper leaves, much more attractive than the real arbor Prince had ripped out. Strings of tiny electric bulbs were hung to create a kind of spiderweb between earth and sky.

Mozart hired a printer to prepare elaborate invitations to the banquet and fete (costumes required). Quaint typography summoned guests to "A Revel in the Forest of Arden." No invitation was delivered to Sunrise.

Electric lights within the house were tested, and a chandelier raised in the three-story foyer. Harry Lehr was on the premises nearly every day. He arranged for eight Naval War College boys ("your best and brightest, please") to attend as extra dancing partners late in the evening. Another custom Mamie Fish loudly criticized was banning these "extras" from parties until after the guests had eaten and drunk all they wanted.

Harry also assumed responsibility for engaging the caterers and the orchestra, to be dressed (at additional expense) in Elizabethan garb. Since Sam and Jenny hadn't as yet chosen furniture, the caterers had the task of furnishing decorated tables and gilt chairs for the guests.

Harry traveled to New York to consult a theatrical design firm and returned to breathlessly announce that he had ordered six scale replicas of the Globe Theater, complete with miniature hand-carved actors as centerpieces for the main tables. Sam held his head and told Mozart he wanted to see none of the bills until after the event.

Next day, however, Mozart mentioned flowers for the ballroom, and costs were forgotten.

The ballroom was located on the south side and elevated a story above the entrance. Previously, Sam had designated the large room as a memorial to his late wife. A full-length portrait of Grace by John Singer Sargent existed, created from the two ambrotypes and the small oil painted by an unknown street artist. The portrait was already crated and on the way from the Fifth Avenue mansion. When Mozart respectfully offered the opinion that it wasn't sufficient decoration since it would hang at the head of the broad stair which divided to left and right ballroom entrances, Sam ordered one hundred dozen red hybrid tea roses. Using his railway connections he chartered a refrigerator car, with all necessary ice of the kind Prince cut in the winter, to freight the flowers from New York.

He sent Harry back to the city to commission a series of large decorative panels to be hung in the ballroom. These were to highlight roses in history: Cupid establishing the rose as the symbol of silence for lovers and conspirators; Cleopatra walking on a thick carpet of rose petals; the house of Lancaster adopting the red flower as its symbol in the War of the Roses. Jenny thought roses in the ballroom and Shakespeare throughout the rest of the house and grounds a disparate, too-garish admixture, but Harry cooed and purred and assured her the denizens of Newport would be "astonished and delighted by the novelty."

Things seemed to hurtle forward with the momentum of a runaway locomotive, Sam and his helpers shoveling ever larger loads of money into the firebox. Red Rose would be spectacularly presentable, if largely unfurnished, on the night of the grand fete—September 4, the first Tuesday of the month, 1894.

Once she'd decided to let her father fret about costs, Jenny faced the approaching event with enthusiasm, because the evening promised to be a success. Favorable replies from invited guests came in quickly. Mamie Fish would be pleased to attend. Caroline Astor and her libertine husband would be pleased to attend. Alva Vanderbilt and her stunning, raven-tressed daughter, Consuelo, would be pleased to attend, Alva no doubt hoping for an eligible European nobleman to be present. Alva's passion to possess a titled son-in-law was well known.

Sarah McAllister replied in stilted prose for herself and her husband, who had been ailing. If recovered, he and his wife would be gratified to attend. The one significant refusal came from Gordon Bennett's private secretary in New York. The

Commodore was at the moment relaxing on a luxury barge on the canals of central France.

Criswell, keeper of the golden apple orchard, accepted, as did Girard St. Ong ("H.R.H. Prince Albert shall be delighted to join you, Her Majesty the Queen regrettably being about royal business elsewhere in the realm"). Mrs. St. Ong had succumbed the preceding winter, which her dotty spouse no doubt had forgotten.

The Howells and the Moulds and others of exalted station accepted—180 in all. It struck Jenny as deliriously extravagant and not a little sinful, occasionally raising memories of her grandfather railing against those who ignored the First Commandment. But Jenny was young, and hopelessly in love with adulation, and riches—in love with the elusive Irish boy too. She mentally rehearsed what she planned to do to cap and climax the monumental evening if she ever again heard from Prince, whose absence, total silence, steadily made her more anxious.

Four days before the gala, she asked Mozart to join her in the evening on the Ocean House veranda. They sat in white wooden rockers. Summer dusk had become the summer night, full of sounds of distant laughter, a melodeon playing somewhere, crickets harping in the shrubs. Mozart insisted on wearing his smoking cap even in the hottest weather, and on filling his pipe with a tobacco mixture redolent of rum.

"Is it something specific you want to discuss, miss?"

"Are you loyal, Mozart?"

"Loyal? Miss Jenny, you know how long I have worked for your father."

"I mean are you loyal to the whole family? Are you loyal to me?"

"I should hope so."

"Then I ask you to find that Irish boy. I've utterly lost track of him. I hope he hasn't left Newport. Try to discover where he lives. I think it's somewhere down on Thames Street."

"Are you referring to the good-looking boy discharged from the building site?"

"Ycs."

"In other words, the young man your father despises?"

"I'm afraid that's the one," she said with a laugh.

"But you don't despise him."

"Far from it. Were you ever in love, Mozart?"

"Once. Long ago. It ended badly." He knocked his pipe on the porch railing, spilling little orange sparks into a freshly turned bed of earth. He watched until all the sparks blinked out.

"Then perhaps you remember how it feels to care about someone. To want to be with someone, no matter what the rest of the world thinks."

Mozart sat on the rail with his cold pipe between his teeth. After a moment he took it out, shook his head.

"By asking me to help you, you're asking me to divide my allegiances in this family."

"I am. I want to find Prince Molloy. Neither Mr. Leland nor Dickie will say why he was let go, or where he might be. If I'm too persistent with questions it raises eyebrows, which I don't want. Can I count on you? I'm not a child anymore. I expect the same loyalty as my father demands."

A night boat whistled in the distance. "You drive a hard bargain, Miss Jenny."

"I'm learning that in Newport there's no other kind. What do you say?"

Mozart drew a deep breath. "I'll help you. This one time. Only. If that's satisfactory."

"It is. Thank you."

"Then good night, Miss Jenny."

She sat rocking and letting the warm night embrace her while Mozart's footfalls retreated into the dark.

Three days before the gala, Harry Lehr brought a large brown package from the express office. He jubilantly rubbed his hands while Sam tried on the papier-mâché ass's head. It was brilliantly lacquered, worthy of any Shakespearean stage.

Harry's elation came to a sudden bad end: Sam lifted the ass's head off his shoulders and flung it across the room. One of the foot-long ears broke on a baseboard.

"They may call me an ass because of the party, but they won't call me an ass because of that damn thing."

"But, sir—"

"Take it away, Harry. Burn it. Throw it on the lawn at Sunrise but get it out of here, I refuse to wear it."

Harry Lehr was devastated but Sam paid the bills.

They settled on a doublet embroidered with gold braid, gold-paned trunk hose with cross-garters of gold ribbon, a stiff neck ruff and a bag hat with an ostrich plume. Harry showed a hasty sketch on his pad.

"It's fifty years past the time of Elizabeth, but who's to know?"

"It still looks like fop's clothing," Sam complained. "They'll laugh at my legs."

"No one will laugh while they're drinking your champagne. You have to wear something. And we're fast running out of time. I'll dash to the telegraph office and we'll have it from a Broadway costumer tomorrow evening."

Later that night, while Sam consumed heavy amounts of Kentucky bourbon and tried to convince himself he wasn't sinking into a bottomless bog for Jenny's sake, Mozart tapped on Jenny's door. She was still awake, reading an English novel about a detective named Holmes. Mozart reported that young Molloy could be found living in a barn garret behind Ye Snug Harbour on Thames Street.

Jenny threw her arms around the curiously stoic man, and kissed his cheek. Mozart fled to the hotel's saloon bar with his face burning scarlet.

As if a lady novelist who wrote in the Gothic style had consulted about the weather, the atmosphere for the great event was heightened by a light ground fog induced by the clash of warm temperature and damp air. Heat lightning, faint but impressive, flickered like a scenic effect in a theatrical spectacle. The little electric lights strung in the artificial arbors had a hazy, almost mystical radiance.

On the second-floor gallery of the foyer, musicians welcomed the guests with an Elizabethan blend of recorder, baroque flute, English horn, trumpet, violin, viola, bass and lute. Mamie Fish arrived sans Stuyvesant, arrestingly gowned in gold lamé, which did nothing for her potato-sack figure but went well with the gold paste she'd applied to her face, neck and hands.

The guests sipped champagne; the noise level increased. Harry Lehr cautiously greeted McAllister, got up as a heavily bearded Lear fresh out of the storm (his wife was the Fool in cap and bells). The hirsute McAllister was hard to identify, but the two eventually shook hands and embraced. Harry was a faun, complete with bare torso, small cloven hooves and horns.

Jenny was radiant as Titania in pink tulle with a diamond tiara Sam had presented to her as a surprise. Caroline Astor wore imitation chain mail and a tartan for her personation of Macbeth. She greeted Jenny warmly, clasping both her hands between hers and whispering that the Drivers would receive invitations to the lady's next winter ball in New York.

"A year away, I'm afraid. I want my new residence on upper Fifth Avenue to be finished and fit for guests. I expect the ball to be the finest I've ever given—a truly memorable occasion, in a truly special place."

"We'll look forward to it, whenever it happens."

"One thing will not change. I oversee each ball from a red velvet dais and invite favorite friends to join me there. I should certainly like to include you in that number. You're a charming addition to our circle. Why it took us so long to recognize that, I can't imagine. Lovely party," she murmured as she drifted away to others seeking her favor. Jenny was ecstatic.

Dinner began at half past seven. Guests were enchanted by the cunning replicas of the Globe on the larger tables. Mamie loudly announced that she hoped dinner wouldn't be another three-hour affair, but it was. Pâté de foie gras was followed by planked terrapin, maraschino cherry sorbet to refresh the palate, then fillets of beef (red and white wines now substituted for French champagne), more sorbet, truffled turkey and on through courses of pudding and Stilton with digestive biscuits. By then Mamie had vacated the table, to protest the length of dinner and perhaps to repair her face; in the heat from innumerable candles added to the overhead electrics, the gold paste on her cheeks had begun to melt and run.

At eleven, Harry Lehr led a quadrille in the rose-festooned ballroom. The musicians had changed their instruments to those more suitable to Strauss waltzes, themes from the New World Symphony, and popular airs such as "Daisy Bell" and "Sidewalks of New York." Jenny mingled and chatted, danced with her father and with Harry (no mean feat, given his imitation hooves).

She partnered with Willie Vanderbilt for a polka. He fondled her bottom until she told him to desist. Dickie Glossop signed her card for one dance and seemed untalkative, out of sorts while they waltzed. About one o'clock, as weary guests began to depart, she was still excited, not only by the evening's success, and the invitation from Mrs. Astor, but by the prospect of what was to come. When she thought about it, her insides seemed to turn to warm jelly; she was frightened, but she had mulled it endlessly, and she was determined.

By two, the party had ended, the last guest reeling to his carriage: This was St. Ong, thoroughly drunk and exclaiming that the Scottish borders were "in revolt," he must rush to the side of the Queen.

Yawning servants extinguished the candles and the electric lights in the arbors. Caterers whisked the last plate and cutlery and crystal out of sight so the hosts wouldn't have to look at an offensive litter in the morning. The musicians packed their instruments and slunk off into the night, where a light drizzle had begun.

Jenny searched for Mozart, dressed for the evening in the drab grays and blacks of a medieval serf. "Have you seen my father?"

"He retired to the master suite ten minutes ago."

"What? There's no bed, no furniture at all."

"He seemed content to lie down on a wooden floor. He was snoring heavily. He enjoyed his own party, perhaps too much."

"You mean he's liquored?"

"Completely squiffed. Unconscious."

"Oh, what a pity." Jenny pulled a long face, although her heart was exultant. "Let's let him sleep it off. I'll fetch my wrap. Will you drive me back to the hotel?"

"Yes, and then return here to close up."

For the rest of the night, Jenny lay wakeful on top of the sheet in her room at the Ocean House. Before daylight she donned a light cloak, pinned her hat in place with a long hat pin, and slipped out past a drowsing lobby clerk, bound for Thames Street with a single red rose from the ballroom.

26
Love Beneath the Rose

Rex woke him by leaping on the bed and lapping at his face. Prince heard a soft knock. He stumbled up to open the garret door. Against the fading stars he saw the silhouette of a woman in a cape and plumed hat. Rex growled.

Even with the caller's features hidden, Prince recognized her. He was nearly paralyzed with embarrassment. Because of the night's warmth he'd worn only the bottom of a suit of old underwear, cut off at mid-thigh.

"Jenny?"

"Please let me in, it's growing light."

He backed up to the bed and dragged an unused quilt around his waist to hide a sudden erection. Rex continued to prowl and growl near the visitor, who brought aromas of the sea and morning damp into the steeply raftered room. Prince shooed the dog outside to run.

Jenny closed the door. Prince tightened the blanket around

his middle. "Praise God," he said. "I was sure I'd never see you again."

"I feared the same. What happened?"

"I'll explain when my head stops whirling. There's a lot to tell, or confess. It has to do with my sainted mother, and things I promised at her grave. With Glossop too; have you seen him?"

She pulled a long pearl-headed hat pin from her black felt hat. "Only at the party last evening. He seemed cross, and cool."

"He has good reason. At least he's kept his pledge."

"Concerning what?"

"I told you I'd explain and I will. Coming down here's a terrible risk for you. What made you do it?"

"You, Molloy. You. Is that plain enough? Will you climb up on that stool and pin this to the rafter?" She handed him a long-stemmed red rose.

"Roman mythology says Cupid gave a rose to the God of Silence in return for a favor. A rose over your head means everything that happens beneath it is secret. *Sub rosa* is the Latin."

"I don't know anything about Latin, or roses."

"Roses are a favorite decoration for ceilings. Papa's instructed the painters to cover the ceiling of our dining room with enameled roses. It's very convenient for guests who drink too much and talk too freely. It's convenient for plotters." She shook out her unpinned hair.

"And lovers."

Dust-moted rays of early light struck through the garret window. He waggled the hem of the quilt. "Please turn your back, I ain't—I'm not dressed right." Jenny laughed but did as he asked.

She discarded her cloak while he pulled the stool into position, stepped up and poked the pin through the stalk of the rose, into the old rafter. When he climbed down he was stunned to see that her dress had disappeared. Her chemise was white silk with a lace hem, her over-corset brocaded in black.

"Jenny, is it wrong? Should we be doing this?"

"Yes and yes. That's why I brought the rose. So we could do what we both want to do. But I must tell you first—it's all new to me."

He took her hand, warm as his.

"We'll go slowly, then."

While Thames Street woke with sounds of clattering drays and rattling milk cans and stevedores shouting and laughing as they tramped down to the docks, Prince bore her back to the tangled bed where they made love, at first with trembling, then, after her one gasp and outcry, with mutual joy.

They lay in each other's arms, the quilt over them for modesty. He felt her heartbeat as she must be feeling his. He could only think of simplistic questions.

"What happens now?"

"Beyond this moment?" She kissed his cheek. "I've no idea. I'm terrified of the possibilities."

"Because it disrupts what you're doing in Newport?"

Her silence was admission.

"Do you really like it? Getting ahead? Trying to meet the best people?"

"The newspapers call it social climbing. My father wants it. Sometimes I like it. Last night, at the party, I liked it immensely. If it helps us live better than we're living now, why not?"

"I don't know how you could live better unless you marry a foreign duke and have a title. You won't live better if you stick with me."

She was silent again, her hip touching his. The drab and ugly garret seemed to recede, blurred away by what they'd shared. She traced the outline of his lips with her finger. "What is it that you want from life?"

The emotional dam broke then, almost as great a release for Prince as the moment when his loins flooded within her.

"I don't know." He flung himself over with his elbow hiding his face. "I thought I knew the answer before I met you. I wanted fancy summer girls to fall in love with me so I could drop them and laugh at them and walk out. I did it more than once."

"Why? Why such a cruel thing?"

"For my sainted mother. All the summer people I've ever known were cruel. My mother changed their nasty linens at the hotel, all stained with—never mind. They didn't care what she had to clean up. They pushed her aside and looked right through her until she died of poverty and shame."

"So is that supposed to be my fate? A seduction, a chance for you to laugh and slam a door in my face?"

"I confess that was the plan, once."

He rolled over again, his mouth inches from hers. "But I love you. I fell in love. I never meant it to happen. When it happened, how it sneaked up on me, damn if I know, but I know I wish my mother had been right."

She waited.

He lifted the cheap chain to show the face of the tin owl. "She swore that a rich man who gave her this was my father. She never told me his name before she died, so I never believed the story. I don't now, but I wish it were true so I could take care of you. As it is—"

He stopped. He didn't need to bring up Samuel Driver, or what he would think of their relationship. Driver wouldn't allow it. Conceivably, Driver, who had a lingering reputation as a brawler, might resort to violence to end it.

Prince slipped his arm under her bare shoulder, pulled her

close to nestle her against his side, breast and thigh. Her hand rested on his stomach.

"You said there was more to tell. About Dickie."

"Ssshh, plenty of time for that." He heard Rex scratching the door.

"Oh, if only we did have time—"

The unfinished sentence died, only the sound of Rex's claws rasping in the silence. He felt tears from Jenny's cheek running on his. After the sweet union she'd risked so much to bring about, they lay in mutual silence, eyes open, contemplating the rose pinned to the rafter. The future didn't have room or accommodation for the two of them together. Prince's mind boiled with alternatives, schemes, solutions, each more hopeless than the last.

Rex scratched and scratched.

"Damn dog. I'll be back."

But the moment was broken.

September yellowed the leaves and changed the slant of the sun. Lighters carried trunks and portmanteaus out to sleek white yachts. Porters bore similar baggage up the gangways to the Fall River boats for New York. A familiar melancholy descended on Newport: The town shivered from the certainty of summer's end.

For Jenny and Prince, only the continuity of their passion remained unchanged. She paid a second furtive visit to Thames Street. They'd been lucky the first time, but Prince insisted they mustn't take chances; he was ready with a small waxed-paper packet, the contents identified as DR. POWER'S FRENCH PREVENTATIVE (1 ONLY).

"I don't know what that is," Jenny confessed.

"Vulcanized rubber. Very safe. Not easy to come by since some old busybody named Comstock passed laws a few years ago."

"How do you know so much about them?"

"Friends," Prince said, turning his back.

Neither of them saw a future together. Jenny swore she loved him. He swore the same. But she was still conflicted, still set on finding approval and acceptance in society. The subject provoked arguments, so he drew back to safer ground.

"I can't stand to wait till next summer to see you again," he said. "I'll get to New York by New Year's. I don't have the money, cutting ice won't pay enough, but I'll get what I need."

"Let me loan it to you."

"No. I'll get it myself. I'll find a way. I promise to see you in New York."

"What a sweet, stubborn boy you are."

She kissed him. They swore eternal love again, without knowing where that road might take them, if anywhere.

He saw her off at the Long Wharf, standing in the dark blue shadow of stacked crates, his cap tugged low over his eyes. Sam Driver was shepherding his daughter. He scowled when Jenny looked back just before disappearing at the head of the gangway.

The whistle hooted; the steamer churned away down Narragansett Bay; the golden ripples on the water smoothed.

Prince trudged back to Thames Street, feeling miserable.

Autumn winds blew. Leaves whirled and filled the gutters of Bellevue Avenue. Titus began his familiar complaints about the absence of the tourists he hated. While Prince and Jimmy Fetch awaited the freezing of the ponds, Jimmy took to the streets with a tambourine and red leather shoes. When Prince questioned him, he revealed the reason.

Some citizens of Newport indulged in private vices, no different in this than their brothers and sisters around the globe. Jimmy had found a way to turn this to his advantage. On the better streets in the finer sections, he lingered outside houses still occupied, rattling his tambourine and shuffling his red shoes in a clumsy dance until someone tipped him or ran him off. This masquerade as a street entertainer allowed him to practice his new vocation, spying.

Criswell, keeper of the golden apples, was one of his early targets. Jimmy followed Criswell to a shabby home on Coggeshall Avenue, considered the town's mews because of the many carriage horses stabled there. Jimmy peered under a window blind. Old Criswell, trembling with lust, unfastened his trousers by candlelight and fell on a scrawny young woman who couldn't have been more than sixteen. In the bedroom doorway, an ax-faced relative—whether father or husband was unclear—stood with folded arms, watching.

Jimmy reported the incident to Mr. Rowe, the local railroad telegrapher whose talcumed cheeks were as gray as the suit he habitually wore. Rowe paid Jimmy $2 for his tip and sent a message over the wires to New York.

The following week, Criswell's sister Eulalia, from Little Compton, nervously approached Colonel Mann's table at Delmonico's. Mann had summoned her in preference to her older brother because reports said Criswell was "not quite right." But he was right enough to want to keep the cleverly worded story of his lascivious behavior from appearing in *Town Topics*. Criswell's sister invested $900, her savings, in an "advertising contract."

Jimmy knew Prince wanted extra money for a trip to New York. He suggested Prince call on the telegrapher and spy for *Town Topics*. Many gardeners and footmen, maids and cooks and stable grooms earned money that way. Prince hesitated, though not for long. He soon learned there was plenty of vice to go around. Tips on two adulterous romances duly reported to Mr. Rowe enriched him at $2 each. One of the finest homes on Bellevue Avenue, inhabited by a refined Episcopalian who practiced pedophilia on weeknights, netted $3 and actually brought a smile to the vulpine lips of the otherwise humorless telegrapher.

Prince was ashamed of his secret occupation, but overcame his scruples by imagining Jenny's face and caresses. Besides, he assumed that Driver must have done similarly bad things in his days as a crony of Fisk and Gould and that crowd, else how could he have gotten everything he wanted?

27
INVINCIBLE

The Pickwick Hotel, a few steps east of Herald Square, was well appointed and unabashedly Dickensian. Portraits of the great man hung in all the public rooms. The hotel was also somewhat passé now that fashionable New York had moved uptown. Politicians, stars of the theater and other notables no longer stopped at the Pickwick. Sam found it ideal for his purpose. He installed Tessa in a penthouse suite occupying half of the sixth floor.

Tessa had given up the high kicks and salacious skirt-waving of the cancan in order to attend to Sam's well-being. She was a tactful realist, never pleading for access to the higher planes of his world. She ardently ministered to his declining sexual urges, but she was far more than a mistress devoted to hedonistic pleasures. For someone who grew up around an Ohio feed and grain business, she'd learned a surprising amount about health, medicine and nostrums of the day.

She filled the cabinet adjoining the water closet with bismuth powder for Sam's bouts of dyspepsia, liniment for sore muscles, Dr. Hazeltine's Celebrated Stomach Bitters for bowel complaints. Sulphate of zinc for her douches kept romantic romps from deteriorating into parenthood; she was still young enough to conceive.

She owned a stethoscope and frequently listened to Sam's heart and lungs. She insisted he bathe three times a week, minimum. She threatened to sue a chemist who sold her a "guaranteed hair restorer" that turned out to be colored lard. She got twice the purchase price returned.

She forbade Sam's use of calomel, a popular purgative, insisting it did no good and rotted the teeth and gums. Sam's teeth she pronounced "healthier than a stallion's," though he did have one silver incisor, wired in place by a dentist Tessa deemed acceptable only after he swore he used no teeth peddled by the poor who went door to door selling their extractions.

Whenever Tessa's mothering became smothering, he absented himself for a few days, but he found he couldn't stay away for long; he was besotted with her. Her lively, always ingratiating way of suggesting this or that improvement in their lives fascinated him and, more often than not, persuaded him that she was right.

One blustery night in October, they lay in her double bed at the Pickwick, Sam drowsing in postcoital contentment while Tessa briskly turned pages of a newspaper.

"Here's an article in the *Herald* that confirms what I've believed for a long time."

"Mmm, arrgh," Sam said, which roughly translated as, "Yes, what?"

Tessa laid her long-handled magnifying glass aside. "Public railway cars and steamships breed infections. The unwashed passengers carry disease. You should own a yacht."

"Agree. Can't stand the crowding on the public boats. Would you like a peek at my Christmas present to myself?"

She tossed the quilt aside and rolled on top of him, cheerfully naked.

"What is it, a picture of a yacht you want to buy?"

"Much bigger than that. Put on your finery tomorrow and I'll have Mozart here with a carriage by half past eight. By ten we'll have breakfast aboard."

"Aboard what?"

"That's my surprise."

The carriage collected them on schedule. Mozart politely handed Tessa into the closed interior, then joined the driver on the high front seat. The heavy black Percheron pulled them south through the clatter of lower Manhattan, to the half-oval where omnibuses and private vehicles discharged passengers at Battery Landing. It was a fine, crisp day, azure skies without a cloud, breeze from the northwest bracing rather than cold. Tessa shielded her eyes against the glitter of the harbor. "Good morning, sir, madam," said a young man in seaman's garb at the head of a gangway descending to a float.

Sam took Tessa's elbow to guide her down the ramp. He indicated a small open boat. "Naphtha launch. She belongs to *Invincible*."

Tessa followed Sam's pointing hand. Amidst the panorama of steam freighters, tugs, fishing trawlers, catboats, a lumbering ferry, a sleek, blue-hulled steam yacht rode at anchor. Not one usually shaken by the large or the extraordinary, this time Tessa couldn't help putting a gloved hand to her rounded mouth. "Good heavens, Sam, is that yours?"

"Indeed it is. A hundred and ninety feet, three hundred tons displacement. She's all the way from the Laird yards in Liverpool. She can make seventeen knots."

"Did you need something so big?"

"To cross the ocean safely and travel the Mediterranean or the Baltic, yes. Come on, Bully will be waiting." He handed her into the launch whose small naphtha-fueled engine was put-puttering comfortably.

"Who's Bully?" she asked.

Mozart said, "Our sailing master. Captain Jasper Jelks. He prefers the name Bully. You may have trouble understanding his English; he's a Yorkshireman."

They bobbed away from the landing in the launch that needed only an ordinary seaman, not a licensed engineer, to pilot her. Tessa held her hat and squinted against the breeze. A round-faced, splendidly mustached gentleman in nautical uniform waited at the rail of the enormous two-masted vessel. Steam yachts of this size were owned only by the richest men who didn't mind spending thirty to fifty thousand a year for wages and up-keep. She'd read all about such floating palaces but never dreamed she'd visit one.

Over the rush of wind and water he said, "A steamer has a big advantage. You're never at the mercy of weather. You don't sit becalmed for hours or days. When you expect to arrive, you do. Isn't she gorgeous?"

"Oh, she is," Tessa agreed, thrilled by the sight of the anchored yacht, its fore and aft deckhouses silhouetted against the towering magnificence of Bartholdi's statue of "Liberty Enlightening the World" on Bedloe's Island.

The portly Captain Bully Jelks assisted Tessa on her precarious trip up the ladder to the main deck. His crew, mostly young men with bushy mustaches, lined up behind him. "We carry a complement of twenty-five," he explained. "All are present but our engineer, our chef and our two stewards readying your breakfast. While you dine and get acquainted with the yacht we shall cruise up the East River into Long

Island Sound—calm and sheltered water all the way to Block Island."

Or that was the approximate content of Bully's remarks, which seemed to be growled and grunted between a few intelligible syllables; Sam provided a full translation over breakfast.

Rashers of bacon and platters of eggs embellished with French pastries and champagne cocktails, California grapes and chicory coffee, waited for them at the long polished table in the dining saloon. Tessa marveled at the chilled grapes. Sam demonstrated a switch set into the cherry paneling; the room blazed with light.

"She's completely electrified. An Edison generator, a hundred and twenty separate fixtures throughout, two searchlights—even our own ice plant." He spoke like a proud father describing his firstborn.

Tessa heard the anchor chain riding up, felt the slight shift and heave as the engine started them on their voyage. Were there stokers below, shoveling coal for the boilers? Yes, Sam said, three, plus the licensed steam engineer required by U.S. maritime law. He was less interested in eating than in praising the virtues of his acquisition, starting with the price, $310,000 when she was launched from the same River Mersey yard that had secretly built the commerce raiders and blockade runners of the vanished Confederacy.

The dining saloon and galley comprised the forward deckhouse, directly under the flying bridge. The aft deckhouse, which Sam showed her when they finished, consisted of a combination smoking room and library, the bookcases fitted with expensive beveled glass doors, and a ladies' lounge with plush banquettes and a Steinway baby grand. Tessa was enraptured; she loved to play and sing, though never for an audience.

An ornamental staircase led down to the main saloon, twenty-two by sixteen, under the main deck. Aft lay three guest staterooms and an owner's suite with Persian carpets, hanging brass lamps, an enormous bed, even a freshwater shower stall.

"And forward?" Tessa asked, unfastening her veil.

"Crew quarters, this deck and below."

"May we see them?"

Sam fell back on the bed, tearing loose his collar. "You've seen closets before."

"That bad?"

"We pay well to compensate."

"Did you name the yacht?"

"No, the Lairds christened her before Captain Bully brought her across. I didn't object. Yachts are supposed to reflect the owner's character, a friend at the New York Yacht Club told me."

"Are you joining that club?"

"If they'll have me. It's the best on the East Coast. They maintain a fine station in Newport Harbor."

"Who's your friend?"

"Howard Gould, one of Jay's four sons. He's young, more of a spendthrift than his father. I can't say we're close friends. I don't like to make too much of those past associations. Now that you've seen my toy, what's your impression?"

Tessa stretched out beside him, tickling his chin.

"Worthy of a potentate. I have only one worry. What if you're cruising and there's a medical emergency?"

"Captain Bully can set a broken bone or cure a stomach complaint. Or we can put in at the nearest port. Stop fretting about me and enjoy the day."

Which they did, first by making love on the satin-sheeted bed, then dressing again and, from wicker chairs on the flying bridge, watching the sunlit splendor of Long Island Sound as the yacht steamed seaward at a leisurely nine knots.

"This all seems so unlike you in a way, Sam. You spend freely when it's necessary, but deep down, you're frugal."

"I suppose," he said with a shrug. "On the other hand, haven't I come far enough in life to indulge myself? In spite of all the pills and good care you give me, I won't live forever." She didn't like the thought, but she didn't protest.

They relished the salt air, the green shores of Long Island and Connecticut slipping by, the scents of brass polish and varnish, engine room oil and Captain Bully's cigars. Tessa hummed. Sam laced his hands over his vest and shut his eyes. He was thankful she hadn't pressed the matter of motivation for his purchase. Yes, *Invincible* was a rich man's toy that would raise his status several notches by flaunting his wealth. But the yacht was something else he'd never admit to his mistress, or his daughter. She was a powerful weapon ready to combat the pernicious influence of the Irish boy, or anyone like him. Jenny would marry well or not at all.

Temporarily content, he fell asleep. Tessa smiled and reached across between the chairs to cover his hands with hers.

28
Prince's Discovery, Sam's Rage

After an overnight ride in an unheated passenger car, Prince arrived in New York in a gray dawn, a week before Christmas 1894.

Snow flurried intermittently. To work up nerve to visit Jenny, he spent the day seeing the sights.

At Battery Park, he peered at Bartholdi's huge statue of Liberty holding her lamp above the harbor. He saw immigrants lining the rail of a North German Lloyd ship for a first glimpse of Ellis Island. He wandered the slushy streets of the financial district where so many of Newport's millionaires had made their fortunes, including Jenny's father, presumably.

In a dingy stale-beer joint in the notorious Five Points, three coarse men mistook him for a tourist carrying valuables. He overturned a table to block them, bolted off and outran them. At dusk, fortified by more beer and aching to see Jenny, he trekked through Printing House Square, which wasn't a square but a triangle. Greeley's famed *Tribune*, nine stories of red stone with a clock tower, was reputed to be the tallest building in New York. He saw the *Sun* and the *Times* and the *World*. He'd never imagined one city held so many papers.

He wandered on Park Row as the snow stopped, coming to a white marble building at Broadway and Ann. The architecture reminded him in an uninformed way of some Frenchified cottages back home. A frieze ran the width of the building above the entrance. Two men in bowler hats and snappy plaid overcoats came out of the building. Prince hailed them.

"Excuse me, which paper is this?"

"Bennett's *Herald*, sonny."

"Why all the carved owls up there?"

"The Commodore's convinced the owl is a good luck symbol for his family." The men hurried on.

Prince dived a hand under his coat, brought out the tin-plate medal. He compared it with the stone owls blindly regarding the dark city. The duplication was exact. Never until this moment had he believed Maureen Molloy's claim about a rich man fathering him. Where hopelessness had been his portion before, now he saw the glimmer of a future.

He dashed north to the Driver mansion on Fifth Avenue. Titus had sent him to a city directory in the Newport library that confirmed the address. Wet and cold from his socks to his wool cap, he ran up the broad front stairs and yanked the bell pull. Electric lights warmed the mansion's windows. Above the door hung a huge evergreen wreath.

A long-nosed butler answered the bell. "We are not receiving tradesmen this evening. When you come back, the entrance is in the rear."

"My name's Molloy. I'm a friend of Miss Driver. I wish to see her."

"I'm sorry, she is occupied."

"But it can't wait, I have important news."

Footfalls in the foyer announced the arrival of Mozart Gribble. They recognized each other. An omnibus went by, a few sightseers huddled inside while the heavily dressed guide blared through a megaphone about "homes of the well-to-do."

"What is it you want, Mr. Molloy?"

"To see Jenny, if you please."

"But I don't. It isn't possible."

"Just to let her know I kept my promise to come to New York? How long can that take? I can do it in five minutes. Less."

"It's beyond my authority to allow—"

Mozart abruptly stopped as a hansom veered across oncoming traffic to the curb. Caped and tall-hatted, Sam Driver flung money at the cabman. One look told Prince that Jenny's father was spoiling for a fight.

Earlier in the afternoon, Sam had kept an appointment with young Howard Gould at 67 Madison Avenue, the clubhouse of the New York Yacht Club. Howard, third of Jay Gould's four sons, turned no heads with his rather bland, ordinary looks, unless the observer told you that he and his brothers George and Edwin had been given their late father's power of attorney as birthday presents.

If Sam needed proof that time and wealth conferred respectability, Howard embodied it. He was an esteemed member of the New York Yacht Club, owner with George of an 85-foot sloop, *Vigilant*, which had successfully defended the America's Cup. Unique among the Goulds whom Sam had met, Howard seemed to carry a certain resentment of his family, probably because his sister Helen had interfered with Howard's courtship of Miss Odette Tyler, a Broadway actress. Helen Gould, like her mother, considered actresses no better than streetwalkers. She hired detectives to probe Odette Tyler's past, discovering a divorce after

"Miss" Tyler's husband abandoned her. Harassed to the limit, the actress flung back Howard's $9,500 ruby engagement ring and left town.

A pleasant stroll around the premises brought Sam and Howard to the Model Room on the second floor, a dark chamber with glowing chandeliers, reading tables and an assortment of burgees hanging at ceiling level. Below, on both walls of the long room, shelves held half-hulled replicas of yachts of different classes and designs. Under his arm Sam carried a slim portfolio of application papers for the club.

"I'm sure you'll find yourself enjoying membership and all the amenities at our stations up and down the coast," Gould was saying as the lacquered door opened.

When he saw Sam, William Brady reacted as though slapped. "I heard someone had let you in the clubhouse."

He and Sam stared at one another like antagonistic bulls. Gould sensed bad feelings without understanding them, tried to put a good face on it. "Mr. Driver will shortly be proposed for membership."

Brady's eyes never left Sam's. "I wouldn't count on it, Driver. You'll never get past the front entrance if I have anything to do with it."

He slammed the door and disappeared. Gould looked perplexed and helpless. Sam said, "Can he keep me out?"

"He's very influential. A longtime member, with friends on all the committees."

They left the club together. Sam knew then that he wasn't destined to be welcomed into the New York Yacht Club, in this life or any other.

"Let's step down the street for a drink," Gould said. "I'm really sorry about Brady's behavior."

"I wouldn't have bothered if I'd known he was a member. The bastard hates me." He flung the useless application papers into a smoldering trash barrel. The framed motto on his wall might never have existed. Bill Brady had got the best of him.

At the taproom, one drink led to another, and by the time Gould handed the older man into a hansom, Sam was not only wobbly, inebriated, but choleric.

On the snowy steps of the mansion, Sam took hold of Prince's frayed sleeve. "What the hell are you doing here?"

"I came to see your daughter."

"I'll not have it. Be off."

"I warned him," Mozart began.

Sam released Prince, pushing him. "Go back to Newport where you belong. We don't want you here. Jenny doesn't want you here."

"Let Jenny tell me that."

Sam hit him.

Prince flailed and tumbled down the steps, sprawling in the sidewalk snow. Mozart looked stricken.

Sam ran down to Prince, who scrambled up, feinted to the left. Sam countered and Prince leaped past him, gaining the third step before Sam stuck out his foot to trip him.

Prince cracked his nose. Blood spotted the marble step. Sam stood over him, fists clenched.

"Never try to best me with tricks, boy."

His hat had fallen off. Mozart jumped to retrieve it, all too aware of his employer's reek of whiskey. Prince rose gamely again but Sam had the advantage. He punched Prince's belly, doubling him. He grabbed Prince and clumsily hauled him down to the curb, flung him in the gutter. Prince lay glaring and gasping and blowing blood from his nose.

Despite the freezing temperature, Sam was perspiring. He climbed the steps again.

"Hire a couple of men to throw him on a train. Pay the

fares and order the men to stay with him to Providence." He stepped closer to whisper a final order.

"Really, sir, do you think it's wise to—?"

"You work for me. You do as I say. I don't want him back under any circumstances."

Rising from the gutter slush, Prince gazed at Sam like an enraged animal. "I didn't know how much you hated me."

"I only hate what you could do to Jenny's future. You could ruin it."

"I'm not good enough for her?"

"No one's good enough unless I say so." Sam accepted his hat from Mozart. "He's never been here. You've never seen him. Remember that."

He hobbled into the foyer. There he leaned against the wall, sucking air, realizing how badly his hands hurt from the beating he'd administered.

The encounter, justified from a father's perspective, nevertheless had unnerved him. The old days—the buccaneering, the carelessness about life—weren't so remote after all. He still lived by little Jay's admonition about never being bested.

Upstairs, he ignored a call from Jenny's room; she'd heard commotion. He fell on his bed fully clothed and slept, dreaming again of Jim Fisk dying.

After midnight the snow changed to sleet, then steady rain. The two Bowery roughnecks, recruited by Mozart after a search of the lowest dives, cornered a conductor in the vast dreary space of the Grand Central terminal. Few employees or passengers were about at this late hour, and those who were looked indifferent, sleepy, or both.

"We got a man trussed up over there. He's going to Providence."

"Trussed up?"

"Handcuffs." He showed the key.

The conductor saw the prisoner leaning against the ledge of a darkened and shuttered ticket window. Young chap, face bruised, patches of dried blood on chin and cheeks, hands out of sight behind his back. His eyes were closed. He swayed left, then right, then left again, as if ready to fall.

"Is he a criminal? Are you coppers?"

"Never mind." Folded bills passed between the roughneck and the conductor. "Which gate?"

"There. Track fourteen."

"Thanks. Let's fetch him, Tim."

"Should we unlock the cuffs?"

"Time for that in Providence, when we finish the job."

They hurried away in the echoing gloom of the vaulted hall. The conductor counted and pocketed the bills. The roughnecks and their foot-dragging captive, barely conscious so far as the conductor could tell, disappeared down the incline leading to the Providence local.

III
1895–1896

29
Season of Anger

An era came to an end on January 31 when Samuel Ward McAllister died.

Funeral wreaths appeared on the door of his residence at 16 West 36th Street in New York. The passing of "the head butler," "the dismissed servant," "the mayor of Cadsville," or "Mr. Ward M'Hustler" as Colonel Mann's *Town Topics* uncharitably called him, received front-page coverage in the *Times*, the *Herald*, the *World* and other major papers. His funeral service was announced for February 10, at Grace Episcopal Church, 10th Street and Broadway, where the McAllisters had kept the same pew for years.

The day of the funeral was monochromatic, the piled-up snow on lower Broadway dirtied with soot, speckled with cinders. Foggy gray skies pressed down. The cortege, a hearse with carriages following, arrived on lower Broadway at 10 a.m., where a crowd spilled over the sidewalk, photographers lurked and a squad of police waited to deal with any rowdiness. Within the church, Pew 113 was filled end to end with bouquets and floral tributes.

The sexton guarded the church door so no "undesirables" entered. In the choir loft, an orchestra conducted by John Lander, whom McAllister had often hired for his fetes, played the mournful "Dead March." Pallbearers carried the coffin up the center aisle and placed it amid banks of flowers, the whole interior of the sanctuary smelling so intensely of blossoms, it might have been a perfumery.

The church was crowded but not with the notables one might have expected. Not only had McAllister's book hastened his downfall, so had columns he'd written for Joe Pulitzer's *World* from the late '80s onward—$50 per weekly insertion of "Ward McAllister's Letters." Pulitzer's paper mocked New York society and he was loathed in turn by his victims. One might have seized on that for some sense of who would mourn the dead man.

There were some Vanderbilts in attendance, a few lower-rank Astors as well. But the so-called upper crust, those grand ladies and gentlemen who had followed McAllister's dictates for so long, were not to be seen, for a variety of publicly announced reasons: previous obligations, absence from the city, ill health. Mrs. Astor excused herself on grounds that she feared photographers who might seek to take her picture.

The Patriarchs, the elite dancing society McAllister founded, neither sent representatives nor floral tributes. No Goelets attended. No Whitneys, Schermerhorns, Roosevelts. O. H. P. Belmont did not attend, nor Mamie Fish. The William Bradys were absent "due to my wife's health." The Drivers were in the Midwest attending ground-breaking for a new hospital. McAllister had served them all, but when they no longer found the association useful—when they no longer needed him—they had discarded him like a suit of old clothes.

After the service, as the coffin was returned to the hearse for transportation to the cemetery across the East River, a near-riot occurred when souvenir hunters swarmed to Pew 113 and made off with memorial flowers. The hearse disappeared into the murk of the winter day, its occupant already half forgotten.

McAllister himself had stressed the sacred obligations surrounding dinner parties. In a frequently quoted quip, he'd asserted that if a guest had a dinner invitation and died unexpectedly, his executor should go in his place.

Mrs. Astor had sent numerous invitations for a dinner party on the night of the funeral. McAllister had told her and told her that under no circumstances should a hostess cancel a dinner.

She didn't.

Eighteen ninety-five was the year of the Cuban insurrection, brought on by a depressed economy that destroyed the sugar industry. President Cleveland wanted Americans to remain neutral but Hearst's *New York Journal* and Pulitzer's *New York World* demanded war.

Eighteen ninety-five was the year of Richard M. Hunt's passing, as though he'd reached the zenith of his career with completion of The Breakers for Cornelius Vanderbilt II. The Breakers was epic; no more grandiose cottage was ever built in Newport town. Those who summered there yearned to be invited inside Hunt's last monument to wealth. Dickie Glossop recognized his debt to his mentor but silently thanked heaven for the decline in significant competition.

Eighteen ninety-five was the year gasoline-powered horseless carriages caught the attention of an affluent few, while cycling became the new sport of millions. It was also the year Alva Vanderbilt shed her married name. She gave a ball at Marble

House to celebrate her divorce, and her intent to marry Oliver Hazard Perry Belmont.

As a result, anti-Newport rhetoric cascaded from pulpits, newspaper editorials and the specious reformist columns of *Town Topics*. The dogs of propriety took up the cry.

"Damme, divorce ain't respectable," old Arleigh Mould bayed from the rusticity of the self-appointed "Queen City."

W. K. Brady fell back on society's pretext for good public behavior: "People in our set provide a necessary model for the lower orders."

And, "No person with her status has ever dared sue for divorce."

And, "Let her arrange trysts and assignations if she must, but don't reveal that kind of behavior in a courtroom."

Even Harry Lehr's china-blue eyes flashed disapproval. The divorced lady seemed unconcerned, if she paid any attention at all.

For Prince it was a year of slow physical and mental recovery. Driver's thugs had dragged him from the train at Providence and pulled him behind an abandoned shed near the depot. The rain had passed, leaving an unusually warm morning for late December. Icicles dripped; snowbanks melted; mud turned to brown soup.

The two men had at him one by one. The first twisted his foot, wrenching his leg so badly he couldn't stand. The other man used a razor to torment him; the result was heavy bleeding and a fishhook-shaped scar on Prince's jaw.

After a half hour the thugs had tired of their recreation. The one closing his ivory-handled razor shook it at Prince as he lay in the mud, clinging to his silent vow that he wouldn't moan or give vent in any way to the pain he felt.

" 'Member what they said in New York. Stay away from that girl or, next time, you'll get worse."

Whistling, the man disappeared in the direction of the depot, arm in arm with his partner, the last Prince ever saw of them.

When he summoned enough strength he crawled around the corner of the old shed but passed out short of the train platform. Ten days later he returned to Aquidneck Island from a hospital charity ward, on used crutches.

He couldn't believe that Jenny had a hand in what was done to him, but as he healed, his opinion began to change. If not an instigator of his brutal treatment, surely she was aware of it. She might have written care of Titus's dramshop to profess innocence, or at least express regret. No letter came. In the angry silence of his mind he began to call her names. He'd been lulled into abandoning his original plan, charmed into falling for her, and what he had to show for it were vile memories, a fishhook scar, a left foot with a flattened arch and a limp that seemed permanent.

He and Jimmy returned to ice-cutting. Less nimble than before, Prince was assigned a sled to drive. Late in March he took up with an Irish maid employed at Chepstow Cottage. Flo Dwyer was a square-faced, buxom redhead, barely literate but good-natured. She satisfied Prince's needs for uncomplicated female companionship. On the first balmy night in May, Prince and Flo rode the new electrified trolley across the island to the windy strand at Easton's Beach—Reject's Beach, some called it. He glanced at the empty pavilion only once. He and Flo concluded the visit with frantic tussling and kissing and the raising of Flo's petticoats under cover of darkness.

Afterward Prince felt empty, not contented or fulfilled. In

his garret he kicked Rex just because the dog tried to jump up to show affection.

June brought warm weather. Prince found work as a groom's helper in O. H. P. Belmont's stable. He filled feed bags, laid fresh hay in stalls, shoveled up manure. He wasn't allowed to handle or even touch the fine linen bedding, monogrammed, that Mr. Belmont provided for his horses. Prince liked being around the animals. Horsemanship, coach-driving and racing were things he knew little about, but he thought he'd like them if he learned more.

One blustery Sunday afternoon he walked to Red Rose. Heavy padlocks and chains secured the front and rear gates. He rang a wrought-iron bell. A shuffling watchman appeared. Prince asked when the Drivers would be arriving.

"They won't be, not this summer, that's the word I got."

"Where are they?"

"Don't know. Not my business so long as Gribble sends my paycheck regular."

When the old man had gone, Prince leaned against the gate, smoking a rolled cigarette. A wind sprang up, whirling apple blossoms around his head and leaving a pink fall on his shoulders. He smoked and loitered at the gate a while longer, as angry as he'd ever been.

Jenny lost eleven pounds and grew sallow over the winter. At twenty, fully matured, she felt her life was over. For a while she harbored a hope that Prince might communicate with her but he didn't. He'd sworn to find her in New York but he hadn't. She seethed with confusion, disappointment, resentment.

Reading, one of her joys, became burdensome. She tried Mr. Crane's *Maggie: A Girl of the Streets* and found it too harsh. She retreated to the vapid and sentimental historical romances of Mrs. Kranze and Lady Danielle Fitz-William, quickly absorbed and quickly forgotten.

To force the listless days to pass, she supervised the emptying of her wardrobe. She sent her everyday skirts to a sewing shop with instructions to shorten hems by an inch and a half, then insert small lead weights around the circumference of each, in preparation for summer bicycling. She didn't as yet own a wheel but expected to buy one.

A relentless question hammered her. One night in February, she tapped on the door of Mozart's workroom. She found him inking figures in a ledger, his queer smoking cap visible above slow-moving layers of pipe smoke. Her face was thinner than he remembered, her eyes sunken, with light brown circles of fatigue marring her good looks. The sight induced guilt.

"You still haven't heard from him?"

"Molloy? I haven't."

Mozart's dark watering eyes reflected the wick of the whale oil lamp on his desk. The household was fully electrified but Mozart clung to old ways, as if to deny the advance of a new century with its dizzying array of new ideas and inventions. Sam had presented him with a typewriting machine that reposed in a corner under a dusty cover, untried.

"He hasn't been to the door?"

"All the way from Newport? I should think not."

"Has he or hasn't he?"

"No. Not once."

"You wouldn't lie to me, would you, Mozart?"

He clicked the stem of his pipe against his teeth. "No, Miss Jenny, I would not."

"Damn him." She beat her fist on the door molding. "He's a sick person. All he wants is vengeance for his mother."

"I beg your pardon?" Mozart said, not following.

"*Damn* him," was all she said in reply. She slipped away into the darkened hall. Mozart dropped his pipe in a bowl and raised a hand to cover his eyes, hating himself.

Next morning he reported the conversation to his employer.

Sam Driver proposed a grand tour of Europe:

"My friend Gordon Bennett's invited us to visit him in France. He has a flat in Paris, a villa at Versailles, another at Beaulieu on the Mediterranean. We certainly should see Rome; that's where all the educated young men begin their tours. We might be gone six months but if you give Mozart instructions, he'll see that Red Rose is furnished by the time we're back."

Cautiously, he added a question. "Would you miss the summer in Newport?"

"I don't care if I never see that place again."

Commiserating, he embraced his daughter. "I know he hurt you, that Irishman. I'm sorry for it. You'll feel better about Newport, and America, if you get away for a season. We'll return in time for Mrs. Astor's ball at her new home next winter, I guarantee it."

She brightened, brushing tears away. "That's grand, Papa. I'll go, gladly."

For her birthday in March, Sam presented Jenny with a leather-bound, gold-stamped gift edition of Mr. Twain's *The Innocents Abroad.* The book was almost thirty years old but still popular. In preparation for the trip, Jenny devoured its satiric descriptions of American tourists at European landmarks.

The night before departure, Sam said a lusty private farewell to Tessa at the Pickwick. She wept, but not so copiously that she forgot to hand him a list of necessary medications and travel precautions. "Eight hours sleep per night. No water from unknown sources. No cohabiting with native women. Oh God, Sam, I'll miss you."

On April 1, Mozart and Mamie Fish saw them off at a Hudson River pier at half past seven. Baggy-eyed because of the early hour, Mamie embraced Jenny and urged her to come back with a rich and titled fiancé. Mozart shook his employer's hand and avoided Jenny's eyes. Captain Bully Jelks strode to the flying bridge and *Invincible* hoisted sail, caught a strong northwest wind and soon plowed into the Atlantic bound for the Continent.

30
Orlov

Baedeker in hand, Sam sailed into unfamiliar waters: the port of Piraeus for the Acropolis and the Parthenon; the port of Naples for the eerily empty houses and avenues of Pompeii and a more cheerful boat ride to Capri. Venice revealed its lagoon; a gondolier sang for them when paid. In the plaza of San Marco, Sam was jostled by a pickpocket who attempted to steal his leather wallet and found it firmly fastened to the owner by a gold chain. Sam grabbed the thief's hair and broke his nose with his fist before the man wriggled away and fled, disturbing a hundred pigeons.

Before they left the Hotel Danieli, once the palace of a doge, Jenny bought four costly pieces of Murano glass for shipment back to New York. Sam speculated that she might be getting over her obsession with the Irish boy.

At the port of Ostia they went up to Rome for the Colosseum, St. Peter's and Michelangelo's chapel ceiling. Sam wondered if lombardy poplars would grow so handsomely in America. The port of Livorno led to the Pitti Palace and Giotto's campanile in Florence; Sam missed a trip to the tower of Pisa due to a traveler's complaint.

Invincible steamed through Gibraltar to the port of Amsterdam for the canals and windmills. A first-class rail compartment took them to Berlin, where they strolled the Tiergarten and Jenny asked whether the Brandenburg Gate really honored peace, as the Germans insisted. The guide pretended not to understand.

To Paris next, for Eiffel's Tower and the Louvre, the Tuileries and the Arc de Triomphe, then a hired carriage out to Versailles. After obligatory visits to the Trianon palaces that had influenced so much of Newport's architecture, their carriage bore them on through the closely forested park.

"Sixty miles in circumference according to Mr. Twain," Jenny said with the book open in her lap. "Louis the Fourteenth spent two hundred million on it and kept thirty-five thousand men working to complete it."

The carriage turned into a long drive between mossy stone walls. At the main doors of Gordon Bennett's sumptuous villa, string music and the voices of revelers drifted in the lowering daylight. Yet another party was in progress.

"But he never entertains before midafternoon," Sam told her. "Wherever he is, he's in constant touch with New York and the other *Herald* in London. He reads every issue. The competition too. If he disapproves of copy in his papers, he roasts the appropriate editors by cable telegraph."

"From Paris?"

"From here, from his apartment on the Champs-Elysées—any of his houses. They're all wired."

The villa was a museum of everything fashionable and expensive: Italian Renaissance tapestries, Louis XIV furniture, Chinese porcelains, Limoges china. Pekes and Pomeranians and German spitz dashed among the legs of the guests, yapping and adding to the din; Bennett adored little dogs, Sam said. Her father must have researched his friend to know so much about him.

Footmen pressed champagne into their hands. The large crowd of guests spoke mainly French. Jenny was at a disadvantage; she'd gone no further than the first chapter of a rudimentary French grammar. The guests seemed mostly older men and younger women. The former had the white side-whiskers and jutting paunches associated with bankers, brokers and the like, though a few younger men in gaudy hussar or cuirassier uniforms leavened the mix. The ladies showed a lot of powdered décolletage and numerous beauty spots pasted below flashing eyes. Jenny felt dowdy in her expensive but plain traveling dress.

"Ah, there's James," Sam said. The lanky publisher, in shirtsleeves, strode through the crowd. He wore a bright cravat painted with the famous image of Montmartre's Moulin de la Galette windmill. A redhead clutched his arm and whispered. He whispered, gestured to the ceiling and sent her off with a pleased look on her painted face.

"My good friend. Welcome. And this is your daughter?" The bachelor publisher bowed and kissed Jenny's hand in lingering fashion.

"How do you do, Mr. Bennett?" How handsome he was, with his rakish mustache and sharp, calculating gaze. A pity he was so old, fifty or so, she guessed.

"Charmed, my dear. Absolutely charmed. There's food and drink aplenty in the dining room."

"Who are all these people?" Sam asked.

"Actresses, a few of their lovers—the ones in uniform—but mostly old walruses who control sizable sums for advertising. I cultivate them for the sake of the paper."

"This is such a large house," Jenny began.

"Fully staffed every day of the year, as are all my places. If I want caviar or a glass of mineral water when I arrive without notice, I expect it to be there. Ah, here's a chap closer to your own age, Jenny. Over here, Count, if you please."

The young man smiled agreeably as he approached. He was a head taller than Jenny, thin as a saber, with wide shoulders and perfect posture. His curly hair, inky black, contrasted with his dark blue eyes, one magnified by a monocle. His swallowtail coat, cut short to the waist in front, showed no wrinkles. The two flared ends of a de Jonville scarf, alternating broad stripes of dark green and slender pink, added a touch of color to his otherwise sober attire.

Gordon Bennett performed the introductions. "Mademoiselle Driver, Monsieur Driver, Count Ismail Orlov."

The young man bowed to the visitors, then kissed Jenny's hand. "Enchanted."

Sam charged right in. "Russian, are you?"

"Formerly. At one time I had the honor of serving with the Moscow Hussars." Orlov spoke English fluently, but with a pronounced accent. He touched the scarf. "These are our uniform colors—green for the jacket, pink for the pelisse. Today it is my pleasure to be a citizen of France. And you, sir?"

"New York."

Gordon Bennett lit a cigar. "And Newport for the summers. Lot of four-in-hand racing in New York and Newport. The count's a formidable whip. Not as good as I am, though."

"My dear Bennett, you never let me challenge that assumption on the open road."

"Someday, Count. Keep practicing, work up your courage, and I will."

A footman with a silver tray of champagne and aperitifs floated by. Gordon Bennett passed drinks to everyone, even Jenny, who resisted at first. She was fascinated by the Russian's good looks and polished manners. He smelled pleasantly of shaving soap. She sipped too much of the bubbling champagne.

"So you're no longer soldiering, Count?"

"Alas, I am not. I have a shop on the Rue de Rivoli, near the Tuileries. I deal in antiques. Estate goods, mostly."

"No gimcracks," Gordon Bennett said. "Nothing specious for defrauding gullible tourists. If it's from Orlov's, you can trust the provenance."

Jenny's cheeks felt warm, her legs wobbly. "What a good recommendation. Do you ever visit the States?"

"As a matter of fact I hope to call at New York later this year. Come, let's search out the edibles and we'll discuss whether our mutual schedules might accommodate a meeting."

He offered his arm in a way that allowed no argument. Jenny laid her hand on his sleeve and they swept away.

"Quite a polished gentleman," Sam said, flirting with an idea about Jenny's future.

"Don't let the good manners fool you. Ismail's a whoremaster. I suppose that's why I like him. He can't set foot in Russia any longer. In St. Petersburg there was an affair with the wife of one of the czar's ministers, much older. The minister's household guard pursued him but he outran them. He's a superb rider and swordsman."

"And likes to drive coaches?"

"Very much so. Doesn't own one presently, but he's been to England twice to inspect and price them."

"Ismail's an odd first name for a Russian."

"His mother was Turkish. Some pasha's daughter. What's perking in that dome of yours, Samuel?"

"Oh, nothing," Sam insisted, "nothing."

"Liar. Finish your champagne and I'll introduce you to some of the ladies. Most accommodating, all of them."

"But I already have a young friend—"

Gordon Bennett was gone, not interested in Sam's protest.

On the road back to Paris, Jenny seemed enthusiastic, fairly warbling to her father. "The count promised to be in touch with us when he's in New York."

Sam studied his daughter's face, alternately sunlit and shadowed as the great trees of the park shuttled by. "You liked him?"

"I did."

"Gordon Bennett said he's a bit of a scoundrel. Chases women."

"Oh, I suppose they're all that way in this part of the world," she answered, so quick and blithe about it that Sam breathed a long inner sigh of relief. At last, an antidote for that black-haired Irish lout.

"If you do plan to see him in a few months, Jenny, let your old papa offer a suggestion. Try to put on some weight. Improve your color. You've locked yourself away far too long."

Her eyes held his soberly. "I suppose I have, haven't I?"

Neither mentioned Prince Molloy, but for a moment his presence hovered between them.

At the Hôtel de Crillon, a bilingual porter delivered a small gift box for Mademoiselle Driver. She unwrapped the gold tissue and found an exquisite hand mirror of some kind of polished reflective crystal, thinly framed in tarnished gold. A scarab ornamented the base of the mirror where the handle began. The obliging porter translated the French-inscribed card.

"'In appreciation of our felicitous meeting, and in keen anticipation of a reunion in your country. This trinket is one of many brought from the Egyptian campaign by the officers of Napoléon Bonaparte. Yours obediently, Orlov.'"

Sam saw the delight on his daughter's face and beamed.

In the drowsy library of Gordon Bennett's *Herald* at 49 Avenue de l'Opéra, Orlov consulted past issues of the paper's New York counterpart. What he'd suspected was true. Driver, whose name he'd not heard previously, was a railroad mogul, worth millions. He had but one child, the young woman Orlov had chatted with at Versailles, doing his best to seduce her verbally, as he did with all women. No doubt she would inherit everything. And she was attractive, a bonus. He'd been seeking an end to the dreary business of hawking stolen antiques to dotty old ladies and their obliging husbands.

Orlov closed the paper and rested his palms on the stack, silent and thoughtful in the chapel-like stillness of the *Herald*'s library off the editorial rooms. When he allowed a smile, it was rich with anticipation.

31
At Mrs. Astor's

Hers was a magic name in New York. Old John Jacob's invasion and domination of the northwest fur trade early in the century, and his later enrichment from Manhattan real estate, had begun the tradition, visible in the widespread display of the family patronymic: Astor Library; Astor House Hotel; Astor Place, where mobs had rioted almost fifty years ago over the then-significant question of whether an English or an American actor was superior.

Mrs. Caroline Astor carried on the tradition. The highlight of the 1896 social season, indeed of almost any season the elite could remember, was Mrs. Astor's grand ball in her new home at 842 Fifth Avenue on the night of February 3. Because it was a Monday, and Mrs. Astor always attended the opera on Mondays, the official starting time was midnight.

Six hundred invitations went out. To keep the evening from being a mere inspection tour of the new mansion, Mrs. Astor had held an informal reception the preceding week, allowing friends in to see her latest extravagance. Sam couldn't attend; he was breaking ground in Terre Haute for a new St. Michael the Archangel hospital, and Jenny wouldn't have presumed to go alone.

So large was the expected crowd, Mrs. Astor prevailed on her brother-in-law, John Jacob III, to open connecting doors between her residence and his. Both Astors had moved from relatively more modest side-by-side homes at 34th and the avenue. A. T. Stewart, "the department store person," had lived on the opposite corner for seven years but he might as well have lived on the moon. The great lady ignored him. "I buy his carpets," she remarked, "why should I invite him to walk on them?" The jealous and vindictive whispered that by building her new mansion, Mrs. Astor had anted into the game of residential leapfrog. The tide of swank homes was rushing north.

It was rumored that Mrs. Astor's husband, William III, might attend the ball (she had bullied him into dropping his middle name, Backhouse, deeming it vulgar). Wags called him Smiling Willie because no one ever saw him smile. Seldom visible in New York, he occupied himself with his steam yachts and his horse farm up in Dutchess County. This year, however, Smiling Willie let it be known that, yes, he would attend the ball, though no one expected him to smile about it.

After the curtain fell on *Carmen* at the Metropolitan Opera House at Broadway and 40th Street, elegant carriages streamed north to 842 Fifth. Side lanterns and lacquered woodwork made a pretty sight in gently drifting snow. Landaus, barouches, victorias, even massive drags for four-in-hand driving delivered gentlemen in white tie and tails, ladies gowned by the leading fashion houses of Paris and London, two or three thousand dollars per gown, and up.

Servants in the dusty-blue livery copied from Windsor

Castle helped Jenny alight from the Driver carriage. For a moment her breath caught in her throat; she'd broken into the highest echelons of American society. Sam had paid for a Worth gown of pale red satin with an intricate bodice of lace and tiny embroidered roses. Her headdress with white aigrettes matched her white ostrich fan.

Sam peered into the dazzling entrance hall, lit by scores of incandescent bulbs of various colors; they spread a rainbow effect over all below.

"I expect Brady will be here."

"Papa, please don't quarrel tonight."

"I promise I won't. Unless he starts it."

The entrance hall measured fifty feet on a side, and reached up to a dizzying height. A full-length portrait of the Mystic Rose done by the French painter Carolus-Duran dominated the room. On canvas Mrs. Astor looked formal, almost severe, in a black Marie Antoinette gown, her left glove removed, presumably for greeting someone.

Wearing pale gray satin, the lady herself received the arrivals in a gold and ivory salon off the entrance hall. Caroline Astor might have passed for a hausfrau, and indeed her husband's grandfather, the fur king, had begun his life in a butcher shop in Germany. Mrs. Astor was of medium height, stocky, with a long jaw, gray eyes, and hair of such vivid, glossy black that it surely had to be dyed; she was, after all, in her middle sixties.

Alone on the salon's scarlet carpet, she blazed with diamonds: her tiara, her 200-stone necklace, her stomacher, her numerous rings and little diamond stars in her hair. "Supper at half past twelve, my dears," she said to Sam and Jenny. "So glad you could be with us." The Drivers obediently moved on to make room for others.

In the crowd Sam recognized many of New York's richest

and most important gentlemen. The level of noise and merriment steadily increased throughout the house. Jenny spied Harry Lehr flitting among the guests; husbands were more amused than threatened by Harry, who was considered a saucy though harmless eunuch. Harry darted to their side.

"Greetings, Drivers. Have you seen the gallery? Tonight it's the ballroom. Come, let me show you."

Arm in arm between them, he guided them to a vast room whose walls were crowded with paintings all the way to the high ceiling. Behind a screen of palms on the gallery, an orchestra played. At one end of the room, on a dais, sat Mrs. Astor's divan, known behind her back as the Throne.

Harry cocked a wrist at the art collection. "Dreadful taste, don't you agree? I've never seen so many Meissoniers in one place. Soldiers and sign painters and tavern layabouts aren't my idea of subjects for painters, even Frenchies."

"They look swell to me," Sam said.

Harry rolled his eyes.

Sam led Jenny to the small tables for eight set in the corridors of the house. He indicated a balding man standing alone by a marble column and staring at the revelers with a confused, almost bereft expression. "Smiling Willie. Come along, I see two places."

A half dozen strangers awaited them at the table, sipping champagne to break down their unfamiliarity with one another. Sam and Jenny approached, as did a tall, distinguished gentleman with an attractive woman at his side. Sam thought he recognized the man as a principal in a Wall Street brokerage. The man offered his hand, and confirmed the identification:

"John Howe, sir. This is my wife, Carole."

"Sam Driver, and my daughter, Jenny."

"Pleased to know you both," the attractive woman said warmly.

"Driver." Howe's smile never wavered, but something in his eyes changed. "Associated with Jay Gould, weren't you?"

"A long time in the past, yes." The past that always seemed to rise up to stigmatize him.

"Carole," Howe said, "I see an important client and his wife. I believe we should have supper with them. You'll excuse us, Mr. Driver—Miss Driver." He guided the attractive woman away.

Gruffly, Sam said to the others, "Shall we sit down?" No one else seemed to care about his former associations.

Souvenirs for male and female guests decorated the center of the table: tam-o'-shanter hats and boutonnieres for the gentlemen, delicate gauze butterflies and Japanese fans for the ladies. Jenny spied a tall, broad-shouldered man in white tie and tails gliding in and out of sight in the crowd. Color filled her cheeks.

"The count's here, isn't that exciting?"

"It is," Sam agreed, for reasons she couldn't guess.

Among the latecomers were the O. H. P. Belmonts, the ex-bachelor's new wife fawned over, even applauded, by some of the guests. Others avoided her. Not only was she divorced, but last year she'd forced her gorgeous underage daughter, Consuelo, into marriage with Charles, ninth Duke of Marlborough. Belmont had sailed with the Vanderbilts on several of their trips on Willie's yacht, *Alva*. It was hard to imagine the mild-mannered and genteel bachelor as the wolf in the henhouse, but those in Newport who spread racy tittle-tattle did their best to promote the idea.

Mrs. Belmont had a reputation as a dictator, but this evening, the forty-three-year old bride of three weeks was giddy, and flushed almost to the color of her hair, the hue of fading roses. She and Ollie had been married in city chambers, by Mayor Strong, because no clergyman would perform the ceremony.

In the midst of the crush, Mamie Fish ran into Harry Lehr. "Howdy-do, Harry." His was one of the few names she never forgot.

"You're lovely as always, madam," he murmured as he kissed her hand with plump pink lips.

"Harry, you don't have to flatter me the way you do with the rest of these stuffed birds. I just saw Alva and Ollie Belmont. I haven't seen a single Vanderbilt."

"Nor will there be at any party she attends. She dumped Willie, after all. Change is everywhere, Mamie. Change, upheaval—what can we do to forestall it?"

"Nothing, I should imagine. Unless you believe in Alva's solution now that she's becoming excessively liberal."

"What solution?"

Mamie raised her right hand. "'Pray to God. She will hear you.'"

Mrs. Astor's personal chef had combined his talents with those of the fashionable caterer Pinard to fill the guests with champagne and claret cup, lemonade and mineral water, hot dishes including terrapin, *filet de boeuf*, roasted duck, then cold dishes including foie gras in aspic, galantine of pheasant with truffles, pigeon à la Richelieu, even assorted sandwiches. "I can't, no more, please," Jenny sighed. But there was much more: cakes and ices, fruits, biscuits and macaroons.

After dinner Sam and his daughter separated. Sam was the one who found Orlov. The young Russian bowed.

"My dear Monsieur Driver. How good to see you again."

"I know you promised to visit this side of the pond, but I didn't know when to expect it."

Orlov popped the monocle out of his eye and buffed it with a white silk handkerchief. "Frankly, sir, the prospect of seeing your lovely daughter lured me here sooner than I expected. Is she with you this evening?"

Pleased, Sam said yes.

"Escorted?"

"Only by me. Have you found the carriage you were hunting when we met in Paris?"

"To my regret, no. Perhaps I shall have better luck in your country, although I will be away most of the spring, joining a party to hunt buffalo on—what is the expression?—the prairies?"

Sam's head buzzed with the excitement of an idea. "That's it, the prairies. Are you planning to spend any time in Newport this summer?"

"I hadn't thought that far into the future."

"I'll make you a proposition. I've always wanted a four-in-hand coach but I know my limitations. I've no experience with horses, let alone handling four sets of reins. If you'll help me choose a coach, I'll buy it and designate you as my instructor and driver for races."

The count's dark blue eyes seemed to sparkle, as though he understood Sam's ploy. "Very agreeable to me, sir. May we discuss it at our leisure?"

"Fine. Shall we search for Jenny?"

Jenny at the moment was the target of Honoria Brady, who rushed to her at the ballroom entrance. "My dear friend. It's been so long. How grand to find you again. Were you away last year?"

"Yes, Honoria, Europe."

"When may I call? When may we make a round of the shops, or see a show?"

"Why, I expect the answer's never."

"Never? Why on earth—?"

Jenny stamped a foot. "Stop the dissembling. You're no friend. I heard of the way you talked about me in Newport the year before last. Not in my presence, of course. I believe you accused me of being a climber. And gauche."

Brady's daughter seemed about to dispute the charges but the set of Jenny's mouth, the anger in her eyes, moved her in a different direction. Her lips peeled back from irregular teeth. "You little bitch. I'll say all of that, and more, to anyone who'll listen."

Jenny did the unexpected; she laughed.

"Good-bye, Honoria. You fooled me for a while but, as President Lincoln said, not forever. Please excuse me, I must speak to Harry Lehr."

Emmeline Brady was too far from the young women to hear what passed between them, but posture and the lividity of Honoria's face showed who'd gotten the worst of it.

"Another claret cup, waiter," Em said to a footman passing by. She'd already drunk too many.

Mamie Fish was right about change infusing society. Manhattan's old Assembly Balls had been courtly affairs, drawing on the cotillion with its carefully executed pairing, dividing and recombining. But new musical fashions—polka, mazurka, the waltz—had made inroads. Mrs. Astor's hired musicians had to satisfy all tastes, although convention prevailed at 1:30, when Elisha Dyer and his partner, John Jacob III's wife, Augusta, led the cotillion. Those not taking part lined the walls beneath the framed Meissoniers, applauding the neatly executed figures.

Afterward, Jenny danced with Harry Lehr, then decorously with her father. Old Arleigh Mould tottered out of the throng to request the pleasure. This brought the clock to 2:20 in the morning. Jenny was sleepy but grew alert when a footman, powdered and gloved, approached.

"Mrs. Astor would be pleased if you would join her on the divan."

Mrs. Astor's married daughter, Mrs. Charlotte Drayton, was just leaving the Throne. Jenny accepted graciously, trying not to dance for joy.

Em Brady watched Jenny ascend the dais. Fat tears filled her eyes and spilled to her cheeks. Her husband returned from the bar to find the Tigress slouched in a gilded chair by one of the small dining tables, mumbling drunkenly.

Jenny sat on one end of the divan with its red throw pillows. Mrs. Astor always took the center; people joked that, seated so, she never had to lean far to hear a remark, and the weight of her diamonds wouldn't drag her down.

"Are you enjoying yourself, my dear?"

"Oh, immensely, thank you."

"Here comes a gentleman with his eye on you."

Jenny hurriedly cooled herself with her ostrich plume fan.

"Miss Driver," Orlov said. "At last I find you."

"Count," she said, inclining her head and hoping her racing heartbeat couldn't be heard.

"Is your card filled? I would be honored to claim the next waltz."

Mrs. Astor sniffed. "Barbaric dance. Too provocative."

"Ah, but that's why we adore it in Paris, you see."

"Shame on you, Count." The Mystic Rose tapped his wrist with her fan; even that slight exertion sent reflections from a hundred diamond facets flashing and swirling, as though an invisible glass ball spun above them.

The hidden orchestra began *The Emperor Waltz.* Jenny feared she'd faint when she stepped into Orlov's arms. His grip was strong—if anything, too strong, possessive. The music seemed to speed up, the waltzing couples to flow around them in a delirium of swirling skirts and flashing patent leather shoes. Jenny began to feel deliciously dizzy.

"The gift you sent was exceptionally beautiful, Count."

"More beautiful in what it now reflects." He flattered her without shame; shamelessly, she welcomed it.

"I wanted to write and express thanks but I had no address."

"Consider the obligation discharged."

"The mirror was looted when Napoléon fought in Egypt?"

"I would not use the word *looted.* The French took legitimate spoils of war. And there is no onus in stealing from illiterate louse-ridden Arabs."

"But Napoléon devastated your country too, didn't he? I read Count Tolstoy's long novel—"

He interrupted, sharply. "I have no special affection for Mother Russia since the czar's police ran me out like a jackal. Let's not dwell on depressing matters."

The waltz concluded; breathless couples clapped.

"Your father surprised me with a sporting proposition. He wishes to acquire a coach for four-in-hand driving."

"Heavens, I hadn't heard that."

"He asked me to help choose it, instruct him and occasionally drive for him. I assume he plans to wager on races."

"When?"

"This summer. I shall be away hunting bison for two or three months but when I return we can anticipate another, perhaps longer reunion."

"Oh, I'd welcome that."

He bowed, and fondled her hand, and she no longer saw any flash of that interior coldness. Maybe she'd imagined it. Orlov took his leave at a few minutes past three. Jenny wondered if she might be falling in love.

She hoped Prince would somehow find out, and be maddened with jealousy.

At half past three, as the ball was winding down and the more elderly guests fell asleep over their scrambled eggs, cognac and cigars, Sam and Bill Brady finally confronted one another. A few minutes earlier, Sam had seen the Tigress helped from the ballroom by servants, trailed by her weeping daughter.

"I trust you observed my wife's condition," Brady blurted without preamble.

"Yes, I'm heartily sorry for her, whatever the ailment."

"I hold you responsible, Driver."

"That's ridiculous, Bill. You've got it backward. You're the constant attacker. You have been all along."

A muscle in Brady's jaw quivered. "And I'll continue until you're beaten—all your fatuous pretensions exposed."

Sam's right hand balled at his side. Brady stepped back. He pivoted too sharply, almost fell. Sam's laugh was involuntary but loud.

Brady turned, glared, rushed on to the entrance hall. A shabbily dressed reporter scribbling on a pad—accounts of the great night would appear in all the dailies—accidentally crossed paths with him. Brady smashed the man with a vicious backhand before storming after his family.

Thus the Drivers ended the great Astor evening: Sam aware of Brady's deepening rage, Jenny holding her father's arm and drowsily smiling at the stars above the smoking chimneys of Fifth Avenue.

"You had a good time?" Sam asked as they closed themselves in the carriage under lap robes.

"Marvelous. Count Orlov told me he's going to drive for you. Did you know he was invited this evening?"

"I did not, and he didn't say how he managed it. I've heard that invitations can be had if you find the right man on the household staff and pay him a thousand or two."

"It's a strange world these people inhabit, Papa."

He patted her hand as the carriage rumbled south. "But you're part of it now, and finding it to your liking."

Jenny laid her head back on the cushion and closed her eyes. "Oh, yes. I can hardly wait for summer."

32
Racing Blood

Loud knocking woke Prince. Rex ran in circles, yapping. Jimmy Fetch pressed close to the building to escape the April rain drizzling from the eave. "Come on, you got to see this."

"Jimmy, for God's sake, I have to report to the stable at six."

"It's only ha' past four, get your pants on. I even brung an umbrella."

Prince succumbed, and shortly set off through the darkness with Rex scampering behind. Prince's left foot still dragged a little, raking up the mud. Probably it always would.

Jimmy led him to the eastern end of the Long Wharf, the terminal of the New York, New Haven & Hartford, which had bought out the Old Colony railroad. Four times a day, passengers and freight arrived from Fall River via a bridge at Tiverton. Wind from the harbor carried mist and a mucky odor from the cove beyond the tracks. Under arc lights, a man in a tall black hat and a fancy wraparound overcoat with a black astrakhan collar watched workmen swarming around slat-sided boxcars. A servant protected the well-dressed man with an umbrella.

Huddled in shadows, Jimmy pointed to the tall hat. "Isn't that the pa of the girl you was sweet on?"

"Yeh. Driver. And his hired bootlicker." Prince hadn't revealed to Titus, Jimmy, anyone, the identities of the man who ordered his beating and maiming and the other who hired the plug-uglies responsible.

"Looks like he's jumping into coaching in a big way. See where they're pullin' off the tarps?"

On a flatcar coupled behind the boxcars, workmen untied wheel ropes to release a monster of a black road coach. Raindrops sparkled on its lacquered sides, bright as a coat of diamonds. Prince read the gold lettering on the forward quarter panel.

" 'Tantivy.' That belongs to him?"

Jimmy shifted the umbrella for better protection. "None other. Girlfriend's brother, he works for the railroad, he told me so. Cost old Driver a kettle of cash, I bet. He queered it for you an' his girl, didn't he?"

"He definitely had a hand in it."

"Going to do anything about it?"

Prince stared at the black coach.

"In due time."

O. H. P. Belmont returned from New York four days later. A cold snap had followed the rain; Prince and the other grooms had already laid warming blankets over Belmont's dozen thoroughbred and half-bred horses. Each blanket carried the family's monogrammed crest. Belmont liked to joke about his horses sleeping on fine Irish linens. "Of course they don't, horses sleep standing up, but it's a nice fiction to enhance the cachet of the place." As if a fifty-two-room Richard Morris Hunt mansion imitating a French king's hunting lodge needed much enhancement.

At half past ten every day, the owner appeared for a tour of the stable, which occupied the entire ground floor of Belcourt. Belmont inspected each horse in its stall; a gold plate bore the animal's name.

Prince approached Belmont cap in hand. He asked his question. He was unprepared for Belmont's abruptness:

"Drive four-in-hand? Impossible, unless you have an inheritance, and seven years to practice."

"Seven—? It takes that long to learn?"

"Molloy, consider. You aspire to handle a vehicle that may weigh as much as twenty-eight hundred pounds. I favor a drag over a road coach, mine weighs only twenty-two hundred—by the way, do you know the difference?"

"No, sir."

"A drag is a private carriage. A coach is exactly what the name says, a modified English mail or passenger vehicle. Wheel and lead horses average eleven hundred pounds each. Coming clear? You have an avalanche behind you, a mountain of expensive horseflesh ahead of you, and you must handle four sets of reins, and a whip, while you're crashing along at ten or eleven miles an hour—faster if it's a road race. The sport is not something you master in a week."

Prince's face showed his embarrassment. Belmont's innate kindliness took over. He led Prince out to the cold sunshine, became almost genial. Perhaps it was German gemütlichkeit. The family hailed from the old country; nonobserving Jews, so it was said. Coming to America, August Belmont, Oliver's father, had converted to Christianity.

"I don't mean to patronize you, lad, only to explain. When I drive four-in-hand, two grooms ride in the rumble for starts, stops and emergencies. I understand you're a good worker.

Quicker than most. With experience and diligence, you might qualify as a groom. I can send you to a friend near Portsmouth who raises horses for the coaching trade. He owes me favors, so I don't believe he'd charge you for some instruction. Not to be done on my time, of course."

"That's very good of you, Mr. Belmont. I'd be grateful."

"Tell me, what inspired this sudden passion?"

"There's someone I want to beat."

"On the road?"

"Anywhere I can."

Jumbo Sullivan wasn't jumbo at all. Nicknamed for P. T. Barnum's prize elephant, he was thin as a stick. Sullivan, up in years, hailed from the Bay State. His little horse farm outside Portsmouth evidenced a struggle against poverty and weather: a patched roof, a boarded window, a well in need of tuck-pointing.

Sullivan peered at Prince through spectacles with lenses a quarter inch thick. He spoke with a strong New England accent; the sentences frequently began with, "Ayah." He invited Prince into the cramped kitchen for a mug of tea.

"I'm a humble man, Molloy. Humble about my circumstances, humble about wealth, which I hain't got any to speak of. About one thing I am not humble, grooming and training the finest coach horses in New England. Morgans aren't a breed as popular as they once were, but I say they're ideal and even the Pope of Rome can't change my opinion. Now what prompts you to take advantage of Ollie Belmont's good nature?"

Prince gave Sullivan the same evasive explanation he'd used at Belcourt. Sullivan leaned back in his creaky chair, skeptical. "Got to throw away that attitude right now. One thing you mustn't carry on the road is anger. It affects judgment. A good whip learns how to drive one horse, then a team, then four, always with sound judgment. You need courage, an' nerve. An' one more thing. Even a single horse, pulling hard, can damn near paralyze weak arms and wrists. Kindly stand up. Take off your shirt."

"What for?"

"So's I can see how you're built. Humble, boy—don't forget humble. You're no different than a new animal being looked over."

Prince pulled out the tails of his faded work shirt and unbuttoned it. His skin prickled; the air was still cool but Sullivan wanted the kitchen door open with a breeze scurrying around the mismatched table and chairs. The kitchen smelled of hay and horse dung from outside.

"Show me your back. Alright, good, now double up those arms. Make 'em as strong as you can."

He inspected Prince's biceps, squeezed the knots of muscle. He pulled each arm to an extended position so he could examine the strength and flex of Prince's wrists.

"Ayah, reckon you're strong enough. You work with your hands?"

"All the time. I've been a gardener's man, an ice cutter, a ball shacker at the Casino—"

"Oh, the hallowed Casino. Never set foot in there myself. Now don't think it's a cake walk if Ollie Belmont or anybody else says come on, ride in the rumble. You got to know the fundamentals, got to be ready to take over in case the driver's injured."

From a crowded bookshelf in the parlor, Sullivan pulled a small volume with heavily thumbed paper covers. "This here was printed in London about ten years ago. Best little book on the subject that I know. Take it home, read it front to back, then read it again. Absorb it."

The author of *Hints on Driving* was one Capt. C. Morley Knight. Prince flipped through several pages, saw marginal notes printed beside certain paragraphs. LEANING FORWARD BAD. LEFT HAND MUST GIVE AND TAKE. RESIN OR WAX ON GLOVES. He shook his head. Sullivan scowled.

"Somethin' wrong? You don't understand English?"

"Way back in school, one of the nuns, Sister Frances Mary, said I couldn't learn, my head was full of sawdust."

"Prove her wrong. Memorize the captain's advice."

"I'll try."

"You'll do better than that or I'm wasting my time. Now fetch me that paper on the counter. I'll show you a contraption you need to build an' practice with till you think your arms are damn near ready to fall off."

On the gray block of foolscap Sullivan drew a crude diagram: a pulley screwed to the floor, another pulley on the wall above, a rectangle resembling a clock weight tied to the end of a cord below the wall pulley.

"Ten pounds'll do for a start. A sprightly team will about match that. On the other end of the cord you tie two straps, reins. You sit in a chair in front of this thing and raise and lower the weight."

"I don't own pulleys, or straps, I don't even own a proper chair."

"You want to learn to drive, or not?"

"I do."

"Then don't whine and snivel and poor-mouth me, son. You find the parts and build what I say."

Prince's chin lifted. "I will."

Jumbo Sullivan polished the thick lenses of his spectacles with an old red bandanna. "Damn if I don't think you may. One thing for sure, you ain't humble."

Prince found a strap, and old rusty pulleys he loosened with Mr. J. D. Rockefeller's "Standard" brand lubricating oil, borrowed from Titus. Jimmy turned up a mysterious lead cylinder stamped USN, surely stolen, though he denied it. Prince spent forty cents on a secondhand chair. He practiced a half hour, sometimes an hour every night after work at Belcourt stables.

Sundays, he trudged out to Sullivan's little farm. On the second visit, Sullivan hitched one of his Morgans to his small trap. "Like me, it's humble. But it serves."

They drove the rolling dusty roads around Portsmouth. With no warning, Sullivan handed over the reins. Prince put too much strain on the Morgan's mouth. The horse bolted.

Sullivan snatched the reins. In a quarter of a mile he stopped the Morgan, hopped down and whispered soothingly in the horse's ear while stroking its muzzle. As he turned the trap around he grumbled, "You got to have a feel for the mouth, son; without that you're wasting your time."

"It sure isn't like driving an old nag pulling an ice-cutting sled."

"Who said it was? You got a powerful lot to learn."

Prince studied Capt. C. Morley Knight's little manual an hour or more each night. He carried it with him to Belcourt and instead of eating lunch, he sat in the shade of a wall, reading. O. H. P. Belmont strolled by once, observed the title on the cover and moved on without any expression other than a brief smile.

Prince drew a calendar and tacked it up where he could see it from his chair. Rex watched on his haunches while Prince worked the cord and weight. The dog cocked his head, as though wondering about the strange nightly ritual.

The first of May, Prince tore down the calendar page and put up a new one. Summer was rushing at him. When he was ready, he'd strike back at Mr. Samuel High Hat Driver.

33
Dickie Changes Course

The turn of the season brought an inevitable lift of Titus's spirits: Nearly every table was filled nearly every night. Once again tourists bought cheap tickets, slept in deck chairs and stumbled off the Fall River boats before daylight.

Down in New York, *Invincible* was soon to emerge from drydock. Sam donated $25,000 to William McKinley's campaign for the White House. Jenny protested that she didn't understand "monometallism" or "bimetallism," or why, as the rival parties claimed, one ism or another meant health or death for the American economy, not to mention American honor.

"They're all blowhards, Papa, those politicians."

"I know, but we must elect our blowhards, not theirs."

Jenny tried to lure him to a performance of *Lear*, starring Henry Irving and his Lyceum company from London. Sam refused, so Orlov graciously took Sam's ticket. It was mildly troubling to Jenny that the count seemed to have only vague answers for questions about political unrest among the serfs, or the czar's court at St. Petersburg. He pleaded that he'd been away too long.

Another passionate farewell with Tessa preceded Sam's departure for Rhode Island. The tall and courtly émigré accepted Sam's invitation to sail as a guest. In Newport, Orlov rented a suite at the Ocean House. Soon "Tantivy" was hurtling through the countryside. Sam clung to his tall silk hat while the count skillfully worked four sets of reins: the near lead uppermost, over his left forefinger, the near wheel and off lead under the forefinger, the off wheel between middle and third fingers. From time to time the count's right hand came into play to flick the whip or shorten reins or execute a turn. Sam doubted he'd ever get the hang of it but Orlov drove effortlessly, laughing and chatting while maintaining fast, even reckless speeds.

One noon a hay wain maneuvered to escape collision with the oncoming coach. Sam shouted a warning to Orlov, ignored. The hay wain veered out of the way, tipped and overturned beside the narrow road. Its rear axle snapped; half its load spilled into a marshy ditch. The farmer crawled from the wreck in time to scream oaths at the black coach. Orlov laughed and whipped Sam's horses, two grays, two bays, to greater speed.

Desirable invitations now arrived frequently at Red Rose. Mrs. Belmont requested their presence at a Pastoral Ball, everyone got up as shepherds and milkmaids. Wearing lederhosen and a jaunty Alpine hat, O.H.P. showed off his stable and attempted to entertain guests with very bad yodeling.

The invitations flattered Sam and Jenny, but Sam had no illusions. The wanted guest was their friend Orlov. He was exactly the sort of polite, attentive extra man that the married matrons liked to have hovering. Orlov danced, flirted, but never overstepped, much as some of the matrons might have wished it. Young heiresses swarmed on him but were disappointed. The count reserved most of his time for Jenny.

Prince sweated through steamy nights of pulling the weight, now at twenty pounds. By late June he drove Sullivan's one-horse trap without mishap. "Ayah, that'll do," the older man said. "Next we'll try you on a team. So don't get the swelled head. Remember humble."

On Thames Street one Saturday afternoon, Prince saw Jenny leaving a stationery shop whose window advertised Fanny Farmer's popular new cookbook. Walking with another young woman, she was engrossed in conversation. She passed by on the other side while Prince leaned against the building, smoking and squinting from under the brim of his cap. Jenny hadn't looked at him but he thought she'd seen him.

Or was that a lingering sense of loss he tried unsuccessfully to deny?

Layers of rum-scented smoke drifted in the hot lamplight. Mozart heard a sound, glanced up. When had Sam opened the door?

Usually cordial, Sam looked less so tonight. The heat stuck his linen shirt to his chest. At the fringe of the lamplight Mozart saw pages of figures in Sam's inky hand.

"These expense totals for the last twelve months at the San Antonio and Sonora—"

"Yes?"

"I thought you checked them."

"I did."

"The figures are wrong in five categories. Under expenditures for coal there's an error of more than seven thousand dollars. You don't usually make mistakes."

Mozart rubbed a thumb under his left eye; the bags had

grown darker, more pronounced, a visible contrast to his yellowed complexion. "I'm sorry."

Sam laid the papers on a clutter of documents, disorder not typical of his longtime assistant. "I've ticked the errors with red ink. Correct them as soon as you can."

Mozart reached for the papers, only to be deterred by a change in Sam's tone. "Mozart, are you ill?"

"No. No, I don't believe so. In this hot weather I don't have an appetite. I don't sleep well."

"A druggist can give you something to help. See to it, for your own sake. Don't let it get the best of you," Sam said as he left.

Mozart laid his arms on the clutter, put his head down.

Past 1 a.m. the same night, still sleepless, still exhausted, he slouched along the Cliff Walk under a sky full of misty summer stars. He heard the ocean but hardly a puff of wind reached him high above the breaking surf. He sat on a rock and stared seaward, admitting to himself that he'd been denying the steady deterioration of his state of mind.

In the dull gleam of the sea he imagined human figures moving. Two men wielding iron pipes, then knives, to hurt a writhing victim. He didn't need to see a face to know the victim was young Molloy. The horrific vision faded only when he closed his eyes.

It's been too much, that's all. I tried to shut it out but it's finally reached me, the sum of too many crimes committed for Mr. Samuel Driver, Esq. Too many judges bribed, too many witnesses suborned, too many earnings statements falsified, too many enemies doped in cribs and discovered with whores but let off because they promised to cooperate. A few deserved what happened to them, but not many. Molloy didn't deserve it.

Out of a misguided loyalty Mozart had offered no protest when Sam sent him off to hire Bowery toughs to brutalize the boy. Not seeing it done enhanced the guilt; in Mozart's imagination the brutality grew that much more vivid and vicious. . . .

Then he'd lied to Jenny, whom he adored. Of course Molloy had come to the house. Of course he'd tried to see her that winter evening.

Back at the cottage, he slept an hour, late in the night. To induce that fitful rest he relied on a quart of whiskey hidden in his wardrobe. In years past, before he lost his parents, brothers, one sister, joined the Sharpshooters, met Sam Driver—in those days he'd drunk so little he could almost be classed a cold-water man. Now, at the low point of nearly every day, he visited the wardrobe.

Next morning he trudged to the apothecary's on Thames Street, a block south of Timmerman's groggery. He explained his problem.

"I recommend laudanum," the apothecary said. "A teaspoon at bedtime."

"Laudanum's opium, isn't it?"

"Opium tincture, yes. Widely used."

"Alright, sell me a bottle. Oh, and do you have anything for the breath?"

Sly eyes showed that the apothecary knew the reason for the question. "Something to mask objectionable odors?"

"Correct."

"Essence of peppermint. It comes in a small flask. We prepare it here. It's not cheap, sir."

"I'll take it."

The peppermint hid Mozart's whiskey breath, but a teaspoon of laudanum did little to promote his sleep. Before a week went by he doubled the dosage.

Even with that, he dreamed bizarre dreams. He saw Molloy clawing a ruined leg awash with blood. . . .

"No," he cried, starting, wide awake.

He knew where he was: the stifling room, the sodden bedding, the whine of an insect near his ear. "No, no, *no.*"

The night was still, and hot, and empty of any hope of redemption.

A modern incarnation of the Olympics had resumed in Athens. The Supreme Court decided that a doctrine of separate but equal facilities for the races was legal. At the insistence of a political operative named Marcus Hanna, William McKinley prepared to campaign from his front porch in Canton, Ohio, foursquare behind the gold standard and "a return to Republican prosperity." The Socialist candidate Eugene Debs rose up like a vulture on the horizon.

William Jennings Bryan toured the country, predicting that only free silver would save America. W. K. Brady III got in a fistfight with a Reading Room newcomer who appeared wearing a silver bug lapel pin. Being an old and respected member of the club, and a gold standard Republican, Brady was admonished. Silver Bug was permanently banned from the premises.

So little of the news was heartening or positive, Sam gave up reading the papers for days at a time. Yet he couldn't altogether avoid hearing of all the new ideas threatening the familiar order of things: horseless carriages; a hookless fastener called a "zipper" (what was wrong with buttons?); pictures that "moved" on a screen in dark music halls; sinister-sounding "X-rays" that peered through a person's skin (was nothing sacred?).

Thousands rushed to the gold strike in the Yukon. Depressed, Sam wished he were young enough to go. Marines landed in Nicaragua to protect American nationals. Angry, Sam felt righteous about suppressing "greasers." Bryan thundered to the Democratic convention that the electorate should not be "crucified on a cross of gold." An alarmed capitalist, Sam believed Bryan should be shot or locked up, and Debs soon thereafter.

Wednesday, the fifth of August, a boy with a spyglass saw the first sails. All morning, fog had beclouded the southern horizon, not dispersed by the light southeast wind. The glass revealed spinnakers set. Faithful as the seasons, sloops and schooners of the New York Yacht Club appeared this time every year. It was the club's annual sail up the eastern seaboard. The contenders were finishing their dash from New London to Newport; a smudgy sky astern suggested the usual flotilla of steam yachts following.

The harbor filled. The Fall River boats disgorged double and triple the usual number of visitors. Stewards from the arriving pleasure craft docked their gigs and naphtha launches at the New York Yacht Club's Station 6 on Sawyer's Wharf. While the owners perused the latest New York papers or telegraphed orders to brokers, the stewards dispersed along Thames Street to replenish their stores. Titus always had a brief but lucrative side business this time of year. He sold haunches of beef, previously bought from cooperative wholesalers, for more than he paid.

Next day, Thursday, bands, a parade and flag-raising in Washington Square preceded races in the harbor. Crews of launches, dinghies and two- and four-oared gigs competed while spectators cheered them on. As night fell, electric bulbs and paper lanterns lit the rigging of anchored vessels, a fairyland sight. The largest crowds would appear tomorrow, for the Goelet Cup races, the nation's most prestigious yachting contest. Silver trophies from Tiffany would be awarded to the fastest sloop and schooner.

Dickie Glossop, cravat and boater firmly in place despite the brutal humidity, searched the festive crowd for an hour before he spied the Bradys. "Good evening to you," he said, tipping his hat.

He hoped Bill Brady wouldn't curse or punch him for abandoning his daughter but he needn't have worried. The Tigress clutched his arm as though he were a lost relative. "Dickie, how grand. We've missed you. Honoria, do turn around and say hello."

Honoria did, frosty at first. Roman candles shot up from the Cove, red and yellow and green lights in the sky. Carefully, almost shyly, Dickie said, "I'm awfully glad to see you again, Honoria."

She gave him a cool, limp hand. "Hello, Dickie. I thought you'd disappeared. Taken up with someone else," she added with a snide edge.

Em Brady steered her husband away from the young couple. Dickie felt a surge of encouragement. The Tigress wanted him to reconnect with her willful child. He invited Honoria to stroll to a booth selling paper cones of shaved ice sweetened with flavored syrup. She didn't seem enthusiastic, but neither did she refuse. He supposed he must expect a certain amount of glacial reserve as his penance.

Loud booms from ascending rockets thrilled the crowd. Dickie dared to grasp Honoria's elbow.

"I know you were hurt and irked over Jenny Driver, but I beg you to understand my side of it."

Honoria smiled for the first time. "I rather like that word *beg*."

"What I did was necessary for the Driver commission. I'm done with Red Rose." Damned if he'd mention Molloy, or the shameful tennis game. He'd been a fool to honor the wager with that low-class nobody, never mind that he'd been caught cheating.

"Well, I suppose I should tell you that father's been contemplating an addition to Sunrise."

"Seriously?"

"Don't annoy me, Dickie. Would I say it if I weren't serious?"

"Sorry, sorry. Has your father engaged an architect?"

"Not yet. Aren't you pushing rather hard? You treated me shabbily when you spent so much time with that tart."

"I thought she was your friend?"

A rocket turned Honoria's face green. "Misinformation," she said with a toss of her curls. "Buy me a strawberry cooler, please. Large."

He knew she'd make him climb a long, slippery slope of small rejections and humiliations. She'd subject him to the nastiness that girls of her class enjoyed meting out. He was willing to suffer it if he could worm back into the good graces of the family. Jenny Driver was under the spell of the flashy Russian strutting around Newport as though he owned it. Sam Driver treated Orlov like a prospective son-in-law. A change of partners was a necessity.

Quiet for a time, he and Honoria munched their flavored ices and enjoyed the fireworks. He'd wait a week or two before broaching the subject of a commission to remodel Sunrise. Possibly Honoria would bring it up sooner.

"Oh, Dickie," she cried, pretending fear as spectacular red lights exploded overhead. She thrust her hip and breast tight against him.

Dickie smiled. If he hadn't yet won the new game, he was a serious player.

34
A Question of Marriage

The morning of the Goelet Cup dawned fair. Moderate wind out of the southwest promised a good race. Before the morning was far advanced, central Newport resembled a deserted village. Bits of trash blew along Bellevue Avenue, glumly observed by a few unlucky employees forced to stay behind and guard the Casino. If there was a single day on the calendar when class barriers were forgotten, it was race day. Since the Goelet Cup was the most prestigious yachting event in North America, it would be unthinkable for owners of the great cottages to be "at home" to anyone. They became spectators, rushing to the shore or sailing out to the course. Thus most of their servants were at liberty as well.

Sam decided against cruising in pursuit of the sloops and schooners. He would drive to Narragansett Bay instead. Lessons from Orlov had boosted his confidence, and he thought a drive more conducive to raising a certain issue with his daughter.

Mozart expressed no interest in joining their outing,

Breathing out fumes of peppermint, he pleaded an unspecified indisposition and retired to his bedroom while the sun was still slanting from the east. The recent changes in Mozart's behavior, his withdrawal, confounded Sam, and generated anger against himself. His longtime associate was a puzzle he couldn't solve. The problem often reminded him of the inscription on the plaque he kept in New York. Thus far he'd not lived up to it; Mozart had gotten the best of him.

In addition to "Tantivy," his American-made private coach adapted from British models, Sam owned a two-wheeled cart and a four-wheeled spider phaeton. He sent a runner to Coggeshall Avenue, where he stabled horses and carriages. A groom returned with the phaeton. Sam would drive the short distance along Ocean Avenue to Castle Hill at the extreme southwest point of the island, where Orlov had promised to meet them.

Jenny appeared in the driveway of Red Rose looking fresh and fetching in a white linen sailing outfit with puffy sleeves and a navy shirtwaist with white polka dots. Her cap and oxfords were white linen as well. Her bow tie repeated the shirtwaist pattern. Sam kissed her cheek and told her she looked lovely. She patted his hand and thanked him.

Seated on the driving box, he took the reins from the groom. Sam's freckled hands were slowly being gnarled by rheumatism but this morning the pain was slight. The groom helped Jenny settle next to her father, then climbed up behind. The groom was already sweating in his frock coat and silk hat. Sam gingerly shook the reins and the obedient nag turned out of the drive.

"Jenny, may I bring up something that's been on my mind lately?" Sam never worried about servants overhearing; he tended to forget Colonel Mann's network of spies.

"Of course you may. You look so serious."

"The future of an offspring is always serious."

She was amused by his sweet sententiousness. She waited quietly for him to continue.

"What do you think of Count Orlov? That is, as a prospective husband?"

Startled by his directness, she didn't answer for a beat or two, and then only tentatively. "Why, he's certainly handsome, and sophisticated. Worldly. I do confess there's something a little remote about him. Unreachable. I have no better word than that."

She wanted to end the conversation. The moment reminded her of the Casino tunnel, the day she met Prince. That was a moment of commitment—a moment to go forward, or retreat. This time Sam was doing the pushing.

"I'm really not prepared to give a proper answer to your question, Papa."

"Not that damned Irish boy still on your mind, I hope?"

"Oh, no, no, he's quite forgotten."

Sam sneaked a glance. Jenny's eyes clouded with what he perceived as confusion.

Is she lying to me? He may be out of sight but I wonder if he's out of her thoughts. By God I wish I'd ordered Mozart to have him killed.

Sensing her father's disappointment, Jenny said, "You must understand, Papa—I don't know the count very well."

"We know a good deal about him. Obviously he's well off. He must have competent managers looking after his business in Paris or he couldn't take so much time away."

She agreed. He turned the plodding horse into a long curve on Ocean Drive. To the west, dust clouds faded the crowds of rushing spectators to pale brown ghosts; beyond them, on a blazing expanse of water, scores of white triangles moved seaward, taut with the wind. Those belonged to people sailing out to the three legs of the Block Island course, a beat of about fourteen miles, a run of eighteen, a final reach of six miles back to the finish.

"I hate to press you, Jenny, but I remind you that you're no longer a child."

She responded with a flash of temper. "Neither am I ready for the grave. I'm only twenty-one."

"Considered an eminently marriageable age. I'll be reasonable about the count. I find him an agreeable gentlemen, but I know people say he's something of a rounder."

"Is there any husband in our set who isn't?"

Our set? Good, she's no longer thinking of herself as an outsider. A helpful sign . . .

"If we put that aside, would you consider him a worthwhile catch?"

"I would, provided I wanted to marry a nobleman. A woman is supposed to love the man she marries."

"You couldn't feel that way about Orlov?"

"Papa, may we drop this? It might be possible sometime, but not yet."

"Alright. Keep him in your sights, that's all I ask."

She touched his sleeve, her next question candid but not unkind. "Because you'd like to have a titled son-in-law?"

He didn't take umbrage. "I won't deny it. Quite the fashion in Newport, husbands with titles. Maybe Orlov can teach me to like the French. Thanks for settling the question, anyway."

She was about to say it wasn't settled by any means when a brass horn sounded "Clear the Road."

Sam swore, hauled on the reins to pull their carriage out of the way of the luxurious George IV phaeton coming up behind, drawn by matched grays. The driver was a grass widow notorious for her independence bordering on rudeness. Sam recollected her as one of Alva Belmont's votes-for-women crowd.

She drove imperiously, passing Sam with a jaunty wave. Her

groom, a dwarf standing behind her, was scarcely as big as his fifty-inch coaching horn. He was another one of those affectations of the wealthy, like pet pigs and tame ocelots. The dwarf tooted "Clear the Road" again; the grass widow left them in the dust.

Sam shook the reins; the plodding nag's clip-clop gait speeded up slightly. The spider phaeton left the road, bumped over weedy ground where horse patties left a pungent smell. The white gossamer balls of dandelion seeds danced on the wind. Bees in the clover threatened to frighten nervy horses, but not Sam's placid animal. A glittering river of wheeled vehicles flowed toward the bluffs overlooking the bay.

Amid the dust and noise, father and daughter sank into private reveries. Jenny felt stifled. When determined—and when was he not?—her father became unstoppable. She wished she'd stayed home.

Sam knew Jenny was stubborn. To argue further wouldn't advance his agenda. He decided he must take steps on his own.

35
On Castle Hill

That same morning, Prince ate a huge breakfast prepared by tall Mary in the dramshop kitchen. His uncle had already left to watch the races from the deck of a friend's dilapidated trawler.

When Prince mopped up the last of his white gravy with the last piece of biscuit, the lean black woman said, "You be careful out there today. Some of them white folks from New York is alright, but the uppity ones, they get pleasure outta stompin' on poor people just 'cause they poor. Makes a body mad."

"Won't happen to me, Mary. I feel good."

"That a promise?"

"Cast in stone."

"You a sweet boy. When you keep the gate closed on your temper," she added with a wink. He grinned and hugged her.

He left Thames Street with Rex trotting beside him. At every other step he jabbed the ground with a walking stick hacked from a fallen oak limb. He looked raffish. A red bandanna wrapping his forehead and knotted over his left ear trailed its tattered ends to his shoulder. With his black hair shining and his face deeply tanned, he could have passed for a gypsy.

By arrangement, he met Jimmy Fetch on the hill leading up to Bellevue Avenue. Jimmy tucked a deck of cards into his pants pocket, tossed his burning cigarette into the street and the two walked east on Narragansett Avenue. Flo Dwyer, red-haired and bovine and companionable, waited for them in front of Chepstow, the Schermerhorn's handsome Italianate cottage.

"Hello, dear boys." She linked arms with them. Of late Flo had made eyes at Jimmy. Prince encouraged it because, once too often, she'd mentioned the wedding mass, or the number of babies the good Catholic fathers would want. Jimmy wouldn't care to hear that, either, but let her find it out for herself.

Along Ocean Avenue the traffic forced them off the road. They dodged a stream of coaches, drags, *char à bancs*, phaetons, hooded gigs with tops down for sunshine, tilburies, cabriolets, broughams, omnibuses packed with day trippers, off-duty hansom cabs from the piers. Ordinary road wagons, surreys and buckboards represented the other end of the wealth spectrum, to which was added all the shank's-mare traffic of the sightseeing poor. Youngsters rolling hoops and playing tag added their yelps and squeals to the racket of grinding axles, jingling chains, creaking leather. It was bedlam, but for a change Prince found it a grand morning to be alive.

Rex paused occasionally to visit a stunted shrub. Then he chose the bright yellow wheel of a slow-rolling victoria carrying ladies in lace bonnets and gentlemen in plaid caps. "Rex, get away from there," Prince yelled, too late. Rex lifted his leg beside the yellow hub.

The coachman, whose face resembled a slab of rare beef, reached down and stung the dog with his whip. Rex showed his teeth and growled. The victoria's passengers expressed degrees of outrage that the driver summed up by shouting, "Dirty son of a bitch."

The victoria drove on. Jimmy laughed. "Who'd he mean, you or your mutt?"

"Jimmy, you're terrible," Flo said. Prince threw a mock punch that Jimmy batted down. The trio marched on through the melee of noise, dust, carriages maneuvering, drivers exchanging words as they vied for choice spots along the bluff.

These were the same blue bloods who had driven Maureen Molloy to her sad end but today Prince felt no animus. Maybe he'd been too long under the gloomy weight of her passing. Whatever the reason, he enjoyed the spectacle of the grooms spreading blankets, the fine ladies in narrow-waisted white flannel decorously settling themselves, the gentlemen breaking out umbrellas, the lids of rear-mounted luncheon boxes opening to reveal platters of oysters and lobster tails, slabs of whitefish in cheesecloth, bottles of red and white wine, jars of lemonade.

A cannon banged, then another. Out on the water the slower race enthusiasts sailed their catboats in the wake of larger craft. The three companions moved along toward the lighthouse, jumping over horse droppings and a smashed beer keg lying in a foaming puddle. Jimmy nudged Prince.

"Hey, ain't that a friend of yours? There, by that phaeton?"

Sam Driver was helping his daughter alight while their groom laid down a blanket. Prince felt like he'd been clubbed.

Flo noticed. "You know them people?"

"Worked for the man for a while. You two go ahead, find a spot, I'll say hello."

Jimmy pulled Flo away, whispering to her. Jenny had seen Prince. What did her expression signify? Shock, yes, but what besides? Revulsion? Wrath? He almost turned back.

Sam saw him, shrank into a sort of protective crouch, eyes darting between Jenny and the intruder, who was ten paces away, then half that. Prince jabbed the ground with the walking stick as he limped to confront them. The fishhook scar fairly blazed on his tanned jaw.

"Miss Driver, Mr. Driver. Wanted to say good day."

Jenny said, "How have you been, Molloy?"

"Oh, just capital."

"Your leg—"

"Minor accident, that's all."

Say this for Driver: He stood his ground, admitting nothing by word or action.

"You look very fit," she said. "Very brown."

"I work at the Belcourt stables. Spend a lot of time outdoors. Mr. Oliver Belmont lets me exercise some of his horses."

"All very interesting," Sam said, "but our picnic is private." He gripped Jenny's elbow to turn her. She reacted with a flare, pulling away.

Prince ignored him. "Miss Driver, if you'll allow me, there's something I need to—" The noisy arrival of a man on horseback interrupted.

By now all but the most sequestered in Newport recognized Count Orlov, Prince no exception. Everyone knew he rode the finest mount he could hire, undoubtedly as a statement about himself. Orlov's stallion was a tawny Arabian, obviously finely bred but high-strung; the horse snorted and pawed the earth repeatedly.

Orlov dismounted with the speed and grace of an acrobat. He wore a smart three-button suit, light gray wool with a large check, a jaunty tweed hat. A gold pin gleamed in his red tie. His eyes were blue, like Jenny's, but much darker. They reminded Prince of holes in winter ice.

He smiled at the others while indicating Prince. "Uninvited guest?"

"The boy worked for one of my contractors," Sam said. "I had to discharge him. He's a rubber plant. Town Irish. Employed by Belmont now, he claims."

"Belmont?"

"Oliver Belmont. Bill Brady's friend."

"Ah." A little smile twitched the count's mouth. "Not a friend of yours, then."

"I've asked the boy politely to move along."

One by one the count peeled off thin gray gloves. He slid the gloves into his right flap pocket. "My young friend, let's resolve this in a gentlemanly way. It's far too pretty a day for us to do otherwise."

Rex growled. The count stepped back. "Keep that mongrel away or I'll make him a gift of a broken spine."

"The hell you will. Jenny, just hear me out, I—" The count wrenched the walking stick from Prince's hand and laid it hard across his forehead.

Jenny gasped. Spectators in nearby carriages treated them to annoyed looks. Rex leaped to chew Orlov's half boot, fine black leather with elastic insets. The count kicked the dog, sent him flying, then ran at him flourishing the stick.

Prince caught the Russian from behind, tripped him, landed him jaw-first in the sere grass. He seized the stick. Jenny's cry stopped him.

"Molloy, please don't. Do as my father asks."

The stick shook in the air above Prince's head. Arms trembling, he lowered it.

Orlov lifted himself out of the dirt. He dusted his knees and elbows with exaggerated annoyance. Prince blinked through blood dripping from an eyebrow. Rex was whimpering and licking his left hind leg. Prince slipped the stick under his arm, picked up his dog and limped away.

Sam Driver shouted at him. "Don't let us see you again."

Farther out toward the lighthouse, he found Jimmy and Flo sitting on a patched quilt, drinking beer from a wire-handled crock. Flo was cool to him; no doubt Jimmy had told her too much. Not that he cared.

"Who slammed you, pal?"

Prince swabbed his bleeding forehead with the tail of his bandanna. "Never mind." Rex squirmed in his arms, leaped free, landed with a yelp.

"Oh, is your doggy hurt?" Flo cooed, maternal all at once. It gave Prince his chance to escape.

"He may be. I'll go see."

He turned his back on Jimmy's smirk, Flo's quizzical squint. Watchers strung along the bluff cheered something on the bright Atlantic water. Prince walked wide of the Driver phaeton so they wouldn't see him.

Colonia won the schooner cup in five hours, four minutes. The sloop *Queen Mab* won her class with an elapsed time of five and a half hours. The sloop *Wasp* ran into a steam yacht and ripped the mainsail, rendering it useless. The schooner *Quisetta*, a favorite, lost a halyard block and withdrew. Prince meantime carried Rex to a Newport horse doctor who assured him that Orlov had done no real damage.

Prince settled his dog in old blankets in his regular bed, a fruit box in the garret. He spent the rest of the day in the deserted grogshop, drinking one tankard of ale after another, fueling his unhappiness, his longing for Jenny.

Did she think he hadn't come to New York as he promised?

He'd botched his moment to set everything straight. Driver too had spoiled it, and that damn thick-spoken Russkie.

Worst of all, Prince had broken his promise to Mary.

Next morning the New York Yacht Club fleet sailed for Vineyard Haven. Sam questioned Jenny about the Irish boy: What had he wanted to say to her?

"I'm sure I don't know, Papa." Her face was calm, her eyes remote. A wall had been raised. He gave up in frustration.

He summoned Mozart to his shuttered study. A clock ticked in the dusty gloom. A few slits of daylight fell through the shutter slats.

"Take the first train to New York. Deliver this to the agent in charge of the local office of Pinkerton's." Sam had high regard for the detective agency organized in the Civil War to spy for the Union. In recent years Pinkerton's had specialized in antilabor activity. The San Antonio & Sonora, of which Sam was still treasurer, had engaged the agency to infiltrate a cell of union organizers and destroy it with cracked heads, bribed sheriffs, jail sentences without due process. Always conscious of deniability, Sam never sought details or signed checks, only authorized cash payments to Pinkerton's verbally.

Sam pointed to the envelope. "That contains my instructions. I'll telegraph New York before you arrive so there's no question as to who you represent. Bring back proposed costs, and the agency's estimate of time involved."

Mute, Mozart fingered the sealed envelope. Anger welled in Sam again, an emotional overflow from the encounter with the worthless but obviously still dangerous Irish boy.

"And make sure you're sober when you transact my business."

"Sir," Mozart said, a mumbled obeisance. He left without

saying more. Who or what had broken his spirit? Age? Alcohol? Events were getting the best of Sam.

"Unacceptable, Goddamn it. *Unacceptable.*"

His fist descended on the desk so violently, everything rattled.

36
The Race

A footman from Red Rose delivered the challenge, signed by the count and S. S. Driver. They proposed a race between four-in-hands on what they termed a simple course, fourteen miles or a little more, the winner to pay the loser $10,000.

O. H. P. Belmont scoffed:

"No course around this island is by any means simple. The roads are sometimes twisty, often narrow, corners are sharp and dangerous, and there are always stray pedestrians and wild fowl wandering into the right-of-way, not to mention our local rustics herding sheep or goats. The trolleys likewise interfere. Do they think I don't know any of that?

He fairly flung the paper back to the messenger.

"It doesn't matter. I accept."

"Yes, sir."

"Inform Messrs. Driver and Orlov that one of my men will call on them tomorrow with a date and time. We must agree on the course. I suspect what's behind this is my cordial relationship with Bill Brady. But you wouldn't know about that, would you, being a proper servant? Good day."

Prince heard about the challenge before the sun went down. He hiked all the way to Jumbo Sullivan's in the twilight. Sullivan's reaction was skepticism:

"Belmont's a fine whip. Too smart to let you touch the reins of an expensive rig like his. I wouldn't."

"But I'm responsible for this. Sam Driver hates me because of his daughter, and he hates Mr. Belmont for being a friend of Brady's. I'll bet Orlov promoted the race to show up Mr. Belmont and impress Jenny's pa."

"So? Tell him your story, maybe he'll let you ride along. But don't count on it. Now sling your hook, it's past my bedtime."

Great changes had come to 690 Bellevue Avenue that summer. Belcourt's new mistress had hired architects and contractors to renovate the ground floor, turning her husband's haven for horses and carriages into an Italian Renaissance reception hall.

She supervised the workers with language only a few shades more purple than her thinning, darkening hair. Alva was the only heiress who owned two Newport cottages, Belcourt by right of marriage, and Marble House a short distance along the avenue at number 600, which her former husband had deeded to her in the divorce settlement.

A crew of carpenters was listening to another of madam's lectures when Prince slipped in next morning. Alva's foghorn bellow faded as he hurried up the dark staircase. He found O.H.P. in the great baronial dining room, in front of the chimneypiece, a spectacular miniature replica of a French château. Belmont was pointing out features to a bearded gentleman with the myopic eyes and threadbare clothing of an academic.

Prince waited quietly, cap in hand, near one of Belmont's prized suits of armor. Finally the professor, as Belmont addressed him, took his leave.

"And what do you want, Mr. Molloy?"

"Permission to ride with you in the race, sir."

"You're a presumptuous fellow, aren't you? I believe you have no experience other than what Jumbo Sullivan may have taught you. My regular grooms will accompany me, thank you very much."

"Mr. Belmont, I think I caused all this."

Belmont's pale brow furrowed. "The challenge? I accepted willingly. Sam Driver's an ass, an upstart—a parvenu in love with himself."

"That may be, sir, but I feel responsible."

Prince quickly described the near-brawl on Castle Hill.

Belmont pushed his spectacles up on his forehead. Using his sleeve, he buffed one of the suits of armor. "Does this have something to do with your new passion for driving?"

"Yes, sir."

"Is one of the challengers the man you want to beat?"

"Originally it was Mr. Driver. Now there's a second one in the picture."

"Orlov. If that's even his name. Pretenders who swarm here in search of wives fabricate all sorts of histories. I can't take you along, Mr. Molloy, you're still too green."

"Would you let Mr. Sullivan speak to that? What if he convinced you I was capable?"

"Doubtful." Belmont brushed his mustache. "But you've proved yourself a good worker. I suppose I'm obliged to listen."

Jumbo Sullivan brought Belmont to Prince's garret. Characteristically polite, neither by word nor expression did O.H.P. indicate disapproval, or any reaction, to Prince's cramped and impoverished quarters.

Inspecting the pulleys and weights, Belmont said to Prince, "You built this?"

"To strengthen my arms," Prince said. "Mr. Sullivan showed me how to do it."

Belmont said, "Let's see."

Prince set his chair in place and demonstrated for five minutes, finishing without shortness of breath, or even sweat on his brow. Belmont addressed Sullivan. "Can he drive?"

"He's competent with a team. More than that, I hain't had time to teach him."

"Given his age, I should imagine not. Would you trust him to drive four-in-hand?"

"Not yet."

"Even in an emergency? My grooms handle starts and stops and road mishaps."

Prince watched the men discussing his fate as though he were miles away. Sullivan glanced at his pupil.

"Well, sir, the answer to that depends on a number of other questions."

"Such as?"

"The drag's in good condition?"

"Prime."

"Are your animals liable to bolt or balk if they're pressed?"

"No."

"You know the roads on the island."

"By heart."

"And you're not plannin' to run down any chickens or children or half-witted tourists tryin' to find the beach?"

"For God's sake, Sullivan."

"Then take him. Let him ride on top. He's a quick lad—quicker'n most give him credit for."

"I'd have to carry only one groom to compensate for weight."

"How much can that hurt?"

"Not a bit unless I pitch over with a seizure."

"Planning to do so during the contest?"

A flicker of a smile. "Alva wouldn't allow it."

"Defense rests."

Belmont eyed Prince up and down. "Alright. We hitch up the drag at half past five tomorrow morning. You're not there on the dot, don't bother to show up."

"Count on me, sir."

"What do you think I'm doing?" Belmont said with a fishy look at Sullivan.

"Greedy mick," snarled the groom Belmont replaced. He was probably sixteen. "Go on, take food off the table of a whole family, then."

"What the devil are you talking about?"

"If Mr. B wins, he'll tip us handsome."

"If I get paid I'll hand it over."

"Yeah? Why would you do that?"

"Because I don't care about the money."

"Crap. Everybody cares about money."

"I want to see the others lose."

The groom let that penetrate for a second. He threw a bundle of clothes at his replacement.

"Well, then, good luck."

Saturday, August 15. Awake at 3:30, Prince paced his garret for a half hour. He fed Rex and donned the undress livery provided by Belmont in consideration of the summer weather: a short roundabout coat, a simple neckcloth, a low-crowned hat. He set out for Belcourt as the blurred stars were paling. Already he could feel a steamy, stifling day coming on.

At the stables, the senior groom, Noonan, a freckled Irish gnome distantly related to Paddy Leland, greeted him by lantern light, but not enthusiastically.

"Heard you was comin' with us. I'll be riding up front this time. You lend a hand if I tell you, otherwise stay out of the way."

Belmont strode in from the dark, knuckling sleep from his eyes. For his horses he'd chosen half-bred mares with docked tails, a black and gray ahead, a gray and black behind. The leaders were lighter and two inches shorter than the stronger wheelers. From Sullivan's instruction Prince knew that to be proper.

Belmont helped hitch the animals to his prize drag, a white beauty with JUGGERNAUT painted in small, dignified letters on the center door panels. All the harnesses were matched black; gleaming brass mountings were engraved with the family crest.

Prince stood by nervously while Belmont climbed small steps built into the side of the carriage box. Noonan said to Prince, "Think you can hand up those reins without tangling them?"

"Yes, sir."

The senior groom sniffed to express doubt. He climbed the box on the other side. Prince handed up the four sets of reins without mishap. Belmont carefully separated and arranged them in his left hand. The horses were fretful; as the sky paled, flies deviled them. Weather that brought a lot of flies wasn't good for high-strung animals.

"For God's sake don't stand there," Noonan snapped, "this train is pulling out." Prince stepped up on a rear wheel spoke and then to the groom's box at the back of the drag. From there it was an easy hop to the roof, where ladies and inexperienced gentlemen could ride during less strenuous outings. Forward and rear roof seats had fold-down backs covered with patent leather. Prince took the forward seat after folding down the back of the other.

Belmont was a cautious, precise driver. He pulled down the goggles made to duplicate his regular eyeglasses. He tested the reins. Noonan pulled the whip from the socket. Belmont grasped it in his right hand. One flick of the whip and "Juggernaut" rolled out of Belcourt's driveway, bound north for the starting line.

A couple of sleepy stable hands waved and shouted good luck, but neither the groom Prince had replaced nor the new Mrs. Belmont had bothered to get up for the departure.

Dawn brought a day that promised to be an unpleasant tag end of summer: overcast, steamy, with thunderheads building above the Atlantic. "Juggernaut" arrived at the intersection of Bellevue and Bath Road at half past six. Orlov and Driver were already waiting with "Tantivy."

The black coach looked enormous in the dull gray light, more like a hearse than a sporting vehicle. The tails of Sam Driver's horses switched like fly whisks, which on this stultifying morning they were. Driver's grooms were dressed in full winter regalia: top hats, thigh-length wool coats, stiff collars. All four faces on the challenger's coach already ran with sweat. Prince wiped his own cheeks and brow frequently; the lighter summer outfit didn't do much to relieve the effects of heat and humidity. Eastward, Prince saw a flicker of lightning.

Word of the race had spread. Perhaps thirty people, citizens of the town, had gathered in carriages and carts and on foot behind the starting line marked with a white flag on a stick. A local ostler had been recruited to officiate.

"Once around the course, first coach to the finish line's the winner," he said. "Drivers, bring your vehicles to the line."

Orlov took "Tantivy" forward. Belmont followed more slowly, pulling up to the right of the black coach. The count glanced over at Prince, and not in a friendly way. A clatter behind them announced Jumbo Sullivan arriving in his trap. He tipped his cap to Prince.

Orlov and Belmont climbed down for the obligatory walk around their vehicles, beginning at the rear. Prince followed Noonan to the ground in case someone needed his services. Jumbo planted his reins under a rock and strolled over to observe the whips inspecting axles, running chains, harness, the adjustment of bits. Prince swatted a fly buzzing at his ear.

Sullivan said, "Driver's got a bad horse. His off leader. He's a kicker. Ought to be sold."

Driver's groom held the near wheeler's headstall while Orlov gingerly stepped between the horses to examine the pole jutting from the carriage. He tested the pole chains. The off leader almost kicked him. Orlov cursed as he stepped back into the road.

"I'll cut across to the West Road," Sullivan told Prince. "Meet you at the finish line. Expect to see you coming home first."

"Sure," Prince said, far from confident.

There was no cordiality between the contenders, no shaking of hands. Belmont and Orlov climbed up to front seats again. Driver took the guard's position on his coach. Noonan and Orlov's groom again handed up the four sets of reins. Prince clambered to the roof. The sweating ostler said, "A few rules, gentlemen. No passing when the road's too narrow or there's wheel or foot traffic to contend with." Deep in a thunderhead, lightning glowed.

"Alright behind?" the starter called.

"Alright," someone returned.

"Stand clear, then."

He dropped his hand.

Belmont was slow to pull out, but slow and steady, six or seven miles an hour, was preferable to a jackrabbit start, which Orlov favored. "Tantivy" was immediately a coach length ahead, rolling down the hill toward the public beach. The deserted pavilion reminded Prince of what had happened there.

Like most roads around Newport, Bath was unpaved; "Tantivy" stirred up a dust cloud that enveloped Belmont's drag. Prince coughed and held fast to the side irons. Despite the drag's good springing, he felt every sway and bounce, every stone in the road. Still, the spectacular view was worth it: the East Passage of Narragansett Bay and, beyond, the hills of Tiverton and Little Compton emerging in the morning light.

Belmont purposely stayed behind Orlov as the coaches clattered past a row of rickety bathhouses on the beach. They climbed a moderate incline along aptly named Purgatory Road, Purgatory Chasm unseen on their right. At the summit, another gorgeous view opened before them—Little Compton across the water to the east, Hanging Rock, a favorite subject of landscape painters, towering thirty or forty feet above the road on the left.

One by one the coaches plunged downward on the steep hill that led into a hazardous S-turn at the bottom. Belmont took a pull at the horses to slow and steady them. With his right hand he seized the brake handle. The blocks locked against the metal of the rear hoop tires; Prince fancied he could smell smoke from the leather-covered wood. Through flying dust, he watched the action of Belmont's left wrist—the give and take, Sullivan called it. Prince's employer was a master of those factors Captain Knight emphasized: pace, distance, interval.

The leading coach plunged down the incline to the hazardous curve. "Tantivy"'s rear wheels slid sideways until Orlov compensated by slowing his horses. He might be experienced but he was reckless, sacrificing safety and sureness for speed.

"Tantivy" remained ahead; Belmont held back because passing on this stretch of road was impossible. A couple of boys enjoying the weather atop Hanging Rock hallooed at the drivers.

The road twisted and turned through dense brush and a few wind-warped trees. A ragamuffin with a fishing pole ran across in front of Orlov's coach, white with fear when "Tantivy" showed no sign of slowing. "Juggernaut" passed the boy as he lay in roadside weeds, sobbing with relief.

Next, Indian Avenue, running roughly northeast for a good distance. A few large houses broke up the woods on the right side of the road. One, Boothden, belonged to the famous actor Edwin Booth; Prince remembered seeing him years ago, pottering in his yard. Flashes of oily water in the East Passage showed between the trees.

Here there was an opportunity to pass. Belmont held the reins taut, applied the whip and swung out on the left. The leader bars on Belmont's front horses were wider than the wheel hubs, so they told Belmont that he had room to go by. Slowly, steadily, "Juggernaut" pulled ahead of "Tantivy." The manes on Orlov's horses flew. Their eyes rolled. Foamy sweat streaked from their flanks. Orlov flung a venomous look at his competitors.

Belmont correctly judged his distance and pulled over in front of the other coach. He slowed the horses and applied the brake to prevent running past the sharp left turn into Old Mill Lane. The tires scraped and slewed, the brake blocks spurted smoke; Belmont brought the drag around the northwest corner with a foot to spare. Orlov almost crashed into a farm family watching behind a fence on the corner. They fled before the coach hit them. Orlov's rear wheel hubs tore the fence apart and left kindling.

The coaches again climbed a slight incline, toward the central spine of the island. Prince clenched his teeth to stop the jolting and jarring in his head. His thighs felt as though someone were pounding them with mallets. Belmont and then Orlov hurtled around another corner, a right turn into Wapping Road. Prince saw places ahead where the narrow road widened near farm entrances. Spectators hung on low stone walls, waving hats and cheering, though Prince was hanged if he knew who they were rooting for.

A cloud dark as slate opened suddenly. Rain poured down so hard, hay fields and grazing cattle and human beings vanished behind wind-driven curtains of water. Prince glanced behind, saw to his alarm that "Tantivy" was going to attempt to pass in the downpour, before the road narrowed again. Noonan saw it too, yelled at Belmont, who grimly whipped up his leaders and wheelers, the best way to forestall an accident if Orlov persisted in his foolhardy driving.

The challengers kept their positions, the drag leading as they veered left into Sandy Point Road, then right again onto East Road, the main artery leading to the bridge off the island. Noonan yelled to clear some wandering pigs from the right-of-way. A buggy emerged from a farm driveway, its dapple gray balking and pawing the air as "Juggernaut" approached. Two elderly ladies in the buggy shrieked under their parasols.

Oakland Farm loomed in bucolic splendor; some servants of Cornelius Vanderbilt II, grandson of the late Commodore, leaped away as the wheels threw a high wall of mud toward them. As suddenly as it began, the thundershower ended. Columns of sun descended between parting clouds.

The drivers took a sharp left into Union Street, in what was known as Lawton Valley, climbing again toward the familiar spine of the island and the magnificent view of Narragansett Bay waiting on the other side.

The drag pounded toward a wooden bridge. The leaders smelled the water in a Newport reservoir; Belmont fought the reins to keep the horses from pulling to the left. On the right, beside the little stream crossed by the bridge, a large, sturdy house was visible in a grove: the home of Julia Ward Howe, the old lady whose international renown had lured so many New York swells to the island.

Prince had mud on his face, mud in his hair, pain in his arms and wrists from gripping the side irons. He could imagine the pain Belmont must be feeling from the constant strain of directing the horses. "Juggernaut" clattered over the little bridge, "Tantivy" right behind.

Orlov wouldn't sit by without making a challenge, no matter how dangerous. Prince guessed it would come on the relatively broad and straight West Road, the route to the finish line. Though less traveled than its eastern counterpart, the West Road led directly south into Newport via Broadway, hence was hard used. Rain had filled ruts and sink holes, effectively hiding their depth.

Prince held the side irons tighter than ever as "Juggernaut" slewed around the corner. The coach suddenly confronted a new hazard—a defiant farmer unhooking his gate to let his flock of three dozen sheep cross the West Road.

Belmont fought to stop the drag. Noonan waved his hat. A ferocious neighing, a grind of wheels, and blue oaths from Orlov and Driver came from behind as Orlov's coach almost rammed "Juggernaut" before it too stopped. A moment later the right-of-way was silent except for the bleating of the sheep and the drip of muddy water from the stalled carriages.

Sam Driver threw his plug hat on the floorboard and trampled on it. Orlov leaped to his feet, abusing the farmer in French. The farmer stood with folded arms while his flock meandered into the pasture on the east side of the road.

The air was steamy, hazy. Blue and green flies swarmed around leaders and wheelers. Orlov's off leader flicked its tail at the flies. The tail tangled with the reins. Orlov screamed at his groom, who jumped down from the rumble and ran forward. Prince groaned when he saw the panicky groom yank on the reins instead of lifting the horse's tail first.

The last of the flock cleared the road. Orlov's horses pulled every which way. When he got them under control, "Tantivy" swung out to pass, sideswiping Belmont's drag. Rocks flew from under the wheels. One smashed Belmont's goggles.

Belmont instinctively threw both gloved hands to his face. Noonan caught the reins and started the drag forward again. "Tantivy" was already two lengths ahead, swaying mightily as Orlov whipped his animals into a gallop past a slowly revolving windmill. Orlov's groom was a pathetic muddy figure abandoned in the center of the road behind the carriages.

"You alright?" Noonan yelled.

A stream of blood ran from Belmont's goggles down the right side of his nose. "Drive," he shouted.

"Juggernaut" lurched, back in the race. What had begun as a decent pairing of whips was ending as a sickening grudge match, one driver already injured, the other flying ahead, ignoring hazards or common sense. Orlov's coach rocked and swayed dangerously as it flew by Two-Mile Road, where the East Road joined. A landscaper's wagon would have collided if the farmer hadn't reined his team. "Tantivy" 's four horses galloped as if devils pursued them.

Belmont's pointing hand flew out. "Noonan, he's too close to the verge."

Before the sentence finished, the near wheels of the big black coach slipped over the left shoulder. Gravity exerted its pull. With a mesmerizing, almost dreamy slowness, "Tantivy" began to topple, dragging its wheelers and leaders even as the coach's momentum hurled it ahead.

Orlov leaped from the coach. He landed in a huge puddle, Driver right behind him. His eyes and Orlov's shone white in masks of mud, like the eyes of minstrel men. "Tantivy" knocked over a telephone pole as it smashed into the ditch. Hooks and iron pins tore free. The main bar and one lead bar splintered like twigs. Three bellowing horses broke loose. The near leader lay in the weeds with heaving flanks and a twisted foreleg.

Noonan fought Belmont's horses to the right, away from the accident. "Juggernaut" rocked and crashed through ruts and potholes. Ahead at the finish line, an intersection known as One-Mile Corner, a Newport Street Railway car swayed to a stop at the line's northern turnaround. The trolley's headlight blazed.

The drag bounced in and out of another deep hole. The jolting motion threw Noonan off the coach to the side. His outcry faded swiftly. With less than a half mile remaining, "Juggernaut" ran straight on a collision course with the trolley.

Prince had no time to recall specifics from Captain Knight's manual, but apparently some things had sunk in. He flung himself over to the front box, grabbing all four reins. At One-Mile Corner spectators were jumping off the trolley car and scattering.

Prince had no idea how to separate the reins and stop the horses except to pull hard with both hands. The drag lost speed, but not enough. He remembered one of Captain Knight's desperation remedies. He threw his right leg over all four reins and pushed down. He leaned back as far as he could. His leg began to tremble.

He seized the brake handle and nearly tore his arm out of its socket applying pressure. Wet as the leather-covered blocks were, they squealed against the wheel rims but they held.

Belmont's drag rocked to a standstill halfway across the intersection. The tossing heads of the leaders shone with eerie halos. "Juggernaut" had stopped two feet shy of the headlight.

Prince bundled the reins and threw them to the ground, far to the left of the wheel horses. That was what a coachman was supposed to do, wasn't it? He couldn't quite remember . . .

Ground fog congealed around the intersection. Prince saw Jumbo Sullivan in his one-horse trap. Jumbo raised his right hand, then his thumb. He was grinning.

O. H. P. Belmont had ripped off his goggles and driving gloves. He pressed a glove to his bloodied face while reaching across with his left hand to squeeze Prince's arm.

"Fine driving. Damn fine. A thousand of the prize money's yours."

Before Prince could thank him, he leaned back, wildly dizzy. The gray-white sky came down like a collapsing ceiling and Prince fainted.

Prince wakened at the roadside. His head rested on his roundabout, which had been rolled into a makeshift pillow.

Jumbo Sullivan drove him back into Newport. Prince ached all over. His head throbbed.

"Their own blasted fault that they lost," Sullivan said. "Ollie's goggles saved his eye. Orlov's reputation as a prime whip's demolished, 'least around here."

On Thames Street, Sullivan delivered him to Ye Snug Harbour. Word had traveled; well-wishers greeted Prince when he climbed down from the cart. Sullivan asked, "You alright?"

"Passable. I'll be better with a drink in me."

"Don't slug down too much."

"Sure, sure."

While the steamy red sun sank, Prince heard the news that Noonan had a broken leg, a broken collarbone, and contusions. Driver's valuable horse had to be put down. Prince ignored Sullivan's advice about drinking. In the smoke and heat of Ye Snug

Harbour, he was soon on his way to inebriation. Jimmy Fetch, who'd come in shortly after Prince arrived, was nearly as drunk.

"Serves 'em right, the bastards," Prince muttered. "Driver 'specially."

"You really got it in for Driver, ain't you?"

"You blame me?"

Prince waved for another tankard. Bound for the kitchen, tall Mary frowned at him. He looked the other way.

"He did this, for God's sake." Prince slapped his leg. "Well, he ordered it done. Same thing."

With a narrowing of eyes, Jimmy said, "Driver did that?"

"I don't mean Mrs. Astor."

"That a fact. You never told me."

"Didn't I? Don't remember. Truth, though. I got this bum leg thanks to Sam Driver. That baggy-faced Gribble actually hired the bozos who did the work. But it was Driver's order. New York, winter before last. Swell Christmas present, huh? We got a bit of our own back today."

He drank, slopping ale over his chin.

"Gribble," Jimmy said. "Christmas before last. Is that a fact?"

37
Confronting the Colonel

The letter bore Colonel Mann's name although evidently written, in a poor hand, by one of his local agents. The anonymous messenger left the grounds before Sam thought to order him stopped and questioned.

The letter was cryptic yet alarming. Words such as *alleged thuggery* and *December before last* prodded him to action. He ordered Capt. Bully Jelks to stoke *Invincible*'s boilers and get up steam for an overnight run to New York. When Jenny asked the purpose of his trip Sam dismissed it as business, an explanation she'd heard many times.

In the heat of late summer, Sam had slept badly since the coaching accident. He dreamed twice of Jim Fisk bleeding all over him, drenching him with guilt, as it were. "Tantivy" was beyond repair at a reasonable price: decorative doors staved in, windows broken, axles cracked—with a fine horse dead in the bargain. He'd written a bank draft for $10,000 payable to Belmont. Greater than the financial setbacks, which counted for hardly anything in his well-financed universe, the defeat itself, his loss of face, the unspoken humiliation, tormented him.

Count Orlov grumbled about accepting blame for the accident. He cited the rain, the treacherous road, the ignorant sheep herder as responsible. When he and his prospective father-in-law sat together with brandies, Orlov nervously polished his monocle and peered at Sam as though wary of hostility. Sam considered redrawing his plans for the future but decided he could find no better suitor for Jenny on the current market.

During the cruise to Long Island Sound and the Hudson piers, Sam continued to sleep badly. At home on Fifth Avenue he found the usual pile of correspondence and glib charity solicitations. Most he threw into the cold empty grate.

A hansom delivered him to Delmonico's at half past noon the following day. The maître d' showed him to the table where Colonel Mann sat gorging on another gargantuan lunch. A starched serviette covered the whole of his front. Dabs of pâté hung precariously in his Father Christmas mustaches. His blue eyes twinkled with cordiality.

"Mr. Driver. What a pleasure to see you again, sir."

"I don't consider this a pleasure. And we haven't met before," Sam answered in a curt way.

"No, sir, regrettably not, but I feel as though I know you. The illustrated weeklies have printed your engraved portrait, and I'm well acquainted with your accomplishments. Won't you join me? Broiled squabs today. I've ordered three for myself. How many would you like?"

"None."

Sam sat down, pulled off his new black homburg with rolled brim and wide ribbon of dark gray petersham, the latest from the hatters at Brooks Brothers. He lodged the expensive hat on an empty chair. "Some flunky delivered your message. Before I could question him, he ran."

The colonel sighed. "Heaven help us. The quality of help these days is shameful." He drank generously from a glass of red wine, identified as claret by the bottle decanted in a wicker basket. "I would make personal visits to Newport except that I can't bear the place. It's a sinkhole of depravity and moral decay. Excluding present company."

"Don't patronize me, Colonel. I assume you brought me here to squeeze me for money."

Feigning horror, the publisher raised both hands. "No, sir, no. A vicious concept. Vicious! I only strive to spare the sensibilities of important people who may not want my little paper printing false information. Such as this item, revealed to us only recently." From under his napkin he took a proof, coarse foolscap, which he laid between them.

"Often I can't attest to the veracity of certain agents of mine on that corrupt isle you inhabit in the summertime. I want to include nothing in my Saunterings column that might prove damaging to the innocent."

The copy was short. As he read, Sam's temples reddened. He clenched his teeth so hard his jaw hurt.

> A year ago last December, we have lately learned, a hard-driving member of the Newport colony may have hired Bowery bullyboys to beat and permanently injure a young man from the town's Irish settlement. The young man's crime? He was said to be an unsuitable match for a rich man's daughter. If this cruel financial denizen is the Spirit of Christmas past . . . forgive him, everyone! Alas, we cannot.

Sam balled the proof and hurled it square into the colonel's face. A passing waiter nearly dropped a water pitcher. Mann's good cheer evaporated. "Sir, you are embarrassing yourself."

Sam's hands dropped under the table. Mann tore the napkin

from his collar and fanned back his lapel to show the ivory grip of his holstered pistol, a move so smooth and quick he'd obviously practiced it often.

"Let me see those hands on the table, please."

Sam glanced at the cutlery, especially a sharp-pointed meat knife suitable for plunging into the pink chins of the fat fraud who was getting the best of him moment by moment. Sam no longer went anywhere armed.

Colonel Mann sensed his thought, reached across and swept Sam's cutlery onto the tiled floor, a dreadful clatter.

"Lucius, a little mishap here. Bring my friend a new place setting."

While a waiter's helper cleared the floor and Lucius ran off to obey orders, Sam leaned toward the colonel. "Someday someone will castrate you for this kind of thing."

Mann recovered his humor. "Someday, perhaps, but not today. Must we continue to discuss this acrimoniously?"

Sam's breathing slowed. "Tell me how much."

"Is there truth in this item?"

"Of course not. But I don't want to spend time kicking reporters off the doorstep and denying ridiculous allegations."

"If there's nothing to it, you might consider engaging a lawyer."

"Damn it, how much?"

The publisher drank claret again. The waiter timorously approached with silverware on a tray. Mann waved him off.

"I am a reasonable man. Seven thousand five hundred will take care of it. We'll call it a commitment to advertise one of your rail investments."

"A check will reach you by close of business tomorrow. But heed me, Colonel. If there are any further references to this piece of garbage—any at all—the *someday* we discussed will come sooner than you expect."

"Mr. Driver, I am offended by—"

"Shut your dirty mouth." Sam heard his heartbeat roaring in his inner ear. "Sit there and stuff your face but don't say another word unless you want me to pick up this table and break it over your head. You think I won't, look me in the eye."

Which Col. William d'Alton Mann did.

Saying nothing.

Sam reached across the table, picked up the proof and tore it in half, then quarters, then smaller pieces. These he strewed like snowflakes in Mann's lap. Smirking, Mann said, "No harm done, I have another." Like a magician producing a pigeon, he brought it forth with a flourish. "Many more, in fact."

Sam swore, grabbed the second proof. Leaving, he nearly knocked the tray of silver from the hands of the hovering waiter.

"I won't be staying for lunch."

Who had talked? How had the story got out? Was Mozart responsible? Sam was willing to believe many things about his old comrade from the Erie wars, but not that. Not yet.

A headache screwed sudden pain between his eyes. The hansom's open windows brought in the grunt of wandering pigs, the jangle of a trolley bell hectoring pedestrians, the noise of a racing fire engine some blocks away. Sam was in a fury. He'd protected Jenny at a price of personal humiliation. Mann had gotten the best of him as few ever had. Sam's concession mocked the motto framed above his desk. Someone had to suffer.

Meanwhile he needed comforting. He pounded the roof of the hansom and shouted, "Pickwick Hotel."

38
Extreme Measures

As August waned, autumn sent its signals of imminent arrival: days growing shorter, nights cooler, blue sky paling, high thin clouds appearing suddenly to mask the low-slanting sun. The familiar fragrant smoke from burning leaves drifted in Newport streets.

Bill Brady's sense of aging sharpened with the conclusion of each summer season, which brought the last outing of the Kat-Bote Club. The exclusive club for gentlemen claimed to be a yachting organization but its primary purposes were fishing and fellowship, down on the sand at Bailey's Beach. The club was small, fifty-two members, each assigned a fanciful rank. Brady's was Extra-Ordinary Seaman.

His driver returned him to Sunrise in the golden dusk, sunburned, sand in his hair, his fine linen beach suit wrinkled and torn at one knee. He alighted from "Rocket," waved the driver on, and abruptly saw the butler waiting at the front door.

"Hamish, what's the trouble?"

"It's the mistress, sir."

"Is she ill?"

"No, sir, I wouldn't say that, but you'll want to see her right away."

"In her bedroom?"

The butler looked elsewhere. "The dining room, sir."

Brady gave a dyspeptic belch as he brushed by; one too many roasted ears of corn sprinkled with black pepper. His footfalls rang on the marble floor. He was about to call Honoria's name when he remembered that Dickie had taken her to the Casino to watch the annual U.S. Lawn Tennis tournament. Ahead, in the dining room, candles burned. What the devil was going on?

The long dinner table was set for fifty, cut flowers in bowls, plate and silver, crystal and napery perfectly arranged. Two servant girls huddled beside the closed door of the dumbwaiter. The only other person in the room was the Tigress. She wore pale yellow satin. Rubies and emeralds flashed on her hands, diamonds at her throat. Brady saw streaks in her powder made by tears.

"In the name of God, Em, what's going on?"

Seated at the far end of the table, Em said, "They haven't come. Not a one."

Brady yanked out the chair at her right, planted his soiled elbows on the tablecloth. "Who are you talking about?"

"The guests. Caroline Astor. Mamie Fish. Tess Oelrichs. Their spouses. All the guests we invited to my banquet."

Brady whipsawed between anger and wild fear. He lowered his voice, reached for her bejeweled hand.

"Em, there isn't any banquet. You sent twenty-four invitations, hand delivered. Three acceptances came back. Three only. Last Friday you sent a second notice that the party was canceled."

A pantry door squeaked, one of the servant girls slipping away. Brady yelled at the other, "Get out, this is private." The door squeaked again. Brady fought for patience.

"Em, surely you remember. You canceled the party."

Her eyes grew glassy as a Christmas doll's. "I don't recall that at all," she said in a sad, little-girl voice. Brady's pointing finger shook.

"You'd goddamn well better remember it, Em. What's causing this? Laudanum?"

"Oh, no."

"Alcohol?"

"A little sherry once in a while—"

"A little, or a lot. You've got to see a doctor. I'll find a specialist in New York."

"Bill, I don't need to see anyone. Please don't force me." The words came between fresh outpourings of tears that cut ravines in her face powder. Brady shouted at her.

"The hell you don't. You're a sick woman."

He stormed from the table into his glass sanctum. She followed, her voice shrill.

"You bastard. You selfish man. You want to be rid of me. You think I'm a liability because I'm ostracized. No one likes me but I'm not sick. I'm not sick. I'm not sick."

The third time, she threw a small brass tripod. He dodged. The tripod shattered a window. Glass fell; the beat of the ocean came through the broken opening. Em slowly folded herself down to the floor, the dying swan.

She hid her face. Her shoulders heaved. Brady watched the spectacle with mingled feelings of disgust and disaster.

Hopper Reynard, M.D., was a Harvard-trained physician with a surgery on Marlborough Street. He maintained a year-round practice but drew most of his income from peak months when the wealthy cottagers were in residence. He supported his wife, seven children, and his exquisite taste by examining eight to twelve patients per hour, shuttling them in and out of tiny consulting rooms like a field general maneuvering regiments. Reynard was always cheerful, always joking. This personal charm garnered and kept more patients than his reputedly mediocre medical skills. Brady trusted him only for attacks of catarrh, stomach distress and similar minor complaints.

Both men belonged to the Reading Room. The night after Em's bout of forgetfulness, Brady spoke to the younger man as they enjoyed whiskeys on the piazza, well away from possible eavesdroppers.

"My wife must see someone. Can you recommend the best man in New York?"

"In what specialty, Bill?"

Brady could hardly say it. He swallowed a half inch of whiskey.

"Neurology."

Which was a polite term for the specialty of an alienist.

Dr. Reynard's smile disappeared. "Is she suffering from hysteria, or an acute case of the vapors?"

"Worse than that, Hopper. She's mentally ill. I fear for her sanity. There'd be no other reason for consulting a neurologist."

Dr. Reynard assumed the sober, pious mien of a bereaved relative. He laid a consoling hand on Brady's fine worsted sleeve.

"I am truly sorry. I will find the right man for you."

"And not a blessed word to anyone."

"None, you have my promise."

The summer gloaming bleached the sky from red to pink. In the direction of the harbor, men and women laughed. Brady found it hateful.

Sam returned from New York that night. Mozart waited for him at the pier and drove him back to Red Rose. On the overnight trip, Sam had decided what he must do. "Take the carriage to the stable," he said as Mozart guided the horse up the drive. "Then come into the study for a drink."

A few minutes later, Sam switched on one small desk lamp, Tiffany, aware of and annoyed by moths flitting to the Edison bulb. Mozart knocked softly. He stepped into the overheated room without removing his tasseled smoking cap.

"I think just water, sir, if you don't mind."

"As you please."

Sam poured a tall glass. Mozart looked more sallow and haggard than even a week ago. Sam swirled three fingers of liquor in a cheap barrel glass he kept for drinking his favorite whiskeys.

"In New York I saw that blackmailer, Mann. I paid him seventy-five hundred dollars to keep this out of his filthy paper."

He showed the second proof. While Mozart read the paragraph, Sam said, "Did you tell him?"

"My God, would I do that? Betray you? Risk jail? The boy has no influence, but he could still involve the police—hire lawyers on speculation."

"If you didn't give this item to Mann's spies, who did?"

"Not those men I hired; they aren't clever enough. I'd be surprised if they know Mann or his paper. Regrettably, for me that leaves one possibility. Molloy himself."

Sam drank again. "My conclusion too. He wants to pay me back."

Mozart didn't disagree.

Sam's forehead showed liverish spots in the multicolored light from the leaded glass lamp shade. He paced, emptying his barrel glass the while.

"Molloy and the colonel have won a round, but only one. Molloy has sniffed Jenny's purse far too long. We'll do what we did in the old days on the Erie. Take the boy out of play. Off the board, permanently."

Mozart's shaky hand spilled water on his trouser leg. "Not more violence. I sleep badly enough as it is."

With sympathy, Sam said, "The laudanum hasn't helped?"

"Only slightly. How will you get rid of Molloy?"

"Hand me your glass, let me pour something stronger. I have a scheme."

An exhausted moth flew from the shade of the desk lamp and spiraled near Sam's leg. Sam set his glass down carefully. He killed the moth with a clap of his hands.

"No violence, but something just as final."

Dearest Jenny

He scratched it out.

My sweet Je

He scratched it out.

In the airless, deeply still August night, Prince hunched at the flimsy table in his garret. A kerosene lamp cast a small blurry circle, enough light for him to see the paper and the pencil with which he was trying to do what a poor education made so hard for him.

I am desprit to explan how I came by my injrys. Ever since the Cup races I have wanted to tell you—as I tried to that day befor your freind the "Count" stopped me—but I have not done because to do so will hurt someone close to you. Even right now I cant decide whether to set down the whol story and then find some way to get this leter to you, but that I am trying to write it says something is driving me namely my feelings for you. If I can push on with the story, make a clean brest, it may be that I as well as you can make a new start, each forgiving "him" who saw to it that never more will I walk with complete

He laid the pencil aside. Something odd, an unfamiliar pungent smell, crept in the garret's open window. Rex lifted his head on the unmade bed. The dog yipped softly. Prince sniffed.

Then he saw the ruddy light.

He overturned the chair, stuffed the wretchedly written letter in his pocket. "Rex! Here!" The mongrel, as terrified as his master, leaped into his arms.

Prince ran to the door but didn't open it; orange-hued smoke was spilling in beneath it. He leaned against the wood, felt the heat radiating. He stepped away, coughing.

His choices were bad. He could leap out the window, a fall of a whole story, or rely on the stair, which no doubt was already burning. From the alley behind the grogshop came Titus's strident voice. "Fetch buckets of water. Someone run for the fire brigade. Prince, are you up there?"

With his free hand Prince flung his shaving basin through the window glass. "I'm here."

"Get out. The stair won't last."

Clutching the whimpering dog, Prince held his breath and crossed to the door through dense smoke. The heated latch stung his fingers but he got the door open. He stepped out; smoke billowed up from beneath the landing. To his left, fire climbed the siding of the old building. In the dimly illuminated alley, men ran, shouted pointless questions. Who in God's name had done this? Driver again? His helper?

He squeezed Rex against his chest, advancing to the rail whose dry wood smoldered. "Hang on, boy, hang on tight." Something flashed farther up the alley, as though a man's glass eye reflected the fire. Prince ducked his head and lunged at the rail, feeling the heat against his thighs. The rail gave way and he jumped, an instant before the landing crumbled, a Niagara of flaming embers.

Rex howled during the sickening plunge. Uncle Titus shouted a question Prince didn't understand. He rolled his shoulder for the impact. He hit the ground. Rex sprang loose, his claws accidentally tearing Prince's shirt. Dizziness sucked Prince deep into a lightless void.

The Pearl of the Ocean, one of Newport's better fish houses, lay four blocks south of Ye Snug Harbour. Sam consulted his heavy gold pocket watch. He'd already waited that long and more. Just as impatience turned to ire, the street door opened precipitously and Orlov rushed in.

"Sorry to be late. My meeting was endless. Nothing came of it but a proffer of worthless junk—crazed mirrors, old commodes, chairs stained with Macassar oil—I don't buy or handle such goods. A wreck on the Providence pike blocked traffic on my return."

Grumpily, Sam waved a menu. "Sit down. Order. The kitchen closes soon."

"Are we to discuss something specific?"

Not just yet. Soon, I trust. . . .

"I thought a friendly dinner, the two of us getting that much better acquainted, would be desirable." The Pearl's plate-glass windows facing Thames Street had a lurid orange cast, which Sam noticed. "Look there. Must be a fire in the neighborhood."

Orlov wheeled around in his chair. The clangorous bell of a racing pumper grew louder. Orlov's monocle caught some of the glare.

"Indeed so," he said. "I trust no one is seriously injured, or killed. Sometimes fires are so fatal."

"Indeed," Sam murmured, his eyes on the menu.

39
Revelations

Newport's melancholy end-of-summer ritual began again.

Locks snapped shut and hammers banged in the great houses as wardrobe trunks closed and fine china disappeared into excelsior packing. Drayage companies experienced the semiannual upsurge in revenue as they removed crates and steamer trunks and portmanteaus, the wheels of their wagons passing over fallen leaves of fading yellow and scarlet and brown.

The social season climaxed with what was, even for a jaded population, a new and novel entertainment: a Dogs' Dinner, conceived by Harry Lehr and sponsored and arranged by Mamie Fish. Pets received invitations care of their masters. The animal's pedigree didn't matter, only that of the owner's.

"I do wish you owned a little doggy so that we could include you, dear," Mamie said to Jenny over tea.

"Frankly, I'm not sure I'd accept." Jenny had been long

enough in Newport so that she spoke not only candidly but, sometimes, tartly. "The whole thing strikes me as rather gross."

"One must humor Harry, even though his ideas tend toward the bizarre. Besides, as we've said many times, the cardinal rule here is to avoid boredom. If you care to discuss what's boring, consider this."

She showed Jenny several sheets bearing columns of signatures. Jenny leafed over a couple of pages but didn't immediately grasp their significance.

"It's Alva Belmont's latest petition. Votes for women. Julia Ward Howe is quite an advocate; perhaps she's inspired Alva. Whatever the truth, it's a genuinely boring idea, don't you agree?"

Sections removed from dining tables were set on trestles on the veranda of the cottage Mrs. Fish was renting that season, Oakview Villa on Bellevue at Narragansett. Ninety-eight canines—collies, wolfhounds, dachshunds, Pekes, pugs, borzois, Chihuahuas, beagles, basset hounds, poodles and other varieties of sniffing, yipping, scratching four-legged guests lapped up bowls of a chef-prepared stew of liver and rice. This course was followed by crushed bones fricaseed in a white sauce, and finally by a dessert of crumbled dog biscuits in cream. The meal was served by the household staff and some hired extras, the latter required to clean up the inevitable accidents under the table. The pet owners took supper inside, chatting amiably and ignoring the barks and occasional dog fights on the veranda.

A servant whispered to Mamie, "We have detained a stranger lurking on the grounds with a vicious bull terrier in a paper neck ruffle."

"A late arrival?"

"Not with the requisite invitation, madam. Before he was ejected, we confiscated his credentials."

The servant lowered his voice still further. "From the *New York Sun*."

Someone's bilious bulldog was carried out, tongue lolling, and unconscious, by two footmen holding the corners of a large towel as a stretcher. Mamie said, "Let's not worry about one unwashed reporter. It would spoil the evening."

Her lack of concern was ill-advised. Back in the city, the party crasher and then his fellow journalists on rival papers circulated details of the Dogs' Dinner in society columns. Clerics again rushed to their pulpits to declare that America's idle class had plumbed new depths of paganism. Colonel Mann's *Town Topics* fulminated against the event, its perpetrators and participants, with all the fury of an Old Testament prophet damning a satanic ritual.

Mamie, who avoided newspapers, shrugged off the criticism. She agreed with Harry Lehr that the dogs' dinner was so successful, they must do it again.

Harry concurred. "To hell with the moralizing majority," he said.

Five days before the Drivers closed Red Rose for the season, a Pinkerton detective arrived on a Fall River boat. The detective had come up from New York on Sam's orders, and at his expense. Sam locked himself in his office and read the detective's report, eleven typewritten pages. He found the contents disappointing though somehow not surprising.

Next morning he read the report again, making notes. He sent a message to Orlov at the Ocean House, suggesting a last excursion on *Invincible*, just the two of them.

Offshore, under sail, the Atlantic a smooth blue surface and Aquidneck Island a thin charcoal stroke on the horizon, the chief steward served a luncheon of consommé, cold lobster salad and chilled Montrachet. Sam and the count sat under an awning at the stern, Orlov visibly nervous, crossing and uncrossing his long legs. Sam began the dialogue:

"In the *Mercury*, I read that the Irish lad is still in Newport Hospital."

"The rubber plant who assaulted me at the races?"

"That's the one. The night we met at the Pearl, someone set the fire at his uncle's barn down on Thames Street. The lad was burned. He'll recover, they say, but slowly."

Sam shook ash from the end of his long green cigar. Sea wind scattered it over the rail. Orlov crossed his legs again.

Sam said, "I loathe that young fellow but I had nothing to do with the fire."

The count pulled his monocle from his eye and tapped it against his knee. "I hope you don't believe I was involved."

Sam drew on the cigar. "Were you?"

"I had nothing to do with it." Orlov sat rigidly in his canvas deck chair, his dark blue eyes like sunken stones under his thick brows. He breathed in, then added, "Personally."

Nothing to do with it *personally.* That told Sam all he needed to know.

He had no illusions about the sort of man he was inviting into his family. Orlov's veiled admission jibed with the behavior described in the Pinkerton report. In a way Sam admired the count for seizing the initiative, hiring firebugs, no doubt to place himself more solidly in Sam's favor. He and Orlov were not dissimilar, although Sam liked to think he had long ago outgrown deeds outside the law. Perhaps Orlov would too.

Time to get down to the issue, then.

Sam signaled the white-coated steward, who disappeared forward, returning to hand Sam a manila file pocket fattened by the typewritten pages. Orlov watched the exchange as if the steward had delivered an asp. Sam enjoyed protracting the moment, letting his guest squirm.

"I have a question, Count."

"Whatever you wish to know, you have only to ask."

"How much money do you want to marry my daughter?"

"What? Do you mean—?"

"Exactly what I said. What's your price?"

The count tripped over his words. "Sam—my friend—I have no indication whatever that your beautiful daughter cares for me, other than as a social companion. Never has she suggested she could look on me favorably as a suitor—a husband."

"In time she will. It's of no importance. You and I will settle the future between us."

"But I have not proposed."

"If we agree, it'll happen."

The count slipped his monocle back in place; it seemed to enlarge the blue-black iris. "Believe me, my friend, I have never for a single moment entertained the idea of—"

"Don't lie. It's a specialty of yours, I've discovered. I won't tolerate it."

Sam opened the folder to show the edges of the typewritten sheets.

"I've had you investigated by America's finest, most trustworthy private police agency, Pinkerton's. They employed correspondent agencies in England, France and Russia."

Abruptly, Orlov rose from his chair, his cheeks discoloring from ruddy to deep scarlet. "I find this insulting. I will not stay here and listen."

"You'd better. It's a long swim back to Newport. Now sit down and quit pretending you're a saint. You're an impostor. Charming, good-looking, plenty of social graces—far more than

I had growing up or working with the Erie crowd. But you employ petty thieves all over the Continent to rob homes and loot collections for pieces you can safely resell. You don't hail from Russia, and your name isn't Orlov. It's Ismail Rudenko. Your father was a Turkish-Hungarian seaman who was found stabbed and drowned in the harbor of Marseille, France, when you were twelve. Your mother was—well, let's spare your feelings and call her a lady of easy virtue. French, I believe."

Orlov was now staring at him with purplish lividity discoloring his face from jaw to hairline.

"You grew up in Marseille. The crime-ridden slum district down by the water, the Vieux Port."

Orlov snidely corrected his pronunciation. Sam stared until the count quailed, looked away.

"You became a roustabout and learned juggling in a traveling circus. You didn't reach Russia until you were in your twenties. For the next few years, the Pinkertons and their colleagues met a number of blank walls. You did serve briefly in the Moscow Hussars but you were cashiered for cheating at cards and reneging on gambling debts. You surfaced in St. Petersburg with a title."

"The title is genuine, one hundred percent. I bought it from Count Vassily Alexei Orlov when he knew he would soon die of tuberculosis. The provenance is unimpeachable. The papers are in order. The Orlovs are old and distinguished members of the Russian nobility. Prince Vladimir Orlov, Fat Orlov as they call him, is a favorite of the newly crowned Czar Nicholas the Second. Fat Orlov descends from a lover of Catherine the Great. Count Vassily Orlov is from another branch of the family, less wealthy, less renowned, but no less proper."

"I want to see the papers."

"They are locked in a bank box in Paris."

"Cable for them. Communication is amazingly fast these

days, not like it was when I was a boy, before the railroad and the telegraph. They won the war for the Union, you know."

Silence. Sam's curly hair, more ginger and gray than brown anymore, tossed in the wind. White horses showed on the Atlantic.

"How were you able to pay for the title? I'd guess it wouldn't have been a small sum."

Orlov relaxed slightly, unbuttoned the two highest buttons of his cream-colored yachting jacket. "Staggering, in fact. Old Vassily was a misanthrope. He had three nephews and a bastard son and despised them all. He wanted to disinherit them and endow a monastery. He wanted more rubles than I had ever seen in my life. Fortunately the asking price was not too high for my wife, Irenee. Very comfortable sort, Irenee. A widow, twenty-two years my senior when we met at a Moscow ballet."

"She died, then?"

"Regrettably, after we had been wed only eighteen months. An accident crossing the Alps in a blizzard. The forward axle broke, the coach tumbled into a crevasse."

And had you hired work done on the axle before it attempted the Alps in a storm?

Sam chastised himself for the thought.

"Go on, please."

The count drew a handkerchief from an inner pocket, wiped his eyes. "I was awaiting Irenee's arrival in Paris, where I had just opened my shop. I delayed the opening and immediately went into mourning."

"Touching," Sam replied with such subtle mockery that Orlov, blowing his nose, missed it.

He and Orlov regarded one another. The count was first to speak. "Have we finished?"

"Nearly. If I take you into the family, I demand only a very few things from you. That you treat my daughter kindly, with affection. That you appear to enjoy her company in public, and never humiliate her. A man must go his own way with women but you had damn well better be discreet or I'll have the police on you. Perhaps the czar's police."

The count sat motionless, cowed.

"I insist on one thing more. Run that business of yours legitimately. Henceforth, no more stolen goods. None."

Above the sea's roar and the mate bawling orders and the crew running on the forward deck, Orlov's answer was almost inaudible.

"I accept that. But I implore you, don't hint of any of this to Jenny. She's a decent, unspoiled young woman."

"I agree. If you marry her, she'll never know. How much do you want?"

Orlov lurched to the polished teak rail, grasped it, leaned over, looking for a moment as though he might heave out his guts. He dabbed his mouth with the handkerchief, recovering.

"A dowry of one and one-half million dollars would be suitable."

"We'll call it two."

"Plus a monthly stipend. Household expenses, entertainment, that sort of thing."

"Draw up a list. If it's legitimate, I'll agree."

"Of course we will need a suitable residence in New York. Also a larger apartment than I now occupy in Paris, and a villa somewhere in the south of France. For the winter warmth."

Sam wagged the stub of his cigar. "No New York, at least not for the next year or two. I want Jenny married and living abroad."

"Because of the Irish boy?"

Sam nodded. "Until I'm satisfied that she no longer cares for him in the slightest."

"Then we shall marry in Paris?"

"A Protestant ceremony."

"Russian Orthodox, Roman Catholic, a civil magistrate—it's immaterial to me."

"You're not the religious type, are you, Ismail?"

The count's florid color faded. "And you, Sam Driver, are *un bâtard*. I trust my memory is clear."

"You've got it wrong. I just hate to lose."

Sam returned the manila report folder to the steward, who had silently glided into their presence. Then he laid a fatherly arm over the younger man's shoulders. "It's the supreme accomplishment in Newport town, snaring a titled son-in-law. We'll all cross the Atlantic on this yacht. I've already informed the captain."

"I must ask Jenny for her hand."

"We'll do it together. We won't ask her, we'll tell her. Tactfully. I'd say this occasions another drink." To the steward: "Break out that magnum of Mumm's in the ice locker."

Invincible's steam horn blared. A Rhody fishing trawler near the yacht's bow gave way suddenly, veering to avoid a collision. Warmed by his success, Sam paid no attention to the protesting cries of the lowly fishermen.

40
Sam's Surrender, Jenny's Grief, Mozart's Penance

Tessa stamped her slipper, dusty-rose satin with gold buckles. She stamped so vigorously the pendants on the Pickwick chandelier tinkled.

"Take your choice, Sam. Paris by yourself, or New York without me. For good."

"But I have to consider Jenny."

"You think she doesn't know about me?"

"I'm certain she does, I've never taken pains to keep from mentioning your name."

"Thank you very much," Tessa said with a flounce of her ample rear. "I've gotten your ultimatum and you've gotten mine. Mine trumps yours. Kindly excuse me, I have a note to write to another gentleman. Before you swallow your tongue, it's my old manager. I'm returning to the stage while you endanger your life mingling with Frogs."

Sam felt as dismal as the autumn day outside: gray rain whipping the windowpanes, plastering an occasional dead leaf before the next gust blew it into the sky. How could she return to the stage when she's gained fifteen pounds in the past two years? Mauve tights would not become her bulky thighs . . .

The thought left unexpressed, he said, "I know people call them Frogs but the term's derogatory. What's wrong with the French, anyway?"

"I've met some in the theater, tourists. Parisians are the worst. They're ruder than New Yorkers, and that's rude. More to the point, they don't wash their vegetables. They relieve themselves at those filthy street corner kiosks. The girls in their music hall revues shamelessly bare their bosoms, leaving nothing to tease the imagination. With no one to look after you, you'll be a wreck when you return. If you're even alive. I love you, Sam Driver. I also realize what a sad, weak, careless little boy you can be. You may have conquered the likes of Commodore Vanderbilt and Daniel Drew but you can't take care of yourself. I refuse to wave good-bye from the pier and let you commit suicide eating dirty vegetables."

The battle was lost. He fell back to a feeble defense position:

"Jenny hasn't agreed to the marriage. She hasn't heard the count's proposal."

"When does the yacht leave?"

"A week from Tuesday if we maintain our schedule."

"Then get to it. Good-bye." She slid the chair out from her writing desk and snapped on the electric lamp. Sam sighed long and soulfully.

"I'll take you along. I'll find a place on the yacht."

"You won't throw me into a hammock among a lot of randy tars, thank you."

"You'll bunk with me, in the owner's suite. The bed is quite large enough for two."

Melting instantly, she cooed, "Oh, I do like that." Her kiss was ardent, her arms strong around his neck. She'd got the best of him but, on balance, it was one contest he didn't mind losing.

They began the evening on West 35th Street, occupying expensive box seats at the Garrick Theatre for the opening night of *Secret Service*, a Civil War melodrama by the handsome leading man and playwright William Gillette. He personated a Union spy posing as a Confederate artillery officer in Richmond. The romance between the spy and the daughter of a rebel general enthralled Jenny, who had no hint that her escorts had planned the outing like a military campaign seeking to overcome an enemy position.

Afterward they repaired to Louis Sherry's at Fifth Avenue and 44th. Sherry, a star in the restaurant and catering trade, had engaged Stanford White to design an entire twelve-story building to house his sumptuous eatery and challenge Delmonico's, now located directly across the street. The man at the podium of the main dining room on the Fifth Avenue side whispered that Pierpont Morgan and party were on the premises, as though the Almighty had descended to pay a special visit.

The meal was certainly grand enough to draw the denizens of heaven to New York: lobster cutlet (Jenny), a pastry shell filled with a timbale of black grouse in a chestnut puree (Orlov), spring lamb (Sam's selection), asparagus in Hollandaise sauce and for dessert Baba au Rhum, which Jenny protested added pounds just from looking at it.

Sam had arranged a secluded table by tall windows overlooking Fifth Avenue. On the far side of the large room J. P. Morgan and half a dozen male friends ate and drank with noisy conviviality. When the noise diminished a little, Orlov signaled and two balding fiddle players appeared, serenading Sam's table with romantic airs by Tchaikovsky. Orlov maintained that the Russian composer's tunes always made young girls cry.

At the end of the meal, a waiter in white tie set a demitasse at each place and retired. Orlov drew a small Tiffany box from his pocket.

"Dear Jenny, I have the honor to offer a gift and make a request."

The diamond in the box was so large and bright, it reflected lights on the eyeglasses of a matron at the next table. She gasped in admiration or, perhaps, envy.

Orlov slid the box across the table. "That is for you. To prove that what I am going to ask is heartfelt. I want you to be my wife."

Jenny sat back, pale beneath her rouge. She looked wary, like a forest animal in a trap.

"I have spoken to your father. He is quite willing."

"Happy about it too," Sam concurred. "Ismail's an intelligent, cultured man. You couldn't find better."

"I'm ever so flattered, but I think I must—" Her voice broke; the matron rubbernecking from the next table had even more to goggle at: Jenny's sudden rise, overturning her gilt chair. "Won't you both excuse me?"

She ran from the dining room.

Orlov rubbed his temples. "*Dieu.* Have we lost already?"

"Hell no. Give her time to collect herself, get over her surprise. Waiter, two more drinks here."

Forty-eight hours later, Jenny tapped at Sam's bedroom door on Fifth Avenue. He laid aside a San Antonio & Sonora balance sheet, brushed cigar ash from the front of his dressing gown, snatched off his pointed night cap. The door opened; Jenny was pale, wearing no powder. She struck him as world-weary—older than her twenty-one years.

"Papa, I'll marry him if he'll have me."

"Child, that's wonderful. No lingering doubts about that Newport boy?"

"I haven't seen or heard from him since he fought with the count."

Sam's frantic maneuvering, in collusion with Mozart, to keep news articles about the Thames Street fire out of the house had worked.

"I know you cared for him."

"I confess I did. But he broke promises."

"He abandoned you."

"Mozart confirmed that."

Sharply, Sam said, "Mozart? When?"

"Oh, some time ago. Don't think badly of it, I forced the admission from him."

"The day of the Cup races, that boy came to Castle Hill to harass you."

"How can we be sure? He never finished saying what he wanted to tell me."

"Threats. Vituperation. Poor people are always playing the victim."

"Well, it's past history. So is he."

"I'm pleased to hear you say it. You'll be very happy living in Paris."

"I'm sure I will," she said in a listless way. "I'm going to bed now. I've hardly slept in two nights. Good night, Papa. You may tell the count if you wish."

She closed the door so quietly, he couldn't hear it. For a moment he wondered what he'd done. For a moment, guilt flayed him.

But then he smiled.

Seasick and heartsick, Jenny Driver crossed the Atlantic in the first of the autumn gales. She seldom left her cabin, drinking tea that refused to stay on her stomach. She'd vowed to study a

French grammar, master it cover to cover during the crossing. She hadn't opened it.

In the darkness, with the yacht timbers creaking and the high waves smashing against the hull, she left her bed and knelt at the side to pray she'd done the right thing, not surrendered thoughtlessly. She prayed that Prince would still find a path to a decent life, free of the vengeful impulses that had drawn him to her.

She prayed he'd find peace.

She could marry Orlov for the prestige, the grand adventures the capitals of Europe promised, but it was a dubious trade-off. She could never love anyone but the impoverished Irish boy from the Casino.

Lightning played around the mast tops as the storm worsened. St. Elmo's fire ran across the spars and down the rigging. The deeply devout among the crew crossed themselves and wished they'd made better plans for their families in case *Invincible* foundered and broke apart, which for several dark hours seemed likely.

The storm terrified Jenny—lured her mind into all sorts of forbidding places. She dreamed or wakefully imagined herself to be in the Casino tunnel for the third time, caught in darkness between the clear daylight of her past and the foggy radiance of an uncertain future.

Grandfather Penny appeared to her, his hammerlike fist upraised, his eyes bright as a burning bush.

Read the law Moses brought down from the mount. "Thou shalt have no other gods before me." You have turned away. You are an idolater. Let this cup pass from my lips for I cannot abide the thought of a child of my own flesh worshipping false gods. . . .

"I'm not," Jenny whispered in the stale dark of the cabin. "I'm not, I'm not."

The storm cracked and roared.

She covered her ears and closed her eyes and fell on top of the coverlet in a tearful swoon.

What happened when the garret landing collapsed, Prince learned in detail only afterward, when Titus visited him in the ward at Newport Hospital on Friendship Street. Prince had been unconscious for twenty-four hours, kept that way by morphine injected to reduce the excruciating pain. It didn't, entirely; when he finally woke, if he'd been a child he'd have cried. His left side from his armpit to his thigh near his knee had been burned when his flannel nightshirt ignited.

Uncle Titus kept a vigil in a bedside chair. Gone, at least temporarily, was Titus's frugality. "They wanted to job you into the charity ward but I said no. This ward's a little better." But not much, as evidenced by the putrid odors drifting in the aisleway; the moans of a man with an amputated leg; the sudden howls and thrashings of a patient severely burned when the boiler on an excursion boat exploded.

"How bad does it hurt, lad?"

"Bad enough," Prince said through dry cracked lips.

Titus explained that Rex had leaped from Prince's arms and landed wide of the fire, jarred but unhurt. "Old Doc Hasselberger, he's put Rex in one of his cages, nice and roomy. He'll be fine till you're out of here."

Under the sheet Prince felt wet dressings on the affected areas. The wetness burned like acid. Even slight movement in the hard bed renewed the pain. He said, "How long will that be?"

A phantom in a beautiful blue frock coat with velvet lapels appeared behind a passing matron.

"I'll answer that. You'll be here a week, perhaps two. I'm Dr. Reynard. I happened to be calling on another patient when you were brought in. I was asked to examine you, and initiate treatment, which I did." Without liking it much, Prince sensed.

"I can't continue to handle your case, I am overdue at my daughter Sophie's harpsichord recital. However, Dr. Meade here"—a second phantom appeared, younger, with a wispy brown goatee—"will see to your care. Dr. Meade trained at the Johns Hopkins hospital. Now if you'll excuse me."

And that was the last Prince ever saw of the well-dressed Dr. Reynard.

Young Dr. Meade was gaunt as a starved refugee, but he was also more concerned, less bored than his colleague. He sat in another chair, next to Titus. "You were burned over a fairly significant area of your left side, but luckily your uncle was quick to act."

"Took hold of your bare legs," Titus began.

"He rolled you in the dirt to help extinguish your burning nightclothes. A woman—"

"Mary. A good nigger."

"—found a blanket and wrapped you in it. I would characterize your burns as superficial, though I know they're painful. I grew up on a farm in Ohio. Our mare kicked a lantern when I was hitching her to the buggy. Hay caught fire and I tried to save the mare. I was bedridden for weeks. I was nine."

"You're right, it hurts, clear down to the bone." Prince turned slightly to relieve pressure on his left side; the pain only worsened.

"We'll continue the morphine for a day or two. The best treatment for burns like yours is warm soaking dressings changed two or three times daily. I'll write the order. We rely mostly on the healing ability of the patient's own constitution. We prefer a natural debridement of the affected area instead of surgical intervention. At Hopkins they're experimenting with silver to fight burn infection, so I'm going to order silver foil applied once a day." Dr. Meade started to pat his arm, looked chagrined when he realized what he'd almost done. "You're a lucky fellow. You'll be out of here soon."

"Scarred?"

"Probably. Where it can't be seen."

"Fucking bastards," Prince groaned, looking at the water-stained ceiling but visualizing Driver, his assistant and that Russian. The scores to settle were mounting.

Visitors whom Dr. Meade allowed during the second week improved Prince's spirits. Jimmy Fetch and Flo Dwyer visited together. They held hands, which required no explanation.

Tom Pettit came from the Casino, and Jumbo Sullivan from north of town. Marcel the baker arrived with a paper bag of Prince's favorite tomato and basil bread sticks. Paddy Leland brought his wife, Ella, whom Prince had never met. Ianelli, sheepish and clumsy at conversation, smuggled in a bottle of red Chianti wrapped in brown paper.

Dickie Glossop sent a stiffly formal card of sympathy.

Tall Mary surprised him with a pail of homemade vegetable soup with okra, carrots, snap beans and a ring bone with marrow flavoring it. Sitting up to sip through a paper spiral straw, paraffin-coated, something Prince had never seen before, was a novelty; he was acquainted with rye grass straws from nature.

Sitting up was also a struggle. It required the help of two matrons. It drove him to the point of tears again.

When Dr. Meade signed him out of Newport Hospital, he walked with a crutch to take weight off his left side. *Bastards.* They'd crippled him, then scarred him.

Titus, forever conscious of overhead, lived in an alcove separated from the grogshop pantry by a curtain. He slept on a secondhand brass bed, shaved at a cracked mirror hanging over a marble washbasin from a churchyard sale. He used the outhouse at the rear of the property; fire hadn't reached there.

He offered to build a similar alcove for his nephew but Prince wasn't eager to spend more time with the old man. Though Titus was family, he wasn't the most lovable or congenial person when focused on business. Prince gladly accepted an offer from Mary and moved into a room recently vacated by her older son, George, as in George Washington, who'd gotten married. Mary's second son, lanky Abraham, named for the emancipation president, worked downstairs from the flat, ironing shirts and pressing pants in Herman's New Steam Laundry. No one thought it peculiar that a white man lived with a Negro family. On Pond Street in the West Broadway district, Newport blacks lived in relative harmony with Irish stevedores, Bohemian carriage finishers, Jewish haberdashers, Swedish bakery owners. What bonded them all together was hard work and a belief in a better future, which at the moment Prince didn't share.

Soon after he moved in, early December, Mary helped tie a muffler around his throat, turned up the collar of his shabby coat and advised him to forgo his trip into the worsening weather.

"Not going far," he said. "Just to Red Rose."

"Ain't nobody there."

"Must be a watchman."

"Just don't overtax yourself. I got a duty to care for you now you're one of mine."

"And you care for me very well." Prince kissed her brown cheek and went out into the night of soughing trees, flurrying snow and a distant ship's horn that sounded as melancholy as he felt. Each step hurt. Under his dressings, burned flesh was blistering. The blister fluid soaked the cloths and stung.

The old gates on Leroy Avenue had long ago been scraped and repainted. An electric lantern shone light on the shiny black bell. Prince rang it by the knotted cord tied to the clapper. After three rings, a firefly glow appeared and floated toward him.

"Get away. House is closed up."

"No one's here?"

"Mr. Gribble, but he ain't in the habit of palavering with strangers."

"Tell him Molloy's at the gate. Prince Molloy."

"Why should I?" snapped the rheumy-eyed old man.

"Because, if you don't, when I'm off this crutch I'll look you up and then you'll wish you'd been a little more accommodating." Prince's bold black eyes shone like stones in the lantern light. "Gribble knows me."

"Shit, ain't no business of mine." The watchman shuffled away.

Presently lantern light returned, carried this time in the hands of Sam's assistant, who'd donned an old Union Army greatcoat, incongruous with his tasseled smoking cap. Mozart Gribble looked shrunken, slumped, less formidable and capable, than in times past. Prince seethed at the sight of him.

"Mr. Molloy," Mozart said, holding the lantern high between them while needles of snow stung their cheeks. "I was happy to hear you survived the fire."

"If you call scars from your ribs to your knee surviving. Why do you care?"

"It was a topic of much interest in Newport." The reply was a monotone, devoid of significance.

"I thought you might be in New York."

"I chose to stay here. There are unpleasant memories in New York. I travel down there only when necessary."

Prince clutched the iron gate with a hand in a fingerless mitten. "Did you start the fire? Oh, I forgot, you don't hurt people personally, you hire it done."

Mozart flinched as though struck. "I can understand your

anger. For thirty years I've done despicable deeds on behalf of Sam Driver. For years I didn't mind but lately I have gone to the poisoned well too often."

"That won't erase the scars. Or cure this limp."

"I am profoundly sorry. I can tell you that I hardly sleep from regretting the whole business."

Looking into the sallow, sagging face, Prince felt pity overwhelming his anger. He let go of the cold iron gate.

"Who set the fire?"

"I don't know."

"Who do you suspect?"

"Orlov. I have no proof."

"But you hired the men who broke my foot."

"God help me, I did. I live with that day and night."

"Where's Miss Driver? In the city?"

"I should imagine she and her father and Count Orlov are approaching the English Channel, if they have not already anchored at Le Havre. You see, Miss Driver"—the admissions were torn out of him like something pulled forcibly from deep within—"she and the count will be married in Paris."

"*Married?* When?"

"Upon arrival in that city."

"Jesus, Joseph and Mary." Prince beat his mittened fist against the iron uprights. "You really did a job, Gribble, you and that Russian son of a bitch. You fixed my wagon twice over. I never dreamed I was such a threat to a great man like Mr. Driver. I don't know how I can get to Paris but I will. My sainted mother taught me to repay debts. As for you, I hope you never sleep solidly again."

Mozart repeated, "I am profoundly sorry. Somehow I will make reparations."

Prince laughed at him, swung and lurched off into the thickening snow. His left side hurt from thigh to shoulder. He was supremely conscious of his uneven gait. He didn't know enough rude words to express his hatred.

Farther along Leroy Avenue, he looked back but the lantern no longer shone at the gate. Darkness enveloped everything, Prince's heart and soul most of all.

Scoppo the carpenter left his ramshackle house before daylight, to fish for inshore cod. Scoppo wasn't a good or even an enthusiastic angler, but he preferred fishing by himself to staying with his wife. The laws of his church prohibited divorce, or murder. Nothing was said about fishing.

Scoppo's path took him by the foul-smelling cove between Long Wharf and better houses on the Point. The setting moon cast his shadow on the water: shoulders bowed, belly protruding as though he were about to deliver twins, his rod over a shoulder, his tackle box in hand.

He saw something peculiar in the gently waving cattails. A long tassel floated there, attached to a round cap.

He fished the cap out of the reeds, let cap and tassel drip awhile, then stored the cap in his tackle box along with sinkers and cork bobbers and line. The moon had set. A milky canopy of stars paled and vanished as daylight approached. Nowhere in the lagoon did Scoppo see evidence of the man who'd worn the cap.

Let the authorities search for the body. Scoppo would fish, then go along to the police station. He'd say that he'd found the cap on his way home. The drowned man wasn't going anywhere, was he?

IV
1897

41
Sign of the Owl

The French had a phrase for it—*fin de siècle*, the close of the century. Old beliefs and traditions crumbled under the attack of new, some thought radical, changes in the social order, artistic technique, even the most fundamental moral precepts. Marxism was in the air. Impressionism. Woman suffrage. Free love, a concept almost eighty years old, was not only widely discussed but widely practiced.

America in 1897 felt the tremors of change. A new president, McKinley, left his Ohio porch to move into the White House. Brooklyn and New York planned to merge to create a new, larger city. A great tomb for U. S. Grant, a superb general but an easily bewildered chief executive, was dedicated on Riverside Drive. A ship loaded with Yukon gold weighed anchor for Seattle.

It was a year for memorable expressions. The *New York Times* announced that its pages contained "all the news that's fit to print." Pugilist Bob Fitzsimmons knocked out the much larger heavyweight champ, Jim Corbett, and said, "'The bigger they are, the harder they fall." A *New York Sun* editorialist answered a young girl's plaintive letter by assuring her that, "Yes, Virginia, there is a Santa Claus."

Prince missed much of this because he couldn't afford newspapers, and his determination had pushed him to another language.

Jumbo Sullivan drove him to Providence. There, from a pushcart peddler, Prince bought a used English–French dictionary and a grammar authored by a French pedagogue named Pierre Larousse. He carried the books to Marcel's shop. Berthe, the baker's stout wife, sat with him for an hour at the end of every day, teaching him the rudiments, correcting his pronunciation and graciously refraining from laughing at his countrified gaffes. Prince was astounded to find he liked the flavor of French words even when he didn't understand them or know how to pronounce them. When glimmers of understanding began to shine through he liked them even more. He wondered why the nuns had called him slow to learn; he gobbled up the new language like a feast set before a beggar. Even Sullivan noticed:

"You ain't so humble anymore, spoutin' your high-toned Frog palaver."

"I'm getting ready to go to Paris."

"Ayah, but how are you going to get there?"

"Don't know. I will, though. There are scores to settle."

"Devil of a way to spend your life."

"No other way, far as I'm concerned. I'm half a freak—scarred up, can't walk straight, thanks to Driver and that Russian."

Sullivan saw no point in continuing an argument he couldn't win.

Early in the last week in April, the steam yacht *Namouna* anchored in Newport Harbor. A member of Paddy Leland's family who worked on the docks told Prince the following day.

He loitered outside the gates of Stone Villa in the long spring evening. After two unsuccessful vigils, watching the bright windows of the publisher's vast house but seeing no human being, he was rewarded by the noise of a coach and four coming out of the drive.

He crouched behind a bank of forsythia, his heart racing. When lanterns on the moving coach lit the drive in front of him, he crashed through the shrubbery, seized the near door and leaped inside.

Startled though he surely was, James Gordon Bennett regarded the intruder calmly. He smelled of talc and his long cigar.

"If this is a robbery, I'll see you in hell first."

"I only want to talk, sir. No danger to yourself."

The publisher answered a knock on the panel behind his head. "No trouble, Elijah. For the moment. Proceed toward Ocean Drive until I say otherwise."

The coach creaked into Bellevue Avenue, heading in a southerly direction beneath the new leaves of old shade trees. Gordon Bennett laid aside his *Paris Herald*. Prince sat well forward on the seat opposite the publisher, sweating in the cool night air. He fumbled under his shirt, drew up the chain, brought out the tin-plate owl that swung with the motion of the carriage.

"What am I supposed to infer from that gewgaw, young man?"

"I saw owls exactly like this one carved all over your building in New York."

"What of it? The owl's the symbol of Minerva, the Greek goddess of wisdom. My father regarded it as our clan's good luck sign. Either state your business or leave me alone."

Over the years Prince must have absorbed some of the audacity of older, richer, more assertive Newport residents because he wasn't deterred by the publisher's belligerence. He twisted the chain so that the owl flashed.

"My mother was a chambermaid at the Ocean House. A gentleman gave her this. She said the gentleman had money. She said he was my father."

The iron-shod wheels ground over the cobbles, striking sparks. Gordon Bennett drew on his cigar. The end threw ruddy light over his saturnine face.

"What was the fellow's name?"

Prince slipped the tin-plate owl into his shirt. "She died before she told me."

"My condolences. Turn your head to the left when we pass the next streetlamp."

Prince did as he was asked.

"I admit there's a slight resemblance between the two of us. I freely admit I gave trinkets like yours to any number of ladies whose company I enjoyed when I was younger. But if I paid off every bastard trying to extort money because of that, I'd be bankrupt."

"I don't want money from you."

"What, then?"

"They say you sail back and forth to France regularly. Give me a berth on your yacht next time you cross."

Prince was astonished when Gordon Bennett laughed, a loud *haw-haw*. "God, that's effrontery. What's your name?"

"Prince Molloy."

"I'll say this, Mr. Molloy. You present me with the most unusual bit of moral blackmail I've ever encountered, and I've encountered plenty. Why do you want to go to France?"

"Personal reason, sir." He didn't want to mention his eagerness to square things with the count, or Sam Driver; Gordon Bennett might be a friend of one or both. "There's a young lady involved."

"Ah. Isn't there always. Well, Mr. Molloy, it happens that *Namouna* is scheduled to cross week after next, although my destination is Beaulieu, on the Mediterranean."

"I need to go to Paris."

"You're daft. However, if a woman's involved, I can understand. Here's the bargain. My crew will land you on the French coast in a small boat. From there you'll have to make the journey alone. Further, you earn your passage. Swab decks. Polish brightwork. Scrub out the shitters. I provide no passport or *permis de séjour*."

Prince cudgeled his memory. "Housing license?"

"Permit for residency. You know the language?"

"No, sir. I'm trying to learn it. I'll get by without those documents."

"Risky, but it's up to you. Tell me where you live. I'll send a man with a notice of our departure. If you're not on the pier when my cutter leaves, find another Samaritan."

He gave Mary's number on Pond Street. Gordon Bennett's carefully plucked brows ticked up and down; he recognized an address in a mixed neighborhood but he didn't comment. He tapped on the panel behind him.

"Elijah, stop at the next corner. Our passenger is getting out."

It was a disquieting finish to what he'd hoped might be a reunion with his flesh-and-blood father. He was elated at finding passage but let down by the abrupt end of the conversation. When the coach halted, Prince opened the door, stepped out, only to have Gordon Bennett's voice stop him.

"She was a lovely lass, Maureen Molloy. I remember her fondly."

Prince peered into the carriage but the publisher sat well back, hidden from the light.

"I didn't tell you her name."

"No, you didn't. Elijah, drive on."

The carriage rolled away, turned right into Shepard Avenue and out of sight.

Under the streetlamp Prince examined the owl medal again. He couldn't see any deeper than the cheap tin surface, couldn't visualize his mother and the publisher as lovers.

He considered his enthusiastic immersion in the French language and wondered whether he'd inherited some of Gordon Bennett's brains.

He laughed at his own conceit, but it cheered him. He set off along Bellevue Avenue whistling.

42
Jenny's Confession

Some weeks prior, *Invincible* called at Boulogne. Sam engaged an entire wagon-lit to couple onto an express and carry them up to Paris. Sam and Tessa took a four-room suite at the Hotel Meurice on the Rue de Rivoli, a few blocks from Orlov's business near the Louvre. Jenny had a suite of her own until the wedding.

A cable waited for Sam at the hotel desk. Jenny saw her father's face fade from ruddiness to a kind of parchment gray. "What is it, Papa?"

"Mozart. He's dead. In Newport. Apparently suicide."

"Mozart? Why?"

"Lately he's acted despondent. Beyond that I've no idea."

He completed the registration and surrendered his folded passport in its leather wallet. Of course he knew, or guessed, the cause of Mozart's death: all the shady deeds Sam had asked him to perform.

An image of Fisk lying in bed, bleeding and expiring, flashed before Sam's eyes. To the bellman he said, "Show us to our rooms," with a savagery that made his daughter stare.

On a morning stroll, the count proudly showed off the gold-leaf lettering in a lower corner of the window of his shop.

ORLOV ET CIE
ANTIQUAIRES

PATRIMOINE ET COLLECTIONS PRIVÉES
VENTES ET ESTIMATIONS
DISCRETION ASSURÉE

Orlov closed out his flat on the Boulevard Haussmann and leased a newer, larger one on the top floor of a building in the Opéra Quarter, near the opera house itself, and the many fashionable hotels, shops and bistros lining both sides of the tree-shaded Boulevard des Capucines. The name commemorated nuns of the Capuchin order who'd once had a chapter house on the boulevard.

On this very street, Orlov explained, the failed Revolution of 1848 had begun on the steps of the Ministry of Foreign Affairs. Fortunately, he said, builders and developers who looked beyond emotional slogans and frivolous concepts such as "democracy" moved in, bought up properties and razed the Boulevard's seedy dance halls and marionette theaters. Thus was created the swank neighborhood which bore few traces of its bloody past, the memories lingering only in the moldering brains of academicians writing histories no sane person would read.

Jenny passed her days in a dull, almost trancelike state of acceptance. Sam took her aside and begged her to be happy. She stared at him, only returning an enigmatic smile like that of Leonardo's *La Joconde* hanging in the Louvre to be gawked at by long files of schoolchildren from Neuilly and tourists from the wilds of Illinois.

She abandoned her failed study of French. When she shopped, she protested that she didn't understand, as when bargaining with a saucy little *grisette* in a *parfumerie*. If her fiancé were with her, she insisted he translate. Learning the language of her new home might be necessary eventually but for the present it seemed uninteresting, not worthwhile. Nothing seemed worthwhile.

The count and her father took her to a small gallery to sneer at the works of certain artists who painted not realistically but to create their "impression" of a scene. Orlov dismissed a canvas depicting the Boulevard des Capucines observed from a great height, much like the view from the new flat. "Worthless madmen, this whole crowd."

Sam agreed. "The picture makes me nervous. The street's so busy."

"Papa, the boulevard is busy day or night."

"I don't care, Jenny, that isn't art—little dibs and dabs and dots. You have to squint to make sense of it."

Tessa invited her to luncheon at the smart Café de la Paix on the Boulevard. Discreetly, Tessa asked whether Jenny needed any particular feminine advice before her first night alone with her new husband. Jenny's smile echoed the one she'd given her father, but she did say that she believed she knew everything she needed to know. Tessa sensed Jenny might be experienced, and secretive about it.

On a Friday evening in January, the dean of the Cathedral of the Holy Trinity, the somber and elegant Anglican church below the Champs-Elysées and above the slow-moving Seine, joined Jenny Driver and Ismail Orlov in holy wedlock.

Jenny's auburn hair shone in muted light flooding the altar. She was superbly dressed, not formally, as a bride, but in smooth white satin with a pearl collar, expensively provided by Europe's finest designer, Charles Worth. He kept his couture firm at No. 7 Rue de la Paix, and astounded the world by repeatedly proving that a humble English draper from Lincolnshire could outshine, and outcharge, the finest French dressmakers.

Sam gave his daughter away with pride but certain formless misgivings. Tessa stood up with Jenny and kissed her warmly at the end of the short service.

Jenny had wanted a wedding trip to Venice. Orlov pleaded the press of business. A consignment of fifty valuable pieces from an estate near Grenoble demanded his presence in Paris. He promised a trip to Italy before long.

The wedding party enjoyed an eight-course champagne supper at the Meurice. At half past twelve in the morning, Orlov called for his carriage to return them to the new flat, for a night that was unforgettable for the wrong reasons.

He brutalized her. He took her the way Prince had, but not tenderly. When she longed to sleep he rolled her on her stomach and entered her again. Bruised, she begged him to stop. He rolled her on her back and flung a hairy leg over her breasts. Only when he gripped her hair with one hand and forced her lips open with the other did she understand what he intended.

She'd heard of it, imagined it with a perverse but arm's-length fascination, never expecting to experience it. Minutes later she ran from the bedchamber, coughing, spitting, wanting to vomit.

Orlov found it amusing. She heard him chuckle as she crouched in the water closet, sick and disillusioned. From the far side of the closed door came the peculiar grassy odor of the brown cigarettes he smoked.

She limped to her own wardrobe, found a clean gown, belted it and curled up on the sateen divan in the reception parlor. She didn't think it possible to sleep but it came rapidly, a blessed escape.

In the morning Jenny's new husband seemed chipper and polite. He sent the concierge's son to a neighboring bistro to order breakfast. He gave the bistro waiter a large tip and enthused over the eggs with caviar, the warm croissants, the chilled strawberries. A single dewy red rose decorated the table in a slender crystal vase.

He'd dressed before she woke—a pale gray suit, high silk hat and gloves. He kissed her cheek almost daintily. He thanked her for being a proper wife and left for his shop without saying when he'd return.

Four days later, the expensive telephone, barrel wood base and gilded handset, announced a caller with a rachetlike noise. " 'Allo?" Jenny said, her mild concession to trying to sound like a native.

A cultured English voice, female, replied.

"Let me speak to Count Orlov, please."

"I'm sorry, he's in Nice, going over an acquisition."

"Really. What's her name?"

"I beg your pardon?"

"With whom am I speaking?"

She was about to say Mrs. Orlov but remembered her location. "Madame Orlov."

"Don't jest, my dear. You're another of his tarts that he's moved in temporarily."

"Count Orlov is my husband."

"Your—?" The woman laughed. "Oh, dear. How rich. Someone he couldn't get round any other way. Are you American?"

"Who is this, please?"

"Just ask the dear boy to ring the Crillon when he returns. Clementine Sandringham. You will be understanding about it, won't you? A French wife is always tolerant of mistresses and other special friends of her husband. *Au revoir*, you poor child."

The line grew scratchy; a switchboard person interrupted with a genuine "'Allo? 'Allo?" that sounded as though it traveled a long distance through a cheap tin horn.

Sam sensed desperation in his daughter's request that he take her driving. He hired an open barouche drawn by two plumed horses and they set out from the Boulevard des Capucines on a bright, balmy May morning. Flower gardens were blooming and even the poorest Parisians seemed cheerful. Jenny looked oddly spinsterish in a gray spring dress, wool, with a high collar and quilted white vestee. The dark gray veil on her picture hat revealed nothing beyond the oval shape of her face.

Sam instructed the driver to take them through Napoléon's triumphal arch to the Bois de Boulogne, 2,100 acres of woodlands artfully enhanced with lakes, gardens, islands and follies by Baron Haussmann's landscape architects, who had followed his instructions to replicate London's Hyde Park. The barouche entered the lovely sprawling wood by the Porte Maillot. On the Allée de Longchamp Jenny undid her veil. Her left cheek, from her eye to her jaw, showed a gaudy yellow and purple discoloration.

"God above. Did some thief attack you?"

"I'm beginning to think so, Papa. You're looking at the handiwork of my esteemed husband, the night he returned from Nice."

Briefly she described the telephone call from the English woman.

"When I told him about the caller he flew into a rage and used his fists on me. I locked myself in my bedroom. I want to know what to do."

"Do?" he echoed in a puzzled way. "What do you mean? You're describing a family quarrel."

"I'm describing a sadistic beating. This marriage has already lasted too long."

Red and embarrassed, Sam put a finger across his lips, pointed to the driver's back. "Let's discuss it while we stroll."

They left the barouche near the Lac Inférieur. Sam told the driver to return in an hour. He and Jenny walked beneath old lime and beech trees. They crossed a wooden footbridge to a café on one of the two islands in the lake. Near their table, swans glided in pairs. Jenny ordered *thé* from the English-speaking waiter, Sam a tall Artois lager.

"Papa, there's no love in my marriage to Ismail. It's a sham. The man's a poseur and a philanderer. I admit you warned me. Also, he may be drugging himself with narcotics. If we had Mr. Holmes the consulting detective here, I'm sure he could tell us; he injected morphine, didn't he?"

Her pallid smile drew no response. Sam missed the literary allusion, as he'd failed to make the connection between a thief and her dowry. Jenny resumed:

"I think I knew most of this about him, or I guessed it, before we left Newport. I said I'd marry him because I wanted to escape all the bad memories. The mistakes."

Sam stamped his foot; two swans, alarmed, swam off, leaving spreading ripples. "Is this another reference to that Irish bum? Is he behind this?"

He'd never seen her in such a fury, albeit silent. Tears fell from her blue eyes but she didn't blubber at him. "That's *over*. He has nothing to do with what's happened. I'm at fault. I want a divorce."

"A—? Oh, no, sweet. You're not that Belmont woman. Look at all she went through. The ostracism. The rude jokes behind her back. She planned to acquire Ollie Belmont like a new possession. She schemed, cast her net, long before she divorced Vanderbilt. You're not that sort. A divorce would ruin your reputation. You'd never find another husband of quality."

"Is that all that matters to you, a husband of quality? A son-in-law you can brag on to your cronies? *I'm* the one Ismail hit. *I'm* the one he nearly raped on our wedding night."

"He—forced himself on you?"

"Yes, yes, isn't that rape?" Jenny calmed a little. "I don't want to be a prude, or an hysterical child, but I made a grievous mistake about the man. I've paid for it, and I want out of the arrangement. If you won't help me I'll do it on my own, damn the consequences."

"You mean you'd seek a lawyer?"

"Isn't a lawyer necessary?"

"Run away from that lovely flat?"

"That *lovely flat* is where I live with a monster. You've heard my side, Papa. Tell me yours."

"I have to think about this."

"Pfaugh. How many times in your days with Jim Fisk and Jay Gould did you knock a man down the instant he crossed one of you? Don't tell me you need time to decide about your own daughter."

"I do, Jenny, I—see here. The carriage should be waiting. We'd best go back. You must give me a day to mull this. You're proposing a dreadfully serious step."

"Because it might hurt your reputation with all those fine, shallow people you've learned to chum with?"

Sam's liver-spotted hands trembled. He touched her elbow. "I'll think about it, I swear. I want you to be happy. I want the best way out of this for all concerned. I'll think about it and let you know my decision."

"Very well," she said, chin high, eyes far away on the spring greenery of the Bois.

They recrossed the footbridge. A white heron stepped daintily in the shallows of the lake. She appeared not to notice. Sam felt he was marching in step with some creature made of marble.

Orlov went to Berlin to confer with a potential customer "of some means." He didn't inform Jenny personally; he left a note on a silver salver. Wooing the customer might take as long as a week, he wrote.

Until she's exhausted you?

Jenny felt she'd made some slight progress with her father. They'd talk again. She'd assault him with her determination, and more details, if she could bring herself to reveal them. It wouldn't happen as quickly as she hoped, that was evident next morning when a messenger from the Meurice presented her with another note, this one in Sam's crude sprawling hand.

He needed more time to think. He and Tessa were boarding a train for the south, there to rendezvous with Capt. Bully Jelks for a short cruise to Gibraltar and Morocco. Sam didn't define what he meant by short. He urged her to remain composed and do nothing until he returned.

Sad and defeated, Jenny threw his note on the carpet. "I can't. I can't."

She knew herself better than that. Of course she could. She looked down at Sam's apology and ground it under her foot.

43
Prince's Journey

Prince found a map of France in the Redwood Library and memorized its basic features. An old issue of the *Newport Mercury*, twittering over the arrival of a Russian nobleman, informed him that Count I. Orlov purveyed expensive antiques from a shop on the Rue de Rivoli, Paris. He wrote it down on the blank inside cover of the Larousse grammar.

He delivered Rex to Jumbo Sullivan, who promised to care for him. He bid a tearful farewell to the Youmanskys, who gave him a list of cheap but worthy restaurants in Paris, coupled with an admission that some or all of them might be out of business. Marcel presented Prince with a sack of tomato and basil bread sticks as a parting gift.

He gave notice to O. H. P. Belmont, explaining only that he had to leave for a while. Belmont expressed regret, complimented him again on good work habits and his pluck and quick thinking during the race. He tipped Prince $20 and wished him godspeed.

On the Atlantic crossing he rediscovered his sea legs, and found a new self-confidence. Gordon Bennett's sous chef, a Portugee named Romeo, nicknamed him Brains because he stuck his nose into one of his books every spare moment. The Newport nuns had dismissed him as a likable but undistinguished lower-class Irish boy of limited intelligence. He studied till his head ached, sometimes under the moon on the heaving deck.

A man was *un homme.*

Driver's daughter was *une fille.*

You said *merci* for thanks, *s'il vous plaît* asking for help.

He thought out how he must proceed, a penniless stranger, in an unfamiliar country. Yes, he'd have to steal occasionally to survive, but to do it he'd do no physical harm to another person. It set limits he was glad to have.

Namouna passed close by the south coast of England and put in briefly at Portsmouth to provision. Already dark brown from the weather, Prince marveled at the sea change in his attitude about travel. As a youngster he'd stayed comfortably close to the bays and harbors of Rhode Island; even the rail trip to New York had created anxiety.

How much greater, then, to sail halfway across the world and find it not alarming, but exhilarating? He remembered old wives' tales of a flat earth with a finite end, a cliff off which great sailing ships dropped, forever lost. Columbus and others had proved the earth was a sphere but Prince saw no sign of it, just a gentle, invisible transition that brought you from one place to another. By the time Gordon Bennett's yacht anchored in sight of the lights of a French fishing village, Prince knew he had nothing to fear from any new land, except the unexpected.

Gordon Bennett came to the ladder where Prince waited to climb down with his canvas rucksack.

"I hope we meet again, Molloy. I'd like to know how your

adventure works out. Here are twenty francs to speed you on your way. Give my greetings to your mysterious lady."

"I will, sir, *merci beaucoup*."

"Your accent's dreadful, but a smile or two should overcome that. Safe journey, *mons fils*."

Several of the deck- and galley hands including Romeo saw him off in the cutter. The last thing Prince heard from the grinning, waving Portugee was, "*Adeus*, Brains, *adeus*."

The map he'd memorized took him roughly southeast, toward the city of Rouen. The onset of summer brought warm days, cool nights. He slept in barns, orchards, haylofts and, twice, the vestibule of a country cathedral. At the first, the priest kicked him awake and ordered him out with choleric accusations of possession by the devil. At the second, the gouty old father invited him to sit down to a platter of sausages and hot bread, prepared by a buxom lady who seemed to pat the cleric with unusual familiarity.

Kilometer after kilometer, he trudged along dusty roads where cattle lowed and sunburned farmers cultivated their fields. Here and there he stole: dark blue pantaloons, a peasant blouse with tight cuffs to ward off insects, a midnight-blue scarf with a faded pattern of stars, work boots, a beret. He stole to eat: apples, small slabs of cheese, warm baguettes, oranges from Provence. He lost weight steadily. His hair hung below his collar. He'd packed a straight razor in his rucksack and every second or third day he scraped his face free of stubble, leaving a small mustache. He examined the mustache in the reflecting waters of a stream and considered it "Frenchified." He looked more like a footloose peasant every day.

His grasp of the language, his vocabulary, grew to fifty words and phrases, then a hundred.

He believed Jenny was lost to him, wrapped in the chains of

matrimony that he had neither the skill nor the wherewithal to break. His pilgrimage had the same kind of purpose that had directed his life when he first encountered Jenny on the Newport quay—revenge. Not against her this time but her husband, the culprit behind the fire, he was convinced. When he disposed of the Russian, he'd consider what to do about Samuel Driver. Since he had no intention of harming Jenny, and presumably she loved her father, that course was less clear.

In Rouen, at three in the morning, he used a rock wrapped in old newspapers to break a pawnbroker's window. He crawled in through the jagged opening and emerged with *un rigolo*, a revolver. He knew nothing about it other than that it appeared to be in good working order.

He followed the meandering Seine. He slept beside level crossings, awakened periodically by smoking, thundering locomotives pulling long trains of cars. He'd been on the road for a month and a half, perhaps two—summer's heat had settled on the land—when, following the tracks, he began to pass through large areas of cement-block tenements from whose tiny balconies came the shrieking of infants, the voices of hectoring wives, the racket of kitchen pots. On a crooked street in the city's western suburbs he came upon a shop whose window glass bore the gold silhouette of a handgun above the words *Le Corse.* A sun-faded show card propped in a corner read BUY – SELL – ENGLISH SPOKEN.

The proprietor, *Le Corse*, the Corsican, was a roly-poly man with straight gray hair to his shoulders and an oil-spotted smock. Prince showed the revolver. The shop owner looked the traveler up and down.

"My, my, young sir," he said in raspy English, "this is a fine piece. Did you come by it from your inheritance? Or as a birthday present from a rich maiden aunt?"

"You're mocking me."

"No, young sir, merely wondering what stroke of fortune brought you into possession of a Galand model 1869, widely used by our officers in the Franco-Prussian War a year after the gun's introduction. Galands performed better than our officers. Of course I never inquire as to where a gun comes from; I only compliment you on its, ah, availability to your hands."

"It's a good piece?"

"Excellent. Double action, open frame—notice, no strap across the top of the cylinder. Rapid fire, to be sure, but you'll discover it has a long trigger pull. This piece has been well cared for."

"Do you sell ammunition?"

"I have nine millimeter, yes. You'll want to practice a bit; it's less accurate at longer ranges than a single action."

Le Corse brought forth a soiled cardboard box. They haggled but the fat *propriétaire* refused to budge on the price. "If, of course, you could show me a passport or, of course, a permit for the weapon, then, of course, I should be obliged to chisel a few sous off the tariff. With this transaction you are asking me to assume risk and, of course, that I cannot do for the sake of my ex-wives, numerous children and grandchildren, and my old age."

Prince had to dip into his shrinking fund of francs. He walked out without telling the Corsican that he wasn't worried about accuracy, he'd use the Galand at close range, to blow a hole in a man's belly. Stomach wounds were almost always fatal.

He walked beside deeply shadowed railroad tracks. Buildings became larger, more fashionable. The tracks took him to the busy Gare St.-Lazare. He darted inside, past an outbound local spouting steam from underneath. He slipped along a crowded platform, his head down, avoiding eye contact. He limped into the street where horse-drawn cabs queued up and horseless Panhard and Benz autos went by, delighting some of the Parisians, infuriating others. A cab horse reared at a honking auto, broke his traces and galloped away.

Prince crossed the city's right bank to the Seine, impossibly lovely and shady, a haven for strolling couples, artists with easels, aggressive streetwalkers, beggars and vagabonds. He rolled out his thin blanket beneath a busy bridge and dropped off to sleep before sunset, exhausted.

He woke suddenly to find a monkey-faced fellow with a long knife menacing his throat. A lighted barge glided by, heading upstream; an unseen musician played a concertina.

The man knelt on Prince's chest, made a grasping motion with his free hand. "*Monnaie, monnaie, Anglais.*" Which was not so hard to translate.

"*Oui, oui, attendent, attendent.*" He hoped he was correctly asking the robber to wait. He shifted his rucksack from under his shoulder, opened it, and with a deft grab, pulled the loaded pistol. He rocked the hammer back, jabbed the barrel in the thief's throat.

The thief dropped his knife and ran. Upstream, the concertina wailed of love or some equivalent sadness. Prince pulled his beret over his eyes and slept without fear.

"*Où est il?*" Prince tapped the scrap on which he'd written *Comte I. Orlov.*

The gentleman behind the counter of *Libraire Percy* smelled sweet. A pink carnation decorated his lapel. He ogled Prince in a disconcerting way. From an upper shelf he took a city directory, which he laid on the counter. He managed to brush Prince's hand as he ran an index finger down a page.

"Orlov, Orlov." He rotated the book and pointed, touching Prince again.

The first entry, with *d'antiquités* following the count's name, referred to an address on the Rue de Rivoli. The second, *résidence*, showed a number on the Boulevard des Capucines. Prince thanked M. Percy, who pouted noticeably as Prince hurried out.

The elderly concierge came out of her cabin inside the elegant marble vestibule. Behind him, hansoms and trams and drays and an occasional auto violated the leafy charm of the neighborhood, where Prince felt distinctly out of place in his country garb. The concierge's frown said she agreed.

He unfolded the scrap bearing Orlov's name. The old woman, who smelled of onions at half past ten in the morning, took the scrap and the two francs, Prince's last, that he'd hoarded for just such an eventuality.

After surveying him from boots to beret, the old woman clicked her false teeth and pointed skyward; he thought she was directing him to the top floor. He snatched off his beret, kissed her hand, and slipped past her. As he climbed, she continued to pepper him with incomprehensible bursts of French—inquiries about the purpose of his call, maybe.

Prince's palms sweated as he rounded one dim and creaky landing after another. What if Jenny was in the flat?

At the flat's enameled door, beneath a dusty skylight where spots of rain had dried, he took his pistol from his rucksack. He checked the loads in the cylinder. He pulled out his blouse, hid the gun in his belt.

Then he knocked.

44
ANOTHER REUNION, THREE FLIGHTS UP

And then he saw her, standing there in an unbecoming day dress, mousy tan with touches of black trim.

Jenny started to speak sharply, as to an unwelcome tradesman. She recognized the face thrown out of kilter by the black mustache, the deeply browned skin. Tears filled the corners of her eyes. "Oh my God. Oh my God. Is it—?"

"*Bonjour*, Jenny."

"You look like a gypsy."

"You look like you've been in a train wreck. What happened?"

She remembered her fading bruise, more yellow-brown than purple now. Her raised hand failed to hide it. Prince meantime reeled inwardly at the pale, shrunken look of her cheeks, her darkly circled eyes.

"I fell."

"I know you better than that. Who hit you? Your husband?"

She glanced away, a confession.

"Where is he?"

"In Hades for all I care." She drew a breath, looked at him directly again with those heartbreaking blue eyes. "I'm going to divorce him."

"Here?"

"No, I'll go home. Newport, or New York. How did you get to Paris?"

"I'll tell you if we don't have to stand in the hallway all day." His old, boyish smile broke through.

She smiled too, or made the attempt, stood back. Plainly flustered, she added, "Come in, then, please. Would you like something? A coffee?"

He followed her through the foyer to the reception parlor of the flat, intimidated by its size, all the fine furniture pieces, mirrors, lamps in every corner and open space. "I'd love a little bread. And whiskey."

She left him perched on the crocheted seat of a chair so insubstantial he feared his weight would break it. She returned with a lacquered tray, cleared a taboret of its parade of five elephants, carved teak, each smaller than the one before.

She watched, not approvingly, as he lifted the shot glass and drained it in quick swallows. He wiped his mouth with the starry bandanna.

"Let me ask you again. Where's your husband? At his shop?"

"So far as I know."

"When does he come home?"

"Evening. What do you want with him?"

"A talk. A little talk," Prince answered, conscious of the revolver under his blouse.

"You're not the same young fellow I met in Newport."

"I hope I'm not as stupid. I traveled across France on foot.

I learned a little of the language. I can do more than I ever supposed."

"How proud I am to hear you say that. Will you come home with me?"

"The United States?"

She nodded.

"If it's possible."

"What do you mean?"

Silent, he tore a chunk from the baguette. He chewed it without meeting her eye.

It was a strange, and strangely tranquil, afternoon, there in the luxurious apartment thousands of miles from where they'd met. Carillons chimed distantly; tenants on the floor below rattled up and down stairs. They sat facing one another across the reception parlor, very decorous, very proper, like a swain paying a call on a maiden. Three tall windows bordered by narrow bands of leaded glass framed gabled copper roofs of identical third-floor flats across the boulevard. The three windows showed a spring sky gradually turning from pale blue to a hazy lavender.

After she'd listened to his long account of his journey, she said, "I honestly thought you'd abandoned me."

"I thought the same. I believe it's what your father wanted. Still wants."

A shake of her head. "I've obeyed my last order from him."

"At the Cup races that day, I wanted to tell you what happened to me, and why. I did come to New York the way I promised."

Violet as the early evening sky in the changing light, her eyes showed astonishment. "I never knew that."

"You weren't supposed to know, that's my guess."

"Does anyone in our household know?"

"We could ask Mozart."

"Mozart's dead. Papa had a cable when we arrived. Mozart drowned himself in a lagoon in Newport."

Prince's mind leaped. He saw a narrow door of escape from the dilemma Sam Driver represented.

She said, "Tell me why you're limping. Was that from New York?"

"It started there. Some roughnecks threw me on a train to Providence, then beat me something fierce when we arrived. I'll never walk straight." His mouth quirked. "You noticed before— I'm not the broth of a boy you met at the Casino."

"Oh, Prince. Do you think it makes any difference? I love you so. I fought it and fought it but every time I turned around, there it was."

"You married the count."

"Papa urged it. I thought you'd gone for good." She ran the back of a hand under one eye, the other, then said softly but clearly, "Who hired the men who hurt you? Was it my father?"

Prince unbent, heard his knees crack as he rose to watch late afternoon crowds hurrying to restaurants and bistros, love affairs and financial transactions. The imaginary door beckoned. . . .

"I expect Mozart Gribble understood your father's feelings and hired those men on his own. Mozart threw me off the stoop on Fifth Avenue, left me groggy on the curb. Next thing I know, two bullyboys were hauling me onto the night local."

"You're saying my father—"

"Had nothing to do with it. Nothing of which anyone could accuse him."

A great mass, a weight of iron, seemed to rise off his shoulders. Jenny's disfigured face shone with joy. *Secrets within secrets,* Prince thought. *Lies within lies.* But he felt better for it.

"What are you going to do to my husband? You didn't travel all the way to Paris for conversation, did you?"

"The truth? I came to shoot him." Prince pulled the Galand from under his blouse.

She reacted neither with alarm nor a great deal of surprise, almost as though it was the most natural thing in the world for someone to want to dispose of Orlov. Instead, she said, "They'll execute you. He's a French citizen. In France they still use the guillotine."

Prince heard a light tread on the stairs. "One thing at a time. You don't have to watch this. I guess I'd rather you didn't."

Footsteps louder.

Jenny unmoving . . .

A key in the lock was immediately withdrawn. Orlov strode through the foyer to the reception parlor, not winded or perspiring, immaculate as though his day had begun only moments ago. "Curious damned business, the door open—"

He saw Prince and the revolver, framed by the middle of the three windows.

Orlov stood his lacquered stick in a tall Japanese jar, perched his black silk hat on the gold knob. He plucked out his monocle.

"All the way from Rhode Island?"

"Yes, sir. Believe it."

Whatever tension or fear flooded up in Orlov, he was expert at hiding it. He let his monocle drop on its dark green ribbon. He jerked the neat points of his folded handkerchief from his breast pocket and wiped his lips, his forehead.

"You insignificant piece of shit. How dare you invade my home? Harass my wife? I'll deal with you, but not here."

The click of the cocking hammer arrested him in midstride. Prince held the revolver in his right hand. With his left he tugged up his blouse to show the narrow ridge of pink and brown scarring that ran from his belt to his armpit.

"I wanted you to see what the fire did."

Jenny said, "What fire?"

"Someone burned the building behind my uncle's shop on Thames Street. Someone set the fire and hoped I'd burn up too. Is this something else they kept from you?"

She pressed white knuckles to her lips, unable to do more than nod. Finally she said, "When this fire started, were you in your garret?"

"Yes, asleep, or trying."

Orlov seized her arm. "How do you know it was a garret?"

"Because I saw it, more than once. Because I made love with him there. That's how I know."

Orlov thrust his hands to her neck, clamped them. "*Catin. Putain.* You betrayed me with him?"

"Let her go," Prince shouted, wanting to shoot, fearful of hitting her. He ran to Orlov, shoving the revolver in his belt to free his hands. Orlov pushed him backward.

Prince's heavy boots slid on the carpet. Orlov seized a heavy silver candlestick, one of a pair ornamenting a side table. Before Prince could right himself, Orlov brained him across the temple with the candlestick.

Prince flailed with both arms. Orlov hit him again, left ear. Blood gushed. Prince fell against an étagère, smashed the glass shelves, spilled the Limoges china and the little wooden stands in an avalanche of broken pieces. Blood leaked from Prince's ear down over his collar and the blue bandanna with the stars.

Orlov wrested the pistol from Prince's belt. He held it in both hands, recocking the hammer Prince had eased off. Prince lay in the wreckage, too dazed to do more than stare into the muzzle. Orlov steadied the Galand for a shot.

A leaping shadow startled him. He twisted around, astonished, but with too little time to be enraged. Jenny swung a Louis XIV chair with both hands.

She stabbed a chair leg into Orlov's throat. He dropped the revolver, seized the chair to tear it away from her, screaming curses, French or Russian, it was hard to tell. Jenny looked sixty years old, her eyes stark blind with hatred, her lips back like a savage mastiff's as she threw her whole weight forward.

In an attempt to save his balance Orlov let go of the chair. He did a peculiar little dance at the edge of the carpet, his momentum dragging him on. He lurched against the left-hand window, shattered it, waving his arms and crying out as he dropped three floors.

He struck the roof of a slow-moving omnibus, crashed through, disappeared. Inside the omnibus, tourists screamed. A gendarme down the way blew a whistle. The omnibus jolted up over the curb, tilting dangerously on two wheels. The terrified nag pulling it dropped huge turds on the cobbles.

A man jumped out of the omnibus, shouting a word Prince knew. It drifted above the excited people who rushed around the omnibus, gesticulating, questioning. Prince heard the word clearly in the purple dusk.

Mort. Mort . . .

Jenny moaned. They had perhaps one or two minutes before the broken window brought the gendarmerie trampling up the stairs. He scooped the revolver from the floor, ran through a door, rejected the kitchen, ran through a hall, found a bedroom decorated with racehorse prints, a man's room. A bottom drawer, the third drawer that he pulled out, held red and white striped nightshirts, blue and white striped pajama suits with patch pockets, all meticulously folded. Prince hid the unfired revolver under the fancy nightwear.

He ran back to Jenny and hugged her, stroking her hair.

"We tell them he fell accidentally. We tell them he found you talking to an old lover and went crazy. We tell them that, nothing more. We'll be alright."

Or so he prayed.

Heavy feet rode up the outer stairs like cavalry.

Secrets within secrets. Lies within lies . . .

Jenny cried while he held her and they waited.

45
Summer's End

The Golden Anchor, a modest town-house inn facing Washington Square, catered to Newport visitors who couldn't afford better. These visitors often came seeking bargains in late September, when the leaves were once again dying and the steamers crowded with departing servants. Prince and Jenny took two connecting rooms because Jenny wouldn't stay at Red Rose, though she bought a red rose from a florist shop and helped Prince stand on a rickety chair to put a tack through the stem, pinning the flower above her bed. They left the door between their rooms unlocked.

Two weeks of police questioning and deposing before a French magistrate had cleared them of any responsibility for Ismail Orlov's death, which was officially designated an accident. Jenny feared Sam and Tessa would return from their cruise before she and Prince escaped but they didn't. An American embassy employee amenable to bribery accepted $500 to draw up an impressive but meaningless "Travel Permit" for Prince

"I am not the secretary of state," he said. "If this doesn't get you past the customs officers, there's nothing more I can do. Tip the way you tipped me, you should have no difficulty."

They took a wagon-lit to Calais, a ferry to Dover—Jenny sick again from the turbulent night crossing—sooty trains to London and then Southampton, where they embarked on the White Star Line's *Germanic*, bound for Boston. At every barrier or turnstile, Prince's bogus permit was accepted and stamped, supplemented only twice with cash.

One of the larger ships of Ismay's Oceanic Steam Navigation Company, *Germanic* offered three classes of passage. Jenny preferred to stay out of first class, so they settled for second. Prince complained that she was paying for everything.

"Because you don't have a penny to your name, sweet." She kissed him. "One day you will."

His smile charmed her. "Yes, I will. I'll make something of myself, when I figure out what I should be. I can do it. France taught me that much."

Once in Newport, Prince hiked out to Jumbo Sullivan's. He found Rex napping in the sunshine in Jumbo's horse corral. He whistled.

Rex opened an agate-colored eye, recognized the whistler, began leaping and barking. Sullivan appeared, a reunion with much laughter and backslapping.

"You plannin' to take the pup?"

"They don't allow animals at the Golden Anchor. If you can look after him a while longer, I'll collect him when we leave the island."

"Ayah, I can do that. Where you headed?"

"Not sure yet. Someplace where I can make some money, and study."

"Study what?"

"To be better than I was around here."

"Just remember this. Wherever you go, stay humble."

"Considering the state of my finances I don't have a lot of choice. One day things'll be different."

Prince ran into Titus on Thames Street, told him where he and Jenny were staying. After Titus finished extolling Prince's rather dashing appearance—Jenny had paid for barbering his long hair—Prince walked off feeling cheerful about the encounter.

Unfortunately it was a misguided complacency. Late the next day, the desk man at the Golden Anchor knocked at Jenny's door. Prince sat up on the bed, wearing drawers and a singlet. Jenny belted her robe and unlatched the door.

"Beg pardon, miss, there's a gent downstairs claims he's your father. Wishes to come up."

Instantly, Jenny said, "No. Let me comb my hair and I'll come down."

The door closed on the desk man gaping at the rose hanging from one of his ceiling beams.

Prince reached for his boots. "I'll go with you."

"Sweetheart, this is mine to do alone."

She slipped out of her robe, naked and lovely and, Prince realized, unable to be argued out of her resolve.

In the lobby, an obese woman with three quarreling brats was just trundling into the street, fanning herself with a tourist map and loudly wishing she were back in Asbury Park. Sam rose from an old couch showing cracks in its leather upholstery. He was smartly turned out in a single-breasted morning coat with a cutaway front, a top hat, black leather button boots with patent leather toes.

"That's a handsome suit, Papa."

"Jermyn Street, London. Is there somewhere we can go to talk?"

"This will do fine. Please sit." She arranged herself on the couch and waited.

Sam eyed the desk man fiercely enough to drive him away behind a partition.

"You can't stay in this shabby place."

"Why not? It's clean. I'm very happy here while we get ourselves organized."

"You and that Molloy."

"He'll be my husband as soon as I'm sure the book's closed on Ismail and the French authorities want nothing more to do with me. I've hired a Newport attorney to stand by in case I need help. We weren't detained at Calais, so I hope the affair of Count Orlov and his unfortunate death is behind us."

"And now you propose to live in sin until you remarry."

Jenny's color was better than at the start of summer; when she laughed, it was hearty. "Oh, Papa. I'm already living in sin, there's no *propose* about it."

"Come home. Red Rose."

"No. Where I am with Prince, that's home."

Sam's struggle came forth when he said, "I'll even tolerate that Irishman in my house."

"That's it, don't you see—? Your house, no one else's. I appreciate what it takes for you to make the offer, and I thank you, but, no, we can't."

"Damn it, you'll defy me again?"

"Not defy, Papa. Please calm down. I'm just not the young woman I was when we saw Newport for the first time. I understand what you tried to do for me, and it was kind, and laudable, but it wasn't right. Not for me. I realized that by degrees. For a long time I wouldn't acknowledge it. I think I changed permanently when Mamie Fish and Harry Lehr amused themselves with a banquet for dogs. For *dogs*, Papa. I remember Mother speaking about her father—"

Sam grimaced. "The old Bible-thumper."

"He believed the First Commandment. Thank heaven he never saw this place—how many false gods are worshipped. Money, never earned the way you earned yours, by hard work, and risk. Fashion is a god. Another is reputation, which means exactly nothing in the grave."

She stroked his age-spotted hand. "I don't want you to feel badly. I'll be perfectly content with Prince the rest of my life."

"Doing what? Running a hash house? A one-room school for brattish little girls?"

"It doesn't matter so long as Prince is happy. He's not the man he was. He's more than people credited him with being."

Sam rose from the couch, fretfully turning his top hat in both hands. "So that's your decision. You are defying me, Jenny. Rejecting everything I've bought, and done, for you. Kindly don't lecture me about Grandfather Penny's so-called wisdom. The old fool died a pauper, intestate. He never wrote a will because he had nothing to leave your poor mother except worthless pieties. As soon as you're through rutting with your Irish stud—"

"I won't listen to such language."

"—you'll be through with him too. Crawling back to New York and Newport, trying to curry favor with old friends."

"No."

Shoulders a little straighter, Sam plopped his tall hat on his graying curls.

"I don't believe you. When you come back, you'll be my Jenny again. Then I'll consider writing you into my will. But not before."

46
The Tigress at Twilight

Brady scheduled departure of *Ozymandias* for early Friday, intending to be at Sunrise by evening. His week in the city had been a disaster three times over. First, his current mistress, a buxom bookkeeper for a Broadway theater, packed her things and waved ta-ta, making it worse by informing him that he was an old, old man, wholly inadequate in bed.

His brokerage firm discovered a loss of $450,000, the embezzler a lowly clerk calling himself Dillard Smathers. The bored detectives who interviewed the embezzler's brother in the slums reported that Diego DiPerla had adopted the name Smathers from some misguided idea that it would transform him from what he was, a greaser. Brady hated greasers. Even more than that, he hated anyone who stole so much as a penny from him.

No, the police could do nothing, Smathers-DiPerla had already left U.S. territorial waters on a banana boat bound for

Honduras. Brady's second day in the clamorous streets of Manhattan ended as had the first, a debacle.

The third blow, the last and heaviest, came when he answered the polite summons of Em's alienist, whom she had been visiting on a twice-monthly basis. Dr. Valentin Glucksmann was Vienna-trained, with a fine reputation. But Brady hated foreigners, especially European Jews.

Dr. Glucksmann, small and soft-spoken, offered him tea, coffee, a slice of his wife's strudel in the lace-curtain sitting room adjoining his consultation chamber. Nearly sleepless for two nights, Brady erupted.

"Why are you stalling? Continue Em's treatment more frequently. I'll pay you anything, only get her well, out of her damned fog."

Brady slapped the fat leather arms of the guest chair. "Why are you shaking your head?"

"There is no easy way to say this, Mr. Brady."

"Then just say it, I'm not paying your outrageous hourly charges to be offered strudel and bromides."

Dr. Glucksmann removed his round eyeglasses. "I cannot in conscience continue to accept your money. I must resign from your wife's case."

"You little Jew shit, I'll find someone to replace you."

Glucksmann's large eyes, moist and brown, expressed remorse rather than anger. "Sir, that is certainly your prerogative. In my opinion the outcome will always be the same. Mrs. Brady is beyond recovery. She needs to be institutionalized."

"No, you're wrong, you're mistaken."

"Shout all you want. It won't change her sorry state of mind. She lives in another era—perhaps five years ago, or twenty-five, I'm not positive. But there's no reality in it, only ghosts."

Brady wanted to beat the little Jew's face to red paste. Perhaps because at heart he knew the alienist wasn't lying, he paid his balance and got out of the office. He visited a brothel near the old Five Points, where he drank half a bottle of whiskey and fell asleep with his trousers at half-mast.

The girl, fourteen, tucked his payment in her bloomers and left the little room, whose only pretense at artistry was a Japanese screen illustrated with drawings of men and women copulating in unusual positions. If she'd shared a cup of tea with the theater bookkeeper, they'd have agreed that poor old William K. Brady III was a dreadful lover.

Brady's plan to reach Newport and hide away ran afoul of a swift nor'easter that overtook *Ozymandias* shortly after the yacht passed Block Island. By the time Brady's captain fought the yacht to her berth in Newport Harbor, Brady was not only full of rage but bilious with seasickness. Rain beat down on the quay. Brady berated his driver for failing to bring an umbrella. His outpouring of foul language startled the driver, who had heard plenty from his employer, but never at such length.

The coach swung up the empty drive of Sunrise. A few watery lights glimmered in the lower windows. Brady drank from a pint flask kept in the pocket of his sodden overcoat. He flung the empty flask into the bushes and ran for the door.

It opened before him, revealing Honoria with Dickie Glossop. Both were pale, clearly unnerved. Honoria clutched the door with her left hand; there she wore the gaudy diamond from Cartier's that had sealed her engagement to the architect. Dickie hovered at her shoulder, an expression of pious concern on his white face.

"Oh, Papa, thank God, we feared for you in this storm."

"Just rain, nothing worse." Brady peeled off his overcoat, dropped it dripping on the marble. He staggered; Dickie caught him, eased him to a bench. Brady covered his eyes, fearing he'd be sick.

"Can you get up?" Honoria asked.

" 'Course, perfectly sober." He demonstrated by standing, then falling sideways. Dickie had to brace him a second time.

"Where's Mrs. Brady?"

"In the dining room," Dickie said, flashing a mysteriously bleak look at Honoria.

"I wouldn't go in there," Honoria said. "She's having another of her spells."

"Her spells?" A bucket of cold brine might have been thrown on Brady, so quickly did he sober. "I'm sick of her damned *spells*. From now on she'll have them in an asylum."

"Father, please," Honoria began, only to have Brady seize her, drag her out of the way. He stormed to the dining room, where sconces and candlesticks flickered and smoked. His shoes left a trail of water.

The Tigress once more sat at the head of the mahogany table, her grayed hair flawlessly done, her wattled throat and mottled hands flashing and gleaming with her collection of diamonds and emeralds, rubies and sapphires.

She chirped prettily as a songbird. "I'm so glad you're in time, dear. We're entertaining sixty people and many of them are already here."

"Where are they? Not in the driveway, it's deserted."

Bewildered, Em passed a hand across her eyes. "Truly? Then they must have parked nearby. In any case, you'll be glad to see who's already arrived."

She spoke to empty places at the fully set table.

"Mamie's here, say hello to Mamie. Dear Harry who's promised to play for us after dinner. Arleigh Mould came all the way from Cincinnati."

One by one she named them; one by one she pointed to vacant chairs.

"Girard St. Ong. Alva Belmont and Ollie. My very dear friend Caroline Astor."

Brady wheeled, shouting for Honoria. She ran to him, Dickie anxiously dry-washing his hands close behind. Honoria embraced her father, pressed her cheek against his damp shirt bosom.

"I didn't want you to see her. She spent all morning supervising the table arrangements, all afternoon dressing and making the maid do her hair. I can't imagine what caused this."

"Not what. Who. I know who did this to her. That tramp who pretended to be your friend."

"Jenny Driver?"

"Yes, isn't she back in Newport?"

"And her father too, a week ago."

Brady's pallor, his disarrayed hair, his sunken eyes made him resemble some grotesque exhibit in a waxwork display.

"The Drivers. Sam Driver. They destroyed a fine woman. They'll do no more damage."

A half hour later Brady left Sunrise on foot, wrapped in a dry greatcoat and silk hat, another half bottle of whiskey in his pocket to fuel his determination. The nor'easter howled in the black vault of night. The rain fell harder, and still harder.

47
Jenny's Defiance

Several hours before the big blow struck the island, Prince put on his cap and trotted off to the Fall River ticket office to arrange passage to New York. After Jenny saw him out the door she decided this was her opportunity; if she told him what she planned, he might try to stop her. She threw her bathing costume into a canvas satchel, hired a horse-drawn cab and arrived at Bailey's Beach under a threatening sky.

The gatekeeper, an octogenarian by now, held his post in his gold-braided finery. "Blustery day, Miz Driver. My sciatica tells me there's a whopper of a storm coming."

"I can guarantee it," Jenny replied with an angelic smile.

She unlocked the Driver cabana, found it filled with drifted sand and the staleness of the damp sea air. The cabana had been so important to Sam at the beginning, and enjoyed so little use anymore. She donned her beach costume, black from hat to shoes, and stepped outside.

A few elderly idlers watched in a bored way as she walked

down to the surf under a darkening sky. In one of the front cabanas, an old lady whose name she couldn't remember spied on her with bird-watching glasses. Jenny took off her black bonnet and sailed it over the white curls of the breaking surf.

She shook out her hair and waved to the old lady with the glasses. The watcher promptly lowered the canvas that hid the beach.

One by one Jenny kicked her square-toed black shoes into the water. She rolled down her left stocking to the ankle, exposing white flesh. She did the same with her right stocking. A gray-haired spindleshanks tottered out of his chair, his eyes bulging.

Jenny unbuttoned her sleeve buttons at the wrist and rolled up both sleeves to the elbow, followed by a hint of cleavage as she opened the neck of her bathing dress. She could sense the stillness of the beach; those watching her sat or stood still as statues sculpted by astonishment.

Showing more white skin than was tolerated on Bailey's Beach, or possibly ever seen there before, Jenny marched back to the road. She paused to speak to the old gatekeeper, who seemed ready for heart failure when he realized she was barefoot and, in other scandalous areas, bare.

"My father's up at Red Rose. Please tell him for me that if he wants to sell or otherwise transfer our cabana to a new tenant, he may. I won't be coming back."

"No," the gatekeeper wheezed, "you most surely won't, not after this display of vulgarity and impropriety."

"Oh, do go stuff yourself," Jenny said with that unwavering angelic smile. She pointed to the boiling sky. "Storm's almost here, I'd take cover."

She proceeded to the waiting cab, sand between her toes, her hair flying in the sea wind, her heart exultant. She imagined she heard another idol crashing down.

48
Brady's Wrath

A minor ailment delayed Tessa's arrival at Red Rose—an unspecified "female complaint"—but she'd sent a special railway express package as a preview of her presence. The carton contained bottles of celery tonic, pills for "nerves," pills for "manly vigor," purgatives in both liquid and tablet form, a new spiky German-designed toothbrush that looked more like a medieval torture device than a health aid, extra gloves, both wool and leather, and shiny rubber overshoes. Except in the army Sam had never worn overshoes and he never would.

Dear Tessa was a bit crazy on matters of health but he'd come to love her for it. He kept the open carton in his bedroom, in plain view, altogether as good a reminder of her as a framed photograph; he had a half dozen of those already.

On the evening of the storm, he brooded alone in his study, one question nagging at him. Why hadn't Molloy accused him of the very real crime of arranging for men to beat and injure him, that night when Sam himself fought the Irish boy on the slushy steps of the Fifth Avenue mansion?

Disconsolate, he tried to make sense of a revised architect's elevation and footprint for a new St. Michael the Archangel hospital in Columbus. Ohio. The blue lines blurred. The dimensions so carefully inked might have been in Chinese.

Sam's head hurt. His eyes watered. Angrily, he broke his reading glasses at the nosepiece and threw both halves in the cold fireplace. He needed new spectacles. He needed a new life. The first one, he could buy.

At five in the afternoon, a member of the Spouting Rock Beach Association board called with a report on Jenny's behavior earlier in the afternoon.

"My daughter no longer lives here," Sam said.

"A good thing, because she'll never be allowed at Bailey's again. She behaved like a tramp."

Sam tugged off his cravat, cracked his knuckles, advanced slowly on the whey-faced caller, an undertaker by trade. "I suggest you haul your nasty ass out of here because if you say one more word about my Jenny, you won't be able to crawl."

"You're not the man we thought you were, Driver. You're not the sort we want in Newport."

"And vice versa. Are you going?"

"Going," the man quavered, backing up, jamming his straw hat on, running nose-first into the door, so blind and hasty was his flight.

Sam poured himself a large barrel glass of whiskey as nature supplied a storm of mounting intensity. He latched the shutters in the study, drew the heavy velvet drapes. He slumped in his reading chair, alternately drinking and leafing the pages of the *Mercury*, trying to read without glasses. Dickie Glossop's wedding was announced for October, according to the bride's parents. Well, well, . . . Dickie the opportunist, secure at last. No doubt he'd build his own cottage in a year or so.

An outer door leading to the side lawn creaked, as though someone leaned against it.

Sam peered at the door with its curtained window light. The door creaked a second time.

His reactions slowed by liquor, Sam lumbered toward it. Whoever was outside exerted heavy pressure again; the lock gave, bringing pelting rain, and the intruder, out of the dark.

"I thought there was a door here. I thought it might get me in."

"For God's sake, Bill, close it."

Sam tried to remember the whereabouts of the servants. His butler had the evening off. He'd sent cook and the maids home early because of the storm. An elderly footman was the only person on duty, sleeping far away in his room beneath the eaves. He was deaf as a post, hardly to be expected to hear unusual noises downstairs, especially with the nor'easter moaning and shaking the roof.

W. K. Brady's overcoat dripped water on the carpet. Sam smelled him, a walking distillery. Sam was drunk, but compared to Brady he might have been sipping mother's milk. Wet strands of hair framed Brady's beaky face like parentheses.

"What do you want here, Bill? We have no business."

"Hell we don't, you gutter lowlife."

"Turn around and walk out that door. Sit in the rain until you sober up."

"Trying to get rid of me? Miserable coward." Brady slurred his words. His hand dropped to an overcoat pocket. He showed Sam the silvery blade of his knife.

"My wife's non compos mentis because of you and that whore daughter of yours. You two conspired to ensure her rejection here in Newport."

"Of all the damn nonsensical—"

"Em will spend the rest of her life in a barred room somewhere, eating bad food and reading her Bible and singing nursery rhymes, if she can remember any. I hold you accountable."

"You're out of your fucking mind."

Sam moved away to pour more whiskey in the barrel glass. His chest hurt. He remembered Fisk, poor Jim, who might have been saved if someone had intervened to foil a killer. Sam drew a breath, pivoted suddenly and threw the whiskey in Brady's face.

Spitting, Brady wiped his dripping cheeks with his coat sleeve. Sam flung himself forward, cracked Brady's knife wrist over his knee.

Brady swore. Sam turned to throw the knife into a corner, a mistake. He heard Brady moving before he saw him charging, both hands raising a fireplace poker seized from the hearth.

The poker slashed down. Sam braced his legs, caught Brady's wrists inches above his head. He sweated and pushed and slowly, slowly raised Brady's arms, and the weapon. Brady's bleary eyes were inches from Sam's, his breathing spasmodic, his yellowing teeth giving off odors of tobacco and a sour stomach. Brady pushed, his wrists descending again. Sam thought of little Jay's motto hanging in his office on Fifth Avenue.

Brady wheezed and grunted, straining against Sam's grip. Sam's hands ached, rheumatism and age taking a toll. He shifted his balance suddenly, leaped aside to let Brady's weight carry him to the carpet with a loud exclamation. Brady's fingers loosened on the poker. Sam scooped it away.

Brady flopped on his back, wild-eyed, drunkenly defiant. "Go on, you son of a bitch, kill me."

Sam's arms shook. He was sorely tempted.

"Go on, what are you waiting for?"

"Bill, get up."

"What?"

"Drag your sorry ass back to Sunrise. Sleep until you sober up. You aren't worth killing. You aren't worth a gob of spit."

Sam stepped back, puzzled by strange expressions that seemed to flash across Brady's face like rapidly changing magic lantern pictures. Brady was pathetically grateful for the reprieve but the next moment angry, *angry* because Sam had spared him. Maybe this spiteful sot was as deranged as his wife.

"Out, damn you!" Sam yelled. He tore the side door open, blasted in the face by rain, by a wind gust with the force of a cyclone.

He left the door swinging, banging, dragged Brady up by his collar, sent him snuffling into the night, mouthing words Sam couldn't understand.

Sam kicked the door shut and leaned against it, dripping rain from his hair and eyebrows.

"God. He's a lunatic."

A lunatic safely out of the house, however. A lunatic bested. Sam found his glass, poured more whiskey.

What had just happened? He wasn't sure. Oh, he grasped the surface details well enough. But those wild changes of expression—Brady wrathful because Sam had spared his life—Sam could neither understand nor explain apart from Brady's drunken state. He sat pondering the imponderable, glad to be alive, while the nor'easter tore shingles from the roof with explosions sharp as gunshots.

Late the next afternoon, Sam glanced up from the hospital plans to see his butler standing at the study door. An inventory of damage to Red Rose had begun that morning. Windows in the kitchen and all along the second floor on the ocean side had been blown out. A large limb from some neighbor's property had sailed into the roof and pierced it like a battering ram. There was much minor damage, all repairable; it was only money.

"What is it?" Sam said.

"Beg pardon, Mr. Driver, there's a gentleman to see you."

"Who is he? I have no appointments today."

"No, sir. He drove up in a buggy. He's from the police department."

Just inside the closed front doors, a short, unremarkable man waited. The man's tight blue suit had been new when his belly was smaller. He didn't know enough to take off his derby indoors. His eyes were rolling like marbles as he tried to absorb the house, its furnishings, the sums they must represent.

"I'm Sam Driver."

"Mr. Driver," the policeman said, shooting out his hand, then drawing it back. He was half Sam's age, plainly intimidated by Sam's seniority. "My name is Elbert Bramble. Detective Bramble. I'm sorry to interrupt your day but I'm afraid I must ask you to come to headquarters."

"For what reason?"

"To answer certain questions."

"Questions about what?"

"Last night, sir. Mr. William Brady of Sunrise Cottage said you telephoned at the height of the storm, requesting that he hurry over."

"I did no such thing."

"He also said that when he arrived, you"—Bramble swallowed—"threatened him with bodily harm. He alleges that you attacked him with a knife, then a fireplace poker."

"He said that?"

"His lawyer, sir. Shortly after noon today."

Like a guilty little boy caught stealing a pie from a kitchen sill, the detective drew a blue-covered document from inside his too-small coat.

"Sir, I have here a warrant for your arrest. Mr. Brady filed a complaint of attempted murder. Do you need any other clothes to accompany me? My buggy's right outside."

49
At the Fall River Boat

Sam woke before dawn. He dressed and let himself out of Red Rose. His stick tucked under his arm, his top hat slightly tilted to the right, his overcoat with the astrakhan collar comfortable but not too heavy, he struck out on foot for the Long Wharf. A ticket agent at the Fall River Line had sent a runner late yesterday to notify him.

Three days had passed since the visit from the reluctant policeman. Sam had been driven to headquarters, a white-painted brick building on Marlborough Street across from the Methodist church. There he endured four hours of interrogation without a lawyer, defended only by his righteous anger. He'd called Brady a liar, a schemer, someone he'd never contacted on the night of the storm. Bramble hesitantly agreed to leave that point open; Newport's limited telephone service had been knocked out by the nor'easter a few minutes before Sam's alleged call.

"But I'm afraid we must keep you as our guest overnight,

until the magistrate arranges bail in the morning," Bramble said, still apologetic.

"If you think I'm going to sleep in one of your drafty little cells surrounded by the town's finest habitual drunks, you're mistaken. Take me back to Red Rose and put a guard there. My daughter's in Newport. Do you think I'm about to abandon her?"

"Shall we notify her for you?"

"If you do, Mr. Bramble, I will see that you are transferred to the most remote, onerous post that can be found in the back woods of this county."

Bramble showed a little spine. "Are you threatening me, sir?"

"Not for a moment, sir. I am promising you. Accept it as a certainty."

Bramble left the room to consult his superiors, including the police chief, Harwood Read, whom Sam knew slightly and considered a good man. Since there were no other witnesses, only Sam's version against Brady's, Bramble returned to say Sam was released on his own recognizance, bail to be set the following day.

Sam heard voices in the corridor. Bramble said, "Two of our off-duty men have been called in. They will return you to your home and stand guard overnight."

"Fine," Sam said, a little more cheerful. "First, however, I want to contact a lawyer. He's in New York, so I'll have to send a telegraph. At your expense."

Sam stared until Bramble mumbled, "Yes, sir."

By late next day, the high-priced criminal lawyer who had agreed to represent him took charge. Hunter Vann, Esq., was closing his Manhattan practice at the start of the new year, to move to San

Francisco with a new wife. In the meantime, he said it would be a pleasure to defend Sam against "the libelous calumnies of that man of no accomplishments, the cowardly socialite Bill Brady."

With Vann's help, Sam retained a judge in Providence with a cash payment of $1,500. The judge assured Vann that the venue could and would be changed to that city, or New York, as Sam and the attorney wished. Sam had no fear of confronting Brady in a courtroom. The man was deceitful, and weak. Such men were mostly bluff, unable to fight as Sam had fought most of his life. He could visualize Brady's face beading with sweat as Hunter Vann tore into him on the witness stand. Sam was annoyed at the bother, the interruption in his life, but confident of the outcome. Little Jay's maxim, *Never let them get the best of you*, would carry the day again.

Sam had asked Bramble to keep the whole affair out of the local paper, ostensibly to protect his name. He was really thinking of Jenny, bargaining for time until she and Molloy left Newport. Bramble's superiors had not exactly kowtowed, but neither had they argued very forcibly after Sam handed over a personal check for $5,000, a donation to a police benevolence fund. Word came back from the chief of Newport's finest that most assuredly, there would be no publicity.

Sam would very much have liked to rid the earth of Bill Brady, yet he was thankful not to have Brady's death on his conscience. He already had the blood of many others there, including, at least in the world of his dreams, that of Jim Fisk. He needed no more.

He'd telegraphed Tessa to do all she could to hurry to Newport; he needed companionship at Red Rose while he waited for the wheels of justice to grind. Considering the way Jenny had behaved at Bailey's Beach—Mamie Fish had already written to express admiration for Jenny's daring deed—flaunting a mistress in his own cottage could hardly worsen his reputation. He saved Mamie's letter because it so ably represented the lady.

> *Sweet lamb, you must come dine with Stuyvesant and myself in New York. We shall jeer at all the pious blowfish who swim in Newport's befouled waters.*

Mamie still couldn't remember names, and she didn't know all those fine words; someone else surely had written them for her. He treasured the letter all the same.

Sam walked briskly toward the harbor. The stars, bits of white ice in a paling sky, told him how chilly it was, as did his pluming breath. He arrived on the pier a few minutes ahead of an omnibus that serviced several of the smaller, cheaper hotels. He saw Jenny and Molloy alight, waiting for two small trunks the porter handed off. Molloy carried a wire-and-canvas pet cage.

Jenny and Molloy watched him approach. Sam tipped his hat. "Good morning. I want to wish you both a safe journey."

"Good morning, Papa," Jenny said.

"Good morning, sir," Prince said, equally wary.

Sam peered at the carrier, saw only an unmoving furry mass. "You have a pet in there?"

Prince said, "My dog. I gave him a saucer of beer to help him sleep. He favors it. Must be some Irish in him."

Sam laughed. Jenny said, "I suppose you heard about Bailey's Beach."

"I'd love to have been there. Serves the stodgy old farts right, wouldn't you say?"

"Not in those words, Papa, but yes, I would."

Prince looked trig in a silk scarf, a tweed peacoat, a billed cap of matching material. No doubt Jenny had paid for the clothes but what did it matter? The chapter was closed. In one sense Newport had gotten the best of Sam. He just didn't care to have posterity record it.

"Molloy, let me speak candidly. I tried to thwart you at every turn. I admit my error. I don't like you any more than I did before, but I respect you a hell of a lot more. I've thought things over and rewritten my will to make Jenny a fifty-percent heir. The other half goes to an eleemosynary trust to build hospitals in my name. Given half a chance, if you succeed in cutting Jenny's purse strings, you might amount to something."

"I'll cut them, sir, don't you worry."

"Please tell me where you settle."

Then Sam made his ultimate peace offering, an age-spotted hand held out to Prince.

Unsmiling, Prince shook Sam's hand. "Sure."

"Might I speak to my daughter privately?"

"I'll wait by the gangway, Jen."

In the rising clamor of the steamer *Puritan* loading passengers and baggage, Sam made his mea culpa.

"I pushed you into marriage with that scoundrel Orlov. His title was the only honest thing he possessed. I knew what he was and chose to ignore it, because he was a member of the nobility, and you know how alluring that is in Newport. I'm deeply sorry for my mistake, but I've made a lot of them, in this family and elsewhere. I regret the day your dear mother died. Things would have turned out more positively if she hadn't. I can look you in the eye and say to you that I failed as a father. I know I failed. But I'll make you proud of me yet."

"I don't have to be proud of you," she said. "You're my father. I'm supposed to love you, right or wrong."

She leaned forward, gripped his left arm, chastely kissed his newly shaven cheek.

"I do."

The steamer whistle hooted twice. The night was waning, a

clear crystal brilliance spreading over the crest of Bellevue Avenue. Jenny ran to the gangway. She and Prince wove through the crush on deck to a place at the stern, waving to him. In the act of waving back, Sam noticed a bright trinket at his feet. He picked it up.

An owl stamped from tin plate, with a few inches of broken chain. Sam surmised that it had fallen, perhaps not accidentally, where Prince stood. If Jenny's young man didn't want the piece of junk, neither did he. He stepped to the pier's edge, dropped the medal into the murky water.

Puritan churned away from the Long Wharf, into the bay. She proceeded slowly, majestically toward the open sea. Samuel S. Driver, worth several hundred millions, facing his fifty-seventh year on earth and burdened by the guilt of a lifetime, stood alone, watching as the steamer disappeared into the new day.

50
Some Citizens of Newport Again

The warmth of the October afternoon faded as the sun sank over Narragansett Bay. Two Rhodys well acquainted with one another sat on a bench in front of Ye Snug Harbour, taking note of pedestrian traffic on Thames Street.

Titus Timmerman held the ends of a plaid shawl together at his collar. He looked more than ever like an old turtle, cane across his knees, eyes cloudy with cataracts. Year after year, the cottagers packed up, the servants followed a week or two later, the streets emptied, the temperature dropped, his business prospects sank. Long days and months stretched away into 1898 and the spring upsurge of his food and beverage trade.

Next to him sat Jimmy Fetch, whittling a stick. A wilting sprig of lily of the valley graced Jimmy's frayed lapel. Jimmy thought it made him look like a sissy but hadn't dared raise an objection when Flo pinned it on him, to celebrate the posting of their banns. His bride-to-be was three months along with the child she was carrying. Jimmy supposed the time had come for him to settle down.

Truthfully he wasn't half sorry, provided the child was his. After Prince Molloy drank too much and babbled the names of the guilty parties who had arranged for his beating, Jimmy had rushed to Mr. Rowe, the telegrapher who fed titbits to *Town Topics*. Rowe paid Jimmy $3. As soon as he'd sobered up and spent the money, Jimmy began to fret about Prince finding out, cornering him, accusing his best friend of betraying him for a few pieces of silver.

He'd lost sleep, but it never happened. Prince and Jenny Driver were settling somewhere far from Aquidneck Island. He had nothing to worry about except eventual adjustment to a more restricted life.

"Went over the books last night," Titus said. "Bad summer. Next one better be an improvement."

"I thought you hated tourists."

"I do. They think they own the town. They knock you down, it's their right—why not?—they're on vacation. I wish I didn't need 'em, God rot every one of them."

"I remember Prince saying you're only happy when you take in more cash than the year before."

"Not sure I ever will again. Something's gone out of this place."

"What?"

"Not smart enough to know. Everybody's older. Everything's different." Titus could have cited a wealth of specifics if he'd cared to: Gribble's unexplained suicide, Jenny Driver disgracing herself by showing flesh at Bailey's Beach, Bill Brady's wife gone to a loony bin near Poughkeepsie, Sam facing a trial for attempted murder but everyone agreeing that foxy lawyers, a bought-and-paid-for judge, maybe some bribed venire men thrown in, would all contribute to sparing him punishment. Of the fancy Russian count, Orlov, no one had heard since he sailed to France with the Drivers last year. No one missed him; another money-grubbing prince or duke would come along to divert the old ladies and fascinate their daughters.

"I can say amen to older," Jimmy agreed; a week ago he'd found some gray hairs over his ears. "Maybe the season's got us, ever think of that? Fall's when things die. Everything's gloomy."

Titus sighed. "Yep. Including this old bird."

The grogshop door opened. Tall Mary stepped forth, a crocheted sweater over her bib apron. "Kitchen's cleaned up fine, Mr. Titus. Suppose you won't need me after today."

"No, Mary, not until next May. I'll figure your wages."

Shadows grew longer. Leaves collected at their feet, then scurried on when a northwest gust caught them. A peculiar popping and clanking came from the far end of Thames Street. Mary put a hand over her brow.

"Lord have mercy, what is it?"

Jimmy said, "One of them bubblers."

Titus poked his head forward. "One what?"

"Horseless carriage. Mr. Oliver Belmont's imported one from France. I can tell you about it."

Neither Titus nor Mary encouraged him but he was eager to talk on one of the few subjects he knew something about. "It's a Panhard Levassor phaeton"—he mangled the words—"last year's model. First four-cylinder ever made. Won a long road race from Paris to Marsales and back. Monsoor Levassor's works manager averaged fifteen miles an hour."

"Trying to kill us all," Mary said.

"I hear Mr. Belmont's got other folks interested. He's planned something on the Belcourt grounds next year. The bubblers will weave around a special course and try to keep from knocking over dummies painted like horses and babies and coppers and such."

"How come you know so much about Belmont?"

"Work for him, Mary. Took Prince's place. Pay's good."

Mary pressed a kerchief to her face. "Just when I got used to horse manure after so many years of covering my nose and watching my step, now we got this menace. That there bubbler thing smells like the oil my boy Abraham squirts on the axle of our dogcart."

"She's gasoline powered," Jimmy said.

Titus rapped the ferrule of his cane on the cobbles. "Who gives a damn? Shut up about it."

The cause of all this reaction to the march of progress coughed and clanked its way out of a cloud of blue smoke, discernible at last in some detail. The Panhard Levassor resembled a one-seat carriage, the rear wheels twice the diameter of those in front. The driver and his companion sat forward of a fold-down top, behind a maroon-lacquered motor box which seemed ludicrously small for such a loud contraption.

Guiding the "auto-mobile" by means of a long handle like a boat tiller, O. H. P. Belmont sported a pale linen duster, cap, tinted goggles. Beside him sat Alva, equally elegant in a duster and a wide hat held in place by a patterned veil tied under her chin. She clutched a bouquet of pink hydrangeas while waving to gawkers, as though she were a dowager empress greeting her subjects. Titus disapproved of the woman and all her radical ideas, which included female suffrage and the public dissemination of lewd facts about birth control.

"Good morning, all," Alva cried as she passed in a cloud of smoke and fumes. She rotated her free hand at the wrist, a supple gesture of condescension. Mary coughed and fanned her kerchief harder.

Titus said, "It's an affront to a white man's peace and quiet," heedless of the woman of color next to him. "I can't stand this. Too much change this fast is immoral."

Mary stepped aside to let him pass. At the dramshop door, he turned for a last look at the Belmont bubbler, now chugging out of sight around a corner with only wisps of blue smoke to mark its passing. Jimmy couldn't tell whether Titus was disdainful or frightened of the machine. Prince could have told them, maybe, but Prince wasn't here.

Titus shook his cane over his head. "It's the end of the good old Newport, I swear it is."

He slammed the door.

Mary tucked her kerchief into her apron pocket.

"Might not be a bad thing," she said. "I been wondering for a long time, who needs sixty, seventy rooms for eight weeks of vacation?"

"Mr. Belmont, Mr. Fish, Mr. Driver, all them cottagers. Everybody knows they don't *need* it; they do it to show off that they can *pay* for it."

"How do you feel, Jim? You fine with that?"

"Suppose I'm not, Miss Mary? Got a feeling one person couldn't stop all those things coming along the pike—things Mr. Titus hates. One person, or ten thousand million."

"Well, I guess I can say the same. 'Scuse me, I got to collect my wages."

She left him sitting in the fading light. Jimmy was as bewildered about tomorrow, and next year, and the new century, as his friends.

A growler of beer would restore his composure. Take his mind off upsetting subjects such as the future of Newport, assuming it had one.

In the distance the stutter of the bubbler died up toward Bellevue Avenue. He walked inside, escaping from a once-familiar town that seemed to be leaving them all behind.

Afterword

I loved writing this novel because I love Newport. I love Newport because it is history preserved. I contrast this with my first adult visit to Boston, a week spent there to research *The Rebels*, the second volume of the Kent Family Chronicles. Eagerly I went to the site of the Boston Tea Party. I found real estate built on landfill, a dull green office building, a bronze plaque.

"Developers" have "developed" and are continuing to "develop" our history out of existence. Their tools are the wrecking ball, bloviation about "progress," "variations" to applicable zoning laws granted by pliant city or county councils, sometimes even cash payments to obtain such exemptions.

Savannah was smart enough to stop that kind of "progress" before all of Governor Oglethorpe's charming squares were destroyed

Newport was smart enough to stop it before most of the great nineteenth-century cottages were destroyed to make room for mini-malls, chain hotels or water fun parks. Various preservation societies stepped in to retain the major cottages "as is," opening most to visits by the public. Even the Newport Casino on Bellevue Avenue looks much as it did when Gordon Bennett financed it.

So if you've never seen Newport, go.

I always wanted to write a novel about Newport because so many famous, wealthy and downright zany people trooped up there to mingle with their peers. These people frequently had nothing to recommend them except enormous fortunes. Few such fortunes were earned (the classic two-word American success story is "Thanks, Dad"). In the 1890s, the height of Newport's social glory, men of "new money" such as Sam Driver were not often welcomed.

The resident millionaires, throwing it around prior to the era of the confiscatory income tax, were, despite their often empty heads, decidedly entertaining. Who wouldn't be entertained by a gentleman farmer who hung fourteen-karat gold apples, pears and peaches on his fruit trees?

Who wouldn't be diverted by Savannah's own Mr. Make-A-Lister, who committed social suicide by—ye gods—writing a book?

By Harry Lehr, who could get away with telling Mrs. Astor her diamonds made her look like an electric chandelier?

By the abusively funny Mamie Fish, or dictatorial Alva Vanderbilt, who forced her daughter into marital slavery with a titled Englishman, then turned around and campaigned for women's rights?

Equally diverting were the robber barons—"Uncle" Dan Drew, who prayed one minute, preyed the next; the proper yet sinister Jay Gould; and my favorite, jolly Jim Fisk, theater impresario, steamship owner (he had a few admiral's uniforms run up), organizer of a military regiment (he had a few colonel's uniforms run up) and crook. Who wouldn't be enamored of a semiliterate Vermont peddler who loved to refer to bosky places "where the woodbine twineth"? Newspapers lampooned him but loved the copy he provided. There is a reasonable suspicion that he loved it too.

Newport, of course, lingered on as a center of high society long into the twentieth century. Some of its denizens lingered as well.

Harry Lehr remained a bachelor until 1901, when he married Elizabeth Drexel of the Philadelphia Drexels. On their infamous wedding night, Harry told his wife that he'd married her for her money, would always treat her well in public, but had no interest in women physically. Apparently the marriage succeeded on those terms. Lehr died in 1928. His widow wrote a memoir of their years together, *"King Lehr" and the Gilded Age.*

"The" Mrs. Astor survived until 1908 but had succumbed long before that to what we may presume was Alzheimer's disease. She spent her last days wandering through empty rooms, wearing her finest gowns and jewels, greeting and carrying on conversations with invisible guests. She was the model for the fictitious Em Brady.

Many people grow increasingly conservative as old age claims them. As mentioned earlier, Alva Vanderbilt Belmont went the other way, becoming a champion of feminist causes, notably votes for women. She expressed regret over forcing her daughter, Consuelo, into an unhappy union with the Duke of Marlborough, but she had no regrets about leaving Willie Vanderbilt despite the scandal of being the first woman of her social standing to seek a divorce.

The passion for opulent steam yachts continued into the twentieth century. The record books tell us that Howard Gould's *Niagara* carried a photographic darkroom. On Gordon Bennett's *Lysistrata*, successor to *Namouna*, guests were invited to observe the engine room from a glass-enclosed gallery, or visit the yacht's self-contained dairy, where two cows in padded stalls patiently submitted to an electric milking machine.

The rascally Colonel Mann died in 1920, but his paper's power to intimidate and extract money from the rich effectively ended fifteen years earlier. In 1905 Mann filed a libel suit against *Collier's* magazine and its editor, who had described Mann's editorial staff as "a gang of blackmailers," and had written, among other encomiums, that Mann's "standing . . . is somewhat worse than that of an ordinary forger, horse-thief or second-story man."

The colonel failed to grasp that a trap had been set by the district attorney. Star witness for the defense in the libel case was none other than O. H. P. Belmont, with many of his society friends seated in a reserved section to add their encouragement. He testified to Mann shaking him down for a $5,000 "stock purchase" or "loan," as he preferred. He didn't prefer, not even when Mann cut his price to $2,000 and suggested that Belmont could either pay or receive constant attention from *Town Topics*, which he did after he said no for the last time. The *Collier's* editor was acquitted of libel in seven minutes.

Mann's legal troubles induced a state of paranoia. He included among his alleged tormentors President Theodore Roosevelt, whom he snidely called "that professional cowboy." During a perjury trial, the colonel's defense attorney didn't deny that Mann had squeezed thousands of dollars from the rich and famous. He concentrated on Mann's Civil War service, coupled with a reminder of his age. The "gallant old soldier" was set free but railed against "the Roosevelt–Collier conspiracy" to the end of his rather unbelievable career.

The craze for "dog dinners" continued in Newport after Mrs. Fish and Harry Lehr arranged the first one. They staged another famous dinner honoring a mysterious European, "Prince del Drago of the Corsican nobility." Prospective guests fought for invitations. Mamie and Harry chortled when the "prince" arrived, a lively monkey in a dress suit.

The prince had an appetite for champagne. After a bit too much, he leaped to a chandelier and began pelting the guests with lightbulbs. Since this notorious affair didn't occur until the new century, with great regret I left it, as the saying goes, on the cutting room floor.

Finally, I have it from a reliable source that in 1902, Prince Molloy settled with his wife and three children in Rochester, New York. He had finished two years of study at a free college and was gainfully employed at a private academy as a well-regarded teacher of history and French. He also coached tennis.

The Gods of Newport grew out of another of those meetings in the publisher's office I've described before. Once again the publisher was my astute longtime friend, Carole Baron, who has since moved on. But she didn't go before she green-lighted the project. She said to me that she saw many parallels in America today, starting with grasping CEOs and a rush to build "McMansions" (I prefer my own term, "Museums of Me") by pretentious people with more cash than taste or brains.

Fortunately a fine editor-publisher named Brian Tart succeeded Carole; he too endorsed the book with enthusiasm.

As always, I thank those who have helped in large and small ways. As always too, I absolve them from any responsibility for how I've handled the information or helpful advice they provided. I convey special gratitude to Jewell Anderson, Librarian of the Georgia Historical Society; Max Bach of the editorial library of the *International Herald Tribune*, Paris; Bert Lippincott of the Newport Historical Society; Deanna Scheffer of the faculty of Episcopal High School, Jacksonville, Florida; and John E. Woods, M.D. (ret.), of the Mayo Clinic, Rochester, Minnesota.

Major thanks are due to two exceptional gentlemen who helped me in countless ways. The first of them is Dan Starer of New York, a genius at digging out nuggets of information that seem to be available nowhere else in the world. Dan's service, Research for Writers, has long been on my radar, and he came through once again.

In Newport, through the good offices of Mrs. Richard Long, an experienced guide, I connected with Pieter Roos. Pieter is executive director of the Newport Restoration Foundation, and a longtime resident of Aquidneck Island. We first met on the pier on a rainy day in September 2005. Since then he has been my "boots on the ground," as they say at the Pentagon. Without Pieter's assistance in ferreting out the elusive answers to questions—what houses did Mrs. Stuyvesant Fish rent in the years before she built Crossways? what route might a four-in-hand coach race have followed? and many more—I could not have written this novel.

Every writer needs and should depend on a good editor. I've been fortunate in having many such in the last three decades. Doug Grad edited three of my novels for Dutton and New American Library before moving on. But I owe a particular debt to three others who, together, taught me more about the craft of writing than I ever could have learned on my own.

I refer to the late Joe Fox, to Herman Gollob, now retired, and Julian Muller, likewise retired. Each in his own way was a genius at structuring and pacing a novel as well as individual scenes. Each was probably in his sixties when we began working together, and that accumulated experience was invaluable. I owe more to this trio of "old gents," as *The Wall Street Journal* once called editors of their generation, than I can ever repay.

I've already named Carole Baron and Brian Tart as two of the many good people at Penguin who helped bring this novel to completion. I must also pay tribute to my agent, attorney and friend, Frank R. Curtis, who has represented me ably for going on thirty years. How he has put up with me for that long I don't know, but he has, and I'm forever grateful.

Finally, the lady who is central to my life kept me on track once again during the difficult months of writing and editing. Her name is on the dedication page. We are coming up on our fifty-fifth anniversary this summer. I was very lucky to find her in the zoology lab (my instructor, who still made me draw the frog correctly even though we were dating), lo these many years ago.

John Jakes
Hilton Head Island,
Newport, and Sarasota
April 2005–April 2006

John Jakes is the bestselling author of *Savannah*, *Charleston*, the Kent Family Chronicles, the North and South trilogy, *On Secret Service*, *California Gold*, *Homeland* and *American Dreams*. Descended from a soldier of the Virginia Continental Line who fought in the Revolution, Jakes is considered one of today's most distinguished authors of historical fiction. He divides his time between South Carolina and Florida.